Linda Howard is an award winning
New York Times bestselling author.
She lives in Alabama with her husband and
two golden retrievers.

To Die For

Linda Howard

PIATKUS

All the characters in this book are fictitious and any resemblance to real persons, living or dead, is entirely coincidental.

Copyright © 2004 by Linda Howington

First published in Great Britain in 2004 by
Piatkus Books Ltd of
5 Windmill Street, London W1T 2JA
email: info@piatkus.co.uk

First published in the United States in 2004 by Ballantine, a division of
Random House, Inc., New York, USA

This edition published 2004

The moral right of the author has been asserted

A catalogue record for this book is available from the British Library

ISBN 0 7499 3529 4

Typeset by Phoenix Photosetting, Chatham, Kent
Printed and bound in Great Britain by
Bookmarque Ltd, Croydon, Surrey

Dedication

This is to my dear high-maintenance friend, who killed a monitor in just such a fashion, and who provided me with so much inspiration for this story. I won't name names—this time.

CHAPTER ONE

Most people don't take cheerleading seriously. If they only knew . . .

All-American girl, that's me. If you look at the pictures in my high school yearbooks, you'll see a girl with long blond hair, a tan, and a wide grin that shows off her perfect white teeth, courtesy of thousands of dollars spent on braces and fluoride washes. The teeth, that is, not the hair and the tan. I had the effortless confidence of the upper-middle-class American teenage princess; nothing bad could happen to me. After all, I was a cheerleader.

I admit it. Actually, I'm proud of it. A lot of people think cheerleaders are both brainless and snooty, but that's only people who have never been a cheerleader. I forgive them their ignorance. Cheerleading is hard work, a demanding blend of skill and strength, and it's dangerous. People frequently get injured, sometimes even killed, doing the cheers. Usually it's girls getting injured: guys are the tossers; girls are the tossees. Technically we're called "flyers," which is really silly because of course we can't fly. We're *tossed*. The tossees are the ones who fall on their heads and break their necks.

Well, I never broke my neck, but I did break my left arm, and my collarbone, and dislocated my right knee once. I can't count the sprains and bruises. But I've got great balance, strong legs, and I can still do a backflip and the splits. Plus, I went to college on a cheerleading scholarship. Is this a cool country, or what?

So, anyway, my name is Blair Mallory. Yes, I know: It's a fluff name. It goes with the cheerleading and the blond hair. I can't help it; it's what my parents named me. My father's name is Blair, so I guess I'm just glad they didn't tag me as a junior. I don't think I would have been Homecoming Queen if my name had been Blair Henry Mallory, Jr. I'm happy enough with Blair Elizabeth, thank you. I mean, show-business people are naming their kids things like *Homer*, for God's sake. When those kids grow up and kill their parents, I think all the cases should be ruled justifiable homicide.

Which brings up the murder I saw.

Actually it doesn't, but at least it's kind of logical. The connection, I mean.

And bad things do too happen to all-American princess cheerleaders. I got married, didn't I?

That kind of ties in to the murder, too. I married Jason Carson right out of college, so for four years my name was Blair Carson. I should have known better than to marry someone whose first and last name rhymed, but some things you learn only from experience. Jason was big into politics: the student council, campaigning for his dad the state congressman, his uncle the mayor, blah blah blah. Jason was so good-looking he could literally make girls stutter. Too bad he knew it. He had thick, sun-kissed hair (that's poetic for *blond*), chiseled features, dark blue eyes, and a body kept in excellent shape. Think John Kennedy, Jr. The body, I mean.

So there we were, the poster couple for blond hair and white teeth. And my body was pretty fine, too, if I do say so myself. What else could we do but get married?

Four years later, we got unmarried, to our mutual great relief. After all, we had nothing in common but our looks, and I really don't think that's a good basis for marriage, do you? Jason wanted to have a baby so we'd look like the all-American couple while he campaigned to become the youngest state congressman, which really, if you want to know, irritated the hell out of me because he'd refused to have a baby before and now all of a sudden it was a campaign plus? I told him to kiss my ass. Not that he hadn't kissed it before, but the context was different, you know?

I made out like a bandit in the divorce settlement. Maybe I should feel guilty; I mean, it isn't exactly a feminist thing to do. Stand on your own two feet, make it with your own accomplishments, that kind of stuff. And actually I do believe in all that; I just wanted to make Jason suffer. I wanted to punish him. Why? Because I caught him kissing my youngest sister, Jennifer, on New Year's Day while the rest of the family was in the den totally zonking out on bowl games. Jenni was seventeen at the time.

Well, being furious doesn't slow me down any. When I saw them in the dining room, I tiptoed away and found one of the disposable cameras we'd been using that day to record the occasion for Jason's campaign album—family stuff, celebrating a holiday, pigging out around a table loaded with all sorts of artery-clogging goodies, watching football. He liked to have pictures of my family get-togethers because my family is so much better looking than his. Jason used any edge he could get in a campaign.

Anyway, I snapped a really good picture of Jason and Jenni, with flash and all, so he knew I had him by the short hairs. What was he going to do, chase me down and tackle me in front of my father, and wrestle the camera away from me? Not likely. For one thing, he'd have to explain, and he knew he couldn't count on me to go along with his story. For another, my father would have drop-kicked him over the televison for daring to harm a hair on his namesake's head. Did I also mention that I'm Daddy's girl?

So I filed for divorce, and Jason gave me everything I asked for, on one condition: that I give him the photograph and negative of him and Jenni. Well, sure, why not? It isn't as if I hadn't had more than one copy made.

Maybe Jason thought I was too stupid to do that. It never pays to underestimate how dirty your competition will play. For that reason, I really don't think Jason will do well in politics.

I also told Mom that Jenni had let Jason kiss her.

You didn't think I'd let the backstabbing little hussy get away with it, did you? Not that I don't love Jenni, but she's the baby of the family, and she thinks she should get anything and everything she wants. Occasionally she has to be shown differently. I've also noticed that *her* name rhymes, too: Jenni Mallory. It's really *Jennifer,* but she's never been called that, so it doesn't count. I don't know what it is about rhyming names, but they're bad news for me. The difference is, I forgave Jenni, because she's blood. No way in hell was I forgiving Jason.

So Mom took care of Jenni, who tearfully apologized and promised to be a good girl or at least show better taste, and my middle sister, Siana, who was in law school, handled the negotiations with Jason. The name "Siana" is supposedly the Welsh form of "Jane," but take it from me, the name really means "man-eating shark with dimples." That's Siana.

With the Mallory women in action, the divorce went through in record time without Daddy ever finding out exactly why we were all mad at Jason. Not that he cared; if we were mad, then he was mad, too, on our behalf. Wasn't that sweet of him?

What I got from Jason in the divorce settlement was a very nice little chunk of change, thank you. I also got the red Mercedes convertible, of course, but the money was the most important because of what I did with it. I bought a gym. A fitness center. After all, you go with your strength, and I know all about staying in shape. Siana suggested calling it "Blair's Beautiful Butts," but I thought that would limit the clientele and maybe give people the impression I also did liposuction. Mom came up with "Great Bods" and we all liked it, so that's what the former Halloran's Gym became.

I blew a bundle on remodeling and refurbishing, but when I was finished, the place practically screamed "high class." The mirrors were polished; the equipment was the best available; the bathrooms, locker rooms, and showers were completely redone; two saunas and a lap pool were added, plus a private room for massages. A member of Great Bods had a choice of yoga, aerobics, Tae Bo, or kick-boxing classes. If the yoga didn't mellow you out, then you could go kick ass without ever leaving the building. I also insisted all of my staff be trained in CPR, because you never know when an out-of-shape executive with high cholesterol will hit the weight machines in an effort to get back his teenage body overnight so he can impress his new secretary, and there you go: heart attack for the asking. Besides, it was an impressive thing to see in an ad.

All the money and the CPR training was worth it. Within a month of opening our doors, Great Bods was going great guns. I sold memberships by the month or by the year—with a discount if you paid for a year of course, which was smart because it hooked you in and most people will use the facility then because they don't want to waste their money. Cars in the parking lot give the perception of success, and, well, you know what they say about perception. Anyway, success breeds like a bunny rabbit. I was thrilled all the way down to my leg warmers—which some of those not in the know consider *passé,* but they're seriously out of touch with what makes your legs look great. High heels top the list, but leg warmers are a close second. I wear both. Not together, of course. Puh-leeze.

Great Bods is open from six in the morning until nine at night, making it convenient for anyone to fit a visit into his or her schedule. My yoga classes languished, at first, with only a few women enrolled, so I hired some buff and handsome college football players to attend yoga classes for a week. The weightlifting and Tae Bo crowd, macho to the teeth, rushed to do whatever it was my handsome young guys did to stay in such good shape, and the women rushed to be in the same class with those same young guys. By the time the week was over, yoga enrollment had quadrupled. Once the macho crowd discovered how tough yoga was, and its benefits, most of them remained— and so did the women.

Did I mention I took some psychology classes in college?

So here I am, several years later: thirty years old and the owner of a successful business that keeps me busy but also makes very nice profits. I traded the red convertible in for a white one, because I wanted to lower my profile a tad. It isn't smart for a single woman living alone to attract too much attention. Besides, I wanted a new car. Love that smell. Yes, I know I could have bought a Ford or something, but it really griped Jason's ass that I drove around town in a Mercedes convertible, which he couldn't do now because it would be bad for his campaign image. He'll probably die begrudging me that Mercedes. I hope.

Anyway, I didn't park the convertible in the public parking lot in front, because I didn't want dings all up and down the car. I had a private parking lot paved in back of the gym for the staff, with our own, much more convenient entrance; my reserved parking slot— which was plenty big so no other cars could get close—was right in front of the door. Being the owner has its perks. Being a gracious owner, however, I also had a large metal awning installed completely across the back of the gym, so we could park under it and be sheltered coming and going to our cars. When it rained, everyone was very appreciative.

I'm the boss, but I don't believe in lording it over my employees. Except for the parking slot, I didn't claim any special privileges. Well, I guess signing their paychecks gave me a huge advantage, and I *did* handle all the money and make all the final decisions, but I took care of them. We had a nice medical insurance package that included dental, I paid them a decent wage—plus they were free to teach private classes on their off days for extra money—and I gave them plenty of vacation time. For that reason, I didn't have a big turnover in staff. Some turnover is inevitable, because lives change and people move away, things like that, but I seldom had anyone leaving for another job in the same field. Continuity in the staff is good for business. Clients like to feel they know their trainers and teachers.

Closing time was nine P.M. and I usually stayed to lock up so my staff could get home to their families or social life or whatever. Don't take that as a sign that *I* have no social life. True, I don't date as much now as

I did right after my divorce, but Great Bods takes a lot of my time and is important to me, so I take care of the business. And I get creative with my dates: we'll go for lunch, which is good if the guy turns out to be not as great as I'd hoped, because "lunch" is finite. You meet, you eat, you leave. That way if I don't care for my date, I don't have to fend him off or make lame excuses for not inviting him in. Lunch is a good concept, dating-wise. If I *do* like him, then other options open up, such as a real date after hours or on Sunday, when Great Bods is closed.

Anyway, on the night in question—I did mention that I witnessed a murder, didn't I?—I locked up, as usual. I was a bit late, because I'd been working on my gymnastic skills; you never know when you might need to do a backflip. I'd worked up a good sweat, so I had then showered and washed my hair before grabbing my stuff and heading toward the employees' door. I turned out the lights, then opened the door and stepped outside under the awning.

Oh, wait, I'm getting ahead of myself. I haven't explained about Nicole.

Nicole "call me Nikki" Goodwin was a thorn in my side. She joined Great Bods about a year ago and immediately began driving me crazy, though it took me a couple of months to notice. Nicole had one of those breathy little voices that make strong men melt. It made *me* want to strangle her. What *is* it about that fake Marilyn Monroe coo that men seem to like? Some men, anyway. Nicole laid on the false sweetness, too, when she talked; it's a wonder everyone around her wasn't bouncing off the walls on a sugar high. At least she didn't do the finger-twisting-in-the-hair thing.

But that was because *I* don't do it—unless I'm ragging someone, that is. Generally I'm more professional.

See, Nicole was a copycat. And I'm the cat she copied.

First it was the hair. Her natural color was kind of blondish, but within two weeks of joining Great Bods she went golden blond, with pale streaks. Like mine, in fact. I didn't really notice at the time because her hair wasn't as long as mine; it was only later when all the little details started falling into place that I realized her hair was the same color as mine. Then she started pulling it into a ponytail on top of her head to keep it out of her way while she worked out. Guess who also pulled her hair up like that while working out?

I don't wear much makeup while at work because it's a waste of time; if a girl glows enough, the makeup disappears. Besides, I've got good skin and nice dark brows and lashes, so I don't worry about going barefaced. I do, however, have a fondness for glistening lotion that makes my skin take on a subtle sheen. Nicole asked me what kind of lotion I used and, like an idiot, I told her. The next day, Nicole's skin had a sheen.

Her workout clothes began to look like mine: leotards and leg warmers while I'm actually in the gym, with yoga pants pulled on when I was cruising around overseeing operations. Nicole began to wear leotards and leg warmers, otherwise bouncing around in yoga pants. And I do mean bouncing. I don't believe she owned a bra. Unfortunately, she was one of those women who *should*. My male members (I love saying that) seemed to like the spectacle, but all that jiggling and swaying gave me vertigo, so if I had to talk to her, I concentrated on maintaining eye contact.

Then she got a white convertible.

It wasn't a Mercedes, it was a Mustang, but still— it was white, it was a convertible. How much more obvious could she get?

Maybe I should have been flattered, but I wasn't. It wasn't as if Nicole liked me and was copying me out of admiration. I think she hated my guts. She over-did the fake sweetness when she talked to me, you know? In Nicole-speak, "Oh, honey, that's just the greatest pair of earrings!" really meant "I want to rip them out of your ears and leave bleeding stumps, you bitch." One of the other gym members—a woman, of course—even commented once, after watching Ni-cole sashay away, body parts bouncing, "That woman would like to slit your throat, pour gasoline over you, set you on fire, and leave you lying in the gutter. Then she'd come back and dance on your ashes after the fire was out."

See? I'm not just making it up.

Because I was open to the public, I pretty much had to allow anyone who wanted to join admittance, which was generally okay, though perhaps I should have made some of the more hairy members submit to electrolysis first, but there was a proviso in the membership agreement—which all members signed upon joining—that if three other members complained about said member's behavior, dressing-room etiquette, or a number of other transgressions, in any single calendar year, then the one being complained about wouldn't be allowed to rejoin when his/her membership expired.

Being the professional that I am, I wouldn't have booted Nicole's ass out just because she annoyed the hell out of me. It griped me, having to be that professional, but I managed. Being Nicole, however, she regularly annoyed, insulted, or generally pissed off just about every woman she dealt with during the day. She made messes in the locker room and left them for others to clean up. She made snide remarks to other women who weren't in the best of shape, and hogged the machines even though there was supposed to be a thirty-minute limit to an individual session.

The complaints were mostly in the form of bitching, but a few women came up to me with fire in their eyes and insisted on filing a formal complaint. Thank you, Jesus.

The number of filed complaints in Nicole's file was way more than three when her membership expired, and I was able to tell her—gently, of course—that her membership wasn't open for renewal and she should clean out her locker.

The resulting screech probably scared cows grazing in the next county. She called me a bitch, a whore, a slut, and that was just as a warm-up. The shrill invective got louder and louder, drawing the attention of just about everyone in Great Bods, and I think she would have slugged me if she hadn't known I was in better shape than she was and would definitely slug her

in return, only harder. She settled for sweeping everything off the countertop—a couple of potted plants,
membership applications, a couple of pens—onto the
floor and flounced out with the parting shot that her
lawyer would be in touch with me.

Fine. Whatever. I'd match my lawyer against hers
any day. Siana was young, but she was lethal, and she
didn't mind fighting dirty. We get that from our
mother.

The women who had gathered to watch Nicole's
tantrum broke into applause as the door closed behind her. The men merely looked bewildered. I was
pissed because Nicole hadn't cleaned out her locker,
which meant I'd have to let her back inside once more
to retrieve her belongings. I thought about asking
Siana if I could insist on Nicole making an appoint-
ment to empty her locker, and having a cop present to
both witness the removal of her personal belongings
and prevent another tantrum.

The rest of the day passed in a golden glow. I was
free from Nicole! I didn't even mind cleaning up the
mess she'd made, because she was gone, gone, gone.

Okay. That's the deal with Nicole.

Back to me leaving that night by the back entrance,
et cetera, et cetra.

The streetlight on the corner illuminated the parking lot, but the shadows were deep. A steady drizzle
was falling, which made me mutter a swear word because the street crud would get my car dirty, and the
night was turning misty on top of that. Rain and fog
are not a good combination. Thank goodness I don't

have curly hair, so I never have to worry about frizz in circumstances like these.

If you ever have the opportunity to be an eyewitness to a newsworthy event, you at least want to look your best.

I had locked the door and turned around before I noticed the car at the back corner of the parking lot. It was a white Mustang. Nicole was waiting for me, damn it.

Instantly alert and faintly alarmed—after all, she *had* turned violent earlier—I stepped back so the wall was at my back and she couldn't catch me from behind. I looked in both directions, expecting her to come at me from out of the shadows, but nothing happened and I looked at the Mustang again, wondering if she was sitting in it waiting for me to leave. What was she going to do, follow me? Try to run me off the road? Pull alongside me and fire some shots? I didn't put anything past her.

The rain and fog made it impossible to tell if anyone was in the Mustang, but then I made out a figure standing on the far side of the car, and I saw blond hair. I reached into my bag for my cell phone, and turned it on. If she made one step toward me, I was calling 911.

Then the figure on the far side of the Mustang wavered and moved, and a bigger, darker shadow separated itself from Nicole. A man. Oh, hell, she'd brought someone to beat me up.

I punched in the 9 and the first 1.

A loud crack of noise made me jump a foot high, and my first thought was that lightning had struck nearby. But there hadn't been a blinding flash, nor did the ground shake. Then I realized the noise was probably a gunshot, and I was probably the target, and I squeaked in panic as I dropped to all fours behind the car. Actually, I was trying to scream, but all that would come out was this Minnie Mouse noise that would have embarrassed me if I hadn't been scared half to death. Nicole hadn't brought muscle; she'd brought a hit man.

I'd dropped my cell phone, and in the dark I couldn't see it. It didn't help that I was trying to watch all around me and so I couldn't really take the time to look for the phone. I just began sweeping the pavement with my hand, trying to locate it. Oh, shit, what if the hit man was coming over to see if he'd hit me with that first shot? I mean, I'd dropped to the ground, so thinking I'd been hit was reasonable. Should I lie flat and play dead? Crawl under the car? Try to get back inside the building and lock the door?

I heard a car engine start, and I looked up just as a dark four-door sedan cruised up the narrow side street and out of sight alongside the building. I heard it slow and stop at the intersection with the four-lane street, Parker, in front, then pull out into the fairly sparse traffic. I couldn't tell which way it turned.

Was that the hit man? If anyone else had been in the parking lot, surely he or she had heard the shot and therefore wouldn't be driving sedately away. The only sedate driver would be the shooter, right? Anyone else would have been getting the hell out of there, just like I desperately wanted to do.

Typical of Nicole to hire a sorry excuse for a hit man; he hadn't even checked to make certain I was dead. But even if the hit man had left, where was Nicole? I waited and listened, but there weren't any footsteps, nor the sound of the Mustang starting.

I got down on my stomach and peeked around one of my front tires. The white Mustang was still sitting in the parking lot, but there wasn't any sign of Nicole.

Nor were there any passersby rushing to investigate the shot or see if anyone was hurt. Great Bods was located in a good district, with small shops and restaurants nearby, but no houses—and the shops and restaurants catered mostly to the surrounding businesses, so all of the restaurants closed by six and the shops not long afterward. If anyone leaving Great Bods later than that wanted a sandwich, the closest place was about five blocks away. Until now, I hadn't realized how isolated that made the employees' parking lot at closing time.

No one else had heard the shot. I was on my own.

I had two choices. My car keys were in my pocket. I had two key rings because the sheer number of the keys I needed for the gym made the ring too bulky to carry around while I did errands or shopped. I could get to my car keys without delay, unlock the car with the remote, and hop in before Nicole could get to me—unless she was standing right on the other side of my car, which I didn't think she was, but anything was possible. But a car, especially a convertible, didn't feel substantial enough to hold off a psycho copycat. What if she was the one with the gun? A ragtop won't stop a bullet.

My other choice was to fish the big set of gym keys out of my bag, feel for the door key, unlock the door, and get inside. That would take more time, but I'd be much safer behind a locked door.

Well, I guess there was a third option, which was to look for Nicole and try to get the jump on her, and I might have if I'd known for certain she didn't have the gun. I didn't know, though, so no way was I playing hero. I may be blond, but I'm not stupid.

Also, fighting like that will break at least two fingernails. It's a given.

So I felt around in my bag until I located my keys. The key ring had a thingamabob in the middle that kept the keys from sliding completely around, so they were always in order. The door key was the first one to the left of the middle thingie. I isolated it, then, staying low, duck-walked backward to the door. The motion looks really awful but is a great exercise for the thighs and butt.

No one jumped out at me. There wasn't any sound at all except for the distant noise of occasional traffic over on Parker, and that was somehow spookier than if she had leaped, shrieking, over the roof of my car at me. Not that I thought Nicole could jump that far, unless her gymnastic skills were way, *way* better than she had let on, and I knew better than that because she was the type to show off. She couldn't even do a split, and if she'd tried to do a backflip, the weight of her boobs would have dumped her on her face.

God, I wished she'd tried a backflip at least once.

My hands were shaking only a little—okay, more than a little—but I managed to unlock the door on the first try. I practically shot through the opening, and really, I wish I had given myself another inch or two of clearance because I bruised my right arm on the doorjamb. But then I was inside, and I slammed the door and turned the dead bolt, then crawled away in case she shot through the door.

I always leave a couple of low-wattage lights burning at night, but they're both in front. The light switch for the back hallway was just inside the door, of course, and no way was I going so close to the door. Because I couldn't see where I was going, I continued to crawl along the hallway, feeling my way past the female employees' bathroom—the men's room was on the other side of the hallway—then the break room, and finally reached the third door, which was my office.

I felt like a base runner sliding into home. Safe!

Now that there were walls and a locked door between me and the psycho-bitch, I stood up and turned on the overhead lights, then picked up the phone and angrily jabbed 911. If she thought I wouldn't have her arrested for this, she had seriously underestimated how thoroughly pissed I was.

CHAPTER TWO

A black-and-white pulled, lights flashing, to a stop in the front parking lot exactly four minutes and twenty-seven seconds later. I know because I timed them. When I tell a 911 operator that someone is shooting at me, I expect fast service from the police department my taxes help support, and I had decided that anything under five minutes was reasonable. There's a little bit of diva in me that I try to keep bitch-slapped into submission, because it's true that people are more cooperative if you aren't snapping their heads off (go figure), and I make it a point to be as nice to people as I can—my ex-husband excluded—but all bets are off when I fear for my life.

Not that I was hysterical or anything. I didn't charge out the front door and throw myself into the arms of the boys in blue—I wanted to, but they emerged from their patrol car with their hands on their pistol butts, and I suspected they'd shoot at me, too, if I ran at them. I'd had enough of that for one night, so though I turned on the lights and unlocked the front door, I stayed just inside the door, where they could see me but I was protected from any lurking psycho-bitch. Also, the drizzle had turned into rain and I didn't want to get wet.

I was calm. I wasn't jumping up and down and shrieking. Granted, the adrenaline and stress had caught up with me and I was shaking from head to toe, and I really wanted to call Mom, but I toughed it out and didn't even cry.

"We have a report of shots being fired at this location, ma'am," one of the cops said as I stepped back and let them enter. His alert gaze was studying every detail of the empty reception area, probably searching for people with weapons. He looked to be in his late twenties, with a buzz cut and a thick neck that told me he worked out. He wasn't one of my clients, though, because I knew them all. Maybe I could show him around the facilities while he was here, after they had arrested Nicole's ass and hauled her off to the psych ward. Hey, never miss an opportunity to expand your client base, right?

"Just one shot," I said. I held out my hand. "I'm Blair Mallory, and I own Great Bods."

I don't think many people properly introduce themselves to cops, because both of them looked taken aback. The other cop looked even younger, a baby cop, but he recovered first and actually shook my hand. "Ma'am," he said politely, then took a little notebook out of his pocket and wrote down my name. "I'm Officer Barstow, and this is Officer Spangler."

"Thank you for coming," I said, giving them my

best smile. Yes, I was still shaking, but good manners are good manners.

They were subtly less wary, since I was obviously not armed. I was wearing a midriff-baring pink halter-top and black yoga pants, so I didn't even have any pockets where I might hide anything. Office Spangler removed his hand from his pistol. "What's going on?" he asked.

"This afternoon I had some trouble with a client, Nicole Goodwin"—her name was dutifully noted in Officer Barstow's little notebook—"when I refused to renew her membership based on numerous complaints filed by other members. She became violent, knocked things off the desk, called me names, things like that—"

"Did she strike you?" Spangler asked.

"No, but she was waiting for me tonight when I locked up. Her car was in the parking lot in back, where the employees park. It was still there when I called nine-one-one, though she's probably gone by now. I could see her and someone else, I think a man, by her car. I heard a shot and dropped to the ground behind my car, then someone—I think the man— drove off, but Nicole stayed, or at least her car did. I stayed low, got back inside the building, and called nine-one-one."

"Are you sure it was a gunshot you heard?"

"Yes, of course." Please. This was the south, North Carolina, specifically. Of course I knew how gunshots sounded. I had even shot a .22 rifle myself. Grampie— my grandfather on my mother's side—used to take me with him squirrel hunting when we visited them in the country. He died from a heart attack when I was ten, and no one ever took me squirrel hunting again. Still, that isn't a sound you forget, even if a television program weren't reminding you every few seconds.

Now, cops don't go blithely walking up to a car where supposedly an armed psycho-bitch is sitting. After ascertaining that the white Mustang was indeed still parked out back, Officers Barstow and Spangler talked into their cute little radios that were attached to their shoulders somehow—Velcro, maybe—and very shortly another black-and-white unit arrived, from which emerged Officers Washington and Vyskosigh. I had gone to school with DeMarius Washington, and he gave me a brief smile before his chiseled dark face once more set into businesslike lines. Vyskosigh was short and broad, mostly bald, and he was Not From Around Here, which is how southerners describe Yankees. To a southerner, that phrase explains everything, from taste in food and clothing to manners.

I was told to stay inside—no problem there—while the four cautiously went out into the darkness and rain to ask Nicole what the hell she was doing.

I was so very obedient—which shows how rattled I was—that I was still standing in exactly the same spot when Officer Vyskosigh came back inside and gave me a very sharp once-over. I was a bit taken aback. This just wasn't the time for ogling, you know?

"Ma'am," he said politely, "would you like to sit down?"

"Yes, I would," I replied, just as politely, and sat down in one of the visitors' chairs. I wondered what was going on outside. How much longer could this take?

After a few more minutes, more cars arrived outside, lights flashing. My parking lot was beginning to look like a cop convention. Good Lord, couldn't four cops handle Nicole? They'd had to call in reinforcements? She must be even more psycho than I'd realized. I've heard that when people go nuts, they have superhuman strength. Nicole was definitely nuts. I had a mental picture of her tossing cops left and right as she strode toward me, and wondered if I should barricade myself inside my office.

Officer Vyskosigh didn't look as if he would let me do the barricade thing. In fact, I was beginning to think Officer Vyskosigh wasn't so much protecting me—as I'd originally thought—as *guarding* me. As in, making sure I didn't do . . . something.

Uh-oh.

Various scenarios began racing through my mind. If he was here to prevent me from doing something, what could that something be? Peeing? Paperwork? Both of which I did actually need to do, which is why they were first on my mental list, but I doubted the police department was interested in either of them. At least I hoped Officer Vyskosigh wasn't interested, particularly in the first item.

I didn't want to go there, so I jerked my thoughts back on track.

Neither were they concerned *I* might suddenly go berserk, rush out, and attack Nicole before they could stop me. I'm not the violent type, unless I'm extremely provoked; what's more, if any of them had been paying the least attention to me, they'd have noticed that I had a fresh manicure—the color was Iced Poppy, which was my newest favorite color. My hands looked really nice, if I do say so myself. Nicole wasn't worth a broken nail, so obviously she was safe from me.

By now it must be fairly clear that I can mentally dance around a subject for pretty much eternity, if there's something I really don't want to think about.

I really didn't want to think about why Officer Vyskosigh was standing guard over me. I really, *really* didn't.

Unfortunately, some things are just too big to ignore, and the truth cut into my mental do-si-do. The shock was almost like a physical blow; I actually jerked back in my chair.

"Oh, my God. That shot wasn't fired at *me,* was it?" I blurted. "Nicole— The man shot at her, didn't he? He shot—" *Her,* I started to say, but instead nausea welled hot and insistent in my throat and I had to swallow, hard. My ears started ringing and I realized I was about to do something ungraceful, such as fall out of the chair flat on my face, so I quickly bent over and put my head between my knees, and took deep breaths.

"Are you all right?" Office Vyskosigh asked, his voice barely audible above the ringing in my ears. I waved a hand at him to let him know I was conscious, and concentrated on breathing. In, out. In, out. I tried to pretend I was in a yoga class.

The ringing in my ears began to fade. I heard the front door open, heard multiple footsteps.

"She okay?" someone asked.

I waved my hand again. "Just give me a minute," I managed to say, though the words were directed at the floor. Another thirty seconds of controlled breathing pushed the nausea away, and cautiously I sat up.

The newcomers, two men, were dressed in street clothes, and they were each peeling off plastic gloves. Their clothes were damp from the rain, and their wet shoes had made tracks on my nice shiny floor. I glimpsed something red and wet on one glove, and the room spun around me. Quickly I bent back over.

Okay, I'm not usually such a fragile flower, but I hadn't had anything to eat since lunch and the time now had to be ten o'clock or even later, so my blood sugar was probably low.

"Do you need a medic?" one of the men asked.

I shook my head. "I'll be okay, but I'd be grateful if one of you would get me something to drink from the refrigerator in the break room." I pointed in the general direction. "It's back there, past my office. There should be a soft drink, or a bottle of sweet tea."

Officer Vyskosigh started in that direction, but one of the other men said, "Wait. I want to check that entrance."

So off he went, and Vyskosigh remained where he was. The other newcomer sat down beside me. I didn't like his shoes. I had a good view of them, since I was still bent over. They were black wingtips, the shoe equivalent of a polyester housedress. I'm sure there are really good quality black wingtips out there, but the style is awful. I don't know why men like them.

Anyway, this guy's wingtips were wet, with water actually beaded on them. The hems of his pants legs were damp, too.

"I'm Detective Forester," he began.

Cautiously I raised my head a little, and held out my right hand. "I'm Blair Mallory." I almost said, *Pleased to meet you,* which of course I wasn't, at least not under these circumstances.

Like Officer Barstow, he took my hand and gave it one brief shake. I might not have liked his shoes, but he had a nice handshake, neither too tight nor too limp. You can tell a lot about a man by the way he shakes hands. "Ma'am, can you tell me what went on here tonight?"

He had manners, too. I eased into an upright position. The red-stained plastic gloves were nowhere in sight, and I breathed a sigh of relief. I launched into a replay of what I'd told Officers Barstow and Spangler; the other man returned with a bottle of sweet tea and even twisted the cap off for me before handing it over. I interrupted myself long enough to say thank you and take a long swallow of the cold tea, then resumed the tale.

When I was finished, Detective Forester introduced the other man—Detective MacInnes—and we did the social thing again. Detective MacInnes pulled one of the visitors' chairs around so that he was sitting at an angle to me. He was a tad older than Detective Forester, a little heavier, with graying hair and a heavy beard shadow. But though he looked chunky, I got the impression he was solid rather than soft.

"When you unlocked the back door and stepped out, why didn't the person you saw with Ms. Goodwin see you?" he asked.

"I turned off the hall light when I opened the door."

"How can you see what you're doing, if you turn off the light?"

"It's kind of a simultaneous thing," I said. "I guess sometimes the light is still on for a split second when I open the door, and sometimes it isn't. Tonight, I locked the dead bolt after my last employee left, because I stayed late and I don't want just anyone walking in. So, my keys are in my right hand, and I used my left to unlock the dead bolt and open the door while I'm turning out the lights with the edge of my hand." I made a downward motion with my right hand, showing him how I did it. You have something in your hands, that's how you do it. Everyone does it that way. If you have hands, that is, and most people do, right? Some people don't, and I guess they use whatever they can, but I obviously had hands—Never mind. It's that mental dance thing again. I took a deep breath and brought my mind back to order. "It depends on the exact timing, but the odds are that half the time there aren't any lights on when I open the door. Want me to show you?"

"Maybe later," Detective MacInnes said. "What happened after you opened the door?"

"I stepped out, locked the door, and turned around. That's when I saw the Mustang."

"You didn't see it before?"

"No. My car is right in front of the door, plus when I step out, I'm already turning back to lock it."

He asked question after question, nitpicking details, and I answered patiently. I told him how I'd hit the ground when I heard the shot, and showed him the dirt stains on my clothes. That was also when I noticed that I'd skinned the palm of my left hand. I wish someone would explain to me how something I hadn't even noticed before began stinging like hell the moment I *did* notice it. I frowned at my palm, and picked at the loosened skin. "I need to wash my hands," I said, interrupting the endless questions.

Both detectives looked at me with cop eyes. "Not yet," MacInnes finally said. "I'd like to get this interview finished."

Okay, fine. I understood. Nicole was dead, we'd had an altercation earlier in the day, and I was the only one there. They had to cover all bases, and on the face of things I was first base, so they were covering me.

I suddenly thought of my cell phone. "Oh, I meant to tell you; I was in the middle of dialing nine-one-one when I heard the shot and hit the dirt, and I dropped my cell phone. I felt around but couldn't find it. Could you have someone check around my car? It has to be there."

MacInnes nodded to Vyskosigh, and the officer took himself off, flashlight in hand. He returned just a few moments later with my cell phone, which he gave to Detective MacInnes. "It was lying facedown under the car," he said.

The detective looked at the little screen on the phone. When you start to make a call, the screen lights up, but it doesn't stay lit; after thirty seconds or so—and I'm guessing, because, while I might time the arrival of cops, I haven't yet timed the light on my cell phone—the screen goes dark, but if you've actually pressed any numbers, they stay on the screen. Sitting in my well-lit reception area, the numbers would be visible even without the backlighting.

I was tired, I was shaken up, and I was sick at the thought of Nicole being shot basically right in front of me. I wanted them to hurry up and get past first base—me—and move on so I could go somewhere private and cry. So I said, "I know I'm the only one here and all you have is my word that things happened the way I said, but isn't there something you can do to speed this up? A lie detector test, maybe?" That wasn't the best idea I've ever had, because I felt as if my heart were trying to run the Kentucky Derby, which is bound to screw up a polygraph. I tried to think of something else to distract the detectives, in case they decided that, yeah, a polygraph administered on the spot might be just the ticket. I don't know if they do things like that, but I didn't want to take the chance. Besides, I've watched cop shows on television, and I know they have ways of proving if someone has fired a gun. "Or how about one of those thingie tests?"

Detective MacInnes sucked in one cheek, which made his face look lopsided. " 'Thingie test'?" he asked in a careful tone of voice.

"You know. On my hands. So you can tell if I've fired a gun."

"Ohhh," he said knowingly, nodding his head and shooting a quick, quelling glance at his partner, who had made a muffled noise. "*That* thingie test. You mean for gunpowder residue?"

"That's it," I said. Yes, I know they were trying hard not to laugh at me, but sometimes the dumb-blond stereotype has its uses. The less threatening I could appear, the better.

Well, Detective MacInnes took me at my word. A crime scene technician came with a tackle box full of stuff, and did an Instant Shooter I.D. test, rubbing my palms with fiberglass swabs, then putting the swabs in some chemical that was supposed to change colors if I had any gunpowder on my hands. I didn't. I had expected them to spray my hands with something and hold them under a black light, but when I asked the technician, he said that was old hat. You learn something new every day.

Not that MacInnes and Forester relaxed procedure in any way after that. They kept asking questions—could I see the man's features, tell what make of car he was driving, and so forth—while my car, the entire building, and adjacent properties were diligently searched, and only after they turned up nothing in the way of wet clothing did they conclude the interview, without even telling me not to leave town.

I knew Nicole had been shot at close range, because I had seen the man standing with her. Since she was lying beside her car at the far end of the parking lot, in the rain, and since I was the only completely dry person there—which was why they had looked for wet clothing, to make certain I hadn't changed clothes—I therefore had not been out in the rain and couldn't have done the deed myself. There were no wet prints other than those made by the officers coming in the front door; the back entrance was dry. My shoes were dry. My hands were dirty—indicating I hadn't washed them—and my clothes were soiled. My cell phone had been under the car, with the 9-1 clearly visible in the window to show I had started to dial 911. In short, what they saw jibed with what I said, which is always a good thing.

I escaped to the bathroom, where I took care of a pressing problem, then washed my hands. The skinned patch on my palm was stinging, so then I went into my office and took out my first-aid kit. I squirted some antibiotic salve on the scrape, then covered it with a giant-size adhesive bandage.

I thought about calling Mom, just in case someone had heard something on their police scanner and called her, which would scare her and Dad to death, but figured it would be smarter to first ask the detectives if making calls was okay. I went to my office door and looked out, but they were busy and I didn't interrupt.

Frankly, my butt was dragging. I was exhausted. The rain was pouring down and the sound made me even more tired, while the flashing lights outside gave me a headache. The cops looked tired, too, and miserably wet despite their rain gear. The best thing I could do, I decided, was make coffee. What cop didn't like coffee?

I like flavored coffees, and always kept a variety of flavors in my office for my personal use, but in my experience men aren't very adventurous when it comes to coffee—at least, southern men aren't. A man from Seattle might not turn a hair at chocolate-almond-flavored coffee, or raspberry chocolate, but southern men generally want their coffee to taste like coffee and nothing else. I keep a nice, smooth breakfast blend for those with Y chromosomes, so I got it out of my supply cabinet and began scooping it into a paper filter. Then I added a dash of salt, which counteracts the natural bitterness of coffee, and just for good measure added one scoop of my chocolate-almond. That wouldn't be enough for them to taste, but would give the brew an added mellowness.

My coffeemaker is one of those two-pot Bunn machines that makes an entire pot of coffee in about two minutes flat. No, I haven't timed it, but I can go pee while it's making and it'll be finished when I am, which means it's pretty damn fast.

I put one pot under the spout and used the other pot to pour in the water. While the coffee was making, I got out a supply of polystyrene coffee cups, creamer, sugar, red plastic stirrers, and arranged them beside the coffeemaker.

Very shortly Detective Forester followed his nose into my office, his sharp gaze noting the coffeemaker as soon as he entered.

"I just made a fresh pot of coffee," I said as I sipped from my own cup, which was a nice cheerful yellow with the words "FORGIVE YOUR ENEMIES—IT MESSES WITH THEIR HEADS" emblazoned in purple around the bottom. Polystyrene is hell on lipstick, so I always use a real pottery cup—not that I had on any lipstick, but that's beside the point. "Would you like some?"

"Has a cat got a tail?" he asked rhetorically, moving toward the pot.

"Depends on whether or not it's a Manx."

"Not."

"Then, yes, the cat has a tail. Barring any unfortunate accidents, that is."

He was smiling as he poured himself a cup. Cops must use telepathy to pass along the word that there's fresh coffee in the vicinity, because within minutes there was a steady stream of both uniformed and plainclothes peacekeepers coming to my door. I put the first pot on the warmer on top, and began making a second pot. Soon I was switching pots again, and the third batch of coffee was brewing.

Making coffee kept me busy, and made the night a little less miserable for the cops. I actually got to drink a second cup myself. I probably wouldn't be able to sleep that night anyway, so why not?

I asked Detective MacInnes if I could I call my mom, and he didn't say no, he just said he'd appreciate it if I waited a while, because if he knew mothers, she'd come rushing down and he'd like to get the crime scene wrapped up first. Put like that—he was a man who understood mothers, all right—I just sat at my desk and sipped my coffee and tried to stop the trembling that kept seizing me at unexpected moments.

I should have called Mom anyway, so she could rush down and take care of me. The night had been bad enough already, right? Well, it got worse.

CHAPTER
THREE

I should have known he'd show up. He was, after all, a lieutenant with the police department, and in a fairly small town like ours—sixty-odd thousand people—murders weren't an everyday occurrence. Probably most of the cops on duty were there, and a good many who weren't.

I heard his voice before I saw him, and even after two years I recognized the deep timbre, the slight briskness that said he hadn't spent his entire life in the south. It had been two years since I'd last seen the back of his head as he walked away from me without so much as a "Have a nice life," and still I felt the bottom drop out of my stomach as if I were riding a Ferris wheel and just beginning the downward arc. *Two damn years*—and still my heartbeat speeded up.

At least I was still in my office when I heard his voice; he was just outside the door talking to a knot of cops, so I had a moment to prepare myself before he saw me.

Yes, we had a history, Lieutenant J. W. Bloodsworth

and I. Two years ago, we had dated—three times, to be exact. His promotion to lieutenant was fairly recent, no more than a year ago, so then he'd been Sergeant Bloodsworth.

Have you ever met someone and every instinct, every hormone, sat up and took notice and whispered in your ear, *"Oh, my God, this is it, this is the real thing, grab him and do it NOW!"*? That was the way it had been from the first hello. The chemistry between us was incredible. From the moment we met— we were introduced by his mother, who belonged to Great Bods at the time—my heart literally fluttered whenever I saw him, and maybe his didn't flutter, but he zeroed his attention in on me the way guys do when they see something they really really want, whether it's a woman or a big-screen plasma TV, and there was that flare of heightened awareness between us that made me feel slightly electrified.

In retrospect, I'm sure a bug feels just the same way as it flies into a zapper.

Our first date passed in a blur of anticipation. Our first kiss was explosive. The only thing that kept me from sleeping with him on the first date was: (A) it's so tacky, and (B) I wasn't on birth control pills. I hate to say it, but (A) was almost more compelling than (B), because my rioting hormones were screeching, *"Yes! I want to have his baby!"*

Stupid hormones. They should at least wait and see how things turn out before doing their mating dance.

Our second date was even more intense. The kissing became heavy making out, with most of our clothes off. See (B) above for my reason for stopping, even though he produced a condom. I don't trust condoms because when Jason and I were engaged, one *shredded* on him and I sweated bullets for two weeks until my period came right on schedule. My wedding gown was ready for the final fitting, and Mom would have blown a gasket if my waistline had started expanding. Normally I don't worry about Mom's gaskets, because she can handle just about anything, but planning a big wedding will stress out even a woman with ironclad nerves.

So, no condoms for me, except for entertainment purposes; you know what I mean. I fully intended to go on birth control pills as soon as I got my next period, though, because I could see into my future and a naked Jefferson Wyatt Bloodsworth figured very large in it . . . very large, indeed. I just hoped I could hold out long enough for the pills to take effect.

On our third date, it was as if he'd been taken over by the Pod people. He was inattentive, restless, constantly checking his watch as if he couldn't get away from me fast enough. He ended the date with an obviously reluctant peck on the lips, and walked away without saying he'd call—which would have been a lie, because he didn't—or that he'd had a good time, or *anything*. And that was the last I'd seen of him, the bastard.

I was furious with him, and two years hadn't done anything to dilute my fury. How *could* he have walked away from something that promised to be so special? And if he hadn't felt the same way I did, then he'd had no business taking off my clothes. Yes, I know that's what guys *do,* and God bless them for it, but when you get out of the teenage years, you expect something else to go along with the lust, for the shallowness of a puddle to have deepened into at least . . . a deeper puddle, I guess. If he had walked away because I'd twice stopped him from consummation, then I was better off without him. I certainly hadn't called him later to ask what was wrong, because I was so angry I wasn't certain I could control myself. I intended to call him when I was calmer.

Flash forward two years. I still hadn't called.

That was my state of mind when he walked into my office in Great Bods, all six feet two inches of him. He was wearing his dark hair just a little longer, but his green eyes were just the same: observant, sharp with intelligence, hard with the hardness that cops have to acquire or get a different job. That hard cop gaze raked over me, and appeared to sharpen even more.

I wasn't happy to see him. I wanted to kick his shins, and I might have if I hadn't been pretty sure he'd arrest me for assaulting a police officer, so I did the only thing any self-respecting woman would do: I pretended not to recognize him.

"Blair," he said, coming over to stand way too close. "Are you all right?"

What did he care? I gave him a startled, faintly alarmed look, like the one women get when some strange man is getting too close and too familiar, and discreetly hitched my chair just an inch away from him. "Uh . . . yes, I'm fine," I said warily, then subtly changed my expression to one of puzzlement as I stared at him, as if I half-recognized his face but couldn't pull a name out of my memory banks to match it.

I was surprised by the flash of potent anger in his green eyes. "Wyatt," he said curtly.

I backed up a little more. "Why what?" I leaned to the side and looked around him, as if making certain there were still cops within calling distance to protect me if he turned violent—which, to be honest, he looked as if he might.

"Wyatt Bloodsworth." The words dropped from his grim mouth like lead balloons. He wasn't finding my little charade at all funny, but I was having a great time.

I repeated the name silently to myself, moving my lips just a little, then let enlightenment dawn on my face. "Oh! *Oh!* I remember now. I'm so sorry, I'm terrible with names. How's your mother?"

Mrs. Bloodsworth had fallen off her bicycle onto the sidewalk in front of her house and broken her left collarbone as well as a couple of ribs. Her membership at Great Bods had lapsed while she was recuperating, and she hadn't rejoined.

He didn't look any happier to hear that his mother was my foremost connection to him. What had he thought, that I'd throw myself into his arms, either crying in hysteria or begging him to take me back? Fat chance. The Mallory women are made of sterner stuff than that.

"She's almost back up to speed. I think what hurt her even more than breaking bones was finding out that she doesn't bounce back as fast as she used to do."

"When you see her, tell her I said hello. I've missed her." Then, because he was wearing his badge on his belt, I lightly smacked myself on the forehead. "Duh! If I'd noticed your badge, I'd have made the connection faster, but I'm a little distracted right now. Detective MacInnes didn't want me to call my mom before, but I notice half the town seems to be in the parking lot, so do you think he'd mind if I called her now?"

He still didn't look very pleased with me. Oh dear, had I hurt his little ego? Wasn't that just too damn bad? "No civilians have been allowed on the scene yet," he replied. "The press is being held off, too, until the preliminary investigation is finished. We'd appreciate it if you didn't talk to anyone until the interviews are finished."

"I understand." And I did, truly. Murder was serious business. I just wished it weren't serious enough to have required Lieutenant Bloodsworth's presence. I stood up and stepped around him—giving him the same amount of personal space I would a stranger—and poured myself another cup of coffee. "How much longer will it take?"

"That's hard to say."

Which was a good nonanswer. I noticed him looking at the coffee and said, "Please, help yourself." I grabbed the plastic pitcher I'd been using to fill the coffeemaker now that both pots were occupied. "I'll just get some water to start another pot." Then I whisked myself out of the office and down to the bathroom, where I filled the pitcher and basked in satisfaction.

He certainly hadn't liked the idea that he'd been so

unmemorable that I hadn't even recognized him. If he'd thought I'd spent the last two years mooning over him and mourning all the might-have-beens, his thinking had now been properly adjusted. And what had he expected, anyway? A rehash of old times?

No, not under these circumstances, not while he was working. He was way too professional for that. But he had definitely expected me to react to him with the unconscious intimacy you use when you've known someone personally, even if the relationship had ended. Too bad for him I wasn't unconscious.

When I came out of the bathroom, Detectives Mac-Innes and Forester were talking with Wyatt in the hallway, their voices pitched low. He was standing with his back to me, and while he was distracted by their conversation, I had an opportunity to really look at him, and damn if it didn't happen again, the heart-flutter thing. I stopped in my tracks, staring at him.

He wasn't a handsome man, not the way my ex was handsome. Jason was model handsome, all chiseled bone structure; Wyatt looked sort of battered, which was to be expected, since he'd spent a couple of years playing defensive end in pro football, but even if he hadn't, his features were basically on the rough side. His jaw was solid, his broken nose had a bump in the middle and was just slightly off-center, and his brows were straight black lines above his eyes. He'd kept the honed physique of an athlete to whom both speed and strength were equally important, but while Jason's body had the streamlined, strong elegance of a swimmer, Wyatt's body was meant to be used as a weapon.

Most of all, he practically dripped testosterone.

Good looks are almost totally irrelevant when a man has sex appeal, and Wyatt Bloodsworth had it in spades, at least for me he did. Chemistry. There's no other way to explain it.

I hate chemistry. I hadn't been able to get serious about anyone else in the past two years because of stupid chemistry.

Like the detectives, he was dressed in slacks and sport coat, with a tie that was loosened at the throat. I wondered what had taken him so long to get here; had he been out on a date, with his pager or cell phone turned off? No, he was too conscientious for that, so it followed that he had been far enough away that getting here had taken roughly two hours. He had also been outside in the rain, because his shoes and the bottom six inches of his pants legs were wet. He must have taken a look at the crime scene before coming inside.

The two detectives were both shorter than he, and Detective MacInnes's face was carefully impassive. The older men must not be happy, I thought, to have a younger man promoted so fast. Wyatt had risen through the ranks like a comet, only partly because he was a good cop. He was also a Name, a local boy made good, a celebrity who had made All-Pro in the NFL his rookie year, then walked away to become a cop in his hometown after just a couple of years in the pros. Law enforcement was his first love, he'd told the media.

Everyone in town knew why he'd played pro ball: for the money. The Bloodsworths were Old Money, meaning they had once had money but were now broke. His mother lived in a four-thousand-square-foot, hundred-year-old Victorian house that she loved, but the upkeep was a constant drain. His older sister, Lisa, had two children, and though she and her husband had a solid marriage and did okay with day-to-day expenses, college tuition would be beyond them. Wyatt had pragmatically decided that replenishing the family bank account would be up to him, so he put off his planned career in law enforcement to play pro ball. A couple of million dollars a year would go a long way toward repairing finances so that he could take care of his mother, send his nephews to college, and so on.

The older guys on the force had to resent him, at least a little. At the same time, they were glad to have him, because he *was* a good cop, and he wasn't a glory hound. He used his name when it was for the benefit of the force, not for his personal gain. And he knew people whom it was important to know, which was another reason why he'd been promoted so fast. Wyatt could pick up the phone and talk to the governor. The chief of police and the mayor would have to be stupid not to see the benefits of that.

I'd stood there long enough. I started toward them, and the movement caught MacInnes's eye, causing him to break off in midsentence and making me wonder what they were saying that I wasn't supposed to hear. All three men turned to look at me, staring hard. "Excuse me," I murmured, sliding past them to enter my office. I busied myself making another pot of coffee, and wondered if for some reason I had regained my position as Suspect Number One.

Maybe I didn't need to call Mom. Maybe I needed to call Siana. She wasn't a criminal defense attorney, but that didn't matter. She was smart, she was ruthless, and she was my sister. Enough said.

I marched to my office door, crossed my arms, and glared at Detective MacInnes. "If you're going to arrest me, I want to call my lawyer. And my mother."

He scratched his jaw and darted a glance at Wyatt, as if saying, *You handle this one.* "Lieutenant Bloodsworth will answer your questions, ma'am."

Wyatt reached out and caught my right elbow, smoothly turning me around and ushering me back into my office. "Why don't you sit down," he suggested as he poured himself another cup of coffee. He must have downed the first cup in one gulp.

"I want to call—"

"You don't need an attorney," he interrupted. "Please. Sit down."

There was something in his tone, other than the flat tone of authority, that made me sit.

He pulled the guest chair around so it was facing me and sat down, so close that his legs were almost touching mine. I backed up just a little, in that automatic way people have when someone gets too close. He didn't have the right to invade my personal space, not anymore.

He noticed my action, of course, and his mouth thinned. Whatever he thought about it, though, he was all business when he spoke. "Blair, are you in any trouble that we need to know about?"

Okay, so maybe that wasn't exactly coplike, and totally unexpected. I blinked at him. "You mean, other than thinking I was being shot at and instead finding out I witnessed a murder? Isn't that enough?"

"You said in your statement that you'd had an incident with the victim earlier this afternoon when you told her that her membership wouldn't be renewed, and that she'd become violent—"

"That's right. And there were witnesses. I've already given their names to Detective MacInnes."

"Yes, I know," he said patiently. "Did she threaten you?"

"No. Well, she said she was going to sic her lawyer on me, but I wasn't sweating that."

"She didn't make any threats to harm you physically?"

"No. I've already told all this to the detectives."

"I know. Just be patient. If she didn't make any threats, why, when you saw her car parked in the back lot, did you assume you were in physical danger from her?"

"Because she's—she *was*—a psycho. She copied everything I did. She colored her hair to match mine; she started wearing clothes like mine; she got the same hairstyle, the same style earrings. She even bought a white convertible because I have one. She gave me the creeps."

"So she admired you?"

"I don't think so. I think she hated my guts. Several of the other members thought so, too."

"Then why did she imitate you?"

"Who knows? Maybe she wasn't able to put together a look on her own, so she just copied someone else. She wasn't very bright. Cunning, but not bright."

"I see. Has anyone else threatened you?"

"Not since my divorce." Impatiently I checked my wristwatch. "Lieutenant, I'm exhausted. How much longer do I have to stay here?" Until all the cops had left the building, that was for certain, so I could lock up. They would be stringing yellow crime-scene tape all over the back lot, but surely they'd let me get my car out first—

That's when it hit me that they would probably cordon off the entire building and two parking lots. I wouldn't be able to open tomorrow, and maybe not the next day either. Or maybe not for a lot longer than that.

"Not much longer," he said, drawing my attention back to him. When was your divorce?"

"Five years ago. Why are you asking?"

"Does your ex-husband cause you any trouble?"

"Jason? Goodness, no. I haven't even seen him since the divorce."

"But he threatened you then?"

"It was a divorce. He threatened to trash my car. He never did, of course." Actually, he'd threatened to trash my car if I ever made certain information public. I had then threatened to make certain information public if he didn't shut up and give me everything I asked for—or at least, Siana had threatened it. I didn't think Wyatt needed to hear all of that, though. That comes under the heading of Too Much Information.

"Do you have any reason to think he might hold a grudge?"

Oh, I hoped so. That was why I still drove a Mercedes convertible. But I shook my head. "I don't see why. He remarried a few years ago, and from what I hear he's very happy."

"And no one else has threatened you in any way?"

"No. Why are you asking me all these questions?"

His expression was unreadable. "The victim is dressed almost identically to you. She was in a white convertible. It occurred to me, when I saw you and realized the similarities, that it was possible you were the intended victim after all."

I gaped at him in astonishment. "No way. I mean, I *thought* I was being shot at, but only because I knew Nicole was bananas. She's the only person I've had any trouble with."

"You haven't had any confrontations that maybe you passed off as minor but someone else could have taken more seriously?"

"No. Not even a snippet of an argument." Because I live alone, my life tends to be fairly peaceful.

"Could any of your employees be angry with you about something?"

"Not that I know of, and anyway, they all know me personally—and they know Nicole. There's no way any of them could mistake her for me. Plus, they all know where I park, and it isn't at the back of the lot. I don't think I'm involved in this at all, other than just being there by an accident of timing. I can't help you by pointing a finger at someone who might have it in for me. Besides, Nicole was the type of person who regularly pissed people off."

"Do you know any of those people?"

"She annoyed every woman who belongs to Great Bods, but men tended to like her because she had this syrupy sex-kitten act. It was definitely a man who shot her, though, which seems wrong, but brings up the question of jealousy. Nicole is—was—the type who'd play the jealousy game."

"Did you know any of her boyfriends, or was there one in particular?"

"No, I don't know anything about her private life. We weren't best buds; we never chatted about personal things."

He hadn't once taken his gaze off my face, which was beginning to make me nervous. See, his eyes are kind of pale, that shade of green that leaps out at you if the person's hair and brows are dark, which his were. On a blond you wouldn't notice eyes like that so much, unless he wore black mascara—never mind. Wyatt wasn't the mascara type. The point is, his gaze was piercing. When he stared at me, I felt sort of pinned.

I didn't like him this close. I functioned much better when he was at a distance. If we had been in a relationship, it would have been different, but we weren't, and after my last experience with him I wasn't willing to put myself on the emotional line with someone who blew so hot and cold. But he was so close I could feel the heat coming from his legs, so I moved back another inch or so. Better. Not perfect, but better.

Damn him, why couldn't he have stayed outside in the rain? Detective MacInnes had things handled in here. If Wyatt had just stayed outside, I wouldn't be having these very acute memories of how his skin smelled, how he tasted, the sounds he made when he was so turned on—

Nope. Don't go down that path. Because when he'd been turned on, *I* had been turned on, too.

"Blair!" he said, a little forcefully.

I jumped and refocused, and hoped he hadn't been able to tell where my thoughts had wandered. "What?"

"I asked if you got a good look at the man's face."

"No. I've already told all this to Detective Mac-Innes," I repeated. How long was he going to keep asking me questions I'd already answered? "It was dark, it was raining. I could tell he was a man, but that was it. The car was a dark four-door, but I can't tell you the make or the model. I'm sorry, but if he walked into this office right now, I wouldn't be able to identify him."

He watched me for a minute longer, then stood and said, "I'll be in touch."

"Why?" I asked in obvious bewilderment. He was a lieutenant. The detectives would be handling the case; he'd just be overseeing the big picture, distribution of manpower, okaying stuff, things like that.

His mouth thinned again as he stood looking down at me. No doubt about it, I was irritating the hell out of him tonight, which gave me a great deal of satisfaction.

"Just don't go out of town," he finally said, though he actually *growled* the sentence instead of *saying* it.

"So I *am* a suspect!" I glared at him, then reached for the phone. "I'm calling my lawyer."

His hand slammed down on mine before I could lift the phone. "You aren't a suspect." He was still growling, and now he was way too close, bent over me the way he was, his green eyes fairly snapping with temper as he glared back at me.

Ask me if I know how to leave well enough alone.

"Then I'll damn well go out of town if I want to," I said, pulling my hand out from under his and crossing my arms.

CHAPTER
FOUR

So that's how I wound up at the police station at midnight, in the custody of a very irate police lieutenant.

He hauled me into his office, plunked me into a chair, barked, "Now, stay there!" and stalked out.

I was fairly bouncing with temper myself. I'd given him what-for all the way down to the station—without using swear words or threatening him, of course, which would probably have given him a reason to arrest me for real, which I'm sure he would have done because he was that mad—but now I'd run out of things to say without getting into personal territory and I didn't want to do that, so I was frustrated on top of being mad.

I surged to my feet as soon as he closed the door behind him, and just to show him what's what I went behind the desk and sat in *his* chair. Hah!

I know. It was childish. And I knew that, childish or not, it would get his goat. Getting his goat was turning out to be almost as much fun as making out with him.

The chair was a big one. It needed to be, because he was a big man. It was leather, too, which I liked. I swiveled all the way around in it. I looked through the files on his desk, but I did it fast, because that was probably a misdemeanor or something. I didn't see anything interesting about anyone I knew.

I opened the middle drawer of his desk and got out a pen, then searched the other drawers for a notepad. I finally found one, plopped it on top of the files, and began writing a list of his transgressions. Not all of them, of course; just the ones he'd committed that night.

He came in with a Diet Coke in his hand, stopped dead when he saw me sitting at his desk, then very carefully and deliberately closed the door and in a low voice of doom said, "What do you think you're doing?"

"Writing down all the things you did so I won't forget any of them when I talk to my lawyer."

He plunked the Diet Coke down on the desk and jerked the pad away from me. Turning it around, he looked at the first item and his dark brows snapped together. " 'Manhandled the witness and caused bruises to her arm,' " he quoted. "That's a load of bullsh—"

I lifted my left arm and showed him the bruises on the underside where he'd gripped my arm while he was bodily forcing me into his car, and he stopped in midword. "Ah, hell," he said softly, temper fading. "I'm sorry, I didn't mean to hurt you."

Yeah, sure; that's why he'd dropped me like a hot

potato two years ago. He had definitely hurt me, no denying that. And then he hadn't even had the decency to tell me *why*, which was what had really made me mad.

He hitched one hip on the edge of the desk and continued reading. " 'Unlawful detainment. Kidnapping'— *kidnapping*?"

"You forcibly took me away from my place of business and drove me to another location where I didn't want to be. Sounds like kidnapping to me."

He snorted and continued reading my list of grievances, which included bad language, a snotty attitude, and poor manners. He hadn't even thanked me for the coffee. Oh, there were other legal terms in there, too, like *coercion, badgering,* and *harassment,* refusing to let me contact my lawyer, but I hadn't let any detail slide.

Damn his hide, he was smiling by the time he got to the end of the list. I didn't want him to smile. I wanted him to realize what an asshole he'd been.

"I brought you a Diet Coke," he said, sliding the can toward me. "You've probably had enough coffee."

"Thank you," I said, to underscore the difference between his manners and mine. I didn't open the can, though. My stomach was already jittery from too much caffeine. Also, as a peace offering, the Diet Coke didn't make the grade, especially since I was well aware he'd left the room more to give himself some breathing space before he snapped and tried to strangle me. The Diet Coke was a last-minute thought, to make it look as if he was being considerate when in fact it was his own skin he'd been protecting, because I'm sure it would be hell on his career if he strangled a witness. Not that I was much of a witness, but in this case I was all they had.

"Now get out of my chair."

I blew my hair out of my eyes. "I'm not finished with my list. Let me have the pad back."

"Blair. Get out of my chair."

I wish I could say I behaved like an adult, but I was already way past the point where I could do that. I clamped my hands on the arms of the chair, glared at him, and said, "Make me."

Damn, I wish I hadn't said that.

A very short and humiliating struggle later, I was back in the chair where he'd originally put me, and he was in his chair, looking angry again.

"Damn it." He scrubbed his hand over his whiskery jaw, where his five o'clock shadow had long ago become darker than that. "If you don't behave— Do you know how close you came to being in my lap instead of that chair?"

Whoa. Where had that come from? I pulled back in alarm. "*What?*"

"Don't act like you don't know what I'm talking about. And I don't buy your earlier act, either. You remember me, all right. I've had you naked."

"You have not!" I said, shocked. Did he have me confused with someone else? I was pretty sure I'd have remembered *that*. Yes, clothing had been shed, but I definitely had not been naked.

He gave a grim smile. "Honey, trust me: when all

you have on is a skimpy little skirt pulled up around your waist, that's naked."

I trembled a little, because this was indeed familiar. I remembered the occasion well. It was the second date. He'd been on the couch; I'd been astride him, his fingers had been inside me, and I'd been an inch away from saying to hell with the concept of birth control, and taking my chances.

I blushed, not in embarrassment, but because the office was becoming uncomfortably warm. The thermostat for the air-conditioning in the building needed to be bumped down just a notch. Just because I felt all squirmy inside, however, didn't mean I was giving up the fight. "Naked means totally without clothes, so therefore by your own description I definitely wasn't naked."

"So you do remember," he said with satisfaction. "And don't split hairs. You were as good as naked."

"There's still a difference," I insisted stubbornly. "And, yeah, I remember that we made out. So what?"

"You mean you get naked with a man so often it doesn't mean anything anymore?" he asked, his eyes narrowing.

I was tired of pretending. He wasn't buying it, anyway. I looked him in the eye and said, "Evidently it didn't mean anything that time, either."

He grimaced. "Ouch. I know I owe you an explanation. I'm sorry—"

"Save your breath. The time for explanations passed a long time ago."

"Did it?"

"I moved on. Haven't you?"

"I thought I had," he said, scowling. "But when I got the call that there'd been a murder at Great Bods and the victim was a blond female, I—" He broke off, then said, "Shit."

I blinked at him, honestly surprised. Come to think of it, his first words to me *had* been *Are you all right?* And he'd gone out in the rain to the crime scene to see Nicole's body before coming inside. Surely by then her name had been broadcast, but maybe not, until her family could be notified. I had no idea who or where her family was, but there was probably a next-of-kin listed in her paperwork at Great Bods, which Detective MacInnes had taken.

Poor Nicole. She'd been a psycho-bitch copycat, but it bothered me that her body had been lying out in the rain for such a long time while the cops worked the crime scene. I knew crime scene investigations took a while, and the rain had hindered the cops as well, but still, she'd lain there for a good three hours before they let her be moved.

He snapped his fingers in my face. "You keep wandering off."

Man, I wanted to bite those fingers. I hate it when people do things like that, when a little wave will suffice to get my attention. "Well, excuse me. I'm exhausted and I witnessed a murder tonight, but it's terribly rude of me not to stay focused on personal matters. You were saying?"

He studied me for a moment, then shook his head. "Never mind. You *are* exhausted, and I have a murder investigation to oversee. I wish you weren't involved in it, but you are, so you'll be seeing more of me whether you want to or not. Just stop pushing, will you? Let me do my job. I admit it, I can't concentrate when you're in my face making me crazy."

"I don't make you crazy," I snapped, incensed. "You were evidently crazy before I ever met you. *May I go home now?*"

He rubbed his eyes and visibly reined in his temper. "In a few minutes. I'll take you home."

"Someone can give me a ride back to Great Bods. I need my car."

"I said I'll take you home."

"And I said I need my car."

"I'll have it brought to you tomorrow. I don't want you messing around the crime scene."

"Fine. I'll take a cab home. No need to put yourself out." I stood and grabbed my bag, ready to head out the door. I'd stand on the sidewalk, even though it was still pouring down rain, while I waited for the cab.

"Blair. *Sit down.*"

That was the bad thing about him being a cop. I didn't know exactly where his official authority ended and the personal stuff began. I didn't know exactly what legal ground I was standing on. I was pretty sure I could walk out and there wouldn't be a thing he could do about it—legally—but there was always the tiny possibility I was wrong, and the big possibility that he'd force me to stay whether it was legal or not, and I didn't want to have another tussle with him. Tussling was bad for my self-control.

I sat down, and contented myself with glaring mulishly. I had a niggling suspicion he intended to get back on a personal footing with me, and I didn't want to go down that road again. With that in mind, the less contact I had with him, the better.

I have a rule: Walk out, crawl back. If a man does the first, then he has to do the second to get back on good terms with me. I can handle an argument, because at least then you're communicating, but to just walk out and not give me a chance to work things out—that's a big no-no.

I know that sounds as if I need to get over myself, but the truth is—and I know I blew it off as the divorce being the best thing for both of us—it hurt like hell when I caught Jason kissing my sister Jenni. Not just because Jenni had betrayed me, but because I had truly loved Jason. Our first couple of years together had been very happy. At least, I'd been happy, and I think he was, too. We did grow apart and I fell out of love with him, but that didn't mean I had given up on our marriage. I was willing to work on it, to try to get close to him again. When I saw him kissing Jenni, it was like a punch in the stomach, and I realized he must have been cheating on me for some time. Not with Jenni; I pretty much thought that was the first time he'd touched her. But he wasn't in love with her, so that meant he'd done it just because she was pretty and available, and *that* meant he'd very likely done it with other women, too.

He hadn't even tried to make our marriage work. He'd dumped me emotionally a long time before, and I hadn't realized it. Once I did realize it, though, I cut my losses. I didn't go crying on everyone's shoulders; instead I built myself a very satisfying new life, but that doesn't mean I'd escaped without some very deep emotional bruises.

Bruises heal, and I wasn't the type to mope around anyway. I learned from the experience, and set new guidelines and standards for myself. One of those guidelines was that if a man walked out without even trying to work things out, then he wasn't worth my effort unless he proved he was serious about getting another chance.

Wyatt hadn't proved a thing yet. And he wasn't the crawling type. So that meant the idea of us getting together again was pretty much a nonstarter.

He pushed the Diet Coke toward me. "Drink it. Maybe it'll cool you down."

What the hell. No way would I be able to sleep tonight anyway. I popped the top on the can and took a sip, then steered my thoughts to a more practical subject. "I assume there's no way I can be open for business tomorrow."

"Good assumption."

"How long will it be before I *can* open? One day? Two?"

"The time varies. I'll try to move things as fast as possible, but I won't cut corners. A couple of days, probably. I'm sorry for your financial loss, but—"

"Oh, I won't lose any money. The vast majority of the membership pays by the year because it's cheaper than paying by the month. I don't offer any memberships shorter than a month. It's the inconvenience to the members that I don't like, and I know that's minor in comparison to a murder, but as the owner of a business it's a hard fact that I have to take care of my customers or the business will suffer."

He eyed me consideringly, as if he hadn't expected me to be that practical. That irritated me, because he'd spent three dates in my company and if he'd been paying any attention at all to anything other than my body, he'd have realized I'm no airhead.

Maybe I should have been surprised he'd recognized *me,* because two years ago he evidently hadn't looked any higher than my breasts.

Bad thought, because he'd definitely looked at my breasts. And touched them. And sucked them. Now, I'm not much on breasts—they're more of an irritant to me than a source of pleasure—but there was no getting away from the intimacy of the memory, and that was what had me blushing again.

"My God," he said, "what are you thinking this time?"

"Why? What do you mean?" Like I was going to tell him what I was thinking.

"You're blushing again."

"I am? Oh. Sorry. I'm going through premature menopause, and I have hot flashes." Anything to re-gain lost ground.

He grinned, a quick flash of white teeth. "Hot flashes, huh?"

"Premature menopause isn't for sissies."

He laughed out loud, and leaned back in his big leather chair to watch me for a moment. The longer he watched, the more uneasy I became. Remember what I said about how his eyes looked? I felt like a mouse being stared down by a cat . . . a mean, hungry cat. In all this time I hadn't given two thoughts about what I was wearing, but I was abruptly conscious of my pink halter top that bared my midriff, and the formfitting yoga pants. The way he was looking at me made me feel as if way too much of my skin was exposed, and that he was remembering seeing even more of it than he was seeing right now. Even worse, that he was planning on seeing more of me again.

That was the effect he'd always had on me: when he looked at me, I became acutely aware of being female—and that he was male, with all the corresponding bits and parts. You know: Tab A fits into Slot B. If I got close to him, all I could think about were tabs and slots.

He picked up the pen I'd been writing with and tapped it in a rapid tattoo on his desktop. "You're not going to like what I'm about to say."

"I haven't liked anything you've said, so that isn't a big surprise."

"Give it a rest," he advised in a hard tone. "This isn't about us."

"I didn't assume it was. And there is no 'us.' " I just could *not* give him an inch, the benefit of the doubt, or a break. I didn't want to deal with him. I wanted Detective MacInnes back.

Evidently Wyatt decided that trying to reason with me was a lost cause. It isn't; I'm normally very reasonable . . . except where he's concerned. For whatever reason, he didn't pick up that verbal gauntlet. "We try to control all the information that's given to the press about a murder, but sometimes it isn't possible. To do an investigation, we have to talk to people and ask if anyone saw a man driving a dark four-door sedan in the vicinity of the crime. That's already begun. Now, we kept the reporters away from the crime scene, but they were right outside the tape with their telephoto lenses and cameras."

"And?" I wasn't getting his point.

"It doesn't take a genius to put two and two together and come up with you as a witness. We were in your place of business, you were with us, you left in my car—"

"Considering *that* scene, they probably think I'm the suspect."

One corner of his mouth quirked as he remembered the struggle to put me in his car. "No, they probably just think you were very upset by what happened." He tapped the pen against the desk again. "I can't keep them from naming you. If a suspect was seen, obviously there was a witness. Your identity is just as obvious. It'll be in the papers tomorrow."

"Why is that a prob— Oh." I was being named in the newspapers as the witness to a murder. The person who would most likely worry was none other than the murderer himself. What do killers do to protect themselves? They kill whoever is threatening them, that's what.

I stared at him, appalled. "Oh, *shit*."

"Yeah," he said. "My thoughts exactly."

CHAPTER
FIVE

A thousand thoughts ran through my mind. Well, at least six or seven, anyway, because a thousand thoughts are a lot. Try counting your own thoughts and see how long it takes you to get to a thousand. Regardless of that, none of my thoughts were good.

"But I'm not even a good witness!" I wailed. "I couldn't identify him if my life depended on it." Again, not a good thought, because it just might.

"He doesn't know that."

"Maybe he was her boyfriend. It's usually the boyfriend or husband, isn't it? Maybe it was a crime of passion and he isn't really a murderer at heart, and when you pick him up he'll confess ." That wasn't impossible, was it? Or too much to ask?

"Maybe," he said, but his expression wasn't all that hopeful.

"But what if he wasn't her boyfriend? What if it's drugs or something?" I got up and began to pace his office, which didn't have enough room for serious pacing and had way too many obstacles, like file cabinets and stacks of books. I dodged around things more than paced. "I can't leave the country. You won't let me even leave town, which under these circumstances is a really crappy position to hold, you know."

Not that he could stop me, I realized, not without arresting me or taking me into protective custody, and since I couldn't identify the killer, I don't think he could justify that to a judge. So why had he even told me not to leave town? And why was he telling me this when the most obvious, most intelligent response would be to get the hell out of Dodge?

He ignored my comment on his edict. "The odds are you're right, and the reason Ms. Goodwin was murdered was a personal one. With luck we'll have this wrapped up in a day or two."

"A day or two," I repeated. A lot could happen in a day or two. For one thing, I could get dead. No way was I going to hang around for that to happen. Despite what Lieutenant Bloodsworth had told me, I was leaving town. To hell with his permission, which I was fairly certain I didn't need anyway; by the time he found out I was gone, it would be too late. I would tell Siana to get in touch with him and tell him that if he needed me, he could contact Siana, because of course I'd tell my family where I was. Great Bods would be closed for a day or so anyway, so I might as well take a short vacation. I hadn't indulged my inner beach bunny in a couple of years; she was due.

When I got home I'd grab a couple of hours' sleep, if I could. If I couldn't, I'd pack. I'd be ready to go whenever my car was delivered to me.

"I can't spare any patrolmen for guard duty, and I

couldn't justify it anyway in the absence of a credible threat—not to mention you aren't exactly a witness, since you can't identify anyone." He leaned back in his chair and gave me a brooding look. "I'll issue a statement to the press that 'unnamed witnesses' saw a man leaving the scene. That should take any focus off of you."

"Hey, that'll work!" I said, cheering up. If there was more than one witness, then killing me wouldn't serve any purpose, right? Not that I intended to hang around to find out. Now that I'd thought of it, a few nice, lazy days at the beach sounded great. I had this great turquoise bikini I'd bought last year and hadn't had a chance to wear. Tiffany—my inner beach bunny—was practically purring in anticipation.

I stood up, picked up the notepad before he could stop me, and ripped off the top page. Like I was going to forget his list of transgressions, right? As I neatly folded the page I said, "I'm ready to go home now. Really, Lieutenant Bloodsworth, you could have told me all this at Great Bods, you know. You didn't have to manhandle me in front of everyone and drag me down here just to prove you're a big macho cop." I made grunting noises like Tim Allen, which I probably shouldn't have.

He just looked amused, and motioned with his fingers. "Hand it over."

I snorted. "Get real. Even if you tore it up, do you think I wouldn't remember what's on the list?"

"That isn't the point. Hand it over."

Instead I tucked the list into my bag and zipped it.

"Then what *is* the point, because I'm missing something here."

He got to his feet with a smooth, powerful grace that reminded me what an athlete he was. "The point," he said as he came around the desk and calmly took my bag away from me, "is that the men in your life probably let you get away with murder—figuratively speaking—because you're so damned cute, but I'm not going to go down that road. You're in my territory and I said hand over the list, so if you don't do it, I'll have to take it away from you. *That's* the point."

I watched as he unzipped my bag and took out the list, which he slipped into his pants pocket. I could have gone for another undignified struggle, but even if I'd won—which wasn't likely—retrieving the list would have meant putting my hand in his pocket and I wasn't born yesterday. This was one battle I'd be smarter not to fight. Instead I shrugged. "So I'll write one when I get home, where, by the way, I would like to have been an hour ago. You should also really work on this problem you have of making everything personal, Lieutenant Bloodsworth." I kept calling him that instead of *Wyatt* because I knew it irritated the hell out of him. "In your job, that could be a real problem."

"What's between us is definitely personal," he retorted as he gave my bag back to me.

"Nope. Not interested. Sorry. May I go home, please?" Maybe if I said it often enough, he'd get tired of hearing it. A big yawn punctuated the end of my sentence, and I swear I didn't fake it. I covered it with my hand, but it was one of those jaw-cracker yawns that just took over and seemed to go on forever. My eyes were watering when it finally ended. "I'm sorry," I said again, and rubbed my eyes.

Damn his eyes, he grinned. "Just keep saying you aren't interested often enough, and maybe by the time you're ninety you'll believe it. Come on, I'll take you home before you collapse," he said before I could respond to his first statement, putting his hand on my waist and urging me toward the door.

Finally! I was so glad to be making progress toward home that I didn't pay proper attention to where his hand was or how it looked. He leaned forward and opened the door for me, and as I stepped through it, what seemed like a hundred pairs of eyes turned toward us. Patrol officers in uniform, detectives in street clothes, a few people who were obviously there under protest—the department was a beehive of activity despite the lateness of the hour. If I'd been paying attention, I'd have noticed the hum of voices and ringing of telephones outside that closed door, but I'd been focused on my battle with Wyatt.

I saw a multitude of expressions: curiosity, amusement, prurient interest. The one expression I didn't see, I realized, was surprise. I spotted Detective MacInnes hiding a grin as he looked back down at the paperwork on his desk.

Well, what had I expected? Not only had they witnessed our very public disagreement that ended with him putting me in his car—only the public part had ended, not our disagreement—but now I realized Wyatt must have said something that indicated we had a personal relationship. The sneaky rat was trying an end run around my objections, but more important, he had made certain none of his people would interfere in our argument.

"You think you're so smart," I muttered as we stepped into the elevator.

"I must not be, or I'd stay the hell away from you," he replied calmly as he punched the button for the bottom floor.

"Then why don't you up your IQ and go after someone who wants you?"

"Oh, you want me, all right. You don't like it, but you want me."

"Wanted. Past tense. As in, not now. You had your chance."

"I still have it. All we did was take a breather."

My mouth was open in astonishment as I stared up at him. "You call two years a *breather*? I've got news for you, big boy: your chance was over by the end of our last date."

The elevator stopped and the doors slid open—it doesn't take long to travel three floors—and Wyatt did the hand-on-my-waist thing again, ushering me out of a small foyer and into the parking lot. The rain had stopped, thank goodness, though the trees and power lines still dripped. His white Crown Vic was parked in the fourth slot down, where a sign saying, "Lt. Bloodsworth," was posted. The parking lot was fenced and gated, so there weren't any reporters waiting outside that entrance. Not that there would be a lot, anyway; our town had one daily newspaper and one weekly, four radio stations, and one ABC affiliate television station. Even if every station and newspaper sent a reporter, which they wouldn't, that was a grand total of seven.

Just to be a smart-ass, I reached for the back door handle. Wyatt growled and pulled me forward as he opened the front passenger door. "You're a pain, you know that?"

"In what way?" I seated myself and buckled the seat belt.

"You don't know when to stop pushing." He closed the door with a solid thunk, and went around to the driver's side. He got in and started the car, then turned in the seat to face me and draped one arm along the back of the seat. "We aren't in an elevator now with a camera watching every move, so tell me again how my chance with you is over and you don't want me."

He was challenging me, actually egging me on so I'd say something rash and give him a reason to do something just as rash, such as kiss me. The parking lot lights were bright enough for me to see the glint in his eyes as he waited for my response. I wanted to fire a verbal blast back at him, but that would have been playing his game and I was so tired I knew I wasn't at the top of my form. So I yawned in his face and mumbled, "Can't this wait? I'm so tired I can't see straight."

He chuckled as he turned around and buckled his own seat belt. "Coward."

Okay, so he didn't buy it. What mattered was that he'd decided not to push the issue.

Well, I showed him. I leaned my head back and closed my eyes, and despite the amount of caffeine I'd had that night, I was asleep before we were out of the parking lot. That was a gift I had; my dad called it

Lights Out Blair. I've never been one to toss and turn at night, but with all the stress and coffee I thought this would be one night when sleep wouldn't come. Not to worry; the lights went out as usual.

I woke when he opened the car door and leaned in to unbuckle my seat belt. I blinked sleepily at him, trying to bring him into focus. "Are we there yet?"

"We're there. Come on, Sleeping Beauty." He picked up my bag from the floorboard, then tugged me out of the car.

I live in the Beacon Hills area—the condos are called Beacon Hills, which is so original—meaning all the streets march up and down hills. Beacon Hills Condominiums comprises eleven separate buildings, each containing four three-story units. I live in the third building, first unit, which means I have windows opening to the outside on three sides, not just two. The end units cost more than the middle units, but to me the windows were worth it. Another big plus was the side portico under which I could park my car. Middle dwellers had to park at the curb. Yes, the side portico also upped the price of the end units. So what? I didn't have to park my Mercedes in the weather, so the portico was worth the cost. Having been there before, Wyatt had parked under the portico.

There was a front entrance, of course, but there was a door connecting the portico and a small entrance nook that also contained my washer and dryer and then led into the kitchen. I almost never used the front entrance unless a date was bringing me home, and the lights beside the side door were on a timer.

They came on at nine P.M., so I never had to fumble my way inside in the dark.

I took my bag from him and dug out my keys. "Thank you for bringing me home," I said politely. I didn't even point out that I would have preferred taking a taxi.

He loomed over me, standing too close, and I automatically tightened my grip on my keys in case he tried to take them from me. "I want to check the locks on your doors and windows."

"Dad can do it tomorrow. I'll be fine tonight, because no one will know I witnessed anything until the papers come out."

"Is your dad knowledgeable about security?"

No more than I was, but, hey, I had an alarm system, and I could check my own doors and windows. "Lieutenant Bloodsworth," I said as firmly as I could around another yawn. "Go home. Leave me alone." As I spoke I unlocked the door and moved so I was blocking him.

He leaned a shoulder against the doorjamb and smiled down at me. "I wasn't intending to force my way in, you know."

"That's good. Why don't we pretend you're a vampire and can't ever come in unless I invite you?"

"You already have invited me, remember?"

Oh. Well, there was that. "I've redecorated since then. That starts everything over. Go home."

"I am. I'm pretty beat, myself. You redecorated, huh? What was wrong with the way things looked before?"

I rolled my eyes. "I'm sure you're so interested in

interior decorating. *Go home.* Leave. But make sure you have someone bring my car to me first thing in the morning, okay? I can't be stuck here without it."

"I'll take care of it." He reached out and cupped my face, his thumb lightly tracing my lips. I drew back, glaring at him, and he laughed. "I wasn't going to kiss you. Not yet, anyway. There might not be anyone around to see at this time of night—or morning, rather—but since your clothes tend to come off when I kiss you, we'd better wait until we're more private and have both had some sleep."

He made it sound as if I started stripping whenever he touched me. I gave him a poisonously sweet smile. "I have a better idea. Why don't you cram—"

"Uh-uh," he cautioned, putting a finger over my lips. "You don't want to let that sassy mouth get you in trouble. Just go inside, lock the door behind you, and go to bed. I'll see you later."

Never let it be said that I don't recognize good advice when I hear it. I always *recognize* it; actually following it is a different category. In this instance, however, I did the wise thing and slipped inside, and locked the door just as he'd directed. Yeah, he might think I was actually following his orders, but it just so happened his orders coincided with my survival instinct.

I turned on my kitchen light and stood at the door waiting until his car pulled away before I turned off the outside lights. Then I stood in the middle of my familiar, cozy kitchen and let everything that had happened that night crash in on me.

There was a sense of unreality to everything, as if I had disconnected from the universe. My surroundings were my own, yet they seemed somehow alien, as if they belonged to someone else. I was both exhausted and jittery, which is not a good combination.

First thing, I turned on all the lights on the ground floor and checked all the windows, which were securely locked. Likewise with the doors. The dining alcove had double French doors leading onto my covered patio, where I keep strands of little white lights outlining the posts and roof edge, and entwined through the young Bradford pear trees. I turn the lights on almost every night that I'm home, because I love how they look, but tonight I felt vulnerable with all that glass and I pulled the heavy curtains closed over the French doors.

After setting the security system, I did what I had been wanting to do for *hours*. I called Mom.

Dad answered, of course. The telephone was on his side of the bed because Mom didn't like answering it. "Hello." His voice was a sleepy mumble.

"Dad, it's Blair. There was a murder at the gym tonight, and I wanted to let you know I'm all right."

"A—*what*? Did you say murder?" He sounded much more awake now.

"One of the members was killed in the back parking lot"—I heard Mom in the background saying fiercely, *"Give me the phone!"* and I knew his possession of the phone was numbered in seconds—"a little after nine, and I— Hi, Mom."

"Blair. Are you all right?"

"I'm fine. I wouldn't have called, but I was afraid someone else would, and I wanted you to know that I'm okay."

"Thank God you did," she said, and we both shuddered at what she might have done if she'd thought any of her children had been hurt. "Who was killed?"

"Nicole Goodwin."

"The copycat?"

"That's her." I might have complained about Nicole a time or two to my family. "She was parked in the back parking lot, waiting for me—we had a slight altercation this afternoon—"

"Do the police think you did it?"

"No, no," I soothed, though for a while I had definitely been Suspect Number One. Mom didn't need to know that, though. "I had just stepped outside tonight and locked up when this man shot her, and he didn't see me. He left in a dark sedan."

"Oh, my God, *you're a witness*?"

"Not really," I said ruefully. "It was dark and raining, and there's no way I could ever identify him. I called nine-one-one, the cops came, and that's all I know. They have just brought me home."

"What took them so long?"

"The crime scene. It took *forever* for them to go over everything." Not to mention I probably would have been home a couple of hours earlier if it hadn't been for a certain lieutenant.

"Um . . . they brought you home? Why didn't you drive?"

"Because my car is inside the area they have taped off, so they wouldn't let me go back there. An officer is supposed to bring it to me in the morning." Morning meant some time after daylight, because technically it was already morning. I expected to see my car between eight and ten, and I would be *so* lucky if an officer and not Wyatt delivered it. "Great Bods will have to be closed for a couple of days, too, maybe longer. I think I'll go to the beach."

"That's a great idea," she said firmly. "Get out of Dodge."

It's scary sometimes how my mom and I think alike.

I reassured her again that I was okay, that I was going to bed because I was exhausted, and hung up feeling much better. She hadn't made any there-there noises, which is so not my mom, but I had headed off any well-meaning gossips who would have upset her.

I thought about calling Siana, but I was too tired to remember my list of grievances off the top of my head. After I'd had some sleep, I'd write them all down again. Siana would get a kick out of my run-in with Lieutenant Bloodsworth, because she knew about our past connection.

There was nothing I wanted more than sleep, so I turned off all the lights except for the dim sconces that lit the stairs; then I climbed up to my bedroom, where I pulled off my clothes and collapsed naked in my cloud of a bed. I groaned aloud with relief as I stretched out— then I ruined the moment of bliss by imagining Wyatt naked and stretching out on top of me.

The damn man was a menace. Before my wayward imagination went any further, I made myself recall and go over every detail of our last date, when he had acted like such a horse's ass.

There. That worked.

Feeling peaceful, I rolled over and went to sleep. Lights Out, Blair.

CHAPTER
SIX

He'd remembered that I drank Diet Coke. That was the first thought on my mind when I woke at eight-thirty. Lying there in bed blinking sleepily at the slowly whirling ceiling fan, I tried to decide whether the Diet Coke was significant. The romantic in me wanted to believe he remembered every little detail about me, but levelheaded me said he probably just had a very good memory, period. A cop had to have a good memory, right? It was part of the job description, reciting Miranda and all of that.

So the Diet Coke thing wasn't important. For all I knew, he just assumed a woman would drink a diet soft drink, which was a really sexist thing to assume, never mind that he'd be right most of the time.

I'd fallen into bed instead of packing, so there went my planned early start for the beach. Not that it mattered, because I didn't have a car. But someone—namely Wyatt—could show up with my car at any time, so I jumped out of bed and into the shower. The shower was a fast one, because I was so hungry I thought I'd be sick. Somehow I hadn't gotten around to eating anything the night before.

Yeah, yeah, I know I shouldn't complain about being hungry when poor Nicole will never eat again. Tough. Nicole was dead and I wasn't, and I didn't like her any more now that she was dead than I did while she was alive.

Even worse, she was the cause of Great Bods being closed for an indefinite length of time. If she hadn't been such a bitch, waiting for me in the parking lot to do whatever damage she'd planned, she wouldn't have been killed on my property. To take this conclusion to the very end, it was also Nicole's fault that I'd been forced to see Wyatt Bloodsworth again.

Last night, I'd felt sorry for Nicole. Today I was thinking more clearly, and I figured it was just like her that, even dead, she was causing trouble for me.

I put on the coffee, grabbed a cup of yogurt from the refrigerator because that was fast, and ate it while I popped two slices of whole wheat bread into the toaster and peeled a banana. One peanut butter, honey, and banana sandwich—and two cups of coffee—later, I was much happier. Sometimes, when I'm really busy at Great Bods, I'll make do with an apple or something like that for lunch, but when I have the time to sit down, I like to *eat*.

Once I felt as if I wouldn't collapse from hunger, I got the morning newspaper from the front steps and, over another cup of coffee, absorbed just how big the paper was playing Nicole's murder. The article was on the bottom half of the front page, and included a picture of Wyatt and me when he was hauling me out of

Great Bods to stuff me in his car. He looked big and grim, and I looked in really great shape, with the pink halter top revealing my toned abs. I didn't have a six-pack, but I didn't go for the really muscular look, so that was fine. I was thinking that my abs were a good advertisement for Great Bods when I read the caption under the photo: *"Lieutenant J. W. Bloodsworth leads witness Blair Mallory from the crime scene."*

"Leads," my ass! *Hauled* was more like it. And why did they have to identify me in the big color photo on the first page, huh? Why couldn't the reporter have stuck my name somewhere toward the end of the article?

I read the entire article, and nowhere did I find Wyatt's official statement about witness*es*, plural. The only mention of a witness was singular—little old me. Probably by the time he'd made the statement, the paper had already gone to press. There would probably be another article in tomorrow's paper, but I was afraid the damage was done.

Right on cue, my phone rang. I looked at the Caller ID and saw the name of the newspaper. No way was I talking to a reporter, so I let the answering machine pick up the call.

Yes, indeed, this looked like a great day to leave town.

I dashed upstairs and dried my hair, then put on pink capri pants, a white tank, and the cutest flip-flops with little pink and yellow shells on the straps. Is that the best beach outfit, or what? I brushed my teeth, put on moisturizer and mascara, then added a little bit of blush and lip gloss just in case. In case what? In case Wyatt delivered the car, of course. Just because I didn't want him back didn't mean I wouldn't take joy in showing him just exactly what he'd turned down before.

The phone kept ringing. I talked to Mom, who was just checking to see how I was doing. I talked to Siana, who was wildly curious about both the murder and the photograph of me with Wyatt, since she had listened to me rant about him two years ago. Other than that, I didn't answer any of the calls. I didn't want to talk to any reporters, nosy acquaintances, or possible murderers.

Traffic on the street outside my condo seemed to be unusually heavy. Maybe it was a good thing my car wasn't parked under the portico; from the street, it must have looked as if no one was home. Still, I had things to do and places to go; I needed wheels.

By ten, my car still hadn't been delivered. I was doing a slow burn as I looked up the number for the police department.

Whoever answered the phone, sergeant somebody, was polite but ultimately unhelpful. I asked for Lieutenant Bloodsworth. He wasn't available. Neither was Detective MacInnes. The sergeant transferred me to someone else, who transferred me to someone else. I had to explain the entire situation each time. Finally—*finally*—I got Detective Forester and went through my spiel again.

"Let me check. I don't think the lieutenant is in the building, but I'll see what I can find out about your car," he said, and put the phone down.

I could hear noise, the kind of noise made by a lot of different voices. I could hear telephones ringing, papers rustling. Days were evidently as busy at the police department as nights were. I waited. I examined my manicure, which was holding up nicely. I began to think about lunch, which could be a problem unless someone—anyone!—delivered my car. I seldom eat lunch at home; I have mostly breakfast food, and I was getting low on that because I hadn't bought groceries in a couple of weeks. I guessed I could have a pizza delivered, but I wasn't in the mood for pizza. I was in the mood to strangle one police lieutenant.

Finally Detective Forester came back to the phone. "Ma'am, Lieutenant Bloodsworth is taking care of your car."

"*When?*" I asked with clenched teeth. "I'm stranded here without it. He was supposed to have it brought to me early this morning."

"I'm sorry for that, ma'am. He's been very busy today."

"Then why can't a patrolman bring the car to me? Or—I know!—I'll take a taxi to Great Bods and someone can meet me there, and move the car from the back parking lot. That would save time and trouble for everyone."

"Hold on," he said, and I held. And held. And held. About ten minutes later he picked up the phone and said, "Ma'am, I'm sorry, but I can't get anything arranged right now."

Okay, this wasn't his fault. I managed to make my tone calm. "I understand. Thank you for checking. Oh—do you have Lieutenant Bloodsworth's cell phone number? I misplaced it, or I'd have called him directly instead of bothering you."

"It's no bother," Detective Forester said gallantly, and rattled off the number.

Heh heh heh. Thanks to Wyatt's high-handed actions the night before, all the cops thought we were involved. Why wouldn't the detective give Wyatt's cell number to me? That was a tactical error on Wyatt's part.

Wyatt might be in the middle of something important, and calling him would be a big distraction. Damn, I hoped so. I started punching in the numbers, then stopped. He probably had Caller ID on his cell, and he might not answer a call he knew was from me.

Smirking, I put down the cordless and retrieved my own cell phone from my bag. Yes, Detective MacInnes had been kind enough to return it to me last night, once he had determined I hadn't shot Nicole. I turned it on and called Wyatt.

He answered on the third ring. "Bloodsworth."

"Where's my car?" I demanded in as menacing a tone as I could muster.

He sighed. "Blair. I'll get to it. I've been a little busy today."

"I'm *stranded. If* you had listened to reason last night, you could have retrieved my car then and we wouldn't be having this conversation, but, no, you had to throw your weight around—"

He hung up on me.

I shrieked in fury, but I didn't call him back, which he probably expected. Okay, he was going to be a jerk.

Fuck him. Well, not literally. Though once upon a time I—never mind. I wasn't going there.

I drummed my fingers and considered my options. I could call Mom and Dad and they would gladly give me a ride to a grocery store, or even lend me one of their cars, which would be an inconvenience for them. Siana would also ferry me around. Jenni *might,* if she didn't have anything else going on, but her social calendar made me exhausted just to think about it.

On the other hand, I could simply rent a car. Several of the name-brand rental agencies would pick you up and take you back to their office to sign the papers and get the car.

I don't dillydally around when I come up with a plan of action. I looked up the number of a rental agency, called them, and arranged to be picked up in an hour. Then I raced around watering plants and packing what clothes I thought I'd need for a few days at the beach, which wasn't many. Makeup and toiletries took up way more room than my clothes in the duffel bag. I added a couple of books in case I felt like reading, then stood at the front door impatiently waiting for the rental car guy to show up.

The traffic had lessened; maybe all the gawkers and/or reporters had decided I was in hiding somewhere, or had maybe gone shopping. Still, when my ride appeared I didn't want to dally around on the front steps, an easy target for either an eager reporter or a desperate killer. I got my keys out to have them ready to lock the dead bolt on the front door, and that was when I noticed I still had my car keys. I was surprised into laughing; there was no way Wyatt could have had my car delivered, because I hadn't given him the keys and he hadn't thought to ask for them.

The car would be all right at Great Bods until I got back. It was locked, and it was under the awning. At worst, Wyatt would have it towed to the city impound lot, which he had better not do because if my car was damaged in any way, I'd definitely sue him.

A red Pontiac with a magnetic sign on the side announcing it belonged to the rental agency pulled to the curb. I grabbed my duffel and was out the door before the guy could get out of the car. I paused only to lock my door, then hurried down the steps to meet him. "Let's go before someone shows up," I said, opening the rear passenger door and tossing my duffel inside, then sliding into the front seat.

The man got behind the steering wheel, blinking in confusion. "Who? Is someone after you?"

"Maybe." If he didn't know who I was, that was all to the good. Maybe no one much read the newspaper anymore. "An ex-boyfriend is really making a nuisance of himself, you know?"

"He's violent?" The man threw me an alarmed look.

"No, he just whines a lot. It's embarrassing."

Relieved, he put the car in gear and drove to our small regional airport, where all the rental agencies were located. After some discussion about the type of car they wanted to put me in—I nixed the bare-bones economy models because they were *too* bare bones (one even had roll-up windows, which I didn't know Detroit still made)—I settled on a sharp black Chevy short-bed pickup. Black isn't the most sensible color in the south, because of the heat, but it's undeniably sharp. If I couldn't have my Mercedes, I thought riding around in a pickup truck would be cool.

I have good memories associated with pickup trucks. Grampie had owned one, and during my junior year in high school, for two whole months I'd dated a senior, Tad Bickerstaff, who drove a pickup. Tad had let me drive his truck, which I thought was the best thing ever. Our romance faded as fast as it had bloomed, though, and Tad and his truck had moved on to another girl.

All the papers signed and the gas tank filled, I tossed my duffel in the seat of the pickup and buckled myself in. Beach, here I come!

I admit, summer isn't the best time to head to the beach if you don't have reservations. Even worse, it was Friday, when all the weekenders were doing the same. But since it was only noon, I figured I had a good head start on the weekend crowd, and among them had to be people like me who trusted they'd be able to get a motel room once they reached the shore. People do that only because—duh—it usually works.

Driving from the western part of the state to the eastern shore takes several hours, especially since I had to stop for lunch. I decided I loved driving a pickup, because sitting higher meant I could see so much better, plus this particular truck had plenty of power and all the extras I could want. The ride was smooth, the air-conditioning was top-notch, the sun was shining, and Wyatt Bloodsworth had no idea where I was. Things were looking up.

Around three, my cell phone rang. I looked at the number that showed in the little window; I had dialed it just that morning, so I knew very well who was calling. I let the voice mail answer, and kept on truckin' down the road.

I was getting very excited about my mini-vacation. A couple of days on the beach would do me a world of good, plus take me away from town while interest in Nicole's murder was so high. Normally I'm very responsible, because Great Bods is my baby, but just this once I thought circumstances warranted that I take a break. Probably I should have posted a sign on the front door at Great Bods, though, telling my members when we might reopen. Oh, my God, I hadn't given a thought to my employees! I should have personally called each of them.

Angry at myself, I called Siana. "I can't believe I did this," I said as soon as she answered the phone. "I didn't call everyone and tell them when I expected to reopen Great Bods."

The great thing about Siana is, growing up with me, she learned to read between the lines and fill in the gaps. She immediately knew I wasn't talking about the members because there were so many of them that calling each and every one would take, like, until Great Bods actually reopened, so obviously I was talking about my employees.

"Do you have a list of their numbers at your place?" she asked.

"There's a printed list folded in my address book, in the top left drawer of my desk. If you'll get it, I'll call you back when I get settled and can write all the numbers down."

"Don't bother with that; I'll call them. Since I'm right here and the calls are local, that makes more sense than using your cell phone minutes. I'll also have Lynn update the voice mail message."

"I owe you. Be thinking about what you'd like to have." I love that girl; it's great having a sister like her. I was calling her at work, and she could easily have said she was tied up and she'd get to it as soon as she could, but it might be tomorrow. Not Siana, though; she handled everything thrown at her as if she had all the time in the world. You'll notice I don't say that about Jenni, who still thinks she's privileged. Besides, I have *not* forgotten that I caught her willingly kissing my husband. I don't bring it up and for the most part get along with her, but it's always there in the back of my mind.

"Don't make open-ended promises like that; I might ask for something more than borrowing your best dress. By the way, someone is looking for you, and he sounds angry. Want to guess his name? Hint: he's a police lieutenant."

I was flabbergasted, not that he was looking for me and that he was angry, but that he had called Siana. I'd told him during one of our dates that I had two sisters, but I'm certain I didn't tell him their names or anything about them. On the other hand, it was silly to be surprised: he was a cop; he knew how to find out things about people.

"Wow. He didn't give you any grief, did he?"

"No, he was very controlled. He did say something about betting that I was your lawyer. What was that about?"

"I have a list of grievances against him. I told him I was taking the list to my lawyer."

Siana chuckled. "What would those grievances be?"

"Oh, things like manhandling me, kidnapping me, snotty attitude. He took my list away from me, so I have to write another one. I'll add to it as time goes along, I'm sure."

She was outright laughing now. "I bet he loved the 'snotty attitude' item. Uh—are you going to need me for real? Are you in any trouble?"

"I don't think so. He told me not to leave town, but I'm not a suspect, so I don't think he can do that, can he?"

"If you're not a suspect, why did he say that?"

"I think he's decided he's interested again. Then again, maybe he was just getting back at me because I pretended not to recognize him. I had him going for a while."

"Then it's probably both. He's interested, and he's getting back at you. Plus he's making certain you stay where he can get to you."

"I don't think it worked," I said as I cruised down Highway 74 toward Wilmington.

CHAPTER
SEVEN

I could have gone to the Outer Banks, but I figured I'd have a better chance of getting a room along the southern coast. Heck, I could always keep going south until I reached Myrtle Beach, if necessary. I wasn't looking for entertainment, though, just a place where I could relax for a couple of days until things cooled down at home.

I rolled into Wilmington around six P.M., and worked my way through the city toward Wrightsville Beach. As soon as I saw the Atlantic, Tiffany—my inner beach bunny, remember?—sighed in contentment. She is so easy.

I lucked out and found a cozy little beach cottage at the first place I stopped; the family that had rented it had just canceled. Wasn't that great? I'd rather have a cottage than a motel room any day, because of the privacy. It was the most darling place, a little blue clapboard bungalow with a screened porch and fire pit on the left side. It was just three rooms, sort of; the front half of the house was a tiny kitchen and eating area, which was open to the living room. The back half of the house was a nice bedroom and bath, and whoever had decorated the bedroom had me in mind, because the bed was wreathed in mosquito netting. I love little touches like that, froufrou feminine things.

While I was unpacking, my cell phone rang again. It was the third time Wyatt's number had shown up on Caller ID, and once again I let the call go to voice mail. The phone kept beeping at me, to tell me there were messages, but I hadn't retrieved any of them yet. I figured if I didn't know what he was saying, I wasn't technically defying him, right? He might be threatening me with arrest or something, in which case I would only be upset if I knew about it, so I was better off not listening to his messages.

After unpacking, I went to this great seafood restaurant and absolutely pigged out on boiled shrimp, which I love. It was one of those places where the atmosphere is casual and the service is fast, and I got there right ahead of the supper crowd. I was in and out in forty-five minutes. By the time I got back to my little cottage, twilight was creeping across the beach and the heat was fading; what better time to take a walk?

Color me contented. After my walk, I called home and let Mom know where she could reach me. She didn't say anything about Lieutenant Bloodsworth calling, so maybe he hadn't bothered them.

I slept like a rock that night, and was up at dawn for a run on the beach. I hadn't had any exercise the day before, and I get antsy if I go longer than that without working my muscles. I did a brisk three miles in the sand, which is great for the legs, then showered and searched out a store where I could buy cereal, milk, and fruit.

After breakfast, I put on my turquoise bikini and slathered on waterproof sunscreen, then took a book and a beach towel, slipped my sunglasses on my nose, and hit the beach.

I read for a while; then when the sun got hot, I took a cooling dip in the ocean, and after that read a while longer. By eleven, the heat was too much for me, so I put on my flip-flops and a beach cover-up, got my bag, and went shopping. I love that about beach towns; no one turns a hair if you go shopping in your bathing suit.

I found a really cute pair of blue shorts with a blue-and-white matching top, and a straw bag with a fish embroidered on it with metallic thread, so it glittered in the sunlight. The bag was great for holding all of my beach stuff. I ate lunch on an open deck looking out over the ocean, where a good-looking guy tried to pick me up. I was there to rest, though, not to look for love of the transient variety, so he was out of luck.

Finally I wandered back to my cottage. I'd left my cell phone on the charger, and when I checked it, there were no new missed calls, so evidently Wyatt had given up. After renewing my sunscreen, I hit the beach again. Same routine: read, cool off in the ocean, read some more. By three-thirty, I was so drowsy I couldn't keep my eyes open. Putting my book aside, I stretched out on the towel and went to sleep.

The next thing I knew, someone was picking me up. I mean literally. The odd thing was, I wasn't alarmed, at least not that I was being kidnapped by some beach maniac. I blinked my eyes open and stared up at a hard, angry face that I knew very well. But even before I'd opened my eyes I'd *known*, whether by some weird skin chemistry or subconsciously recognizing the scent of him; my heart did that crazy dance.

He was carrying me toward the cottage. "Lieutenant Bloodsworth," I said in acknowledgment, as if he needed any.

He scowled down at me. "Jesus. Just shut up, okay?"

I don't like being told to shut up. "How did you find me?" I knew Mom wouldn't tell him, just because she's Mom and would figure if he couldn't keep track of me, that wasn't her problem, and if I'd wanted him to know where I was, *I'd* have told him.

"You paid by credit card." He reached the cottage, which wasn't locked, since I'd been lying on the beach right in front of it, and turned sideways to get me through the door. The air-conditioning raised goose bumps on my bare, sun-heated flesh.

"You mean you *tracked* my credit card as if I was a common criminal—"

He released my legs but kept his grip on my upper body, and I grabbed at his shirt for balance. The next thing I knew, he had me lifted off my feet again and his mouth was on mine.

I think I've mentioned that I went into major meltdown whenever he touched me. Two years down the road, that hadn't changed. His mouth felt the same and tasted the same; his body was hard and hot against me, his muscled arms like living steel around me. Every nerve ending in me revved to immediate attention; it was like a mild electrical current running through me, magnetizing me so that I was pulled to him. I actually whimpered as I wound my arms around his neck and my legs around his hips, and kissed him back as hungrily as he was kissing me.

There were a thousand reasons why I should have stopped him right there, and I didn't listen to any of them. The only coherent thought I had was: *Thank God I'm on birth control pills*, which I had gone on and stayed on after my previous experience with him.

My bikini top came off on the way to the bedroom. Frantic to feel his bare skin against me, I yanked and jerked at his shirt, and he obliged me by raising first one arm and then the other so I could pull it off over his head. His chest was broad and hairy, and hard with muscle. I rubbed against him like a cat as he fought to unbuckle his belt and unfasten his jeans. I guess I didn't help any, but I didn't want to stop.

Then he tossed me on the bed and peeled off my bikini bottom. His eyes were glittering as he stared down at me, stretched naked across the bed. He visually searched every inch of my skin, that hot look lingering on my breasts and hips. He pushed my legs apart and looked at me, making me blush, but then he eased two big fingers into me and I forgot about blushing. My knees came up and my hips lifted as sheer delight fizzed through me.

He said, "Fuck," in a strained voice, and pushed his jeans down, letting them drop to the floor. I don't know how he got rid of his shoes; for all I know, he took them off before walking down on the beach to get me, which would have been the best thing to do. But he stepped out of his jeans and then he was on top of me, and the diabolical fiend bit the side of my neck as he entered me with a hard push that took him all the way in.

I went off like a rocket. If I'd had any self-control left, it was destroyed by that bite.

When I settled, I opened my heavy eyelids to find him looking down at me with a fiercely triumphant expression in his eyes. He stroked my hair out of my face and nuzzled my temple with his lips. "Do I need a condom?"

He was already inside me, so it was a little too late to be asking. I managed to say, "No. I'm on the pill."

"Good," he said, and got started on me all over again.

That was the good part about letting passion override common sense. The bad part was when common sense returned. No matter how many orgasms you have, if you have any common sense to begin with, it always comes back.

Daylight was almost gone when I woke from an exhausted, satiated nap to stare in disconcertion at the naked man beside me. Not that he wasn't great to look at, with that strongly muscled body, but I had not only gone against my own rules, I had also lost a huge amount of tactical ground. Yes, the battle of the sexes is like fighting a war. If everything works out, you both win. If it doesn't work out, you want to be the one who loses the least.

Now what? I'd just made love with a man I wasn't even dating! *Used* to date, yes—very briefly. Absolutely nothing between us had been settled, and I had given in like a total surrender-monkey. He hadn't even had to ask.

How humiliating that he was right: all he had to do was touch me, and I started shedding clothes. It didn't help that actually making love with him had been just as good—better—as that damn chemistry reaction between us had promised. That shouldn't happen. It should be illegal or something, because how was I supposed to ignore him the way I wanted to when actually *knowing* how good we were together was so much worse than imagining how it might be? If I'd been tempted before, the feeling would be ten times worse now.

I realized I'd been staring at his penis for a good ten minutes, and in that length of time it had changed from soft and relaxed to not so soft. I looked up to find him watching me, his green eyes both sleepy and hungry.

"We can't do this again," I said firmly, before he could reach for me and undermine my resistance. "Once was enough."

"Must not have been," he said lazily, trailing a finger over my nipple.

He had me there. Damn it. Never go back for seconds.

I brushed his finger away. "I mean it. This was a mistake."

"I don't agree. I think it was a great idea." He raised up on his elbow and leaned over me. A little panicked, I turned my head away before he could kiss me, but he wasn't going for my mouth.

Instead he pressed his lips just under my ear and

trailed sucking little kisses down the side of my neck, following the ligaments that led straight to the soft little hollow where my neck joined my shoulder. Heat flooded through me, and though I opened my mouth to say "no," or something like it, nothing came out except a moan.

He licked and bit and sucked and kissed, and I shuddered and squirmed and generally went crazy. When he slid on top of me again, I was too far gone to do anything except grab him and hold on for the ride.

"That isn't fair!" I stormed at him as I stomped into the bathroom half an hour later. "How did you know that? *Don't do it again!*"

Laughing, he followed me into the shower. I couldn't throw him out unless he let me, so I turned my back on him and concentrated on showering off the heady combination of sunscreen, saltwater, and man.

"Did you think I wouldn't notice, or remember?" He put one big warm hand on the back of my neck, and his thumb stroked up and down. I shuddered.

"You were naked in my lap—"

"I had on a skirt. I was *not* naked."

"Close enough. At any rate, honey, I paid attention. If I touched your breasts, you barely noticed, but when I kissed your neck, you'd almost come. What was so tough about figuring *that* out?"

I didn't like him knowing so much about me. Most men assume that if they touch or kiss your breasts, they're turning you on and can maybe talk you into doing something you don't really want to do. My breasts are pretty much nothing to me, pleasure-wise.

Sometimes I envy women who get pleasure from their breasts, but I'm not one of them, and anyway, I figure keeping a cool head more than offsets the lack.

Kiss my neck, however, and I melt. It's a weakness, because a man can kiss your neck without taking your clothes off, so I don't go around blabbing about it. How had Wyatt noticed so fast?

He was a cop. Noticing details was part of who and what he was. That's fine when he's after a criminal, but he shouldn't be allowed to use that skill in a sexual situation.

"Keep your hands *and* your mouth off my neck," I said, turning around to glare at him. "We are *so* not doing this."

"You have a remarkable talent for ignoring the obvious," he said, grinning down at me.

"I'm not ignoring it; I'm making an executive decision. I don't want to have sex with you again. It's not a good thing for me—"

"Liar."

"—in any way other than sexually," I finished, glaring harder. "Just go back to your life and I'll go back to mine, and we'll forget this ever happened."

"That's not going to happen. Why are you so dead set against us getting together again?"

"We were never *together*. The term implies a relationship, and we never got that far."

"Stop splitting hairs. I couldn't forget about you and you couldn't forget about me. Okay, I give up: not seeing you didn't work."

I turned my back and began shampooing my hair, so angry I couldn't think of anything to say. He *wanted* to forget about me? I'd be glad to help him. Maybe if I hit him in the head with something hard—

"Don't you want to know why?" he asked, sliding his fingers into my hair and massaging my scalp.

"No," I said stonily.

He moved closer, so close his naked body was pressed against me as he worked the suds through my hair. "Then I won't tell you. One day you'll want to know, and we'll talk about it then."

He was the most exasperating man I'd ever seen. I clamped my teeth together to keep from asking him to tell me.

Frustration and resentment built, and finally I relieved it by saying, "You're such an asshole jerk."

He laughed and pushed my head under the shower.

CHAPTER
EIGHT

I don't know how I ended up going to dinner with him. Actually, I do. He wouldn't leave.

I had to eat, and I was starving. So after I got out of the shower, I totally ignored him while I dried my hair and got ready, which actually doesn't take all that long because I didn't bother with anything more than the basic makeup—mascara and lipstick. The summer heat meant I'd just sweat off anything more, so why go to the trouble?

He irritated me no end by actually bumping me away from the bathroom sink with his hip so he could shave. I stared at him openmouthed, because that just isn't the way things work. He looked at me in the mirror and winked. In a snit, I marched into the bedroom and threw on some clothes, which again didn't take long because I didn't bring much in the first place, and what I did bring was color coordinated. Now that I wasn't in a fog of lust, I saw a small black duffel sitting open on the floor at the foot of the bed; that was evidently where the razor and shaving cream came from.

Come to think of it, the closet was fuller . . .

I whirled and opened the closet again. Yes, pushed to the side were a pair of jeans and a polo shirt.

I grabbed them off the hangers and turned to stuff them back into that duffel where they belonged. He came out of the bathroom in time to say, "Thanks for getting these out for me," as he took them from my hands and put them on.

That was when I realized he was out of control, and the best thing I could do was escape.

While he was pulling on his jeans, I rushed through the living room and grabbed my bag and keys on the way out. A rental sedan—a white Saturn—was parked beside the truck, another little detail I'd missed in my earlier delirium. I opened the truck door and slid behind the steering wheel . . . and just kept on sliding, pushed by his big body as he forcibly took my place behind the wheel.

I shrieked and tried to push him out; when he didn't budge, I pulled my feet up and pushed with them, too. I'm strong for a woman, but he was like a rock sitting there. And the jackass was smiling.

"Going somewhere?" he asked as he neatly filched the keys from the floorboard where I'd dropped them.

"Yes," I said, and opened the passenger door. I was sliding out when he caught me under both arms and hauled me back into the truck.

"There are two ways we can do this," he said calmly. "You can sit there like a good girl, or I can handcuff you. Which do you choose?"

"That isn't a choice," I said indignantly. "That's an ultimatum. Neither is what *I* want to do!"

"Those're the only two alternatives I'm offering. Look at it this way: you put me to the trouble of chasing after you, so you're damned lucky I'm giving you even this much of a choice."

"Hah! You didn't have to follow me and you know it. You had no reason other than being an arrogant jackass for telling me not to leave town, so don't act so put upon. You got laid, didn't you? I didn't notice you acting like I was a lot of trouble when you were tossing me on the bed."

He reached across me and grabbed the seat belt, pulling it around to buckle it. "I'm not the only person in this truck who got laid. Fun was had. Rocks were got off. It was a mutual thing."

"Which shouldn't have happened. Casual sex is stupid."

"Agreed. But what's between us isn't casual."

"I keep telling you there is no 'us.' "

"Sure there is. You just don't want to admit it yet." He started the truck and put it in gear. "Nice truck, by the way. It surprised me. You strike me as a luxury-car kind of person."

I loudly cleared my throat, and he looked at me with raised brows. I stared pointedly at his seat belt, which he hadn't fastened. He grunted and put the truck back in park. "Yes, ma'am," he said while he buckled himself in.

As he backed out of the driveway I returned to the argument. "See? You don't know what kind of person

I am. I like driving pickups. You really don't know anything at all about me, so therefore we have nothing between us except for physical attraction. That makes the sex casual."

"I beg to differ. Casual sex is scratching an itch, and nothing more."

"Bingo! My itch has been scratched. You can go now."

"Are you always like this when your feelings get hurt?"

I set my jaw and stared out the windshield. I wished he hadn't realized that hurt feelings *were* behind my hostility and resistance to him. You have to care about someone before he can hurt your feelings, because otherwise what he said or did wouldn't even blip on the old radar screen. I didn't want to care about him; I didn't want to care about what he did or whom he saw, if he was eating properly or getting enough sleep. I didn't want to be hurt again, because this man could hurt me big-time if I let him get really close. Jason had hurt me bad enough, but Wyatt could break my heart.

He reached out and put his hand on the back of my neck, gently massaging. "I'm sorry," he said gently.

I could tell I was going to have trouble with him when it came to my neck. He was like a vampire, going straight for it whenever he wanted to influence me. The apology wasn't playing fair, either. I wanted him to crawl, and here he was undermining my resolve with that simple apology. The man was sneaky.

The best thing to do was fight fire with fire, and tell him exactly where he stood and what the problem was. I reached up and removed his hand from the back of my neck, because I couldn't think straight while he was touching me there.

"Okay, here it is," I said steadily, still focusing on what was outside rather than in the truck with me. "How can I trust you not to hurt me again? You cut and ran instead of telling me what the problem was, instead of working on it or giving *me* a chance to work on it. My marriage failed because my husband, instead of telling me something was wrong and working with me to fix it, started running around on me. So I'm not real big on trying to build relationships with people who aren't willing to put some effort into maintaining it and repairing the breakdowns. You do that for a car, right? So my standard is, a man has to care as much about me as he does about his car. You failed."

He was silent as he absorbed all of that. I expected him to start arguing, explaining how the situation looked from his side of the fence, but he didn't. "So it's a trust thing," he finally said. "Good. That's something I can work with." He slanted a hard look at me. "That means you'll be seeing a lot of me. I can't earn your trust back if I'm not around. So from now on, we're together. Got it?"

I blinked. Somehow I hadn't foreseen he would take a lack of trust and make it seem as if that meant I *had* to be in a relationship with him so he could re-earn my trust. I'm telling you, the man is diabolical.

"You've had a brain fart," I pointed out as kindly as possible. "Not trusting you means I don't *want* to be with you."

He snorted. "Yeah, right. That's why we tear each other's clothes off every time we get within touching distance."

"That's a chemical imbalance, nothing more. A good multivitamin will take care of that."

"We'll talk about it over dinner. Where do you want to eat?"

That's right, distract me with food. If I hadn't been so hungry, his ploy would never have worked. "Someplace with champion air-conditioning where I can sit down and some nice person will bring me a margarita."

"That works for me," he said.

Wrightsville Beach is actually on an island, so we drove across the bridge to Wilmington, where, in short order, he was escorting me into a crowded Mexican restaurant where the air-conditioning was cranked up on high and the menu boasted a huge margarita. I don't know how he knew about the restaurant unless he'd been to Wilmington before, which I guess isn't that much of a stretch. People go to beaches the way lemmings do whatever it is that lemmings do. There are a lot of beaches in North Carolina, but he'd probably been from one end of the coast to the other back in his hell-raising, college-ball-playing days. I'd been a cheerleader, and *I* certainly had hit almost every beach in the southeast, from North Carolina down to the Florida Keys and back up the Gulf Coast.

A young Hispanic man brought our menus and waited to take our drink orders. Wyatt ordered a beer for himself and a frozen Cuervo Gold margarita for me. I didn't know what Cuervo Gold was, and I didn't care. I assumed it was a special kind of tequila, but it could have been regular tequila, for all I knew about it.

The glass they brought it in wasn't a glass. It was a vase. This thing was *huge*. It wasn't actually a vase, but I wouldn't call it a glass, either. It was more like a gigantic clear bowl perched on a skinny pedestal.

"Uh-oh," Wyatt said.

I ignored him and gripped my margarita with both hands, which I needed to lift it. The huge bowl of the glass was frosty, and salt sparkled around the rim. Two slices of lime were perched on top, and a bright red plastic straw provided access to the contents.

"We'd better order," he said.

I sucked on the straw and downed a sizable gulp of margarita. The tequila taste wasn't very strong, which was fortunate, or I'd have been on my butt before I was halfway finished with the thing. "I like burritos rancheros. Beef."

It was amusing watching him watch me while he gave the order. I took another big sip through the straw.

"If you get drunk," he warned, "I'm going to take pictures."

"Why, thank you. I've been told I'm a very cute drunk." I hadn't, but he didn't know that. I had actually never been drunk before, which probably means I had an abnormal college experience. But I'd always had cheerleading practice, or gymnastics—or something unexpected, like an exam to take—and I didn't think any of those would be a happy experience while suffering a hangover, so I simply stopped drinking before I got drunk.

The waiter brought a basket of hot, salty tortilla chips and two bowls of salsa, hot and mild. I resalted half the tortilla chips and dug one into the hot salsa, which was delicious and definitely hot. Three chips later I broke out into a sweat and had to reach for my margarita again.

Wyatt reached out and moved my vase—my glass—out of reach.

"Hey!" I said indignantly.

"I don't want you getting pickled."

"I'll get pickled if I want."

"I need to ask you some more questions, which is why I didn't want you to leave town."

"Nice try, Lieutenant." I leaned forward and retrieved my margarita. "For one thing, the detectives are working the case, not you. For another, I didn't see *anything* other than a man was with Nicole, and he left driving a dark sedan. That's it. Nothing else."

"That you know of," he said, snatching away my margarita just as I guided the straw to my mouth for another sip. "Sometimes details will surface days later. For instance, the car's headlights. Or the taillights. Did you see them?"

"I didn't see the headlights," I said positively, intrigued by the question. "The taillights . . . hmm. Maybe." I closed my eyes and replayed the scene in my head. It was shockingly detailed and vivid. In my imagination I saw the dark car sliding past, and to my surprise my heartbeat picked up in response. "The street is at a right angle to me, remember, so anything will be a side view. The taillight is . . . long. It isn't one of those round ones; it's a long skinny one." My eyes popped open. "I think some models of Cadillac have taillights that shape."

"Among others," he said. He was writing down what I'd said, in this little notepad he'd evidently dug out of his pocket, because it was bent like a pocket dweller.

"You could have asked me this over the phone," I pointed out acerbically.

"Yes, if you were answering your phone," he replied in the same tone.

"*You* hung up on me."

"*I* was busy. Yesterday was a ballbuster. I didn't have time to worry about your car, which, by the way, I couldn't get anyway because you didn't bother giving your keys to me."

"I know. I mean, I didn't know then. I found them a little later. But the paper only identified *me* as a witness and that made me feel uneasy, and Tiffany was whining, so I rented wheels and came to the beach."

He paused. "Tiffany?"

"My inner beach bunny. I haven't had a vacation in a long time."

He looked at me as if I'd grown two heads, or had admitted to having multiple personalities or something. Finally he asked, "Is there anyone besides Tiffany living inside you?"

"Well, I don't have a snow bunny, if that's what you're asking. I've been snow skiing once. Almost. I tried on those boots and they're so uncomfortable I can't believe people actually wear them without having a gun held to their heads." I drummed my fingers.

"I used to have Black Bart, but he hasn't shown up in a while, so maybe that was just a kid thing."

"Black Bart? He was your inner . . . gunfighter?" He'd started grinning.

"No, he was my inner maniac who would go berserk and try to kill you if you hurt one of my Barbies."

"You must have been hell on the playground."

"You don't mess with a girl's Barbies."

"I'll remember that the next time I have the urge to grab a Barbie and stomp it."

I stared at him, aghast. "You'd actually do that?"

"Haven't in a long time. I must have gotten the Barbie-stomping out of my system by the time I was five."

"Black Bart would have hurt you bad."

He seemed to notice his little notebook on the table and got a puzzled expression on his face, as if he couldn't figure out how the conversation had devolved from headlights to Barbies. Before he could reroute, however, the waiter brought our plates and set them down in front of us with the admonition to be careful because the plates were hot.

The tortilla chips had kept me from total starvation, but I was still mega-hungry, so I dug into the burritos with one hand while I took advantage of his distraction to retrieve my margarita with the other. Being ambidextrous has its uses. Not that I can write or anything with my left hand, but I can definitely retrieve kidnapped margaritas.

Like I said, the drink wasn't strong. There was a lot of it, though. By the time I finished my burritos, I'd downed about half the drink, and I was feeling very happy. Wyatt paid for the meal and kept his arm around me as we walked to the truck. I don't know why; I wasn't staggering or anything. I wasn't even singing.

He lifted me into the truck as though I wasn't capable of sliding in on my own. I gave him a bright smile and hooked one leg around his. "Want to get it on, big boy?"

He choked on a laugh. "Can you hold that thought until we get back to the cottage?"

"I may be sober by then, and remember why I shouldn't."

"I'll take my chances." He gave me a lingering kiss. "I think I can get around that."

Oh, right. My neck. He knew about my neck. I could see I'd have to invest in some turtleneck sweaters.

By the time we got back across the bridge to Wrightsville Beach, the happy glow had indeed faded, leaving me sleepy. I slid out of the truck under my own steam, however, and was walking toward the front door of the cottage when Wyatt scooped me up. "Does that offer still stand?"

"Sorry. The glow has faded. Alcohol-induced lust is a transient thing." He carried me as if he barely noticed my weight, which, by the way, since I'm toned and muscled, is more than you'd think. But he was ten inches taller and muscled himself, which meant he outweighed me by at least eighty pounds or more.

"Good. I'd rather you want me for reasons other than being looped."

"My brain is back in control, and my earlier reasoning still stands. I don't want to have sex with you." Boy, was that a lie. I wanted him like crazy, which didn't mean I should have him or that things would work out between us. Our little talk hadn't reassured me in any way, because actions matter way more than talk and one afternoon together didn't amount to much.

"I bet I can change your mind," he said as he opened the door, which was unlocked because I'd been in a hurry to escape and he'd been in a hurry to catch me.

An hour later, a thought surfaced just as I drifted off to sleep. Forget turtlenecks. To hold him at bay, I needed full body armor.

CHAPTER
NINE

I woke during the night, cold and disoriented. The cold wasn't surprising, because Wyatt had the window air conditioner in the bedroom turned on the "Frost" setting. I must have been dreaming, because a loud noise like a gunshot startled me awake, and for a moment I didn't know where I was.

Maybe I made a sound, or jerked the way you do when you're startled. Wyatt said, "Are you all right?" in an instantly alert voice as he sat up in bed, and the question jerked me out of the weird moment. I stared at him in the darkness, able to make out only the outline of his body framed against the slightly lighter background of the window. I reached out and touched him, my hand finding the warmth of his bare stomach just above the sheet pooled around his hips. Touching him was automatic, an instinctive need for contact.

"I'm cold," I muttered, and he lay back down, pulling me against him and tucking the covers up around my shoulders. I cradled my head on his shoulder and put my hand on his chest, comforted by the warmth and hardness of his body, the substantial presence of him beside me. I hadn't wanted to sleep with him—I mean in the literal sense, because I was still desperately trying to preserve my boundaries—but I'd fallen asleep in the middle of the argument and he'd obviously taken advantage of my unconscious state. I suspected it was a deliberate tactic: exhaust me with sex, so I couldn't stay awake. But now I was glad he was here beside me in the night, snuggling me close and keeping the chill away. This was exactly what I had wanted from him before, this intimacy, the companionship, the link. The depth of my contentment now, in his arms, was frightening.

"What were you dreaming?" he asked, rubbing my back with a slow, soothing stroke. His deep voice was roughened by sleep, and the sweetness of lying there like that with him wrapped itself around me like a quilt.

"I don't know. I don't remember anything. I woke up, and it was one of those creepy times when I didn't know where I was, plus I was cold. Did I say something?"

"No, you just made a funny sound, like you were scared."

"I think I heard a loud noise, but it may have been in my dream. If I was dreaming."

"I didn't hear anything. What kind of loud noise?"

"Like a gunshot."

"No, there definitely wasn't anything like that." He sounded absolutely certain. I supposed, since he was a cop, he was attuned to things like that.

"Then I must have been dreaming about the murder. I don't remember." I yawned and cuddled closer, and as I did a wisp of memory floated back. I hadn't been dreaming about Nicole's murder, but about *mine*, because before the cops found Nicole's body, I'd thought the shot had been aimed at me. For about ten minutes, until the cops arrived, I'd been terrified.

"Wait, I *do* remember a little. I dreamed I was being shot at, which at first I thought was what had happened. I guess my subconscious is working that out."

His arms tightened around me. "What did you do? That night."

"Stayed down, duck-walked back to the door and got inside the building, then locked the door and called nine-one-one."

"Good girl. That was exactly the right thing to do."

"I left out the panicking part. I was scared to death."

"Which proves you aren't an idiot."

"And it also proved I didn't shoot Nicole myself, because I didn't go out into the rain to check things out. I was completely dry. I asked them to do a gun-powder residue test, though, because I was tired and didn't want to be taken in for questioning, which as it turned out was a wasted effort because you dragged me in anyway." That was still a sore point with me.

"Yeah, I heard about the 'thingie' test." His tone was dry. Evidently he thought I'd played like a dumb blond to allay the detectives' suspicions. I can't imagine where he got an idea like that.

"I couldn't think of the name right then," I said innocently. "I was rattled." Half of that was the truth.

"Uh-huh."

I think he didn't believe me. Moving right along, I said, "I don't know why I'd dream about being shot now. Why not the first night? That was when I was so shaken up."

"You were exhausted. You probably did dream, but you didn't wake up enough to remember them."

"Then what about last night? I didn't dream then, either."

"Same theory. You'd had a long drive on not much sleep. You were tired."

I snorted. "Hah! You think I wasn't tired tonight?"

"Different kind of tired." He sounded amused now. "The other was stress. Tonight was pleasure."

That was for certain. Even fighting with him was pleasure on some level, because I got so much enjoyment out of it. I was alarmed because he seemed to be winning all the battles, but I was still exhilarated by the fight. I imagine moths are happy while they're flying right into the fire, too. If Wyatt burned me again, I didn't know what I'd do. He'd already gotten to me way more than he had before, witness the fact that I was in bed with him.

I pinched him. Just because.

He jumped. "Ow! What was that for?"

"For not even courting me before you got me into bed," I said indignantly. "You make me feel as if I'm easy."

"Honey, nothing about you is easy. Trust me." His tone was wry.

"I must be." I managed to put some tears into my voice. Hey, if I can't win the battles, at least I can mess with him, right?

"Are you crying?" He definitely sounded suspicious.

"No." That was the truth. Can I help it if the word quivered a little?

His big hand touched my face. "You are not."

"I said I wasn't." Damn, did he accept nothing on face value? We definitely had an issue with trust here. How was I supposed to get away with anything?

"Yeah, but you were doing that little guilt-trip act. You know damn good and well that all you had to say at any time was 'no' if you really didn't want it."

"You sabotaged me with the neck thing. That has to stop."

"What are you going to do, get rid of your neck?"

"Does that mean you won't promise to leave my neck alone?"

"Are you kidding? Have I ever struck you as the type to cut my own throat?" He sounded lazily amused.

"I'm serious about not having sex. I think it's the wrong thing to do this soon. We should have waited to see if a relationship gets going between us."

" '*Gets* going'?" he echoed. "Seems to me we're halfway around the track already."

"Not really. We haven't left the starting line yet. We haven't even been out on a date. This time, I mean. Two years ago doesn't count."

"We had dinner tonight."

"That doesn't count, either. You used your physical strength against me, then coerced me with threats."

He snorted. "Like that would have stopped you from screaming your head off if you hadn't decided you were hungry and I might as well pay for it."

There was that, of course. Plus I was never in the

least worried that he might actually hurt me. I felt remarkably safe and secure when I was with him—from everything except *him*, of course.

"So here's the deal. I go out with you the way I would if we were starting all over again. That's what you want, isn't it? Another chance? That means no sex, because sex clouds the issue."

"The hell it does."

"Okay, it clouds *my* issues. Maybe when I get to know you better, and you get to know me, we'll decide we don't like each other that much, after all. Or maybe you decide you don't like me nearly as much as I like you, because like I said, sex clouds the issue for me. Maybe men aren't that influenced by having sex with someone, but women are. You'll be saving me a lot of possible heartbreak if we back off and take our time with this."

"You're asking me to close the barn door after the horse is already out."

"So round it up and put it back in your pants—barn, I mean."

"That's your point of view. In mine, it goes against every instinct to *not* make love to you as often as possible, because that's how a man makes sure a woman is his."

From his voice I could tell he was getting testy now. I sort of wished a light were on so I could read his expression, but that would have meant he'd be able to read mine, too, so I left well enough alone. "*If* we were that far along in our relationship, I'd agree with you."

"From the evidence at hand, I'd say we are."

So we were both naked and in bed together. So what?

"But we aren't. We're very much physically attracted to each other, but we don't *know* each other. For instance, what's my favorite color?"

"Hell, I was married for three years and I never knew her favorite color. Men don't think about colors."

"You don't have to think about something to just kind of notice it." I glossed over the fact that he'd been married before. I'd known it, of course, because his mother had told me before she ever introduced us, but I didn't like thinking about it any more than I liked thinking about my own failed marriage. In Wyatt's case, however, I was just plain jealous.

"Pink," he said.

"Close, but no cigar. That's my second favorite color."

"Good God, you have more than one?"

"Teal."

"Teal's a color? I thought it was a duck."

"Maybe the color comes from a duck. I don't know. The point is, if we had spent a lot of time together and really gotten to know each other, you'd have noticed that I wear a lot of teal and you might have guessed it. But you couldn't, because we *haven't* spent a lot of time together."

"The solution to that is to spend more time together."

"Agreed. But without sex."

"I feel as if I'm banging my head against a brick wall," he said to the ceiling.

"I know the feeling." I was beginning to get exasperated. "*The point is,* I'm afraid you'll break my heart if I let you get too close to me. I'm afraid I'll fall in love with you and then you'll walk away again. I want to know you're with me every step of the way if I *do* fall in love with you. How can I know that if we're having sex, when sex means so much to a woman and it doesn't mean much more to a man than just jerking off? It's chemistry, and it short-circuits a woman's brain, sort of drugs her, so she doesn't notice she's sleeping with a rat until it's too late."

There was a long pause; then he said, "What if I'm already in love with you, and I'm using sex to show you that, and to get closer to you?"

"If you'd said 'infatuated,' I might have believed you. I repeat, you don't really know me, therefore you can't truly love me. We're in lust, not love. Not yet, and maybe not ever."

Another long pause. "I understand what you're saying. I don't agree with it, but I understand it. Did you understand what *I* said, about using sex to show you I care?"

"Yes," I said guardedly. What was he leading up to? "And I don't agree."

"Then we're at a stalemate. You don't want to have sex and I do. So let's make a deal: any time I put the move on you, all you have to do is say no and I promise I'll stop, regardless. I may be on top of you about to put it in, but if you say no, I'll stop."

"That's not fair!" I wailed. "What's my record so far in saying no to you?"

"Two years ago, you were two for oh. This time, it's four-zip in my favor."

"See! You're two-thirds better at this than I am. I need a handicap."

"How in hell do you handicap sex?"

"You can't touch my neck."

"Uh-uh. No way in hell are you putting your neck out-of-bounds." Just to prove his point, he hauled me up his body so I was level with him, and before I could stop him, he buried his face in the curve of my neck and shoulders and lightly bit me. Lightning pleasure shot through me and my eyes rolled back in my head.

Yes, he cheated.

A while later, bracing himself over me on his arms, both of us sweaty and our lungs pumping like mad, he said, with great satisfaction, "Make that *five*-zip."

I *hate* it when a man gloats, don't you? Especially when he cheats.

"We'll fly home," he said as we packed our bags after breakfast.

"But my truck—"

"We'll turn the rentals in here. My car's at the airport at home. I'll take you to pick up your car."

Finally I was getting my car back! That part of it was a good plan. But I don't like flying all that much; I do it, occasionally, but I'd much rather drive. "I don't like to fly," I said.

He straightened and stared at me. "Don't tell me you're afraid."

"I'm not *afraid*, exactly, not gasping for breath and things like that, but it isn't my favorite thing. The squad was flying to the West Coast once for a ball game, and we hit some turbulence and dropped far enough that I thought the pilot would never be able to pull us out. Since then I've been uneasy about it."

He watched me for another minute, then said, "Okay, we'll drive. Follow me to the airport so I can turn in my rental."

Well, blow me down. For a minute there I'd expected to be strong-armed onto a plane; I'd told him so many fibs these past few days, why should he believe the truth? But he evidently had a Blair Truth Detector like the one Mom had, and realized that if anything, I was understating a little how much it bothered me to fly. Just a little, because I truly don't panic or anything.

So I followed him to the airport, where he turned in his rental, and then waited behind the wheel while he stored his gear beside mine in the bed of the truck. He surprised me yet again by getting in on the passenger side and buckling himself in without even asking to drive. Only a man secure in his own masculinity will let a woman do the driving in a pickup truck . . . either that or he was very sneakily buttering me up. Whatever. It worked. I was feeling much more mellow with him during the long drive back home.

It was late afternoon when we got to our small regional airport, where he'd left his car. I turned in the rental truck and we transferred everything to his Crown Vic; then he drove me to Great Bods to get my car.

To my dismay, the yellow crime-scene tape was still strung around most of my property. About half of the front parking lot was taped off, and all of the building and the back parking lot. He pulled into the section of parking lot that was open. "When will I be able to reopen?" I asked as I handed over my car keys to him.

"I'll try to get the scene closed tomorrow. If I do, you'll be able to open on Tuesday—but I'm not making any promises."

I stood beside his car while he walked around back, and a moment later he reappeared driving my Mercedes. He pulled in on the other side of the Crown Vic, closest to the street, and stopped beside his car. Leaving the Mercedes running, he got out and transferred my duffel to my small backseat, then stepped back only a little, so that he was standing very close beside me when I started to get into the car. He caught my arm, his big hand warm on my skin.

"I have to work tonight, shuffle some papers around. Will you be at your parents' house?"

Thoughts of him had so completely consumed me for two days that my nervousness about being named as *the* witness to Nicole's murder had almost completely calmed down. "I don't want to do anything stupid, but is there really much of a chance this guy will try to eliminate the witness, namely me?"

"I can't discount the possibility," he said, looking grim. "It isn't likely, but it isn't impossible. I'd feel better if you were either at your parents' or if you came home with me."

"I'll go to their house," I decided, because if he thought I should be worried, then I was worried. "But I need to go home and get more clothes, pay bills, that sort of thing."

"I'll go with you. Get what you need, and do your paperwork when you get to your parents'. Better yet, tell me what you need; I'll get it and bring it to you."

Right, like I was going to let him go through my underwear drawer?

No sooner did I have that thought than I mentally shrugged. Not only had he seen my underwear— some of it, anyway—he'd taken it off me. Besides, I like pretty underwear, so it wasn't as if there was anything there I'd be embarrassed for him to see.

"Give me your little notepad and a pen," I said, and when he produced them from his pocket, I wrote down detailed descriptions of exactly what clothes I wanted him to get for me, and where my unpaid bills were filed. Since I already had my makeup and hair products with me, he was getting off easy.

When I gave him my house key, he looked down at it with a strange expression on his face.

"What?" I asked. "Is something wrong with the key?"

"No, everything's fine," he said, and bent his head. The kiss was warm and lingering, and before I knew it, I was on tiptoe with my arms laced around his neck, kissing him back with enthusiasm, plus interest.

When he lifted his head, he slowly licked his lips, tasting me. My toes curled and I almost told him to take me home with him, but common sense resurfaced at the last moment. He stepped back to give me room to get into the car.

"Oh, I need to give you directions to Mom and Dad's house," I said, remembering at the last moment.

"I know where they live."

"How do— Oh, yeah, I forgot. You're a cop. You checked."

"When I couldn't find you on Friday, yeah."

I gave him the old Beady Eye, which is what Siana called it when Mom knew we had been up to something and would try to stare a confession out of us. "I think you have an unfair advantage, and you throw your cop weight around. That has to stop."

"Not likely. That's what we do," he said, smiling as he turned to go to his car.

"Wait! Are you going to my house now and bringing my things, or are you going to work and bringing them later?"

"I'll bring them now. I don't know how long I'll have to work."

"Okay. See you there." I tossed my bag into the passenger seat, but the toss fell short and the bag hit the console, falling back into the driver's seat. I leaned down to pick up the bag and give it another toss, and a sharp crack reverberated on the street. Startled, I jumped sideways, and a sharp knife of pain sliced through my left arm.

Then a ton of concrete hit me and knocked me to the pavement.

CHAPTER
TEN

The concrete was hard and warm, and was swearing a blue streak. And as I said, he also weighed a ton. "Son of a fucking bitch!" he said between clenched teeth, spitting out each word like a bullet. "Blair, are you all right?"

Well, I didn't know. I'd hit the pavement pretty hard and banged my head, and I was kind of breathless from being squashed beneath him, plus my arm hurt like a mother. I felt sort of boneless from shock, because I'd heard that same crack before and I pretty much knew what was wrong with my arm. "I guess," I said without much conviction.

His head moving from side to side as he kept a watch out for any approaching killers, Wyatt levered himself off me, then hauled me to a sitting position and propped me against the front tire, saying, "Stay!" as if I were Fido. Didn't matter. I wasn't going anywhere.

He pulled his cell phone off his belt and pressed a button. Talking into it as if it were a handheld radio,

he said something hard and fast, of which I understood only "Shots fired," and then our location. Still
swearing, he moved at a fast crouch to his car and
wrenched the back door open. He reached in, and
came out with a big automatic pistol in his hand.

"I *cannot* fucking believe I forgot to get my weapon
out of my bag," he growled as he plastered himself,
his back to me, against the rear tire of my car and
risked a quick look over the trunk, then ducked back
down. "Of all the fucking times—"

"Do you see him?" I interrupted his muttered
stream of profanity.

"Nothing."

My mouth was dry, and my heartbeat was ham-
mering wildly at the thought of the shooter rounding
the car and firing at both of us. We were sandwiched
between the two cars, which should have seemed secure, but instead I felt horribly exposed and vulnerable, with those unprotected spaces at each end of the
cars.

The shot had come from across the street. Very few
of the shops that lined the street were open on Sunday, especially this late in the afternoon, and traffic
was almost nonexistent. I listened, but didn't hear the
sound of a car leaving, which to my way of thinking
wasn't good. Leaving was good; staying was bad. I
wanted the man to leave. I wanted to cry. And I was
seriously thinking about throwing up.

Wyatt glanced over his shoulder at me, his expression grim and focused, and for the first time, got a
good look at me. His whole body stiffened. "Ah, shit,
honey," he said softly. He took another quick look

over the trunk, then moved in a crouch to my side. "Why didn't you say something? You're bleeding like a stuck hog. Let me see how bad it is."

"Not very, I don't think. It just sliced my arm." I thought I sounded just like a cowboy in an old western movie, bravely reassuring the pretty farm-woman his wound was just a scratch. Maybe I should get Wyatt's pistol and return fire across the street, just to complete the illusion. On the other hand, maybe I should just sit here; it took less effort.

His big hand was gentle as he turned my arm so he could examine the wound. Personally, I didn't look. With my peripheral vision I could see way too much blood anyway, and knowing it was all mine wasn't a good feeling.

"It isn't too bad," he murmured. He took another look around, then briefly put his weapon down to take a handkerchief from his pocket and place it, folded, against my wound. He had the big pistol in his hand again less than five seconds after he'd put it down. "Hold this as tight as you can against your arm," he said, and I reached up with my right hand to do as he'd directed.

I struggled not to feel indignant. *Not too bad?* It was one thing for me to be brave and dismissive about being shot, but how dare he? I wondered if he'd be that blasé if it were *his* arm that felt as if it were on fire, if *his* blood was soaking his clothes and beginning to pool on the pavement.

Huh. That pooling on the pavement part couldn't be good. Maybe that was why I felt light-headed and hot and nauseated. Maybe I'd better lie down.

I let myself slide sideways, and Wyatt grabbed me with his free hand. "Blair!"

"I'm just lying down," I said fretfully. "I feel sick."

Supporting me one-handed, he helped me to lie down on the pavement. The asphalt was hot and gritty, and I didn't care. I concentrated on taking deep breaths and staring at the blueness of the late-afternoon sky overhead, and gradually the nausea began to fade. Wyatt was talking on his cell phone/radio, whatever it was, requesting medics and an ambulance. Already I could hear sirens as units responded to a call that their lieutenant was under fire. How much time had lapsed since the shot? A minute? No more than two, I was certain of that.

To one part of me, everything seemed to be moving in slow motion, but another part of me felt as if too much was happening simultaneously. The result was a total sense of unreality, but one in which everything seemed to be crystal clear. I couldn't decide if that was good or not. Probably a little fuzziness would be nice, because I really didn't want to have clear memories of this.

Wyatt crouched over me and put his left hand to my neck. Good God, was he coming on to me *now*? I glared up at him, but he didn't notice because his head was up and he was checking in all directions, his weapon steady in his right hand. Belatedly, I realized he was checking my pulse, and he looked even more grim than before.

I wasn't dying, was I? People didn't die from gun-shot wounds to the arm. That was silly. I was just a little shocky from losing blood so fast, the way I got whenever I gave blood at the Red Cross. It was no big deal. But he'd radioed for an ambulance, which to my way of thinking was for serious stuff, and I wondered if he could see something I couldn't, like maybe an artery spurting out blood like Old Faithful. Not that I had really looked, because I'd been afraid I'd see exactly that.

I pulled the folded handkerchief away from my arm and looked at it. It was totally soaked with blood.

"Blair," he said sharply, "put that back over your wound."

Okay, so maybe I might die. I added up the pieces— a lot of blood, shock, ambulance—and didn't like the picture. "Call my mom," I said. She would be so royally pissed if I had a medical crisis and no one let her know.

"I will," he replied, and now he was trying to sound soothing.

"Now. I need her now."

"You're going to be all right, honey. We'll call her from the hospital."

I was outraged. I was lying there bleeding to death and he refused to call my mother?! If I'd had more energy, I might have done something about it, but as things were, all I could do was lie there and glare, which wasn't having much effect because he wasn't watching me.

Two patrol units, lights flashing and sirens blaring, slid into the parking lot, and two officers, weapons drawn, bailed out of each. Thank goodness each officer driving killed the sirens just before stopping, otherwise we'd have been deafened. There were other units on the way, though; I could hear more sirens, and they seemed to be coming from all directions.

Oh, man, this was going to be so bad for business. I tried to imagine how I would feel if I belonged to a fitness center where there were two shootings in four days. Safe? Definitely not. Of course, if I died, I wouldn't have to worry about it, but what about my employees? They'd be out of a job that paid above the average, plus benefits.

I had visions of the empty parking lot sprouting weeds through the pavement, windows broken, roof sagging. Yellow crime-scene tape would forlornly droop from poles and trees, and kids would walk by and point at the decaying building.

"Do *not*," I said loudly from flat on my back, "string even one inch of that yellow tape in my parking lot. Enough's enough. No more tape."

Wyatt was busy giving instructions to the four officers, but he glanced down at me and I thought he struggled not to smile. "I'll see what I can do."

Here I was bleeding to death, and he was smiling. *Smiling.* I needed to start another list. Come to think of it, I needed to rewrite the one he'd confiscated. He'd distracted me with sex, but now I was thinking clearly again and the list of his transgressions would probably take up two pages—assuming I lived to write them.

This was all his fault.

"*If* a certain lieutenant *had listened to me* and brought my car to me on Friday *the way I asked,* this wouldn't have happened. I'm *bleeding,* and my clothes are *ruined,* and it's *all your fault.*"

Wyatt paused briefly in the middle of my condemnation, then continued talking to his men just as if I hadn't said anything.

Now he was ignoring me.

A couple of the officers seemed to be coming down with something, because they had simultaneous coughing fits—either that or they were trying not to laugh in their lieutenant's face, which I didn't like because, again, I was the one lying there bleeding to death and they were laughing? Excuse me, but was I the only one who didn't think it was funny that I'd been shot?

"*Some* people," I announced to the sky, "have better manners than to laugh at someone who's been shot and is bleeding to death."

"You aren't bleeding to death," Wyatt said, his voice showing some strain.

Maybe, maybe not, but you'd think they'd give me the benefit of the doubt, wouldn't you? I was almost tempted to bleed to death just to show him, but where's the profit in that? Besides, if I died, then I wouldn't be around to make his life miserable, now would I? You have to think these things out.

More vehicles arrived. I heard Wyatt organizing a search-and-destroy mission, though he didn't call it that. It was more like, "Find this bastard," but I knew what he meant. A couple of medics, a young black woman with cornrowed hair and the prettiest chocolate eyes I'd ever seen, and a stocky red-haired man who reminded me of Red Buttons, arrived toting tackle boxes full of medical supplies and gear, and hunkered down next to me.

They quickly did the basics, such as checking my pulse and blood pressure, and slapped a pressure bandage on my arm.

"I need a cookie," I told them.

"Don't we all," said the woman with some sympathy.

"To get my blood sugar up," I explained. "The Red Cross gives cookies to people who give blood. So a cookie would be nice. Chocolate chip. And a Coke."

"I hear you," she said, but no one was making any effort to put the requested items in my hand. I made allowances, because it was Sunday and none of the nearby shops were open. I guess they didn't carry cookies and soft drinks in the medic truck with them, but, really, why didn't they?

"With all these people around, you'd think at least one person would have some cookies in the car. Or a doughnut. They *are* cops."

She grinned and said, "You're right." Raising her voice, she yelled, "Hey! Does anyone have anything sweet to eat in his car?"

"You don't need to eat anything," the red-haired man said. I didn't like him nearly as well as I did her, despite his sweet Red Buttons face.

"Why? I don't need to have surgery, do I?" That was the only reason I could think of not to eat.

"I don't know; that's for the doctors to decide."

"Naw, you won't need surgery," she said, and Red glared at her.

"You don't know that."

I could tell he thought she was being way too free with the rules, and actually I understood his point.

She, however, understood *me.* I needed reassurance, and a cookie would be just that, putting my blood loss on the same plane as giving blood at the Red Cross. If there were sweets available and they wouldn't let me have any, then that meant I was in Serious Condition.

A patrolman appeared, duck-walking between the cars even though no other shots had been fired and any murderer with an ounce of sense would have left the scene as soon as reinforcements arrived. He held a package in his hand. "I got Fig Newtons," he said. He looked puzzled, as if he couldn't understand why the medics needed something to eat and just couldn't wait.

"That'll do," she said, taking the package and tearing it open.

"Keisha," Red said in warning.

"Oh, hush," I said, and took a Fig Newton from the proffered pack. I smiled at Keisha. "Thanks. I think I'll live, now."

Three more Fig Newtons later, I wasn't feeling dizzy at all, and I sat up to prop myself against the tire once more. Red objected to that, too, but he had my well-being in mind, so I also forgave him for wanting to deny me the Newtons. I noticed that the multitude of cops milling around were walking upright now, so evidently the shooter had long since disappeared.

Wyatt was nowhere in sight. He had joined the search-and-destroy mission, and hadn't yet returned. Maybe this time they'd found some clues, though, that would lead them right to the shooter's door.

I was loaded into the back of the boxy ambulance. The back part of the gurney was raised instead of lying flat, so I was in a sitting position. I didn't feel like walking anywhere, but I was definitely up to the task of sitting.

It seems as if nothing at a crime or accident scene is ever done with any haste. Honest. There were a lot of people walking around, most of them uniformed, and most of them not actively doing anything other than talking to other people who were doing the same thing. Radios squawked, and people talked into them. Evidently they'd found the spot from which the shot was fired, and forensics people were going over the area. Red talked on his radio. Keisha repacked stuff. No one was in any hurry, and that was reassuring, too.

"I need my bag," I said, and Keisha retrieved it from my car to set it on the gurney beside me. Being a woman, she understood how much a woman needed her bag.

I fished in the bag for a pen and my date book. I flipped to the back to the blank pages for taking notes, and began writing. Man, this list was getting *long*.

Wyatt appeared at the open doors of the ambulance. His badge was clipped to his belt, and his pistol was in a shoulder holster worn over his polo shirt. Lines bracketed his mouth. "How are you feeling?"

"Fine," I said politely. I wasn't, not really, because my arm was really, really throbbing and I felt weak from blood loss, but I was still mad at him and not inclined to lean on him. See, men *want* you to lean on them, because it satisfies their protective instincts, which are pretty much hardwired, and by refusing his sympathy, I was telling him he was in the dog house. You have to read between the lines on these things.

His green eyes narrowed. He got the message all right. "I'll follow the ambulance to the hospital."

"Thank you, but there's no need. I'll call my family."

The eyes got even more narrow. "I said I'll follow you. I'll call your parents on the way."

"Fine. Do what you want." Which meant, *I'll still be mad.*

He got that message, too. He put his hands on his hips, looking all macho and masculine and disgruntled. "What has you in such a snit?"

"You mean, other than being shot?" I asked sweetly.

"I've been shot. It didn't make me act like a—" He stopped himself, evidently thinking better of what he'd been about to say.

"Bitch? Spoiled brat? Diva?" I supplied the choices myself. Up front, Red was sitting very still as he listened to the argument. Standing off to the side, waiting to close the doors, Keisha was pretending to look at a bird in the sky.

He gave a grim smile. "You choose the ones that fit."

"No problem. I can do that." I wrote another item on my list.

His gaze arrowed in on the date book. "What are you doing?"

"Making a list."

"Jesus Christ, another one?"

"The same one. I'm just adding to it."

"Give me that." He leaned forward into the ambulance as if to snatch the date book away from me.

I jerked it back. "This is my book, not yours. Don't touch it." Over my shoulder I said to Red, "Come on, let's get this show on the road."

"Blair, you're pouting—"

Well, yes, I was. When I felt better I might relent, but until then I felt my pouting was well-deserved. You tell me, if you can't pout when you're shot, just when is it called for?

As Keisha closed the ambulance doors, I said, "Just see if I ever sleep with you again!"

CHAPTER
ELEVEN

"You're sleeping with Lieutenant Bloodsworth, huh?" Keisha asked, grinning.

"I have in the past," I said, and sniffed. So what if the past was just that morning? "He shouldn't hold his breath waiting for the next time." I was a bit chagrined that I had blurted out something as personal as details of my love life, but I'd been provoked.

It seemed to me that Red was driving inordinately slow. I didn't know if he was always that careful—which might not be a good thing when you have someone dying in your ambulance—or if he just wanted to listen to as much of our conversation as possible before we arrived at the hospital. Other than Keisha, no one, absolutely *no one,* seemed to think my condition was worth any extra worry or attention.

Keisha, however, was a woman after my own heart. She'd given me Fig Newtons, and she'd got my bag for me. Keisha understood.

"That would be one hard man to turn down," she commented thoughtfully. "No pun intended."

"A woman's gotta do what a woman's gotta do."

"I hear you, sister." We shared a look of total un-
derstanding. Men are difficult creatures; you can't let
them get the upper hand. And thank God Wyatt was
being difficult, because that gave me something to
think about other than that someone was trying to
kill me. I just wasn't ready to deal with it yet. I was
safe for the time being, and that gave me some breathing space, which was all I needed. I would concentrate on Wyatt and my list until I felt better able to
handle the situation.

At the hospital, I was whisked away and put in a
private little cubicle—well, as private as anything can
be that has a curtain for a door—and a couple of
friendly, cheerfully efficient nurses cut away my blood-
soaked top and bra. I really hated that the bra had to
be sacrificed, because it was this beautiful seafoam
lace and matched my underpants, which I would now
be unable to wear unless I bought another matching
bra. Ah, well. The bra was ruined anyway, because I
doubted any treatment would get bloodstains out of
silk, plus I now had bad memories associated with it
and probably wouldn't have worn it again anyway. I
was draped in a blue-and-white hospital gown, which
was in no way fashionable, and made to lie down
while they did a preliminary workup.

They also peeled the bandage off my arm, and by
now I felt steady enough to get a look at the damage
myself. "Ewww," I said, wrinkling my nose.

Now, there's no place you can get shot that you
won't have muscle damage, except maybe in the eye,

in which case you don't have to worry about it because you're probably dead. The bullet had torn a deep gouge in the outside of my upper arm, just under the shoulder joint. If it had gone any higher, it would likely have shattered the joint, which would have been much more serious. This looked bad enough, because I didn't see how the gouge could be closed with a few stitches.

"It isn't so bad," said one of the nurses. Her name tag said Cynthia. "It's a flesh wound; nothing structural's damaged. Hurts like the dickens, though, doesn't it?"

Amen to that.

My vital signs were taken—my pulse was a bit fast, but whose wouldn't be? Respirations normal. Blood pressure a little elevated over my norm, but not by much. All in all, my body was having a rather mild reaction to being shot. It helped that I was healthy as a horse, and in great shape.

There was no telling what sort of shape I'd be in by the time this arm was well enough for me to work out again, I thought glumly. In a couple of days I'd start doing cardio, then yoga, but there wouldn't be any gymnastics or weight training for at least a month. If getting shot was anything like the other injuries I'd had in the past, muscles took a while to get over the trauma even after the initial symptoms were gone.

They gave the wound a thorough cleaning, which didn't make it hurt any worse than it was already hurting. I was lucky in that my top had been sleeveless and there weren't any fabric fibers caught in the wound. That greatly simplified things.

The doctor finally came in, a lanky guy with wrinkles in his forehead and cheerful blue eyes. His name tag said MacDuff. No joke. "Rough date, huh?" he asked jokingly as he pulled on plastic gloves.

Startled, I blinked at him. "How did you know?"

He paused, startled in turn. "You mean—I was told it was a sniper."

"It was. But it happened at the end of my date." If you could call being followed to the beach and taken by surprise a "date."

He laughed. "I see. Gotcha now."

He took a look at my arm and rubbed his chin. "I can suture this for you, but if you're worried about a scar, we can call in a cosmetic surgeon to do the honors. Dr. Homes here in town has a nice touch with scars; he can make them practically go away. You'll be here a while longer, though."

I was vain enough not to be crazy about the idea of a long scar on my arm, but I also hated the idea of being shot and not having anything to show for it. Think about it. Would this be a great show-and-tell for my future children and grandchildren, or what? I also didn't want to hang around the hospital any longer than necessary, either.

"Go for it," I told him.

He looked a tad surprised, but he went for it. After numbing my arm, he painstakingly pulled the edges of the gash together and began stitching them closed. I think my choice appealed to his pride, and he set about doing an exemplary job.

In the middle of the procedure, I heard a commotion outside and said, "There's my mom."

Dr. MacDuff glanced up at one of the nurses. "Ask everyone to stay outside until I get finished here. Just another few minutes."

Cynthia slipped out of the cubicle, pulling the curtain firmly closed behind her. The commotion got louder; then I heard Mom's voice rising above everything, saying in that tone of finality, "I want to see my daughter. Now."

"Brace yourself," I told Dr. MacDuff. "I don't think Cynthia can hold up against Mom. She won't scream or faint or anything; she just wants to see for herself that I'm alive. It's a mom thing."

He grinned, blue eyes twinkling. He seemed to be an easygoing kind of guy. "They're funny that way, aren't they?"

"Blair!" That was Mom again, disturbing everyone else in the emergency department in her frantic need to find her wounded offspring, namely me.

I lifted my voice. "I'm okay, Mom; I'm just getting some stitches here. We'll be finished in a minute."

Did that reassure her? Of course not. I had also assured her, at the age of fourteen, that my broken collarbone was just a bad bruise. I'd had some lamebrained idea that I could wrap an Ace bandage around my shoulder and still perform, never mind that I couldn't move my arm without screaming. That wasn't one of my better judgment calls.

I'm much better now about assessing my injuries, but Mom would never forget and now wanted to See For Herself. Therefore, I wasn't surprised when the curtain was whisked open—thanks for preserving my privacy, Mom—and my entire family stood there. Mom,

Dad, Siana, even Jenni. Nor was I surprised that Wyatt was there with them, still looking both grim and irritated.

Dr. MacDuff looked up and started to say something along the lines of, "Get out," though he probably would have phrased it more like, "If you people will step outside, we'll be finished in a minute," but he never got that far. He saw Mom and forgot what he was about to say.

That was a common reaction. Mom was fifty-four and looked maybe forty. She was a former Miss North Carolina, tall and slender, blond, and gorgeous. That's just the only word for her. Dad was nuts about her, but that was okay because she was nuts about him, too.

She rushed to my side, but once she saw that I really was mostly in one piece, she calmed and brushed my forehead with her cool hand just as if I were five years old again. "Shot, huh?" she asked gently. "What a tale to tell your grandchildren."

I told you. It's scary.

She switched her attention to Dr. MacDuff. "Hello, I'm Tina Mallory, Blair's mother. Is there any permanent damage?"

He blinked and resumed suturing. "Ah, no. She won't be doing much with this arm for a week or so, but in a couple of months she'll be as good as new. I'll give you some instructions for the next few days."

"I know the drill," she said, smiling faintly. "Rest, keep an ice pack on the arm, antibiotics."

"That's it," he said, smiling back at her. "I'll write her a prescription for pain, but she may be able to handle it with just OTC meds. No aspirin, though; I don't want this bleeding."

You notice he was talking to Mom now instead of me. She has that effect on men.

The rest of my family had crowded into the cubicle, too. Dad moved to Mom's side and slipped his arm around her waist, consoling her through yet another crisis involving one of their children. Jenni moved to the lone visitor's chair and sat down, crossing her long legs. Dr. MacDuff looked at her and started blinking again. Jennifer has Mom's looks, though her hair is darker.

I cleared my throat and brought Dr. MacDuff back to earth. "Suture," I whispered to him.

"Oh—yeah." He winked at me. "Forgot where I was for a minute."

"It happens," Dad said in sympathy.

Dad is tall and lanky, with sandy brown hair and blue eyes. He's calm and laid-back, with this really nutty sense of humor that came in handy a lot during our childhoods. He played baseball in college but majored in electronics, and he handled just fine the pressure of being the only man in a house with four females. I know he was anxious during the drive to the hospital, but now that he knew I was basically all right, he'd settled back into his usual unruffled demeanor.

I grinned at Siana, who was standing by the bed. She grinned back, and cut her eyes to the right. Then she looked back at me with raised brows, which is sister shorthand for: *What's with the hunk?*

The hunk in question, Wyatt, was standing at the foot of the exam table practically glaring at me. No, not glaring, and not even staring. He was *focused* on me, his eyes narrowed, his jaw set. He was leaning forward a little, gripping the footrail, and the powerful muscles in his forearms were taut. He was still wearing his shoulder holster, and the big black weapon rode under his left arm.

My family might have relaxed, but Wyatt hadn't. He was in a very bad mood.

Dr. MacDuff tied off the last stitch, then slid his rolling stool over to a counter, where he scribbled on a prescription pad and tore off the top page. "That's it," he said, "except for the paperwork. The scrip is for both an antibiotic and pain medication. Take all of the antibiotic, even if you feel fine. That's it. We'll get you bandaged up and you can go."

The nurses took care of the bandaging, applying a huge amount of gauze and tape that wrapped around my upper arm and shoulder and would make it virtually impossible for me to get into any of my own clothes. I grimaced and said, "This is so not going to work."

"How long before we can change the bandage?" Mom asked Cynthia.

"Give it twenty-four hours. You can shower tomorrow night," she said to me. "I'll give you a list of instructions. And unless you want to wait while someone goes to get some clothes for you, you can wear this beautiful gown home."

"The gown," I said.

"That's what they all say. I don't understand it my-self, but, hey, when you like something you like it." She left to go do whatever paperwork needed to be done, pulling the curtain closed behind her with a practiced jerk.

The gown in question was half on, half off, with my right arm threaded through one of the armholes but my left arm bare. I'd been preserving my modesty by holding the gown in place over my breasts, but no way could I get the thing the rest of the way on with-out flashing everyone.

"If you men don't mind stepping out," I began, only to be interrupted when Mom picked up my date book, which was lying beside my leg because that's where Keisha had put it.

"What's this?" she said, frowning a little as she read. " 'Unlawful detainment. Kidnapping. Manhan-dled the witness. Snotty attitude—' "

"That's my list of Wyatt's transgressions. Mom, Dad, meet Lieutenant J. W. Bloodsworth. The *J* stands for *Jefferson*, the *W* for *Wyatt*. Wyatt, my parents—Blair and Tina Mallory—and my sisters—Siana and Jennifer."

He nodded at my parents while Siana reached for the list. "Let me see that."

She and Mom put their heads together. "Some of the things on this list are prosecutable," Siana said, her dimples nowhere in sight as she leveled her lawyer's stare at him.

" 'Refused to call my mom,' " Mom read, and turned an accusing look on him. "That's indefensible."

" 'Laughed while I was lying on the ground bleeding,' " Siana continued.

"I did not," Wyatt said, frowning at me.

"You smiled. Close enough."

"Let's see, there's coercion, badgering, stalking—"

"*Stalking?*" he said, doing a wonderful imitation of a thundercloud.

" 'Casual about severity of my wound.' " Siana was having a great time. " 'Called me names.' "

"I did *not*."

"I like the idea of a list," Mom said, taking the date book back from Siana. "It's very efficient, and that way you don't forget anything."

"She never forgets anything anyway," Wyatt said, aggrieved.

"Thank you very much for putting this list thing in Tina's head," Dad said to Wyatt, and he wasn't being sincere. "Way to go." He put his hand on Wyatt's arm and pulled him around. "Let's go outside so they can get Blair dressed, and I'll explain a few things to you. Looks to me like you need the help."

Wyatt didn't want to go—I could see it in his face—but neither did he want to pull any of his snotty attitude with my dad. No, he saved all of that for me. The two men walked out, and of course didn't pull the curtain closed again. Jenni got up and did the honors. She was holding her nose in an effort not to laugh out loud until they were out of hearing distance.

"I'm particularly fond of the 'snotty attitude,' " Siana said, then slapped her hand over her mouth to stifle the giggles.

"Did you see his face?" Mom whispered, grinning. "Poor man."

Poor man, indeed.

"He deserved it," I groused, sitting up and trying to find the left armhole in the gown.

"Just be still; I'll do it," Mom said.

"Don't move your arm at all." That was from Jenni, who had moved around behind me. "Let Mom thread the gown up your arm instead."

Mom did, being very careful around the huge bandage, though it was so thick I doubt I could have felt anything through it anyway, even if Dr. MacDuff hadn't numbed my arm before he started stitching. Jenni pulled the gown's edges together in back, and tied the little strings.

"You aren't going to be able to use that arm for at least a couple of days," Mom said. "We'll pick up some of your clothes and take you home with us."

That was what I'd already figured, so I nodded. A few days of being coddled by my parents was just what the doctor ordered. Well, he hadn't, but he should have.

By the time Cynthia returned with forms for me to sign, a list of instructions, and an aide with a wheel-chair, Dad and Wyatt had also returned. Wyatt may not have been in a better mood, but at least he wasn't scowling at everyone.

"I'll go get the car," Dad said when the aide appeared with the wheelchair.

Wyatt stopped him. "I'll get my car. She's going home with me."

"What?" I said in surprise.

"You're going home with me. In case you've forgotten, honey, someone is trying to kill you. Your folks' house is the first place anyone would look. Not only is it not safe for you, are you willing to endanger them, too?"

"What do you mean, someone's trying to kill her?" Mom demanded fiercely. "I thought it was a random—"

"I guess there's a slight chance the shooting could have been random. But she witnessed a murder last Thursday, and her name was in the paper. If you were a murderer, what would you want to do about a witness? She'll be safe at my house."

"The killer saw you, too," I said, thinking fast. *Saw you kissing me.* "What makes you think he wouldn't track me to your place, too?"

"He wouldn't know who I am, so how could he find out where I live? The only way he'd even know I'm a cop was if he hung around afterward, and trust me, no one was there."

Darn it, he made sense. I didn't want to endanger any of my family—or Wyatt either, come to that—so the last thing I should do was go home with them.

"She can't go home with you," Mom said. "She needs someone to take care of her until she can use her arm."

"Ma'am," said Wyatt, steadily meeting her gaze, "I'll take care of her."

Okay, so he'd just told my family we were sleeping together, because we all knew that "taking care of" meant bathing, dressing, and so on. Maybe I had shouted in front of all his men that I wouldn't sleep with him again, but that was different. For me, anyway. This was my *parents*, and this was the south, where of course such things went on, but you generally didn't announce it to the world or your family. I expected Dad to take him by the arm and lead him out again, for another little talk, but instead Dad nodded.

"Tina, who better to take care of her than a cop?" he asked.

"He has a list of transgressions two pages long," she replied, indicating her doubt that he was capable of taking care of me.

"He also has a gun."

"There is that," Mom said, and turned to me. "You're going with him."

CHAPTER TWELVE

"You know," I said as Wyatt drove me to his place after stopping to get my prescriptions filled, "this guy saw your car, and it has 'cop' written all over it. Who else drives a Crown Vic—I mean, who under the age of sixty drives a Crown Vic except for cops?"

"So?"

"You kissed me there in the parking lot, remember? So he might very well figure we have a thing, you're a cop, and work it from there. How hard can it be?"

"We have over two hundred people in the department; narrowing down which one I am could take time. Then he'd have to find me. My home phone number isn't listed, and sure as hell no one in the department would give out information on me or any other member. If anyone wants to contact me about work, they call this," he said, tapping his cell phone. "And it's registered with the city."

"All right," I conceded. "I'm safer at your place. Not totally safe, but safer." *Someone was trying to kill me.* Despite my best efforts not to think about it just yet, the hard truth of that was pushing in on me. I knew I'd have to come to grips with it pretty soon— say, sometime tomorrow. I'd been sort of expecting it . . . not really, but the possibility had been in the back of my mind . . . but I hadn't factored in the shock of actually being shot. That was totally unexpected.

Just like that—boom!—my life had gone out of control. I couldn't go home, I didn't have my clothes with me, I was in pain, I felt weak and shaky, and God only knew what would happen to my business. I needed to get that control back.

I looked over at Wyatt. He was driving out of the city proper; we had left all the streetlights behind, so his face was lit only by the dash lights, and I shivered a little at how tough he looked. This whole situation with him was out of control, too. I'd tried my best to put on the brakes, and instead here I was, going home with him. He'd seen an opportunity and grabbed it, though I was really surprised, considering how pissed he'd been about my list.

Who would have thought a little thing like that would annoy him so much? Touchy, touchy. And here I was, totally at his mercy. There wouldn't be anyone else around—

I had a horrible thought. "How are you at doing hair?"

"What?" he asked, as if I'd said something in a foreign language.

"Hair. You'll have to do my hair."

He gave a quick glance at my hair. "You were wearing it in a ponytail Thursday night. I can do that."

Okay, that was acceptable, and was probably best until I was more functional. "That'll do. I don't even have my hair dryer with me, anyway. It's still in my car."

"I got your bag. It's in back with mine."

I could have kissed him, I was so relieved. Most of the clothes in the bag needed washing, of course, but to be on the safe side I'd taken an extra outfit to the beach. I had underwear, something to sleep in, and even makeup if I felt like putting some on. I had my birth control pills, thank God, though I figured I was safe from him tonight, at least. All in all, things were looking up. Until Siana could pack more clothes for me tomorrow and meet Wyatt with them, I had enough to get by.

We'd been driving for miles, and now there was nothing around except for the occasional house, but they were spaced far apart. I was getting impatient to get there and see how this was going to work out. "Where on earth do you live?"

"We're almost there. I was making certain no one followed us, so I've been taking some extra turns. I live just inside the city limits."

I was dying to see his house. I had no idea what to expect, and part of me was braced for the typical bachelor den. He had made some money playing pro ball; he could have built anything from a log-cabin-style lodge to a fake château.

"I'm surprised you don't live with your mother," I said, and I was. Mrs. Bloodsworth was a nice old lady with a wicked sense of humor, and Lord knows she had enough room to house half the block in that big old Victorian she loved.

"Why? You don't live with your mother," he pointed out.

"It's different for women."

"How so?"

"We don't need anyone to cook for us or pick up after us or do the laundry for us."

"News flash, honey: I don't either."

"You do your own laundry?"

"It's not exactly rocket science, is it? I can read labels and set the controls on a washer."

"And cook? You can actually cook?" I was getting excited.

"Nothing fancy, but yeah, I can get by." He glanced at me. "What about it?"

"Think, Lieutenant. Do you remember eating at any time during the past"—I checked the time on the dashboard clock—"five hours? I'm starving."

"I heard you had a cookie."

"Fig Newton. I had four of them, and it was an emergency. That doesn't qualify as eating."

"It's four Fig Newtons more than I've had, so to me it qualifies."

"That's beside the point. Feeding me is now your duty."

His lips twitched. "Duty? How do you figure that?"

"You commandeered me, didn't you?"

"Some people might think it was more along the lines of saving your life."

"Details. Mom would have fed me extremely well.

You took me away from her, so now you have to step up to the plate."

"Interesting woman, your mother. You came by the attitude honestly, didn't you?"

"What attitude?" I asked in bewilderment.

He reached across and patted my knee. "It doesn't matter. Your dad told me his secret to handling you."

"He didn't!" I was appalled. Dad wouldn't have sided with the enemy, would he? Of course, he didn't know Wyatt was the enemy. For all I knew, Wyatt had told him we were engaged or something and that was why Dad hadn't batted an eye about Wyatt taking me home with him.

"Of course he did. We men have to stick together, you know."

"He wouldn't *do* that! He never told Jason any secret. There isn't any secret. You just made that up."

"Did not."

I fished out my cell phone and furiously punched in Mom and Dad's number. Wyatt reached over and neatly confiscated the phone, punching the *end* button, then slipping it in his pocket.

"Give me that!" I was seriously hampered by my wounded arm, since he was sitting to my left. I tried to turn in the seat, but I couldn't move my arm much at all and it sort of got in the way, and I bumped my shoulder against the back of the seat. For a moment I saw stars.

"Easy, honey, easy." Wyatt's crooning voice reached me through the waves of pain, but it was coming from the right, which was very disorienting.

I took a few deep breaths and opened my eyes, and

found that his voice was coming from the right because he was leaning into the car from the open passenger door. The car was stopped in a driveway, the motor still running, and a dark house loomed in front of us.

"Are you going to pass out on me?" he asked as he gently straightened me in the seat.

"No, but I might throw up on you," I answered honestly, and let my head drop back while I closed my eyes again. The nausea and pain receded at the same rate.

"Try not to."

"It was probably an empty threat. I haven't eaten, remember?"

"Except for four Fig Newtons."

"They're long gone. You're safe."

He brushed his hand over my forehead. "Good deal." He closed the car door, then came back around and got behind the wheel.

"Isn't this your house?" I asked in confusion. Had he pulled into the first driveway he came to?

"Sure is, but I'll park in the garage." He hit a button on the garage-door opener clipped to the sun visor, and simultaneously an exterior light came on and a double garage door in the side of the house began sliding upward. He put the car in gear and pulled forward, then turned to the right and smoothly slotted the car into its place. He punched the button again, and the door began sliding down behind us.

His garage was neat, which impressed me. Garages tend to be catchalls, getting choked with everything except the cars they were meant to house. Not Wyatt's.

To my right was a tool bench, with one of those big, red, multidrawered tool chests like mechanics have parked off to one side. An array of hammers, saws, and other guy stuff hung neatly on the pegboard wall. I stared at them, wondering if he knew what to do with all of them. Men and their toys. Huh.

"I have a hammer, too," I told him.

"I bet you do."

I hate being condescended to. You could tell he thought my hammer was nowhere in the ballpark with his collection. "It's pink."

He froze in the act of getting out of the car, staring at me with an appalled expression. "That's perverted. That's just not right."

"Oh, please. There's no law that says a tool has to be ugly."

"Tools aren't ugly. They're strong and functional. They look like they mean business. They aren't *pink*."

"Mine is, and it's just as good as yours. It isn't as big, but it does the job. I bet you're against women joining the police force, too, aren't you?"

"Of course not. What does that have to do with a friggin' pink hammer?"

"Women are mostly prettier than men and mostly not as big, but that doesn't mean they can't get the job done, does it?"

"We're talking *hammers* here, not people!" He got out of the car and slammed the door, then stalked around to my side.

I opened the door and raised my voice so he could hear me. "I think your aversion to a tool that's attractive as well as functional—mmmph." I glared at him over the hand he'd clapped over my mouth.

"Give it a rest. We'll argue about hammers when you don't look like you're about to fall over." He raised his eyebrows in question, waiting for me to agree, and he kept his hand over my mouth while he waited.

Disgruntled, I nodded, and he removed his hand, then released my seat belt and gently lifted me out of the car. He hadn't thought this through, because if he had, he would have unlocked the door leading into the house before he picked me up, but he handled it with only a little juggling. I couldn't help him because my right arm was trapped between my body and his, and my left arm was useless. Tomorrow I would be able to use it a little, but I knew from experience that right after a trauma the damaged muscle just refuses to work.

He got me inside, turning on light switches with his elbow, and deposited me in a chair in a breakfast nook. "Don't try to get up for any reason. I'll get the bags out of the car, then carry you wherever you want to go."

He disappeared down the short hallway that led into the garage, and I wondered if the doctor had told him something about my condition that hadn't been passed along to me, because I was perfectly capable of walking. Yes, I had gone all woozy in the car, but that was because I'd hit my arm. Other than feeling a little shaky—and my arm hurting like blue blazes—I was okay. The shaky feeling would be gone tomorrow, because this was how I always felt when I gave blood. It wasn't even bad shaky, just a little shaky. So what was up with the "Don't try to get up for any reason?"

Hah! The phone.

I looked around and saw an actual corded phone hanging on the wall, with a really long cord that would reach anywhere in the kitchen. Please. Why not just get a cordless? The units are so much more attractive.

I already had the number dialed and it was ringing by the time Wyatt, carrying both bags, reappeared at the other end of the little hallway. I gave him a "you didn't fool me" smirk, and he rolled his eyes.

"Daddy," I said when Dad answered the phone. I call him Daddy when I mean business, sort of like using someone's full name. "Just what did you say to Wyatt that he thinks is the secret to handling me? How *could* you?" I was in full indignant wail by the time I finished.

Dad burst out laughing. "It's okay, baby." He calls all of us baby because, well, we did used to be his babies. He never calls Mom that, though. Uh-uh. He knows better. "It's nothing that'll undermine you; it was just something he needed to know right now."

"Like what?"

"He'll tell you."

"Probably not. He's stubborn that way."

"No, he'll tell you this. I promise."

"You'll beat him up for me if he doesn't?" That was an old Dad-joke, that he'd beat up any man who made any of his girls unhappy. That's why I didn't tell him about Jason kissing Jenni, because I figured in that case he would really do it.

"No, but I'll beat him up if he hurts you."

Reassured, I said good-bye and turned to find Wyatt leaning against the cabinets with his arms crossed, regarding me with amusement. "He didn't tell you, did he?"

"He said you would, and that he'd beat you up if you didn't." So I stretched the truth a little. Wyatt hadn't been able to hear what Dad had actually said.

"It wasn't anything bad." Straightening, he went to the refrigerator. "How about some breakfast? That's the fastest thing I can do. Eggs, bacon, toast."

"That sounds great. What can I do to help?"

"With that arm, not much. Sit down and stay out of the way. That'll be a big help."

I sat, and looked around the breakfast nook and kitchen while he got out what he needed and started the bacon cooking in the microwave. To my surprise, the kitchen looked kind of old. The appliances were top-notch and fairly new and there was an island with a cooktop occupied the center, but the room itself had that solid, established feel to it.

"How old is this house?"

"Turn of the century. The last century. So it's a little over a hundred years old. It was a farmhouse, and it's been remodeled a couple of times. When I bought it, I did a major remodeling, tore down some interior walls, opened it up for a more modern look, added a couple of bathrooms. There are three bathrooms upstairs, a half bath down here. It's a nice-size house, a little over three thousand square feet. I'll show you around tomorrow."

"How many bedrooms?"

"Four. There used to be six small ones, with just one bathroom, so I took that extra space to make the other bathrooms and enlarge the bedrooms and closets. That'll make it easier to sell if I ever decide to move."

"Why would you?" That was a lot of room for just one person, but from what I could see, there was a nice, homey feel to it. The kitchen cabinets were a warm golden color, the countertops were a greenish granite, and the floor was polished pine with colorful rugs strewn about. It wasn't a fancy kitchen, despite the granite, but one that looked well-arranged and comfortable.

He shrugged. "This is my hometown and I'm comfortable here, plus this is where my family is, but a better job may open up somewhere else. You never know. I may spend the rest of my life here; I may not."

It was a sensible outlook and one I held myself. I loved my home, but who knew what might happen? A smart person was flexible.

In short order he had plates of scrambled eggs, bacon, and toast set on the table, with glasses of milk poured for both of us. He also opened the bottle of antibiotic pills and put two of them beside my plate, plus one of the pain relievers.

I didn't fuss about taking the pain reliever. I'm no idiot. I wanted to quit hurting.

By the time I finished eating, I was yawning. Wyatt

rinsed the plates and put them in the dishwasher, then plucked me out of my chair and sat down in it himself, with me in his lap.

"What?" I asked, surprised by my perch. I'm not much for sitting on men's laps—it strikes me as ungainly—but Wyatt was tall enough that our faces were level and his arm around my back was wonderfully supporting.

"Your dad said that when you get scared, you get mouthy. How mouthy and demanding you get is in direct proportion to how scared you are." His big hand rubbed my back. "He said it's how you cope until you aren't as scared anymore."

It's no secret in my family, that's for sure. I let myself lean against him. "I was petrified."

"All except for your mouth." He chuckled. "Here we were, conducting a search for an armed murderer, and I hear you behind the car loudly demanding a cookie."

"I wasn't loud."

"You were loud. I thought I'd have to kick my men's asses to make them stop snickering."

"It's tough to get my mind around the fact that someone tried to kill me. It's impossible. Things like that just don't happen. I live a nice, quiet life, and within the space of a few days everything has turned upside down. I want my nice, quiet life back. I want you to catch this guy, and do it now."

"We will. We'll get this nailed. MacInnes and Forester were working all weekend, following leads. They have a couple of good ones."

"Is it Nicole's boyfriend?"

"I can't say."

"You don't know, or you literally can't say?"

"I literally can't talk about an ongoing investigation." He kissed my temple. "Let's get you upstairs and tucked into bed."

It's a good thing I fully expected him to take me to his bedroom instead of one of the guest rooms, because that's exactly what he did. I could have walked, even gone up the stairs, but he seemed to want to carry me around and, hey, why not? He set me down in the roomy master bathroom, with its double vanity, garden tub, and large shower. "I'll get your bag. The towels and washcloths are in there," he said, pointing to the door of the linen closet.

I got a towel and washcloth, and managed to untie the neck of the hospital gown with just my right hand. I couldn't manage the second tie, though, which was halfway down my back. Didn't matter. I let the huge thing drop off of me, and stepped out of the circle of fabric.

I surveyed my half-naked form in the mirror. Ugh. My left arm was mostly orange with Betadine, but there were still dried streaks of blood on my back and under my arm. I wet the washcloth and had removed all the blood I could reach by the time Wyatt returned. He took the cloth from me and finished the job, then helped me out of the rest of my clothes. It was a good thing I had gotten used to being naked with him, or I'd have been embarrassed. I looked longingly at the shower, but that was off-limits. The tub, though, was an option. "I could take a tub bath," I said with obvious hope.

He didn't even argue. Instead he ran the water, and helped me into it. While I was happily soaking, he stripped down himself and took a quick shower.

I leaned back in the tub and watched as he stepped out and toweled dry. A naked Wyatt Bloodsworth was a fine sight, broad-shouldered and slim-hipped, with long, muscled legs and a very nice package. Even better, he knew how to use that package.

"Have you finished lolling around?" he asked.

I can loll with the best of them, but I had finished bathing, so I nodded and he helped me to stand, then steadied me to make certain I didn't slip as I stepped out of the big tub. I could have dried myself one-handed, maybe a bit awkwardly, but he took the towel and gently wiped me down, then got my toiletries out of the duffel so I could tone and moisturize. Skin care is important, even when a murderer is after you.

I had a T-shirt to sleep in, but when I dug it out, I saw that no way was it going to go over the bulk of that huge bandage, not to mention I couldn't lift my arm to put it on anyway.

"I'll get one of my shirts," Wyatt said, and disappeared into the big walk-in closet that opened off the bedroom. He came back with a button-up white dress shirt, and gently worked the sleeve up over my arm. The shirt hung halfway down my thighs, and the shoulder seams drooped down my arms. He had to put three turns into the cuffs before my hands poked out. I turned in front of the mirror and checked out the fit. I just love the way men's shirts look on women.

"Yes, you look hot," he said, smiling. He slipped his hand under the shirt and rested it on my bare butt. "If you're a good girl for the rest of the night, tomorrow I'll kiss your neck and make you happy."

"No neck kissing. Remember our deal. We aren't having sex again."

"That's your deal, not mine." Then he picked me up and took me to bed. He settled me between the covers of the king-size bed, I rolled onto my right side, and it was Lights Out, Blair.

CHAPTER
THIRTEEN

I woke some hours later shivering with cold, hurting, and generally miserable. I couldn't get comfortable no matter how I squirmed. Wyatt woke and stretched to turn on the lamp, and mellow light flooded the room. "What's wrong?" he asked, putting his hand on my face. "Ah."

"Ah, what?" I asked fretfully as he got out of bed and walked into the bathroom.

He came back with a glass of water and two tablets. "You're feverish. The doctor said you probably would be. Take these; then I'll get another pain pill for you."

I sat up to take the two tablets, then huddled under the covers until he came back with the other pill. After I took it, he turned out the light and got back into bed, cuddling me close and sharing his body warmth with me. I pressed my nose against his shoulder, inhaling the heat and scent, and my heart turned over. No doubt about it: he cranked my tractor. I could probably be near death and he'd still turn me on.

I was still too cold and uncomfortable to go back to sleep, so I decided I might as well talk.

"Why did you get divorced?"

"I wondered when you'd get around to that," he observed in a lazy tone.

"Do you mind talking about it? Just until I get sleepy?"

"No, it's no big deal. She filed for divorce the day I quit pro ball. She thought I was crazy to walk out on millions of dollars to be a cop."

"Not many people would disagree with her."

"Do you?"

"Well, see, I'm from your hometown, so I've read the articles in the newspaper and I know that being a cop was what you always wanted, that you majored in criminal justice in college. I would have expected it. She was surprised, I take it?"

"Big-time. I don't blame her. She signed on to be the wife of a pro football player, with the money and the glamour, not the wife of a cop, with never enough money and never knowing if he's going to come home or die on the job."

"You didn't talk about the future before you got married? What you wanted?"

He snorted. "I was twenty-one when we got married; she was twenty. At that age, the future is something that happens in five minutes, not five years. Throw in rioting hormones, and there you go, one divorce in the making. It just took us a couple of years to get there. She was a good kid, but we wanted different things out of life."

"But everyone knows—everyone *assumes*—you made millions while you were playing ball. Wasn't that enough?"

"I did make millions—I had four of them when I quit, to be exact. That didn't exactly turn me into Donald Trump, but it was enough to turn things around for the family. I took care of all the repairs and renovations on Mom's home, set up college funds for my sister's kids, bought this place and remodeled it, then invested the rest. There wasn't a huge amount left, but if I can leave it untouched until I retire, it should give me a comfortable retirement. I took a hit when the stock market bottomed out five, six years ago, but my stocks have come back all the way, so things look okay."

I yawned and settled my head more comfortably on his shoulder. "Why didn't you buy a smaller place? One that didn't need so much work?"

"I really like the location, and I thought it would be a good house someday for a family."

"You want a family?" I was a little startled. That usually isn't something you hear a bachelor say.

"Sure. I'll get married again someday, and two or three kids would be nice. What about you?"

The bottom dropped out of my stomach, and it was a moment before I realized that wasn't a very offhand proposal. The pain medication must be kicking in, if I was getting that punchy. "Sure, I want to get married again," I said sleepily. "And have a munchkin. I have the perfect setup. I could take a baby with me to work, because it's my business and it's an informal, relaxed setting. There's music, no television, and lots of adult supervision. What could be better?"

"You have it all planned out, huh?"

"Well, no. I'm neither married nor pregnant, so everything is still hypothetical. And I'm flexible. If circumstances change, I'll adjust."

He said something else, but I was in the middle of another yawn and missed it. "What?" I asked when I could talk.

"Never mind." He kissed my temple. "You're fading fast. I thought it would take the pill half an hour or so to work."

"I didn't get much sleep last night," I mumbled. "Accumulative effect." He was the reason I hadn't had much sleep the night before, because he kept waking me every couple of hours to have sex. My toes curled at the memory, and for a moment I flashed to how it felt when his big body settled on mine. Wow. I definitely wasn't cold now.

I wanted to climb on top of him and take care of matters, but I'd told him no sex, so I couldn't violate my own edict. Probably I should have put on underwear before getting in bed with him, though, because of course the shirt had ridden up to my waist. That's what shirts do when you sleep in them. He'd been very gentlemanly, not feeling me up or anything, but that was only because I was hurt. I expected that would change, because being a gentleman was probably a strain for him. Not that he didn't have great manners, because he did, but his instincts were aggressive and competitive. That was what had made him such a good athlete. Besides the physical ability, he had that ruthless drive to come out on top. I wondered how long he would be considerate because of my arm.

I went to sleep on that thought, and found out the answer around six in the morning when he gently turned me on my back and settled between my legs. I was barely awake when he started, but wide awake when he finished. He was careful with my arm, but ruthless in his attack on my neck.

When he finally let me up, I stormed into the bathroom. "That was so not fair!" Delicious, but not fair. "That was a sneak attack!"

He was laughing when I slammed the door. Just to be on the safe side, I also locked it. He could use one of the other bathrooms.

I definitely felt better this morning, not as shaky, and the pain in my arm was more of a dull throb now. Checking myself in the mirror, I saw that I didn't even look pale. How could I, when Wyatt had just done me? My cheeks were flushed and it wasn't from fever.

I cleaned up, then rummaged one-handed through my duffel, which was still parked in the middle of the bathroom floor. I found my clean underwear and managed to pull it on, then brushed my teeth and hair. That was the limit of what I could do by myself, though. My clean clothes were wrinkled and needed to be run through the clothes dryer, but even if they had been newly pressed, I couldn't have coped. I couldn't put on a bra. I could move my arm a little more this morning, but not enough to extend to dressing.

I unlocked the door and stomped out. He was nowhere to be seen. Just how did he expect me to harangue him if he didn't stay where he could hear me?

Fuming, I gathered my clean clothes in my right arm and went downstairs. The stairs led me to a great room with ten-foot ceilings, leather furniture, and the required big-screen television. There wasn't a plant in sight.

The smell of coffee made me turn to the left, which led through the breakfast room and into the kitchen. Wyatt, barefoot and shirtless, was busy at the cook-top. I looked at that muscled back and brawny arms, the deep furrow of his spine and the slight indenta-tions on each side, just above the waistband of his jeans, and my heart turned over again. I was in deep trouble here, and not just because some idiot mur-derer was after me.

"Where's the laundry room?" I asked.

He pointed to a door that opened off the short hall leading to the garage. "Need any help?"

"I can manage. I just need to get the wrinkles out of my clothes." I went into the laundry room and put my clothes in the dryer, then turned it on. Then I went back to the kitchen and took up the battle. Well, first I poured myself a cup of coffee, using the cup he had set out for me. A woman needs to be alert when she's dealing with a man as underhanded and sneaky as Wyatt Bloodsworth.

"You have to stop doing that."

"Doing what?" he asked as he flipped a buckwheat pancake.

"The sneak attacks. I told you no."

"You didn't tell me no while I was doing it. You said some interesting things, but *no* wasn't among them."

My cheeks got hot, but I brushed that aside with a wave of my hand. "What I say during doesn't count. It's that chemistry thing, and you shouldn't take advantage of it."

"Why not?" He turned aside and lifted his own coffee cup. He was smiling.

"It's almost date rape."

He spewed coffee all over the floor. Thank goodness he'd turned away from the pancakes. Outraged, he glared at me. "Don't you even start down that road, because it isn't funny. Date rape, my ass. We have a deal, and you know it. All you have to do is say no and I'll stop. So far, you haven't said it."

"I said a blanket no beforehand."

"Those aren't our rules of engagement. You can't stop me before I get started. You have to say it after I've made a move on you, to prove you really don't want me." He was still scowling, but he turned to rescue the pancakes before they burned. He buttered them, then got a paper towel and mopped up the coffee. Then he very calmly went back to the skillet he was using and poured more batter into it.

"That's the point! You keep short-circuiting my brain, and it isn't fair. It's not as if I can short-circuit your brain, too."

"Want to bet?"

"Then why are you winning and I'm losing?" I wailed.

"Because you want me, and you're just being stubborn."

"Hah. *Hah!* Using that logic, your brain should be just as fried as mine if we were on the same footing, in which case you wouldn't be winning all the time. But you are, so that means you don't want me." Okay, I knew there were holes in the argument, but it was all I could think of to sidetrack him.

He cocked his head. "Wait a minute. Are you saying I'm fucking you because I don't want you?"

Trust him to immediately see the holes, and drive a verbal truck through the argument. I didn't see anywhere to go with that, so I backtracked. "The thing is, whatever the reasoning, I don't want to have sex anymore. You should respect that."

"I will. When you say no."

"I'm saying no now."

"Now doesn't count. You have to wait until I touch you."

"Who made these stupid-ass rules?" I bellowed, frustrated beyond control.

He grinned. "I did."

"Well, I'm not playing by them, understand? Flip the pancakes."

He glanced at the skillet and flipped the pancakes. "You can't change the rules just because you're losing."

"Yes, I can. I can go home and not see you again."

"You can't go home, because someone's trying to kill you."

There was that. Fuming, I sat down at the table, which he had already set with two places.

He walked over with the spatula in his hand, and bent down to kiss me warmly on the mouth. "You're still scared, aren't you? That's what this is all about."

Just wait until I saw Dad again. I was going to tell

him a thing or two about giving information to the enemy camp.

"Yes. No. It doesn't matter. I still have a valid point."

He ruffled my hair, then returned to his pancakes.

I could see arguing with him wasn't going to work. Somehow, I'd have to keep my wits about me enough to tell him no when he got started again, but how could I do that if he kept jumping me when I was asleep? By the time I was awake enough to think, it was already too late because by then I didn't *want* to say no.

He took the bacon out of the microwave, divided it between our plates, then dished out the buttery pancakes. Before sitting down, he freshened our cups of coffee, and also got a glass of water for me and set out the antibiotic and a pain pill.

I took both pills. Though my arm felt better, I wanted to stay ahead of the pain.

"What am I doing today?" I asked as I dug into breakfast. "Staying here while you go to work?"

"Nope. Not until you can use that arm. I'm taking you to my mother's house. I've already called her."

"Cool." I liked his mother, and I really wanted to see the inside of that giant Victorian she lived in. "I assume I can talk to my family whenever I want, right?"

"I don't see why not. You just can't go see them, and I don't want them coming to see you, either, because they could lead this guy straight to you."

"I don't see why y'all are having such a hard time finding out who he is. He has to be a boyfriend."

"Don't tell me how to do my job," he warned. "She didn't have an exclusive relationship going on. We've checked out the guys she was dating, and they're clear. There are some other angles we're exploring."

"It wasn't drugs, or anything like that." I ignored his rude comment about telling him how to do his job.

He looked up. "How do you figure?"

"She belonged to Great Bods, remember? She didn't have any of the signs, and she was in good shape. Not great; she couldn't have done a backflip if her life had depended on it, but she wasn't a druggie, either. It has to be a boyfriend. She came on to all the guys, so I figure it's a jealousy thing. I can talk to my employees, find out if they noticed anything—"

"No. Stay out of it. That's an order. We've already interviewed all your employees."

Insulted that he seemed to be totally dismissing my views on the subject, I finished eating in silence. Typical man, he didn't like that either.

"Stop sulking."

"I'm not sulking. Realizing that there's no point in talking is not the same as sulking."

The dryer dinged, and I got my clothes out while he cleaned up the table. "Go on upstairs," he said. "I'll be up in a minute to help you get dressed."

He came up while I was brushing my teeth again, because pancakes make my teeth feel sticky, and he stood beside me at the vanity, using the other basin while he did the same. Brushing our teeth together made me feel strange. That was something married people did. I wondered if one day I'd do all my tooth-brushing here in this bathroom, or if some other woman would be standing in my place.

He crouched down and held my capri pants for me,

and I balanced myself with one hand on his shoulder while I stepped into them. He zipped and buttoned, then eased his shirt off me and slipped my bra in place and hooked it.

My blouse was sleeveless, which was good, but the bandage was so big the armhole was just barely big enough. He had to tug the cloth across it, which had me wincing and mentally thanking Dr. MacDuff for the dope. He buttoned the tiny buttons that marched up the front of the blouse, then I sat on the bed and eased my feet into sandals. I continued to sit there, watching him as he dressed. The suit, the white dress shirt, the tie. The shoulder holster. The badge. The handcuffs clipped to the back of his belt. The cell phone clipped to the front. Oh, man. My heart was jumping like crazy, just watching him.

"Are you ready?" he asked.

"No. You haven't put up my hair yet." I could have gone with it down, since I wasn't working out today, but I was still pissed at him.

"Okay." He got the brush, and I turned so he could gather my hair in a ponytail at the back of my head. When he had it all caught in one hand, he said, "What do I put around it?"

"A scrunchie."

"A *whatie*?"

"Scrunchie. Don't tell me you don't have a scrunchie."

"I don't even know what the hell a scrunchie is."

"It's what you use to hold up ponytails. Duh."

"I haven't worn a ponytail lately," he said drily. "Will a rubber band do?"

"No! Rubber bands break the hair. It has to be a scrunchie."

"Where do I get a scrunchie?"

"Look in my bag."

He was very still behind me. After a few seconds, without saying a word, he let go of my hair and went into the bathroom. Now that he couldn't see me, I grinned to myself.

"What the hell," he said about half a minute later, "does a scrunchie look like?"

"Like a big rubber band with cloth on it."

More silence. Finally he came out of the bathroom with my white scrunchie in his hand. "Is this it?"

I nodded.

He started the process of gathering my hair again.

"Put the scrunchie on your wrist," I directed. "Then you can just slide it off around the ponytail."

His thick wrist just about stretched my scrunchie to the limits, but he grasped the theory at once and got my hair in a decent ponytail without any more delay. I went into the bathroom and checked out the results. "That's good. I think I can go without earrings today, if that's all right with you."

He rolled his eyes up to the ceiling. "Thank you, Lord."

"Don't be sarcastic. This was your idea, remember."

As we went down the stairs, I heard him mutter behind me, "You little shit," and I grinned to myself again. It was good that he knew I'd got back at him, because otherwise what would be the point?

CHAPTER
FOURTEEN

I loved Mrs. Bloodsworth's house. It was white, the gingerbread and trim were painted lavender, and her front door was robin's egg blue. You have to respect, and possibly fear, any woman who has the guts to paint her house those colors. The porch, which wrapped around two sides of the house, was wide and gracious, filled with ferns and palms, and ceiling fans had been installed to provide a breeze whenever nature fell down on the job. Roses of various hues provided explosions of color. Dark green gardenia bushes, heavy with the fragrant white blooms, punctuated each side of the wide steps leading up to the porch.

Wyatt didn't park so we could go up the front walk, though; he continued down the driveway and parked behind the house. I was escorted to the back door, which opened into a small back foyer and then into the kitchen, which had been modernized without sacrificing the style. His mother was waiting for us there.

Roberta Bloodsworth wasn't the type of woman

who is ever described as matronly. She was tall and slim, with a short, chic hairstyle. Wyatt had inherited his sharp green eyes from her, and his dark hair. Hers wasn't dark now, though; instead of doing gray, she'd gone blond. As early as it was, not even eight o'clock, she already had on makeup and earrings. She hadn't dressed up, though; she was wearing tan walking shorts with an untucked aqua T-shirt, and regular flip-flops. Her toenails were painted fire-engine red, and the left foot sported a toe ring.

She was my kind of woman.

"Blair, honey, I couldn't believe it when Wyatt said you'd been shot," she said, putting a careful arm around me for a hug. "How are you feeling? Would you like some coffee, or hot tea?"

Just like that, I was in the mood to be mothered. Since my own mom was forbidden to do it, Wyatt's mom had stepped into the breach. "Tea sounds wonderful," I said fervently, and she immediately turned to the sink to fill an old-fashioned kettle with water and put it on the stove to start heating.

Wyatt frowned. "I'd have made tea for you if you'd said you wanted it. I thought you liked coffee."

"I do like coffee, but I like tea, too. And I've already had coffee."

"Tea gives you a feeling that coffee doesn't," Mrs. Bloodsworth explained. "You just sit at the table, Blair, and don't try to do anything. You must still be feeling shaky."

"I'm a lot better than I was last night," I said as I obeyed her and took a seat at the wooden kitchen table. "I actually feel fairly normal today. Last night was—" I made a rocking motion with my hand.

"I imagine so. Wyatt, you go on to work. You need to catch that creep and you can't do it standing in my kitchen. Blair will be just fine."

He seemed reluctant to leave. "If you have to go anywhere, she should probably stay here," he said to his mother. "I don't want her seen out in public right now."

"I know; you've already told me."

"She doesn't need to do anything strenuous, after losing that much blood yesterday."

"I know; you've already told me."

"She'll probably try to talk you into—"

"Wyatt! I *know*!" she said in exasperation. "We went over all of this on the phone. Do you think I've gone senile?"

He was smart enough to say, "Of course not. It's just—"

"It's just you being overprotective. I get it. Blair and I will do just fine, and I'll exercise my God-given common sense by not parading her down the middle of Main Street, okay?"

"Okay." He grinned and kissed her cheek, then came to me and rubbed his hand down my back before squatting beside me. "Try to stay out of trouble while I'm gone," he said.

"Excuse me, but how is any of this my fault?"

"It isn't, but you do have a talent for the unexpected." He reversed the direction of his hand, sweeping it up my spine to brush the side of my neck with his thumb, then laughing at my alarmed expression.

"Be good, will you? I'll check in during the day, and pick you up late this afternoon."

He kissed me, tugged on my ponytail, then rose to his feet and went to the back door. Pausing there with his hand on the doorknob, he looked again at his mother, and this time he was wearing his cop face. "Take *very* good care of her, because she's the mother of your future grandchildren."

"I am not!" I shrieked after a split second of pure shock.

"I thought so," his mother said at the same time.

He was out the door by the time I got there. I wrenched it open and yelled at him, "I am *not*! That is *so* underhanded, and you know you're lying!"

He paused with the car door open. "Last night, did we or did we not talk about having children?"

"Yes, but not *each other's*!"

"Don't fool yourself, honey," he advised, then got in the car and drove away.

I was so mad I did a Rumpelstiltskin, punctuating each stomp with "Shit!" and of course the jumping up and down hurt my arm, so it went like this: "Shit! Ow! Shit! Shit! Shit! *Ow!*"

Then I realized I was doing this in front of his mother, and I turned a horrified look on her. "Omigod, I'm so sorry—"

Except she was leaning against the sink laughing her head off. "You should have seen yourself! *'Shit! Ow! Shit! Ow!'* I wish I'd had a video camera."

I could feel my face burning. "I'm so sorry—" I began again.

"For what? Do you think I've never said 'shit' before, or a lot worse? Besides, it does me good to see a woman not rolling over for Wyatt, if you know what I mean. It's against the natural order of the world for a man to always get what he wants, and Wyatt always has."

Holding my arm, I went back to the table. "Not really. His wife divorced him."

"And he walked away without a single backward look. It was his way or nothing, no compromising. She—her name is Megan, by the way, but I don't know her last name because she remarried within the year— always deferred to him. I suppose she had stars in her eyes because he was this big football star, and as rough and dirty as football is, the NFL is a glamour job. She didn't understand it and couldn't handle it when, without talking things over with her, he quit playing ball and walked away from everything she expected out of life. What she wanted didn't matter to him. It's always been like that; he's never had to work for a woman, and it has driven me crazy. So it's nice to see someone standing up to him."

"For all the good it's doing," I said glumly. "He seems to be winning every battle."

"But at least there *is* a battle, and he's aware there's resistance. What made you so mad about what he said?"

"Because he's trying to do an end run around me, and I'm not certain it means anything. I told him 'no'—for all the good it did—and he's so frickin' competitive it's like waving a red flag at a bull. So did he say that because he loves me, or because he can't stand to lose? I vote for number two, because he doesn't know me well enough to love me, and I've told him that I don't know how many times."

"Good for you." The water for the tea began boiling, the kettle making a whistling sound. She turned off the stove, and the whistle slowly died while she put tea bags in two cups, then poured the hot water over the bags. "How do you take your tea?"

"Two sugars, black."

She put sugar in mine, and sugar and cream in hers, then brought both cups to the table. I thanked her as she set my cup in front of me, and she sat down across from me. A thoughtful frown between her brows, she stirred her tea. "I think you're handling him exactly right. Make him work for you, and he'll appreciate you a lot more."

"Like I said, he's winning all the battles." Dispirited, I sipped my hot tea.

"Honey, ask him if he would rather have played in a hard, close-fought game, or a runaway. He *loved* the games where it was toe-to-toe until the very end, and he loved making those bone-crunching tackles to stop the ball carrier. He'd be bored within a week if you made things easy for him."

"He's still winning all the time. It isn't fair. *I* want to win every now and then."

"If he's sneaky, you have to be sneakier."

"That's like saying I have to be more of a Hun than Attila." But I suddenly felt more cheerful, because I could do it. I might not win the battle of the neck, but there were other battles where we were more evenly matched.

"I have faith in you," Mrs. Bloodsworth said. "You're a smart, savvy young woman; you have to be, to make such a success of Great Bods at your age. And you're a hottie. He's dying to get in your pants, but take my advice and don't let him."

I managed to keep from choking on my tea. There was no way I was going to tell his mother he'd already been in my pants. I was sure *my* parents had already figured it out, since Wyatt insisted on taking me home with him last night, but I couldn't admit it to *his* mother.

Out of guilt, I steered the conversation away from Wyatt and my pants, and asked if she'd mind showing me through her house. It was a good choice. She beamed and jumped up, and we were off.

My best guess is the house had at least twenty rooms, most of them with those lovely octagonal lines that must have been a nightmare to build. The formal parlor was done in cheerful yellow and white, the dining room had cream-and-green-striped wallpaper, with the table and chairs in a very dark wood. Each room had a very definite color scheme, and I had to admire her resourcefulness in coming up with so many different schemes, because after all there are only so many colors from which to choose. The entire house showed the love she had poured into it, the effort.

"If you get tired during the day and want a nap, use this room," she said, showing me into a bedroom with polished hardwood floors, mauve paint on the walls, and a four-poster bed with a mattress that looked like a cloud. "It has it's own bathroom."

About that time she noticed the way I was cradling my arm, which was still throbbing from the jarring it took. "I bet your arm will feel better if it's supported in a sling. I have the perfect thing for it."

She went to her bedroom—done in shades of white—and returned with a beautiful soft blue shawl. She folded it and fashioned a very comfortable sling for me, which did indeed take some of the stress off the stitches.

I was certain I was hindering her, getting in the way of her normal routine, but she seemed happy to have my company and chattered away. We watched television some, read some. I called Mom and talked to her, and told her what Dad had done. That would fix him. After lunch I did get tired, and went upstairs for a nap.

"Wyatt called to check on you," Mrs. Bloodsworth said when I woke an hour later and came back downstairs. "He was worried when I told him you were lying down. He said you had a fever last night."

"That's normal after you get a wound, and it was just high enough to make me uncomfortable."

"I hate that, don't you? It's such a miserable feeling. But you aren't feverish now?"

"No, I was just tired."

While I'd been half-dozing, I'd been thinking about Nicole, and how Wyatt had brushed off my ideas about her murderer. Where did he get off, thinking he knew more about her than I did, just because he was a cop and could investigate people? He was wrong, and I knew it.

I called my assistant manager, Lynn Hill, and got her at home. When she heard my voice she gasped. "Omigod, I heard you were shot! Is that true?"

"Sort of. It kind of grazed my arm. I'm okay; I didn't even have to stay overnight at the hospital. But I have to stay mostly out of sight until they catch the guy who murdered Nicole, and I'm ready for this to be over. If Great Bods reopens tomorrow morning, can you handle things?"

"Sure, no problem. I can do everything except meet payroll."

"I'll handle that, and get the checks to you. Listen— you talked to Nicole some."

"When I had to," she said drily.

I understood that completely. "Did she say anything about a special boyfriend?"

"She was always making mysterious hints. My guess is she was running around with married men, because you know how she was. She always wanted what some other woman had. She wouldn't have been interested in some single guy, other than as a temporary boost to her ego. You're not supposed to speak ill of the dead, but she was a piece of work."

"Married men. That makes perfect sense," I said, and it did. Lynn had nailed Nicole's personality.

I said good-bye, and called Wyatt's cell phone. He answered immediately, not even saying hello. "Is something wrong?"

"Do you mean other than being shot and someone trying to kill me? Not really." How could I have resisted that line? "Anyway, I checked out something and the word is Nicole was seeing a married man."

He paused. "I thought I told you to stay out of police business." There was an edge of anger to his voice.

"Kind of hard to, in this situation. Are you going to be so stubborn you aren't going to check this out?"

"You didn't leave the house, did you?" He didn't answer my question, instead asking one of his own.

"No, of course not. I'm still tucked away nice and safe."

"Good. Stay there. And, yes, I will have this checked out."

"It isn't exactly something the guy will admit to, running around on his wife. Want me to try finding out—"

"No! No. I want you to do nothing, understand? Let us handle the investigations. You've already been shot once, wasn't that enough?" He hung up.

He hadn't exactly been gracious about my pointer. Okay, so he was worried something else would happen to me, and I wasn't crazy about the idea of putting myself in danger, either. But I could call people, couldn't I? I was using my cell phone, so there was no way I could give away my location. The ordinary person didn't have cell-phone tracing capabilities.

And if you can't win one battle, go find a battle you *can* win.

CHAPTER
FIFTEEN

Belatedly it occurred to me that the detectives had already questioned all my employees, so Lynn should have already told them her married-man theory. In that case, had Wyatt been trying to spare my feelings by saying he'd have it checked out? Oh, that was galling.

I called Lynn back. "What you said about Nicole seeing married men, did you tell that to the police?"

"Well, no," she admitted. "For one thing, I don't *know* anything; I'm just saying she's the type. Actually, what the detective asked was if I knew who she had been seeing, romantically speaking, and I said no, because I don't. He didn't chat and say, hey, was she likely to do this or this, you know? But I was thinking about it later, and that's when it hit me that she was always flirting with the married guys at Great Bods, you know, and while she came on to every man breathing, there was still something about the way she went after the married ones. You saw her in action; you know what I'm talking about."

I knew exactly. Nicole had been forever *touching*, whether it was to ostensibly straighten a collar or a pat on the arm or an arm around the waist as she walked beside a guy—touching. Men aren't stupid; they knew exactly what she was offering. The smart ones had maybe been flattered, but they hadn't been hooked. The ones who weren't so smart, or who were sleazeballs, had responded, so you just knew there was contact going on away from Great Bods. Once she bagged a guy, though, Nicole had always been ready to move on.

"Did you notice any one guy in particular who paid a lot of attention to her?" I asked Lynn because at Great Bods I was tied up doing office work a lot, so she saw more than I did. "It would also be great if you knew what color car he drives."

"Let me think. No one recently, because it's been mostly our regulars and they were wise to her. A couple of months ago I did spot Nicole coming out of the men's bathroom, looking so smug I just wanted to bitch-slap her, and a few minutes later one of the guys came out, so I figure they were getting it on in the john."

"Why didn't you tell me?" I shrieked. "I'd have tossed her ass out right then!"

"You could do that? For doing it in the john?"

"She was in the *men's* john. I'm surprised they didn't get caught."

"I doubt she would have cared. They were probably in a stall. Maybe she was giving him a blow job, but that wasn't her style, either. At a guess, I'd say she did all the taking and none of the giving."

"Do you remember the man's name?"

"Not offhand. He didn't come often, and I don't think he's been in at all since then. He wasn't one of the regulars; he paid for a month and worked out a couple of times, then didn't renew. I'd recognize his name if I saw it, though. Do you keep a separate file on the ones who didn't renew?"

"Not a paper one. He'd be in the computer, though. Do you have any plans for the rest of the day? I'm going to put a call in to the cops"—*my* cop, specifically—"and they might want you to meet them at Great Bods to go through the computer files."

"No, I'll be around. If I do happen to be out, you can catch me on the cell phone."

"Okay. I'll get back to you."

"That sounded interesting," Mrs. Bloodsworth said, her green eyes bright with interest. She didn't bother to pretend that she hadn't been eavesdropping. After all, I was sitting in the same room with her.

"I hope so. Now, if Wyatt just won't hang up on me again—"

"He hung up on you?" Now the green eyes fired. "I taught him better manners than that. Let me drop a little word in his ear—"

"Oh, no, don't do that. Come to think of it, it would be best if I didn't call him again. I'll just call Detective MacInnes." I found the detective's card, and dialed the number on it.

When he answered, I said cheerfully, "Hello, this is Blair Mallory—"

"Uh—wait just a minute, Ms. Mallory, and I'll get the lieutenant—"

"Oh, there's no need. I'll just talk to you. The thing is, I was just now talking to my assistant manager, Lynn Hill, about her taking over for me at Great Bods when it reopens tomorrow—it *is* reopening, isn't it? You have all of that ugly yellow tape down?"

"Uh—let me get back to you on that—"

"Never mind. I'll find out about that later. Anyway, Lynn is the one who mentioned that she thought Nicole had a sort of thing for married men. You know—the challenge, taking something away from another woman. Lynn said she didn't say anything about that to the detective who interviewed her because she didn't think of it at the time, but later on she was running things through her mind and thinks it's very likely, because of the way Nicole acted."

"Uh—" He tried to interrupt again, but I just plowed right over him.

"Lynn and I were talking about possibles, and she said a couple of months ago she caught Nicole and this guy in the men's john doing, well, each other. She can't remember the man's name, because he only came to Great Bods a couple of times and hasn't been back, but she's sure she'll recognize the name when she sees it, and if you want, she can meet you over at Great Bods and she'll go through the computer files of the members who didn't renew. Are you following this?"

"Yeah," he said, sounding much more involved and with me now.

"Good. It's a place to start. That particular guy may not pan out, but knowing she liked married men puts a different spin on things, doesn't it?"

"Sure does." Now he sounded almost cheerful.

"Just in case you don't have Lynn's number handy, here it is." I rattled it off. "She's waiting to hear from you. And if she isn't at home, here's her cell number." Rattled off another one. Then I chirped, "Have a nice day, Detective," and hung up after he mumbled an automatic reply.

"I'm impressed," Mrs. Bloodsworth said, grinning from ear to ear. "You're doing a good imitation of a ditzy blond, but you're spewing out information so fast he probably couldn't write it all down."

"Then he'll call back," I said airily. "Or someone will."

Someone did, of course, within about five minutes. He was royally pissed, too. "If you have information about the case, you call me, not one of my men," he said very tersely.

"Are you the same man who has hung up on me twice now? I can't imagine *ever* calling you again, about anything."

Silence as deep as the Grand Canyon fell between us. Then he muttered, "Oh, shit," in the tone of a man who has just realized he's gonna have to suck it up and apologize, because, no doubt about it, he'd been rude. Not only that, he knew that I was with the mother who had raised him to have better manners than that. This was just one teeny little battle, but he'd been outflanked and I got a great deal of satisfaction out of it.

Finally he heaved a sigh. "I'm sorry. I'll never hang up on you again. I promise."

"Apology accepted," I said briskly. "Now, will

Lynn be able to open Great Bods tomorrow?" There's no sense in beating a horse to death, now is there? I'd won, so I'd be an adult and move on.

"I'm ninety percent certain she will."

"Good. Is my car still sitting in front of it?"

"No. I got your keys out of your bag and had it moved to your condo this morning. It's safe and sound."

"When did you get my keys?" I asked curiously, because I hadn't seen him do it.

"Last night. You were already sound asleep."

"I'm guessing everything was all right at my house, no windows shot out or anything?"

"The patrolman checked, said everything was still locked up, the windows were locked, no bullet holes that he could see."

"Did he climb the fence and check the French doors in back?"

"He said he checked all the doors. Let me buzz him and ask about that particular door." He left the phone, and came back a minute later. "Simmons said he didn't have to climb the fence; he just opened the gate and walked in."

A chill ran down my spine. "I always keep my gate locked." My fingers tightened on the phone. "I *know* it was locked."

"Shit. I'll get someone back out there right now. You sit tight."

"Like I could do anything else," I said wryly. We both very politely said good-bye, so neither could accuse the other of hanging up on anyone; then I reported the latest happening to Mrs. Bloodsworth.

That was when I remembered Siana. She was supposed to go to my place today and pack clothes for me. What if by some awful coincidence she was at my house when whoever unlocked my gate—which could only be unlocked from the inside—was there? Siana was blond. She was a little taller than I was, but Nicole's killer wouldn't know that. She had her own set of keys to the place, in case I lost mine.

She could have gone at any time to get my clothes: first thing this morning, or at lunch, or she might wait until she was finished with work for the day—but I didn't think she would wait that long, because she had to meet Wyatt somewhere to give the bag to him and sometimes she had to work until eight, nine o'clock at night.

"What's wrong?" Mrs. Bloodsworth asked, watching my face.

"My sister," I said in a faint tone. "She was supposed to pack a bag for me today and give it to Wyatt. He didn't mention it, so she might have been—"

She might have been mistaken for me. Oh, dear God.

Praying harder than I'd ever prayed in my life, I dialed Wyatt again. He sounded wary when he answered. "Siana was supposed to be at my house getting my clothes," I said rapidly. "Have you heard from her today?"

"Calm down," he said, his tone switching to soothing. "She's fine. She brought your bag over first thing this morning."

"Thank God. Oh, thank God." Tears burned my eyes. "I just realized . . . She's blond; she's about my size; the killer wouldn't know the difference between us." I was appalled that I hadn't thought of that before, and judging from the muttered curse I heard, our resemblance hadn't registered with Wyatt, either, at least not in that context. People who knew us would never get us mixed up, because we don't favor each other all that strongly, but on the surface, to the casual observer . . .

Because Wyatt was a cop, he asked, "Could Siana have opened your gate?"

I wiped the tears away. "I'll call and ask her, but I can't imagine any reason why she would."

"I'll call. I have more questions I need to ask her. I have a question for you, too: Is your security system set?"

I opened my mouth to automatically say, "Yes, of course," but abruptly shut it as I remembered the last time I'd been at home, on Friday, waiting for the rental car company to come pick me up. I'd waited at the door, and when the man drove up, I had bolted. I had a distinct memory of locking the door, but none at all of setting the alarm.

"It wasn't," I finally said. "Unless Siana set it this morning when she left. She has the code."

"All right. I'll handle things here. Stay calm, and with any luck I'll pick you up in a couple of hours. Okay?"

"Okay." I was grateful he hadn't lectured me about forgetting to set the security alarm. What on earth had I been thinking? Oh, yeah: the beach. I'd been in a hurry to get away.

The killer could have gotten in at any time during

the weekend, and made himself comfortable while he waited for me to come home. Only, he hadn't. Maybe he'd staked out my place and, when my car was never there, decided I must be staying with someone. But if he'd gone back to Great Bods, he would have seen my car and then maybe figured that was the best place to wait for me, because I was sure to collect my car.

That plan had worked, up to a point; it was only by chance that I was still alive. What would he have done next? No, wait—he might have thought the plan *had* worked yesterday evening, because I'd hit the ground and obviously he hadn't hung around to check things out. He must have thought he'd killed me, until the news at ten told him otherwise—or maybe not even then. The hospital didn't give out condition statements the way it used to. The police would have held their cards close to their chests last night, until Wyatt had me stuffed somewhere safe—like his bed was safe, but whatever. The morning news, though, would probably have said I was treated at the hospital and released.

So what would be his next move? Maybe he was in my house now, waiting for me. Maybe he'd just been checking things out, looking for a way to get inside. The French doors were the best bet, and the privacy fence would give him concealment while he jimmied them open, or whatever.

That would be stupid of him, though. The security company's sign was plainly posted on my front window. He wouldn't have any way of telling whether or not the system was on, so he wouldn't chance it—not if he had a brain in his head.

I jerked out of my thoughts when Mrs. Bloodsworth finally got my attention, anxiously asking if Siana was all right. "She's fine," I said, and wiped the last tear away. "She packed my clothes early this morning, and gave the bag to Wyatt. He's calling her to see if she turned on the security system."

The odds were she had. Siana wouldn't have left my house unguarded, even if the system had been off when she arrived. So, since no alarm had gone off, my home hadn't been invaded. No killer waited there. He might have jumped the fence and tried to look in the French doors, but I had pulled the curtains closed over them and he wouldn't have been able to see a thing. Everything was all right.

I breathed a huge, mental sigh of relief.

"There's no telling what time Wyatt will get here," Mrs. Bloodsworth said. "I'm going to go ahead and start supper for us. If he doesn't make it in time to eat with us, I'll just keep things warm for him."

"Is there anything I can do to help?" I asked, hoping there was, because it was getting kind of old just sitting around all day and letting someone wait on me.

"One-handed?" she asked, and laughed. "Other than setting the table, I can't think of a thing. Just come into the kitchen and keep me company. I don't get to cook all that often now, with just me in the house. There's no point, is there? I'll eat a sandwich for supper, and sometimes in the winter I'll open a can of soup, but food's pretty boring if you don't have company."

I followed her into the kitchen, and took a seat at the table. There was a formal dining room, of course, all true Victorians had them, but you could tell most of the Bloodsworth meals had been eaten at this very table. "You sound a little bored. Have you thought about rejoining Great Bods? We have some great new programs."

"I've thought about it, but you know how it is. Thinking about something and actually getting around to doing it are two different things. After my bicycle accident, I'm afraid I became a bit of a slug."

"Who took care of you when you were hurt?"

"My daughter, Lisa. It was misery. The collarbone was bad enough, but the ribs—that was agony. I couldn't move without hurting, and I couldn't find a comfortable position, so I was constantly moving. My left arm is still weak, but I've been exercising it and I'm almost back up to normal. Six months! It's ridiculous to take that long to recover, but I suppose that shows my age."

I snorted. It wasn't an elegant sound, but it got my point across. "I've broken a collarbone, too, when I was on the high school cheerleading squad. I had to work hard to get back in shape for the next year. It's a good thing the squad didn't do pyramids and flying stunts for the basketball games, or I couldn't have managed. Six months sounds like a good recovery time to me."

She smiled. "But I'm not doing handstands, am I? You were."

"Not then, I wasn't. I couldn't; my shoulder just wouldn't hold up."

"Can you still do a handstand?"

"Sure. And a backflip, cartwheel, splits. I try to work on my gymnastics at least twice a week."

"Could you teach me how to do a handstand?"

"I don't see why not. It's balance and strength, and practice. You need to do some light weight-lifting to get your arm and shoulder stronger, though, before you start. The last thing you need is to fall and break something else."

"Agreed," she said fervently.

"I can do a one-handed handstand," I said, bragging a little.

"You can?" She turned from the stove and stared at my injured arm, wrapped in the blue-shawl sling. "Not now, you can't."

"I probably can, because I use my right arm, since it's strongest and because I'm right-handed. I always tuck my left arm behind my back, anyway, so it won't wave around and upset my balance."

Well, the upshot of that conversation was that by the time the pork chops, green beans, mashed potatoes, and biscuits were finished, we were both dying to see if I could manage the handstand. Mrs. Bloodsworth kept saying no, I shouldn't take the chance of injuring myself even more, since the stitches were new and I'd lost blood, things like that, but I pointed out that in a handstand what blood I had left would be rushing to my head, so I wasn't likely to faint.

"But you're weak."

"I don't feel weak. I was shaky last night, just a little shaky this morning, and now I feel fine." To prove it, of course, then I *had* to do the handstand.

She fussed around me like she wanted to stop me

but didn't know how, and at the same time I could tell she was really interested. We took the sling off my left arm, and though I could move the arm a little today, I still didn't have a lot of range, so she moved it for me and tucked it behind my back. Then, in a stroke of genius, she tied the shawl around my hips and over the arm to keep it in position.

I got on the other side of the table, away from the stove and in the wide entry into the dining room, so there was plenty of space. I bent over, placed my hand on the floor with my elbow braced against my right knee, centered my gravity over my arm, and slowly slowly slowly began to curl, lifting my feet off the ground.

So that's what Wyatt saw when he came in the back door. We'd been so engrossed we hadn't heard the car in the driveway.

"Holy shit!" he said, the words exploding out of him and making his mother and me both jump.

That wasn't a good thing, because it ruined my balance. I began to topple, Mrs. Bloodsworth grabbed for me, and Wyatt vaulted the table. Somehow he caught my legs, keeping me from tipping over, then wrapped a brawny arm around my waist and gently flipped me upright.

There was nothing gentle about his tongue, though. "What in hell do you think you're doing?" he roared at me, his face dark with temper, then turned to Mrs. Bloodsworth. "Mother, you're supposed to stop her from doing something stupid, not *help* her!"

"I was just showing—" I began.

"I saw what you were 'just' doing! For God's sake,

Blair, you were shot just twenty-four hours ago! You lost a lot of blood! Tell me how, under those conditions, doing a handstand is even remotely reasonable?"

"Since I did it, I'd say it was within the realm of possibility. If you hadn't startled me, I'd have been just fine." My tone was remarkably mild, because we had frightened him. I understood. I patted his arm. "Everything's okay. Why don't you just sit down and I'll get you something to drink. Iced tea? Milk?"

"You'll be okay," his mother said soothingly. "I know you had a scare, but really, we had everything under control."

"*Under control?* She—you . . ." He stopped sputtering and shook his head. "She isn't any safer here than she would be at home. A broken neck can kill her just as dead as a bullet can. That's it. I'm going to have to handcuff her to the vanity in the bathroom, and leave her at my house all day."

CHAPTER
SIXTEEN

Needless to say, supper wasn't a very cheerful occasion. We were mad at Wyatt, and he was mad at us. That didn't interfere with my appetite; I had to rebuild my blood supply, you know.

His mood didn't improve when, as we were leaving after he'd helped his mother clean up the kitchen, she delivered a parting shot by hugging me and then saying, "Take my advice, honey, and don't sleep with him."

"Gee, Mother, thanks," he said sarcastically, which earned him a sniff and a cold shoulder.

"I completely agree with you," I told her.

"Will you be back tomorrow?" she asked me.

"No," he sourly replied, even though she hadn't asked *him*. "You're a bad influence on each other. I'm going to chain her in the bathroom just like I said."

"I don't want to go with you," I said, scowling at him. "I want to stay with her."

"Tough. You're going with me, and that's that." He clamped a strong hand around my right wrist and, on that note, hauled me out to the car.

It was a silent drive to his house while I ruminated on what this latest show of temper meant. From him, not from us. I knew what was up with us, so there was no point in thinking about it.

I'd scared him. Not just momentarily, as I'd thought at first, the way someone is startled by something unexpected, but all the way to the bone. He'd been stricken with fear.

That was it, plain and simple. He'd seen me shot right in front of him; then the very next day he'd stashed me at what he thought was the safest place in town, his mother's house, and after a stressful day he'd walked in to find me trying my level best, in his view, to break my neck or at least tear out all my new stitches.

In *my* view, one adult apology deserved another. If he could do it, so could I.

"I'm sorry," I said. "I didn't mean to scare you, and we shouldn't have teamed up on you."

He gave me a brooding glance and didn't reply. Okay, so he wasn't as gracious about accepting apologies as I was. I let that slide, because his surliness meant he did care for me, after all; he wasn't driven just by sexual chemistry and that competitive streak of his. Whether he cared about me enough for us to have something to build on was still up in the air, but at least I wasn't in this alone.

Just before we reached his house, he muttered, "Don't ever do that again."

"What?" I asked in bewilderment. "Scare you, or team up on you? You can't mean doing a handstand, because you, like, know what I do for a living, right?

I practice gymnastics every week. The members of Great Bods see me practicing and they're reassured that I know what I'm doing. It's good business."

"You could kill yourself," he growled, and with shock I realized that in fact he was, in a very manlike way, seizing on what he saw as the cause of his scare.

"Wyatt, you're a cop, and you want to lecture me on how dangerous *my* job is?"

"I'm a lieutenant, not a patrol officer. I don't serve warrants, make traffic stops, or do undercover drug buys. The guys on the street are the ones in danger."

"You may not do them now, but you did. You weren't hatched out of the academy as a lieutenant, after all." I paused. "And if you were still a beat cop and I pitched a fit because of the danger, what would you do?"

He didn't say anything as he turned into his driveway and pulled into the garage. As the door was coming down behind us, he said grudgingly, "I'd tell you it was my job and I'd do it to the best of my ability. Which has absolutely nothing in common with you doing a handstand in my mother's kitchen the day after being shot."

"That's true," I agreed. "I'm glad you realize it. Just stay focused on what you're mad at so we don't get sidetracked into arguments about how I run my business."

He came around to open the door for me and help me out of the car, then got the bag with my clothes Siana had packed from the backseat, and led the way inside. Then he dropped the bag on the floor, put his arm around my waist, and pulled me to him for a long, hard kiss.

I was kissing him back with enthusiasm when, belatedly, my danger signals began buzzing at me. Breathless, I managed to pull back. "You can kiss me, but we can't have sex. There. I said it after you touched me, so it counts."

"Maybe all I planned on was kissing," he murmured, and kissed me again.

Yeah, and Napoleon's venture into Russia was just a little day trip. Uh-huh. Did he really think I was buying that?

He kissed me until my knees were wobbly and my toes were curled, then released me with a smug look on his face. He couldn't hide the woody in his pants, though, so I felt pretty good myself.

"Did Lynn find the name of that man in the files?" I asked. Maybe I should have asked that much earlier, but the handstand thing had kind of thrown us into a no-talking zone for a while. We were over that, so I wanted to know.

"Not yet. MacInnes was going to call me as soon as they got the name and he did some preliminary checking. Lynn was having some trouble with the computer."

"What trouble? Why didn't she call? She knows how to use the programs, so what's wrong?"

"It crashed."

"Oh, no. The computer can't crash. We're supposed to open again tomorrow. We *are* opening tomorrow, aren't we?"

He nodded. "We finished processing the crime scene, and all the ugly yellow tape is down." He put little verbal quotation marks around "ugly yellow tape," and I knew MacInnes had probably given him—and the entire department—a verbatim replay of our conversation.

I waved that aside. "The computer," I said urgently.

"I sent one of our computer guys over to see what he could do. That was right before I left work, and I haven't heard anything since."

I dug out my cell phone and called Lynn's cell. When she answered, she sounded a little distracted. "Blair, we have to get another computer. This one's possessed."

"What do you mean, possessed?"

"It's doing weird stuff. It's speaking in tongues. Typing in tongues, anyway. This is gibberish. It isn't even English."

"What does the computer cop say?"

"I'll let him tell you."

A moment later a man said, "It's a major crash, but I can salvage most if not all of your files. I'm going to uninstall your programs and reinstall them; then we'll see what we have. Do you have a backup?"

"No, but I'll get one there tonight if you say we need it. What caused the crash?"

"It's what they do," he said cheerfully. "Right now, other than the gibberish on the screen, it's totally frozen. Mouse won't work, keyboard won't work, nothing will work. Don't worry, though; I'll unfreeze it again—this is the third time it's frozen—and we'll dig those files out."

"What about the new computer tonight?"

"Wouldn't hurt," he said.

After we hung up, I explained the situation to Wyatt. Then I called one of the big office supply superstores, told them what I wanted, gave them my credit card number, and told them to get it ready because a policeman was coming by to pick it up. Wyatt was on his phone already getting that arranged. Then I called Lynn back and told her a new computer was on the way. There was nothing we could do after that except wait for the cop computer-guru to work his magic.

"That was a couple of thousand dollars I hadn't planned on spending," I grumbled. "At least it's tax deductible."

I looked up to find Wyatt grinning. "What's so funny?"

"You. You're such a piece of fluff; it's funny hearing anything businesslike coming out of your mouth."

I was so appalled and taken aback that I'm sure my mouth fell open. "Piece of *fluff*?"

"Fluff," he said firmly. "You have a pink hammer. If that isn't fluffy, I don't know what is."

"I am *not* a piece of fluff! I own a business, and I'm good at what I do! Fluffs don't do that; fluffs let other people take care of them." I could feel a really serious snit coming on, because I hate being put down, and being called a piece of fluff definitely felt like a putdown to me.

He framed my waist with both hands, still grinning. "Everything about you is fluffy, from that Pebbles hairdo to your fancy little flip-flops with the shells on them. You wear an anklet all the time, your toenails are hot pink, and your bras match your panties. You look like an ice cream cone, and I could just lick you all over."

Hey, I'm human; I'll admit to being a bit distracted by that part about licking. By the time I dragged my mind back to the argument—at least I was arguing, he was evidently having fun—he was kissing me again, and before I knew it he was licking and biting my neck and my willpower crumbled. Again. Right there in the kitchen, I lost my pants and my control. I *hate* it when that happens. Even worse, he had to help me back into my pants afterward.

"I'm starting another list," I said furiously to his back as he made his smug way up the stairs afterward, carrying my bag. "And I'm showing this one to your mother!"

He stopped and looked at me over his shoulder, a wary look entering his eyes. "Are you talking to my mother about our sex life?"

"I'm talking to her about you being an absolute manipulative *snot*!"

He grinned and shook his head, then said, "Fluff," and continued upstairs.

"Not only that," I yelled after him, "you don't have a single plant in this house and it depresses me to be here!"

"I'll buy you a bush tomorrow," he called back over his shoulder.

"If you're any kind of cop at all, I won't need to be here tomorrow!" There. Let him top that, if he could.

When he came back downstairs, he had changed out of his suit and was wearing jeans and a white

T-shirt. By that time I'd found a pad of paper and had settled in the big leather recliner in the great room, and I had the television remote tucked into my sling. The television was on the Lifetime channel.

He looked at the television and winced. Then he looked at me. "You're in my chair."

"The lamp is here. I need light."

"We've been through this before. That's *my* chair." He purposefully advanced on me.

"If you hurt my arm, I'll—" I broke off and shrieked as he lifted me high in his arms, then sat down in his chair with me on his lap.

"There," he said, nuzzling the back of my neck. "Now we both have the chair. Where's the remote?"

Still in my sling, by the grace of God, and that was where it was staying. I was clinging to the pad and pen with my right hand while I tried to ignore what he was doing to my neck. At least I was fairly safe right now, because I doubted he could get it up again so soon after the kitchen episode. "It was right here," I said truthfully, looking around. "Did it fall behind the cushion?"

He had to check, of course, so I got removed from his lap and he stood to check behind the cushion. He looked all around the recliner; then he turned it upside down to see if the remote had worked its way into the recliner's innards. He turned a gimlet eye on me. "Blair. Where's my remote?"

"It was right there!" I said indignantly. "Honest!" Again, I wasn't lying. It had been right there until he moved me.

Unfortunately, he was a cop, and he knew all about hiding places. His gaze fell on my sling. "Hand it over, you little sneak."

"Sneak?" I began to back away. "I thought I was just a harmless little piece of fluff."

"I never said you were harmless." He took a step toward me, and I broke and ran.

I'm a good runner, but his legs are longer and my sandals didn't get good traction, so that didn't last long. I was giggling as he caught me in one arm and rooted the remote out of its hiding place.

He wanted to watch a baseball game, of course. I'm not into baseball. So far as I know, baseball doesn't have cheerleaders, so I never learned anything about the game. I know football and basketball, but baseball is probably a snooty sport, so I don't want anything to do with it. But we both sat in the big recliner with me draped across his lap working on my list while he watched the game, and except for occasionally grunting when he saw an item that he considered questionable on my list, he did his thing and I did mine.

After I finished my list I was bored—how long do those stupid games last, anyway?!—and I got sleepy. His shoulder was right there, his arm was supporting my back, so I cuddled up and went to sleep.

I woke as he was carrying me upstairs. The lights were off downstairs, and I assumed it was bedtime. "I get a shower tonight," I said, yawning. "And a new bandage."

"I know. I'll get everything ready before we get in the shower."

He got the gauze and sterile pads ready, then carefully cut and unwound the thick layers of gauze until he got to the pad that was stuck directly over the stitches—and I do mean stuck. After a careful tug, I decided to get in the shower and let the water loosen the gauze from the stitches.

He turned on the shower so the water would get warm, then stripped me and then himself. Considering my stance about not having sex with him—yeah, like that was even slowing him down—I probably shouldn't have been naked with him, but the truth was I liked it. A lot. I liked seeing him naked and I liked the way he looked at me when I was naked. I liked the way he touched me, as if he couldn't help himself, cupping my breasts and rubbing his thumbs over the nipples. He hadn't paid much attention to my breasts since he'd found out about my neck, but I could tell he did my neck for my benefit, and my breasts were for his. He liked them, and he showed it.

When we got in the shower and our bodies were all wet and slippery, and we had to stand close together so he could peel the pad off my arm, we wound up belly to belly and slowly moving against each other in a sensual water dance. I found out that enough time had lapsed for him to get it up again, and I quickly said, "No sex!" He laughed, as if it didn't matter, and began washing me. And I found out why he thought it didn't matter. Look, I tried. I really did. I just hadn't been prepared for all the places he washed me, or how long he took.

"Don't pout," he said afterward, as I sat on the

vanity chair and he rebandaged my arm in a much more sensible manner. "I like that you can't resist me."

"I'm working on it, though," I muttered. "I'll manage it yet."

He took my hair down out of the ponytail and brushed it, though I could have done the brushing. I handled brushing my teeth, didn't I? But he wanted to, so I let him. I did the skin-care routine, then asked for the drawstring pants and tank top I wanted to wear to bed. He snorted. "Like you'll need them," he said, picking me up and taking me to bed just the way I was, which was bare.

Poor Detective MacInnes, I'd forgotten about him, putting in long hours while Wyatt was at home with me. The phone rang just as Wyatt was getting into bed beside me; he had the receiver in his hand before the first ring had finished. "Bloodsworth. You got it?" He looked at me and said, "Dwayne Bailey. Ring a bell with you?"

An image shot to mind, that of a burly man about six feet tall, with a lot of body hair. "I remember him," I said. "He needed electrolysis."

"Could he have been the man you saw?"

I have very good visual spatial skills, and I could mentally place Dwayne Bailey standing beside Nicole's car, comparing him to the man I had seen. "There's no way I could recognize his face, but he's about the right size. About six feet, a little on the heavy side. He was kind of surly, too, like he had a bad temper." I remembered that because he'd been in an argument with another of our members, a regular, over using one of the weight machines. Evidently he'd been in a hurry and hadn't liked waiting while the other man finished his sets.

"Good enough. We'll go see him tomorrow," Wyatt said. "MacInnes, grab what sleep you can."

"Why don't you roust Bailey out tonight?" I asked, a little indignant. They might have found the man who killed Nicole and shot me, and they weren't going to pick him up right away?

"We can't just arrest him," Wyatt explained as he turned out the light and slid under the covers. "We don't have probable cause, and no judge in town would sign a warrant. We'll interview him, see what shakes loose. That's how you investigate, honey, by talking to people."

"And in the meantime, he's running around shooting at innocent pieces of fluff. Something's wrong with this picture."

He chuckled and ruffled my hair, then settled me against him. "I never said you were innocent, either."

I pinched his side. "Just think," I said with fake anticipation. "This time tomorrow night, I could be in my own bed."

"But you won't be."

"Why not?"

He chuckled again. "Because the piece of fluff can't dress herself."

CHAPTER
SEVENTEEN

The next morning I could move my arm more, though very gingerly. While Wyatt was downstairs cooking breakfast, I brushed my teeth and hair, and just to show him, even got partially dressed. I found my clothes hanging in the closet next to his, which gave me butterflies in my stomach, seeing them together like that. He must have unpacked my bag when he brought it up last night, because I certainly hadn't. I searched for my underwear and found it in a dresser drawer, all neatly laid out the way I would have done it instead of jumbled together the way I'd expected. The man had depth to him.

I looked through the rest of the drawers to see how he treated his underwear, and found that he was neat. His T-shirts were folded and stacked, his boxers were folded, his socks were matched and mated. There was nothing unusual about his underwear, just regular guy stuff. I liked that, because a relationship between two vain people can really cut into mirror time. One needed to be normal.

I admit that I'm vain. A little. I'm not as bad as I used to be, when I was a teenager, because as I got older I guess I got a little more confident about how I looked. Strange, isn't it? When I was sixteen, which you have to admit is probably a peak year for body and beauty, I would spend hours fixing my hair and putting on makeup, trying on outfit after outfit, because I wasn't sure I looked good enough. Now that I'm thirty, I'm much more comfortable, even though I know I don't look as good as I did at sixteen. Having dewy skin takes an effort now. I have to work out like mad to keep my weight under control. When I'm going out for a big date or something more formal than my usual stuff, I can still make a big deal out of hair and makeup, but for the most part I don't bother. A little mascara, a little lip gloss, and that's about it.

I still loved clothes, though, and was perfectly capable of trying on every item of clothing I had in an effort to find just the right combination. And some days I couldn't decide what color underwear I wanted. Was it a blue day, or a pink day? Or red? Or black? White, maybe?

Today was one of those days. First I had to decide what I was wearing, because that determines the color of your underwear. No dark underwear under white pants, right? I was feeling colorful, so I finally picked out a pair of aqua shorts, and teamed it with a pink tank top. My tank tops have wide shoulder straps, by the way, because I can't stand the bra-strap-peeking-out style. I think it's just tacky. Anyway, the pink tank top dictated that I couldn't wear anything really dark underneath, so that meant a pastel. Pink would have been the obvious choice, but maybe too obvious.

Wyatt appeared in the bedroom door. "What's taking you so long? Breakfast is ready."

"I'm deciding what color underwear I want today."

"Jesus," he said, and left.

Yellow! That was it! Maybe you think yellow wouldn't look good with pink, but the lingerie set was a pale yellow, and it looked great under the pink. Not that anyone other than me would see it—well, Wyatt would, because I still couldn't manage a bra— but it made me feel like the ice cream cone he had mentioned yesterday. Maybe it would put licking in his mind again.

Food was calling, so I carefully pulled on the underpants and shorts, but I got one of Wyatt's button-up shirts from the closet to wear until he could help me with the tops. I slid my feet into flip-flops—these had aqua sequins on the straps—and went downstairs.

He eyed me as I entered the kitchen. "Flip-flops and one of my shirts took half an hour to choose?"

"I'm wearing shorts, too." I lifted the hem of the shirt to show him. "You'll have to help me with the rest." I sat down at the table, and he took a plate of eggs, sausage, and whole wheat toast off the warmer and set it in front of me. A small glass of orange juice and a cup of coffee completed my feast. "I could get used to this," I said as I dug in.

"Do you cook at all?"

"Well, of course. I just don't get waited on all that

often. And I usually eat on the run, because Great Bods opens so early."

"You open *and* close?" He took his own plate and sat down across from me. "That makes for a long day."

"From six in the morning to nine at night. But I don't do both every day. Lynn and I work it out between us; if I need to stay late, she'll open, and vice versa. One day a week, on Monday, I do both so Lynn can have a two-day weekend. All of my employees get two days off, but they're staggered. That's why yoga classes aren't offered every day, things like that."

"Why Monday? Why not Saturday, if she wants a two-day weekend?"

"Because Saturday is our busiest day, and Monday is our slowest. I don't know why, but it's that way for beauty shops, too. Most of them are closed on Monday."

He looked as if he didn't know where to go with that bit of information. As a cop, you'd think he would see the value in knowing things like that. What if someday he had to arrest a mad hair stylist? He could save time by not going to the shop, if it was Monday.

"So," I said, changing the subject, "why did I even bother to get dressed today if you're chaining me in the bathroom? I hope you've thought this out, because besides the obvious benefit of being there, just how am I going to get something to eat?"

"I'll make some sandwiches and put them in a cooler for you." His eyes held a glint of laughter.

"Just for the record, I do *not* eat in the bathroom.

Yuck. Just think of all the bathroom cooties waiting to jump all over your food."

"I'll make it a long chain so you can stand just outside the door."

"You're all heart. A warning, though: when I get bored, I get into trouble."

"Now, what trouble could you get into in the bathroom?"

Right off the bat I could think of several things, but I didn't share them with him. He must have read something in my face, though, because he shook his head. "It's tempting, but no way would I leave you on your own all day."

"So it's back to your mother's, right?"

"I'm afraid so. I've already called her this morning."

"And apologized for being a sorehead, I hope."

"Yes, I apologized," he said wearily. "I think I might as well make a recording and give it to you so you can play it whenever you think it's needed."

I thought that totally missed out on the spirit of an apology, and told him so. "That's the idea," he replied, and I saw I hadn't gained as much ground as I'd thought.

This time I helped him clean up the kitchen. I was very careful when I moved my arm, but it was time to start giving it some gentle movement and exercise. Then we went upstairs to get ready, and again it had that comfortable, intimate feeling, as if we'd been doing this together for years. He liked the yellow bra, and insisted on pulling down my shorts so he could see my matching yellow underpants. That was his excuse, anyway. The hand he slid inside my underpants gave away his true intentions, though. I swear, the man was a lech.

I quickly said, "No!"; and with a wink, a pinch, a pat, and a teasing probe of his finger that put me on my tiptoes, he withdrew his hand.

Oh, damn him. My heart was pounding and I felt flushed. Now I had to deal with being horny all day at his mother's house.

I got back at him. I bent down and lovingly kissed my way down his zipper. He jerked, and threaded his hand through my hair. "Just think," I purred, "how it would feel if these pants weren't in my way." His hand tightened, and he shuddered.

I straightened and said briskly, "But they are, and you need to get to work."

"That's dirty," he growled, eyes hot.

"That's payback. If I'm going to be horny all day, so are you."

"Gonna be interesting tonight," he mused as he restored my clothes to proper order.

"It might not. I'm getting better at heading you off," I said with satisfaction.

"Then I'll just have to get to your neck faster."

I had another uneventful day at Mrs. Bloodsworth's house. I talked to Lynn and she gave me an update on the computer situation, plus how many members had returned now that we were reopened. I was gratified when she told me, because I'd expected a slow couple of weeks. Evidently the weight room was full, the cardio machines were occupied, and almost everyone had asked if I was okay. The comments about Nicole's murder ranged from "I didn't care for her, but she didn't deserve that" to "I'm not surprised." One person asked for his membership to be extended because our facilities hadn't been available for his use for three days. I told Lynn to give him a four-day extension. There's an asshole in every crowd. When she told me who he was, I wasn't surprised. He was one of the city bigwigs who thought he was privileged. What he was, was tolerated. Barely.

I called Mom, and brought her up to date. I didn't tell her Dwayne Bailey's name, just in case he was innocent. I did tell her about my computer woes, and she filled me in on hers. Mom's in real estate, and she keeps all her records on a computer in her little office at home. Her electronics were evidently in a state of revolt against her. In less than a week, her printer had died, her copy machine had to be taken in for repairs, and her computer had experienced two minicrashes. She was in the middle of preparing her quarterly taxes, and her frustration level was high. I hadn't helped by getting shot.

I made soothing noises to her, and promised to keep her apprised of my situation. She asked after Wyatt, which I guess is normal, since he'd insisted on taking her daughter home with him. She liked him. She said he was a hottie. I thought about him naked, and agreed with her.

Business taken care of and the home front covered, Mrs. Bloodsworth and I settled in for another uneventful day. She worked in her flower garden for a while, and to be on the safe side, I didn't. I doubted

Nicole's murderer was going to drive by Mrs. Bloodsworth's house and spot me pulling weeds in her
flower garden, but until Wyatt sounded the all clear, I
wasn't taking any chances. I had a very sore arm to
remind me of how dangerous this guy was.

I read. I watched television. I watched the clock. I
didn't call Wyatt, though I was tempted. I knew he'd
call when he had anything, so there wasn't any point
in harassing him.

I did some light yoga, to keep my muscles limber.
Mrs. Bloodsworth came in while I was doing it, and
was intrigued. She changed into less restrictive clothing, got her exercise mat, and got on the floor beside
me. I showed her some basic yoga positions, and we
stretched our muscles and entertained ourselves until
it was time for lunch.

Around two, Wyatt called. "MacInnes and Forester
interviewed Dwayne Bailey this morning, in the presence of his wife. Evidently she'd had some suspicions
he was cheating on her, and the family scene got intense. Bailey broke down and confessed on the spot;
his story is that Ms. Goodwin was threatening to tell
his wife if he didn't come through with some money
she needed, so he shot her. He's in custody."

I went weak with relief, and collapsed back against
the sofa. "Thank goodness! I don't like this hiding-
out stuff. So I can go home? And go back to Great
Bods? It's all over?"

"Looks like."

"Was he the one who opened my gate?"

"He denies that. He also denies shooting you,
which is smart on his part. A good lawyer can get him

second-degree on Ms. Goodwin's murder, but shooting you would be premeditated and automatically carry a longer sentence."

"But you can prove it, right? Ballistics and all that."

"Actually, we can't. Two different weapons were used. We found the weapon he used to kill Ms. Goodwin, but nothing that matches the caliber of the slug that hit you. That just means he ditched the second weapon, but without it we can't prove squat."

I didn't like that, because I guess I wanted official vengeance or something. If he wasn't charged with shooting me, then it was like he got away with it. I wanted him to get that longer sentence.

"Will he get out on bail?"

"Probably. Now that the jig is up, though, there's no point in killing the witness, right?"

He was right, but I was still unhappy about the man wandering around loose. He might snap, and decide he needed to finish the job.

"If it helps," Wyatt said, "he isn't a homicidal maniac. He was a man desperate to keep his wife from finding out he cheated on her; then he was desperate to keep from getting charged with murder. Both of those things have already happened, so he isn't desperate anymore. He's cooperating."

Okay, I could understand that. You only fear something that hasn't happened. Once it has happened, all you can do is deal with it.

"Is it okay if I tell Mom and Dad?"

"Sure. It'll be on television tonight anyway, and in the papers tomorrow."

"That's wonderful news," Mrs. Bloodsworth said, when I told her about Dwayne Bailey. "But I'll miss having your company during the day. I think I'll rejoin Great Bods; I've been bored since my accident, and I didn't realize how much."

I called Mom and gave her the good news, then Siana, then Lynn. I told her I'd be back at work tomorrow, but asked her to open up again in the morning. Until I could use my arm more, doing anything in a hurry was off the table.

I thought Wyatt would take me to Mom's house, which was logical. She could spoil me for a couple of days until I could handle dressing by myself, and then things would get back to normal.

I was ready for a little normalcy. For almost a week my entire life had been topsy-turvy, and I wanted everything to settle down. I evidently had a lover, try as I might to keep him under control, and he was bound to complicate things. But now with this threat out of the way, we could settle down into the routine of real life and find out if we had something lasting between us, or if the chemistry would go flat with time.

Things were looking up. I could hardly wait to get started on this new situation between us: routine.

CHAPTER
EIGHTEEN

I felt like a bird out of a cage. Even though I'd been under constraints for less than forty-eight hours, it felt much longer than that. I still wasn't able to do everything for myself, but at least my movements weren't hampered. I could *go* somewhere if I wanted; I didn't have to stay indoors; I didn't have to sneak in back doors.

"I'm free, I'm free, I'm free," I sang as I practically boogied out to Wyatt's car when he came to pick me up. It was later than it had been the day before; the sun was almost down, so it was after eight.

"Not exactly," Wyatt said as he buckled me into the seat.

"What do you mean, 'not exactly'?" I yelled at him. I yelled because he was walking around the car, and he wouldn't have heard me otherwise.

"You still look incapacitated to me," he said as he got behind the wheel. "You can't dress yourself, you can't wash your hair, and you can't drive with both hands on the wheel."

"*You* don't drive with both hands on the wheel," I pointed out.

"I don't have to, because I'm in charge. You're not."

I snorted, but let that bit of provocation slide past. "As for all of that, the only reason I didn't go to Mom's in the first place is because you said Dwayne Bailey might look for me there and I could be endangering Mom and Dad as well as myself. Well, Dwayne Bailey's been arrested, and there's no reason for him to look for me anymore. So I can go to Mom's."

"Not tonight," he said.

"I'd like to know why not."

"Because I'm not taking you there."

"Do you have something you have to do tonight? She can come pick me up."

"Stop being deliberately obtuse. I'm not buying it. I've got you right where I want you, and I'm keeping you there."

My temper began to fray. "I am *not* going to be your little sex toy for you to play with whenever you get the urge. I have a life to get back to. I have to go to work tomorrow."

"You can go to work tomorrow. But I'll take you, not your mother."

"That makes no sense whatsoever. What if something happens and you have to work? I'm correct that you can be called in at any time, right?"

"It's possible, but I'm not called on to go to the crime scenes very often. That's what my detectives are for."

"I don't need to be taken to work anyway. My car

has an automatic transmission, and I can buckle my seat belt one-handed. I'm perfectly capable of driving, and don't start with that two-hands-on-the-wheel stuff again." I was as determined now to leave as he was determined for me to stay. I hadn't been before, but he was calmly assuming he could tell me what to do, and I had to nip that in the bud, now didn't I?

He was silent for a moment; then he completely undermined me with a quiet, "Don't you want to be with me?"

I stared at him, mouth open. "Of course I do," I blurted before I could catch myself; then reason reasserted itself and I said indignantly, "I can't believe you're that underhanded and sneaky. That was a *girl* argument, and you used it against me!"

"Doesn't matter. You admitted it." He gave me a smugly triumphant smirk, then blinked. "What's a girl argument?"

"You know, appeal to the emotion."

"Damn, if I'd known it worked that well, I'd have used it before." He reached over and squeezed my knee. "Thanks for the tip."

He winked at me and I couldn't help laughing. I swatted his hand away. "I realize circumstances got in the way, but you haven't lived up to our bargain. You haven't courted me at all. So I want to go home."

"I seem to remember having this discussion before. Your idea of courting and mine aren't the same."

"I want to go out on dates. I want to go to movies, to dinner, dancing—You do dance, don't you?"

"Under great protest."

"Oh, dear." I gave him the BSE—big sad eyes. BSEs

are just one step below tears in the arsenal. "I love dancing."

He darted an alarmed look at me, then muttered, "Shit. All right. I'll take you dancing." He said it with a long-suffering air.

"I don't want you to do it if you don't want to." If that wasn't the perfect place for the classic feminine low-blow, I'd never seen one before. If he took me at my word, he knew he was disappointing me, but if he did take me dancing, he had to pretend he was enjoying it. This is one of the ways women get back at men for not having periods, you know.

"*But*—after the date is over, we do what I want to do."

Two guesses what *that* was. I pulled a shocked look. "You want me to *pay* for a date with *sex*?"

"Works for me," he said, and squeezed my knee again.

"Not going to happen."

"Good. Then I don't have to go dancing."

Mentally I added *Uncooperative and not willing to do things for me* to his list of transgressions. The way that list was going, it was going to be in volumes like the encyclopedia.

"No comeback?" he prodded.

"I was just thinking of things to put on your list."

"Would you forget about that damn list! How would you like it if I made a list of all *your* mistakes and shortcomings?"

"I'd read it and try to work on my problem areas," I said righteously. Well, I'd read it, anyway. What he considered a problem and what I considered a problem might be two very different things.

"That's a crock. I think you actively cultivate your problem areas."

"Such as?" My voice took on a very sweet tone.

"Your smart-ass mouth, for one thing."

I blew him a kiss. "You liked my mouth this morning when I was kissing my way down your zipper."

That reminded him, all right, and he visibly shuddered in response. "You're right," he said thickly. "I liked it a lot."

I knew what he meant. All day, I'd been harboring some longings myself. I wanted to forget all this jockeying about as we fought for the upper hand and for once just eat him up, enjoy him, wallow in sex and pleasure. Maybe when I got him home—Until then, though, there was no point in letting him think he'd won.

"You also like my Pebbles hairdo, even though you made fun of it."

"I didn't make fun of it. And, yeah, I like it. I like everything about you, even when you're being a pain in the ass. You're a walking wet dream, you know."

I gave him a doubtful look. "I don't know if that's good or not." The image in my mind was decidedly sticky and icky.

"From my point of view, it is. Personally speaking, not professionally. You're playing hell with my concentration at work. All I can think about is getting you naked. Probably when we've been married a year or two that'll slack off, but right now it's pretty intense."

"I haven't said I'll marry you," I said automatically, but my heart was doing a tap dance and my own concentration kept wanting to slide off our conversation and instead focus on getting *him* naked.

"It's gonna happen and we both know it. We still have some details to get ironed out, like this trust thing you're so worried about, but I figure in a couple of months I'll have that under control and we can maybe have a Christmas wedding."

"Definitely *not* gonna happen. Even if I said yes, which I haven't, do you have the tiniest clue of how long it takes to plan a wedding? This Christmas would be impossible. Next Christmas, maybe—I mean, it would be possible to plan a wedding in that length of time, not that I want to get married next Christmas, because even if we did get married, it wouldn't be at Christmas because our anniversary would get lost in all the holiday hoopla and I'd *hate* that. Anniversaries should be special."

He grinned at me. "You said 'our anniversary.' That's tantamount to an acceptance."

"Only if you don't understand the English language. I said 'if,' not 'when.' "

"The Freudian slip overrode that. It's a done deal."

"Not yet it isn't. Until and *if* I say those three little words, I haven't committed myself to anything."

He gave me a thoughtful look, as if until now he hadn't realized that neither of us had said "I love you." I don't think men put as much importance into saying "I love you" as women do. For them, it was more about doing than it was about saying, but while they might not understand why it's important, at least they get that it *is* important to women. The fact that I hadn't said it to him got his attention, though, made him realize that perhaps things weren't as cut-and-dried between us as he assumed.

"We'll get there," he finally said, and I was relieved that he hadn't said "I love you" as a means of prompting me to say it too, because then I would have known he didn't mean it. Lord, this man-woman stuff was complicated; it was like a game of chess, and we were equally matched opponents. I knew what I wanted: total reassurance that he was in this for the long haul. I *hoped,* but until I *knew,* I was holding back a little part of myself. He was having fun, I thought; I was having fun, even when we argued. At some point the chess game would be over and then we would see where we stood.

He took my hand. It was my left hand, of course, since he was driving, so I couldn't move my arm very much. He gently slid his hand under mine, and laced our fingers. No doubt about it, he was a damn fine strategist.

That night was far different from the first two nights. He did laundry, both his and mine, and impressed me by not messing up. He cut the grass, even though it was dark by the time he got around to it. His riding lawn mower had headlights on it and he also turned on his outside spotlights. I felt as if I were Ms. Bower Bird, watching Mr. Bower Bird build his nest with all sorts of interesting sparklies to show what a good provider he was, then parading in front of it, hoping to lure Ms. Bower Bird inside. This was

Domestic Wyatt in action. To be fair, though, his yard was well-maintained anyway; I could tell he regularly mowed the grass.

It was ten o'clock when he came in, shirtless and dirty, sweat gleaming on his chest because it was still hot outside even though it was dark. He went straight to the sink and downed a big glass of water, his strong throat working as he swallowed. I wanted to jump on his back and wrestle him to the ground, but my darned arm wasn't up to the action.

He set the glass in the sink and turned to me. "You ready for your shower?"

Maybe it was a tactical error, but tonight I didn't feel very hard to get—well, not that I'd ever been all that difficult for him anyway. Give me points for *trying* though. Tonight I didn't even want to try. "Can we wash my hair tonight, too?"

"Sure."

"Blow-drying it won't take long."

"Doesn't matter." He gave a slow smile. "I'll enjoy the scenery while I'm working."

It doesn't take a genius to figure out how the next hour went. We were both wet and slippery and turned on, and I said to hell with controlling myself—just this once—and threw myself into our lovemaking. It started in the shower—then a panting time-out was called while he dried my hair—and ended in the bed.

He rolled off me with a groan and lay on his back, one arm thrown over his eyes while he sucked in huge gulping breaths. I was breathing fast and hard myself, and I was almost limp with mingled pleasure and exhaustion. Almost. I found the energy to climb on top of him and stretch out while I kissed his jaw, his mouth, his neck, and any other place I could reach.

"Uncle," he said weakly.

"You're giving up before you even know what I want?"

"Whatever it is, I can't. I'm mostly dead." His hand settled on my bare butt, patted once, then dropped limply to the bed.

"It's postcoital glow. I want to cuddle."

"Cuddling I can manage." His lips twitched in a smile. "Maybe."

"You can just lie there and I'll do the work."

"Why didn't you say that ten minutes ago?"

"Do I look stupid?" I settled my head in the hollow of his shoulder and sighed with contentment.

"No, I told you, you look like an ice cream cone."

And he'd licked me right up, too. I shivered as I remembered. If I'd been standing up, my knees would have wobbled. His knees had wobbled, too, I thought with satisfaction. He wasn't the only one who could play that card.

I smiled, thinking of doing it again. Not right now, though. After a while. I yawned, and the lights went out in mid-cuddle.

Mom called while we were eating breakfast the next morning. I didn't know it was her, though. Wyatt answered the phone, said, "Yes, ma'am," twice, then said "Seven," and "Yes, ma'am," again before hanging up.

"Your mother?" I asked as he returned to his food.

"No, yours."

"My mom? What did she want? Why didn't you let me talk to her?"

"She didn't ask to speak to you. She invited us to supper tonight at seven. I said we'd be there."

"We will? What if you have to work late?"

"To quote you, do I look stupid? I'll be there. And so will you, if I have to drag you kicking and screaming out of Great Bods. Make arrangements with Lynn for her to stay until closing."

I rolled my eyes, prompting him to say, "What?" in a testy tone.

"Before you start issuing orders, Lieutenant, you might ask what arrangements I've already made."

"Okay, what arrangements have you already made?"

He was such a smart-ass. "Lynn opened, then she goes home when I get there, and I work the middle chunk of the day. She comes in again at five and stays until closing. So she's working three hours this morning, and four tonight. That's just until my arm is better, because there's stuff that has to be done in the mornings and at night that would be hard to do with just one good arm. So your orders weren't necessary."

"Good deal." He winked at me.

It was easy to figure out why Mom invited us. Half of it was to get in some coddling of her injured first-born, and the other half was to check out Wyatt. She must be half mad with curiosity, and having to wait because he'd had me hidden out would have made it worse. Mom deals with frustration just fine—up to a point. Beyond that point, she causes tsunamis.

I was filled with excitement over the coming day. I was getting my car—finally!—and I was going to work, and after work, I was going to my own home. I had packed my bags and Wyatt hadn't argued, though he hadn't looked pleased. That morning I had managed to dress myself, even my bra. I still couldn't twist my arm up behind my back to fasten the bra that way, but I had turned it backward so the hooks were in front, fastened it, then turned the bra around on my body and worked the straps up my arms. That method didn't look as sexy as the other way, but it worked.

"Take it easy today," he instructed as he drove me to my house so I could get my car. "Maybe we should stop at a medical supply store and get a sling for you, so you'll remember not to move your arm very much."

"I'll remember," I said wryly. "Trust me." If I tried a fast movement, the stitched-together muscle reminded me in a hurry.

A few minutes later he said, "I don't like you being away from me."

"But you knew my staying at your house was just temporary."

"It doesn't have to be temporary. You could move in with me."

"Uh-uh," I said without hesitation. "That wouldn't be a good idea."

"Why not?"

"Because."

"Well, that's enlightening," he said sarcastically. "Because why?"

"A lot of reasons. That would be rushing things way too fast. I think we need to back off and give ourselves some breathing room."

"You gotta be kidding me. After the past five days, you think moving in with me would be *rushing things*?"

"Well, look at everything that's happened. Nothing has been normal, not one single minute has been routine since last Thursday night. We've sort of been in an emergency situation, but that's over. Now our real lives kick in, and we need to see how things go under those conditions."

He didn't like it at all. I wasn't crazy about the idea myself, but I knew moving in with him would be a big mistake. I personally don't think a woman should ever live with a man unless they're married. I guess there are some really great guys out there who wouldn't take advantage of having a live-in cook and maid, but guess how those arrangements usually turn out? No, sir. That's not for me.

I was raised by a woman who knows her own worth, and her daughters firmly believe that life is much better for a woman when a man has to work really hard to get her. It's human nature to take better care of something you've worked for, whether it's a car or a wife. In my opinion, Wyatt hadn't worked nearly hard enough for me to make up for what he'd done two years ago. Yes, I was still mad at him for that. I was beginning to get over it, but not enough to move in with him even if I hadn't thought that it was, in general, not a good thing for a woman to do.

We got to my condo, and there was my sweet little white convertible parked under the portico where it belonged. Wyatt pulled in behind it, and then got both my bags from his back seat. He still had a disgruntled expression, but he wasn't arguing. At least, right then he wasn't arguing. I knew I hadn't heard the last of it, but right then he was backing off the way I'd asked. He was probably busy planning a sneak attack.

I unlocked the side door and went in; the beeping noise from the security system proved that Siana had indeed set it when she left after packing my clothes. I disarmed it, then stood in my kitchen gloriously surrounded by my own Stuff, which I had missed dreadfully. Stuff is important in a woman's life.

I told Wyatt which bedroom upstairs was mine, if he wasn't capable of simply looking in the door and telling. He'd been in my condo, but had never been upstairs. Our scene of passion had been played out on my couch, which I had since had reupholstered, not because of stains or anything, because the scene of passion hadn't gone that far, but because it was my version of washing that man right out of my hair. I had also changed the furniture around and painted the walls a different color. Nothing in my living room looked the same as when he had been there.

The message light on my answering machine was blinking. I walked over and saw that there were twenty-seven messages, which isn't a lot considering how long I had been gone and that the day I'd left reporters had been trying to find me. I punched the play button and started deleting messages as soon as I verified they were from reporters. There were a couple of personal messages, employees wanting to know when Great Bods would reopen, but Siana had called everyone Friday afternoon and it was now a moot point anyway.

Then a familiar voice came out of the machine, and I listened in disbelief.

"Blair . . . this is Jason. Pick up if you're there."
There was a pause, then he continued. *"It was on the news this morning that you'd been shot. Sweetheart, that's awful, though the reporter said you'd been treated and released, so I guess it isn't too bad. Anyway, I was worried about you and just wanted to see how you're doing. Give me a call."*

Behind me, Wyatt said, *"Sweetheart?"* in a dangerous tone.

"Sweetheart?" I echoed, but my tone was totally bewildered.

"I thought you said you haven't seen him since the divorce."

"I haven't." I turned and gave him a puzzled look. "Unless you want to count the time I saw him and his wife shopping in the mall, but since we didn't speak, I don't think that qualifies."

"Why would he call you sweetheart? Is he trying to get something started between the two of you again?"

"I don't know. You heard the same message I did. As for calling me sweetheart, that's what he called me when we were married, so maybe it was just an unconscious thing."

He made a disbelieving noise. "Yeah, right. After five years?"

"I don't know what's going on. He knows I'd never get back with him, period, so I have no idea why he'd call. Unless—Knowing Jason, he was just doing something for his political résumé. You know: 'The candidate has remained on friendly terms with his former wife, phoning her after an incident in which she was wounded by gunfire.' That sort of thing. Setting it up so, if a reporter happened to ask me, I'd say yes, that he'd called. He does stuff like that, always thinking about future campaigns." I hit the delete button and erased his noxious voice from my answering machine.

He put his hands on my waist and pulled me to him. "Don't you dare call him back. The bastard." His green eyes were narrow, and his face had that hard look a man gets when he's feeling territorial.

"I wasn't going to." Now was the time for mildness, not for zinging him, because I knew how I'd feel if his ex-wife suddenly got in touch with him and left a message like that. I put my arms around him and nestled my head in the hollow of his shoulder. "I'm not interested in anything he has to say, anything he feels, and when he dies, I won't go to the funeral. I won't even send flowers. The bastard."

He rubbed his chin against my temple. "If he calls you again, *I'll* give him a call."

"Yeah," I said. "The bastard."

He chuckled. "It's okay, you can let up on the *bastard*s. I get the idea." He kissed me and patted my butt.

"Good," I said cheerfully. "Now may I go to work?"

We both went out and got into our respective cars—I remembered to set the security system on my way out—and Wyatt reversed out of my short driveway into the street, backing up far enough to give me room to back out in front of him. I wondered if he intended to follow me all the way to Great Bods, maybe to make certain no ex-husband was lurking, waiting to talk to me.

I backed out of the driveway and shifted the gear lever to *Drive*. The engine purred as I gave it the gas, and Wyatt fell in behind me.

A hundred yards down the street was a stop sign, where the street intersected with a busy four-lane. I put on the brakes, and the pedal went right to the floor. I sailed through the stop sign and straight into four lanes of traffic.

CHAPTER
NINETEEN

My life didn't flash before my eyes. I was too busy fighting the steering wheel and screaming *"Shit!"* to pause for any navel-gazing.

I wasted a precious few seconds desperately pumping the brake pedal, praying it would suddenly, miraculously work. It didn't. Just before I went past the stop sign, as a last-ditch effort I stomped on the emergency brake pedal, and the car went into a hard spin, tires screaming and smoking, as I shot into the intersection. My seat belt snapped tight, jerking me back against my seat. I tried to get control of the spin, but an oncoming car, its own tires screaming as it tried to stop, clipped my right rear bumper and added to the momentum. It was like riding a very fast merry-go-round. In the split second I was facing traffic, I had a lightning flash of a red pickup coming right at me; then there was a hard jolt as my car hit the concrete bumper of the median and jumped it, backward, before slewing sideways across the grass and into the other two lanes of traffic. Terror-stricken, I glanced to the right and, through the passenger window, saw a woman's face frozen in horror, and time itself seemed to freeze, too, in the instant before the impact. An enormous shock wave hit me like a body blow, and the world went black.

The blackness lasted for only a few seconds. I opened my eyes and blinked, both aware and surprised that I was still alive, but I couldn't seem to move and even if I'd been able to, I would have been too afraid to check out what damage I'd sustained. I couldn't hear anything; it was as if I was alone in the world. My vision was misty, and my face felt numb, but at the same time it *hurt*. "Ouch," I said aloud into the strange silence, and with that sound everything popped back into focus.

The good news was: the air bag worked. The bad news was: it needed to. I looked around me at my car and almost moaned aloud. My beautiful little car looked like a twisted pile of scrap metal. I was alive, but my car wasn't.

Oh, my God, *Wyatt*. He'd been right behind me; he'd seen everything. He had to think I was dead. I fumbled with my right hand for the seat belt and unclipped it, but when I tried to open my door, it wouldn't budge and I couldn't throw my weight against it because my hurt arm was on that side. Then I noticed the windshield had been popped out, so I laboriously hauled myself out from behind the steering wheel—it was like playing Twister—and gingerly crawled through the space where the windshield had been, careful of the broken glass, and out onto the hood, just as Wyatt reached me.

"Blair," he said hoarsely, reaching for me, but he froze with his hands outstretched as if he was afraid to touch me. His face was paper white. "Are you all right? Is anything broken?"

"I don't think so." My voice was thin and shaky, and my nose was running. Embarrassed, I swiped at it, then saw the bright smear of red on my hand and the additional red dripping from my nose. "Oh. I'm bleeding. Again."

"I know." He gently lifted me off the hood and carried me to the grassy median, picking his way through a tangle of cars. Traffic in both directions had come to a complete halt. Steam rose from the crumpled hood of the car that had hit me, and other motorists were helping the woman inside. On the other side of the four-lane, two or three cars rested at weird angles in the road, but the damage there seemed to be mostly in the fender-bender range.

Wyatt set me down on the grass and pressed a handkerchief into my hand. "If you're all right, I'll go see about the other driver." I nodded and waved a hand, indicating he should see what he could do. "Are you certain?" he asked, and I nodded again. He briefly touched my arm, then strode off, talking into his cell phone, and I lay back on the grass with the handkerchief pressed to my nose to stop the bleeding. I remembered being hit in the face really hard; that must have been the air bag deploying. My life was well worth a bloody nose.

A man in a suit came over and squatted down beside me, positioning himself so he blocked the sun out of my face. "Are you all right?" he asked kindly.

"I dink so," I said nasally, holding my nose pinched together.

"You lie right there and don't try to get up, just in case you're hurt worse than you realize and don't feel it yet. Is your nose broken?"

"I don't dink so." It hurt; my whole face hurt. But my nose didn't hurt worse than anything else, and all in all, I thought it was just a bloody nose.

Good Samaritans came out of the woodwork, offering aid in a variety of means: bottles of water and baby wipes, even a few alcohol wipes from someone's first aid kit, to help clean up the cuts and wipe away blood so you could tell how bad a cut actually was; emergency ice packs; Band-Aids and gauze; cell phones and sympathy. There were seven walking-wounded with minor injuries, including me, but the driver of the car that had T-boned me was injured severely enough that they hadn't taken her out of the car. I could hear Wyatt talking, his voice calm and authoritative, but I couldn't hear what he was saying.

Reaction seized me and I began trembling. I slowly sat up and looked around at the chaos, at the bloody people sitting on the median with me, and I wanted to cry. I had done this? It was an accident, I knew it was, but still . . . I was the cause. My car. Me. Guilt ate at me. I kept my car in good running condition, but had I overlooked some key maintenance? Not paid attention to a warning sign that my brakes were about to fail?

Sirens were shrieking in the distance and I realized only a few minutes had passed. Time was crawling so slowly it felt as if I'd been lying there on the grass for at least half an hour. I closed my eyes and prayed hard that the woman who had hit me would be okay. Because I felt weak and a little dizzy, I lay back down and stared up at the blue sky.

Suddenly I had a weird sense of déjà vu, and I realized how similar this scene was to the one Sunday afternoon, only then I'd been lying on the warm parking lot instead of fragrant green grass. But sirens had been shrieking and cops swarming, just the way they were now. Maybe more time had passed than I thought; when had the cops got here?

A medic went down on one knee beside me. I didn't know him. I wanted Keisha, who gave me cookies. "Let's see what we have here," he said, but he was reaching for my left arm. He must have thought the bandage was covering a new cut.

"I'm okay," I said. "That's stitches from minor surgery."

"Where's all this blood from?" He was taking my pulse, then flicking a tiny penlight from eye to eye.

"My nose. The air bag gave me a bloody nose."

"Considering what could have happened, God bless air bags," he said. "Were you wearing your seat belt?"

I nodded, so then he checked me for seat-belt injuries, and wrapped a cuff around my right arm to check my blood pressure. Guess what? It was elevated. Since I was structurally all right, he moved on to someone else.

While other medics were working with the woman in the car, stabilizing her, Wyatt came back and squatted beside me. "What happened?" he asked quietly. "I

was right behind you, and I didn't see anything unusual, but all of a sudden you started spinning." He
still looked pale and grim, but the sun was in my eyes
again and I couldn't be sure.

"I put on my brakes for the stop sign, and the pedal
went all the way to floor. There was nothing. So I put
on the emergency brake, and that's when I started to
spin."

He glanced over at my car where it rested in the far
lane, the two front wheels up on the curb. I followed
his gaze, stared a moment at the wreckage, and shuddered. I'd been hit so hard the frame had wrapped in
a U shape, and the passenger side was nonexistent.
No wonder the windshield had popped out. If it hadn't
been for my seat belt, I probably would have popped
out, too.

"Have you had trouble with your brakes lately?"

I shook my head. "Nothing. And I have it serviced
regularly."

"The patrolman who drove it to your place didn't
report any problems with it. You go on to the hospital and get checked out—"

"I'm okay. Honest. My vitals are steady, and other
than getting popped in the face by the air bag, I don't
think anything else is wrong."

He rubbed his thumb over my cheekbone, the
touch light. "All right. Should I call your mother to
come get you? I'd rather you not be alone for the next
few hours, at least."

"After the cars are moved. I don't want her to see
my car; it'll give her nightmares. I know you need my
insurance card and registration," I said woefully, still

staring at the tangle of sheet metal. "They're in the glove compartment, if you can find the glove compartment. And my bag is in there, too."

Briefly he touched my shoulder, then stood and walked across the two lanes to my car. He looked in the window, walked around the car to the other side and back, then did something odd: he got down on the pavement, on his back, and slid his head and shoulders under the car just behind the front wheels. I winced, thinking of all the glass that must be on the pavement and hoping he wouldn't get cut. What was he looking for?

He slid out from beneath the car, but didn't come back over to me. Instead he went to one of the uniformed officers and said something to him, and the officer went over to my car and he, too, slid underneath it, just the way Wyatt had. I saw Wyatt talking on his cell phone again.

A small convoy of wreckers began arriving, to tow the damaged vehicles away. An ambulance arrived, and the medics began the process of gently removing the woman from her car. One of them held an IV bag over her. Her face was drenched in blood, and they'd fitted a cervical collar on her. I whispered another prayer.

Sawhorse barricades were put on the street, and officers in both directions were directing traffic in a detour. The wreckers sat there idling, but none of the cars were moved. More police cars arrived, driving down the median to reach the accident scene. These were unmarked cars, and to my surprise I saw my pals

MacInnes and Forester. What were detectives doing working an accident scene?

They talked to Wyatt and the officer who had been under my car. MacInnes got down on his back and slid under my car himself. What was up with that? Why was everyone looking under my car? He slid out, said something to Wyatt; Wyatt said something to an officer; and before I knew it, the officer came over and helped me to my feet, then led me to a patrol car.

Good God, I was being arrested.

But he put me in the front seat; the motor was running and the air-conditioning was on, and I turned a vent to blow right on my face. I didn't adjust the rearview mirror to see how I looked. My whole face might be black-and-blue, but I didn't want to know.

At first the blowing air felt good, but within a minute chill bumps were popping out on my skin. I closed the vent, but that didn't help much. I hugged my arms.

I don't know how long I sat there, freezing to death. Normally I would have adjusted the air-conditioning controls, but somehow I didn't have the initiative needed to mess with a cop's car. If it had been Wyatt's car, yeah, but not a patrol officer's. Or maybe I was just too dazed to take action.

After a while Wyatt came over and opened the door. "How are you feeling?"

"Fine." Except for a growing stiffness, and a general feeling of having been bludgeoned. "I'm cold, though."

He pulled off his jacket and leaned in, tucking the

garment around me. The fabric was warm from his body and felt blissful to my cold skin. I hugged the jacket to me, and stared wide-eyed at him. "Am I under arrest?"

"Of course not," he said, cupping my face and running his thumb over my lips. He kept touching me, as if reassuring himself that I was all in one piece. He hunkered in the V of the open door. "Do you feel up to going to the station, giving us a statement?"

"Are you sure I'm not under arrest?" I said in alarm.

"Positive."

"Then why do I have to go to the station? Is that woman dead? Will I be charged with vehicular homicide?" Growing horror consumed me, and I felt my lips tremble.

"No, honey, calm down. The woman will be all right. She was conscious, and talking sensibly to the medics. There's a possibility of a neck injury, so they were being very careful moving her."

"It's all my fault," I said miserably, fighting tears.

He shook his head. "Not unless you cut your own brake line, it isn't," he said in a hard tone.

Dwayne Bailey had posted bond, but he was hauled in again and questioned. I wasn't allowed to be in on the questioning, which is probably a good thing because by then I'd worked myself into a state. My brake line had been cut. My car had been deliberately sabotaged. I could have been killed; others who had nothing to do with witnessing Nicole's murder could have been killed. I was furious. Wyatt wouldn't let me anywhere near Dwayne Bailey.

Now I knew why Wyatt had the patrol officer put me in his car: to protect me. I'd been totally exposed, sitting there on the grassy median, in case someone— namely Dwayne Bailey—wanted to take another shot at me. I couldn't think why he would, or why he would sabotage my car, since he'd already confessed and there was no need to kill me—not that there ever had been, but he didn't know that. Well, maybe now he did, though I doubted the cops would have told him that I couldn't have identified him anyway.

I washed off in the ladies' restroom, using paper towels to scrub the dried blood off my face and out of my hair as best I could. I have no idea how blood from a nosebleed got in my hair, but it was there. I had blood in my ears, behind my ears, on my neck, my arms—and another bra was ruined, damn it! I even had blood on my feet.

There was a small cut across the bridge of my nose, and both cheekbones were red and swollen. I suspected I would have two black eyes in the morning. I also suspected I would have so many other aches and pains that I wouldn't care about a black eye, or eyes.

Wyatt hadn't found my bag, so I didn't have my cell phone. The bag had to be in the car . . . somewhere . . . and the car was in the police lot, secured behind a locked fence. The forensics team had gone over the car there at the scene, at least the exterior, so the wrecker could haul it in without destroying any evidence. They would do their best to check out the interior, too, and Wyatt said they'd find my bag then. I could do without everything that was in it, except my wallet and checkbook. Having to replace all my credit cards, my driver's license, insurance cards and all the others, would be a pain, so I hoped they found it.

I hadn't called Mom yet, because telling her someone had tried to kill me—again—was infinitely worse than telling her I'd been in an accident.

The cops kept bringing me stuff to drink and eat. I guess, having heard tales of the cookie situation on Sunday, they thought I needed sustenance. One woman, who looked stern and businesslike in her blue uniform and with her hair tightly braided, brought me a bag of microwave popcorn and apologized because she didn't have anything sweet to offer. I drank coffee. I drank Diet Coke. I was offered chewing gum, and cheese crackers. Potato chips. Peanuts. I ate the peanuts and the popcorn, and refused everything else or I'd have been bloated. They did not, however, offer me the one thing I was waiting for. Excuse me, but just where were the doughnuts??? This was a cop station, for crying out loud. Everyone knows cops eat doughnuts. Of course, considering it was now lunchtime, probably the doughnuts were long gone.

The officer, Adams, who had been the primary accident-scene investigator, went over the sequence of events at length with me. He had me draw diagrams. He drew diagrams. I got bored and drew smiley faces, too.

They were keeping me occupied, of course. I knew that. It was probably on Wyatt's orders, so I wouldn't be tempted to interfere in Dwayne Bailey's interrogation, as if I would. Hard as it may be to believe, I know when to butt out. Wyatt, however, evidently had doubts.

Around two, Wyatt came to collect me. "I'm taking you to your place to get cleaned up and your clothes changed; then I'm taking you to your mom's for right now. It's a good thing your bags are still packed, because you're going back to my house with me."

"Why?" I asked as I got to my feet. I'd been sitting in his chair, at his desk, making a list of everything I needed to do. Wyatt frowned a little when he saw the list and turned it around so he could read it. His brow cleared when he realized the list wasn't about him.

"Bailey swears he didn't touch your car," he said. "He says he doesn't even know where you live, and that he has an alibi for his time from Thursday night on. MacInnes and Forester are checking things out, but just to be on the safe side, we're going back to Plan A, which is keep you hidden."

"Bailey is here, right? Is he under arrest?"

Wyatt shook his head. "He's in custody, but he isn't under arrest. We can hold him for a little while without officially filing charges against him."

"Well, if he's here, then who am I hiding from?"

He regarded me soberly. "Bailey's the most obvious person—if the sabotage was done before yesterday and he didn't tell us about the car because then we'd figure he was the shooter on Sunday and the car was just another attempt to kill you. On the other hand, if his alibi checks out, then we have to consider that someone else is trying to kill you and used this opportunity while someone else had the motive for doing it. We had this conversation the night Ms. Goodwin was murdered, but we need to have it again—have you been in an argument with anyone?"

"You," I said, pointing out the obvious.

"Other than me."

"No. Believe it or not, I don't get in many arguments. You're the exception."

"Lucky me," he muttered.

"Hey. How many people have *you* had arguments with in the past month, other than me?" I asked indignantly.

He rubbed his face. "Good point. All right, let's get moving. I'm having your ex-husband interviewed, too, by the way."

"Jason? Why?"

"It struck me as a little odd that he'd call you like that, after five years of no contact at all. I don't believe in coincidence."

"But why would Jason try to kill me? It isn't as if he's the beneficiary of any insurance policy I have, or that I know anything he wouldn't want—" I stopped, because I did know something about Jason that would hurt his political career—and I had the picture to prove it. He didn't know I had the picture, though, and I wasn't the only one who knew he was a cheating scumbag.

Wyatt's eyes had that hard, piercing cop look. "What?" he said. "What do you know?"

"It can't be that I know about him cheating on me," I said. "That doesn't make sense. For one thing, I haven't said anything for five years, so why would he all of a sudden get worried about it? And I'm not the only person who knows, so bumping me off wouldn't accomplish anything."

"Who else knows?"

"Mom. Siana and Jenni. Dad knows Jason cheated; Mom eventually told him that much, but he doesn't know any specifics. The women he cheated *with* certainly know. Probably his family. And it isn't as if knowledge that he cheated on his first wife, over five years ago and with someone who isn't his current wife, would wreck his political career. Dent it, maybe, but not wreck it." Now, if it were generally known that he'd been caught coming on to my seventeen-year-old sister, *that* would wreck his career, because that put him in the category of pervert.

"Okay, I'll give you that. Anything else?"

"Not that I can think of." Like I said, Jason didn't know I had copies of those pictures, so I was safe on that count. "Anyway, Jason isn't violent."

"I thought you said he threatened to trash your car. To me, this is definitely in the same ballpark."

"But that was five years ago. And he threatened to trash my car if I went public about him cheating on me. He was running for the state legislature at the time, so that would definitely have hurt him. And to be fair, he only did that when I threatened to go public on him if he didn't give me everything I wanted in the divorce settlement."

Wyatt tilted his head back and surveyed the ceiling. "Why doesn't that surprise me?"

"Because you're a smart man," I said, and patted his butt.

"Okay, if you don't think it's your ex-husband—I'm going to check him out anyway—do you have any other ideas?"

I shook my head. "Dwayne Bailey has the only reason I can think of."

"C'mon, Blair. Think."

"I am thinking!" I said in exasperation.

He was getting exasperated, too. He put his hands on his hips and looked down at me. "Then think harder. You're a cheerleader; there must be hundreds of people who'd like to kill you."

CHAPTER
TWENTY

My resultant shriek stopped the hum of voices that came from outside his closed office door. *"You take that back!"*

"All right, all right. Pipe down," he muttered. "Shit. I take it back."

"No you don't. You *meant* it." As a rule of thumb, you never let a man take something back on the first attempt. Section three, paragraph ten, of the Southern Women's Code states that if one (meaning a man) is going to be a shithead, one must pay for it.

"I didn't mean it. I'm just frustrated." He reached for me.

I drew back before he could touch me, jerked the door open, and swept out. Just as I had thought: everyone in the big, busy open room was staring at us, some openly, some pretending not to. I stalked silently to the elevator, and let me tell you, various aches and pains were making themselves felt, so stalking *hurt*. Creeping would have been better, but there's just no way to creep with attitude. My feelings were hurt, and I wanted him to know it.

The elevator doors opened and two uniforms got out. Well, the uniforms had men in them, but you know what I mean. Silently Wyatt and I entered the elevator, and he punched the button.

"I *didn't* mean it," he said as soon as the elevator doors closed.

I shot him a dirty look but didn't say anything.

"I've seen you get nearly killed twice in four days," he said raggedly. "If Bailey didn't do it, then you have an enemy somewhere. There has to be a reason. You know something, but you may not know that you know it. I'm trying to dig out some information that will point me in the right direction."

I said, "Don't you think you should check out Bailey's alibi before assuming there are 'hundreds' of people who want to kill me?"

"Maybe that was an exaggeration."

Maybe? An *exaggeration*? "Oh? Just how many people do you *really* think want to kill me?"

He shot me a glittering glance. "I've wanted to strangle you myself a time or two."

The elevator stopped, the door opened, and we stepped out. I didn't respond to that last statement because I figured he was trying to get me mad enough to say something rash myself, like maybe accuse him of tampering with my brakes, since he admitted having wanted to kill me, and then I'd have to apologize because of course he didn't really mean that, either, and I knew it. Rather than surrender the high ground, I played dirty and kept my mouth shut.

When we walked out into the parking lot, Wyatt caught me around the waist and turned me to face him. "I really am sorry," he said, lightly kissing my forehead. "You've been through a lot these past few days, especially today, and I shouldn't have teased you, no matter how frustrated I am." He kissed me again, and his voice roughened. "When you spun into the intersection and that first car hit you, I thought my heart would stop."

Well, hell, there was no point in being petty, was there? I leaned my head against him and tried not to think about the sickening terror I'd felt this morning. If it was that bad for me, what had it been like for him? I know how I would have felt if I'd been behind him and watched him get killed, which is what I'm sure he thought had happened to me.

"Your poor little face," he murmured, stroking my hair back as he examined me.

I hadn't been just sitting in the police station all day waiting for my face to swell up and my eyes to turn black. One of the cops had given me a plastic sandwich bag, and I'd filled it with ice and applied it, off and on, to my face, so however bad I looked wasn't as bad as it could have been. I'd also put an adhesive strip across the cut on the bridge of my nose. I thought I looked like a boxer who'd just finished a fight.

"J. W.," someone said, and we both looked around as a gray-haired man in a gray suit approached. With his hair, I personally thought he should have worn a suit with more color in it, or at least a nice blue shirt, so he wouldn't have given such a blah impression. I wondered if his wife had no fashion sense. He was short and stocky, and looked like a businessman, except that when he got closer, I could see he had that distinctive sharp gaze.

"Chief," Wyatt said, from which I deduced (duh!) that this was the chief of police, Wyatt's boss. If I'd ever seen him before, I didn't remember it; in fact, at that moment, I couldn't even remember his name.

"Is this the young lady the entire force is talking about?" the chief asked, studying me with great curiosity.

"I'm afraid so," Wyatt said. "Chief, this is my fiancée, Blair Mallory. Blair, this is William Gray, chief of police."

I resisted the urge to kick him—Wyatt, not the chief—and instead shook hands. Well, I would have shaken hands, but instead Chief Gray just sort of gently held my hand as if he were afraid of hurting me. *I* was afraid I looked a lot worse now than I had the last time I'd checked myself in a mirror, what with Wyatt's "poor little face" and now the chief treating me like a piece of fragile glass.

"It was a terrible thing that happened this morning," the chief said solemnly. "We don't have a lot of homicide in this town and we want to keep it that way. We'll get this solved, Miss Mallory; I promise you."

"Thank you," I said. What else could I say? Hurry up? The detectives knew what they were doing, and I trusted they were good at it—just as I was good at certain things. I said, "Your hair is a really great color. I bet it looks fantastic when you wear a blue shirt, doesn't it?"

He looked startled, and Wyatt surreptitiously pinched my waist. I ignored him.

"Well, I don't know about that," Chief Gray said, giving the laugh that men do when they're both flattered and a little uncomfortable.

"I do," I assured him. "French blue. You probably have ten shirts that color, don't you, because it looks so good on you?"

"French blue?" he murmured. "I don't—"

"I know." I laughed. "To a man, blue is blue is blue, and don't bother you with all those fancy names, right?"

"Right," he agreed. He cleared his throat and took a step back. "J. W., keep me up-to-date on how the investigation is going. The mayor is asking about it."

"Will do," Wyatt said, and hurriedly turned me toward his car while the chief continued on into the building. Wyatt hissed, "Were you actually giving the chief of police *fashion advice*?"

"Someone needed to," I said in self-defense. "The poor man."

"Wait until news of this gets around," he said under his breath as he opened the passenger door and helped me ease into the seat. I was becoming more stiff and sore by the minute.

"Why's that?"

He shook his head. "You're practically all everyone in the department has talked about since last Thursday night. They either think I'm getting my comeuppance, or that I'm the bravest man walking."

Well. I didn't know what to think about that.

* * *

I closed my eyes when we got to the intersection where the wreck had taken place. I didn't know if I'd ever be able to stop at that stop sign again without reliving everything. Wyatt turned onto the street that led to my condo and said, "You can open your eyes now."

I shook away the memory of screaming tires and opened my eyes. With the intersection behind me, everything looked normal and familiar and safe. My building loomed on the right, and Wyatt pulled under the portico. I looked around, remembering that my fence gate had been unlocked when the officer brought my car home. Had whoever tampered with my brakes—I still thought Dwayne Bailey was the most likely suspect—been lurking around then? Had he seen my car being delivered and figured if he couldn't get to me in one way, he would in another?

"I think I'm going to move," I said vaguely. "I don't feel safe here anymore."

Wyatt got out and came around to open the door for me, and helped me out. "That's a good idea," he said. "While you're recuperating, we'll get your stuff packed up and moved out to my house. What do you want to do with your furniture?"

I looked at him as if he were an alien. "What do you mean, what do I want to do with my furniture? I need my furniture for wherever I move to."

"I already have furniture at my house. We don't need more."

Ah. I was a little slow on the uptake, because I just then realized what he was saying. "I didn't mean move in with you. I just meant . . . move. Sell the condo and buy another one. I'm not ready for a house, I don't think, because I don't have time to take care of yards and flower beds and things."

"Why make two moves when one will do?"

Now that I knew what track he was on, I could easily follow him. "Just because you told Chief Gray I'm your fiancée doesn't make it so. You not only have the cart before the horse, you forgot to get the poor thing out of the stable. We haven't even gone on a date yet, remember?"

"We've barely been apart for five days. We bypassed the dating thing."

"You wish." I stopped in front of the door and in that moment, like a blow, realized that I couldn't get in my own house. I didn't have my bag, didn't have my keys, didn't have control of my life. I gave him an appalled look, then sat down on the stoop and burst into tears.

"Blair . . . honey," he said, but didn't ask what was wrong. I think I would have hit him if he had. Instead he sat down beside me and put his arm around me, cradling me close to him.

"I can't get in," I sobbed. "I don't have my keys."

"Siana has a set, doesn't she? I'll call her."

"I want my own keys. I want my bag." After everything that had happened that day, not having my bag was the crowning blow, the one that sent me over the edge. Evidently realizing I wasn't capable of being reasonable, he simply held me, rocking me back and forth while I cried.

While he rocked, he unclipped his cell phone and called Siana. Because of the investigation none of my family had yet been told what happened that morning, and Wyatt kept the explanation brief: I'd been in a car accident that morning, the air bag had deployed and I wasn't hurt, hadn't even gone to the hospital, but my bag hadn't yet been retrieved from my car and I couldn't get in my house. Could she come unlock the door for me? If she couldn't, Wyatt said he would have a patrolman stop by to get the keys.

I could hear Siana's voice, the tone of alarm, but I couldn't make out exactly what she was saying. Wyatt's calm responses reassured her, though, and when he disconnected the call, he said, "She'll be here in about twenty minutes. Do you want to get back in the car in the air-conditioning?"

I did. I wiped my face—very gingerly—and asked him if he had a tissue. He didn't. Men are so unprepared.

"I have a roll of toilet paper in the trunk, though, if that will do."

Okay, I didn't want to know why he had the toilet paper, but I changed my mind about him being unprepared. Diverted from my tears, I went to stand beside him as he popped the trunk, to see what else he had back there.

The main thing was a large cardboard box, which contained the toilet paper, a pretty extensive first aid kit, a box of plastic gloves, several rolls of duct tape, folded sheets of plastic, a magnifying glass, measuring tape, paper bags, plastic bags, tweezers, scissors, and a bunch of other stuff. There was also a shovel, a pickax, and a saw. "What's with the tweezers?" I asked.

"You just keep them handy in case someone's eyebrows need plucking?"

"Evidence collection," he replied as he unrolled some toilet paper and gave it to me. "I had to have it when I was a detective."

"But you aren't a detective now," I pointed out. I folded the toilet paper, then wiped my eyes and blew my nose.

"Habits die hard. I keep thinking I might need some of this."

"And the shovel?"

"You never know when you'll need to dig a hole."

"Uh-huh." I understood that, at least. "I always carry a brick in my trunk," I confided, then felt a twinge as I remembered what shape my car was in.

He closed the trunk, a frown between his eyes. "A brick? Why do you need a brick?"

"In case I need to break out a window."

He paused, then said to himself, "I don't want to know."

We sat in the car until Siana arrived, driving a new model Camry. She got out, looking smart and sexy in a taupe suit with a red lace tank under the jacket. Her shoes were taupe sling-backs with three-inch Lucite heels. Her golden blond hair was cut in a sleek shoulder-length bob, the simple lines doing great things for her heart-shaped face. Despite her great dimples, Siana had a look about her that said, "Be afraid. Be very afraid." Between us, my sisters and I pretty much had all the bases covered. I was pretty enough, but mostly I was athletic and business-oriented. Siana was maybe less even-featured, but her intelligence shone

in her face like a beacon, plus she had great boobs.
Jenni was taller than either of us, with darker hair,
and drop-dead gorgeous. She couldn't settle on a career, but she was making good money doing local
modeling jobs. She could have gone to New York and
tried her luck there, but she wasn't interested enough.

Wyatt and I both got out of the car. Siana took one
look at me, gave a low cry, and burst into tears as she
rushed toward me.

She looked as if she wanted to throw her arms
around me, but she stopped short, started to pat me,
then drew her hand back. Tears dripped down her
face.

I looked at Wyatt. "Do I look that bad?" I asked
uncertainly.

"Yeah," was his answer, which perversely reassured
me, because if I'd been in truly bad shape, he would
have been coddling me.

"I do not." I began reassuring Siana, patting her.

"What happened?" she asked, blotting her eyes.

"My brakes failed." The full explanation could
come later.

"What did you hit? A power pole?"

"Another car hit me. On the passenger side."

"Where's your car? Can it be fixed?"

"No," said Wyatt. "It's totaled."

Siana looked horrified all over again.

I sidetracked her by saying, "Mom invited us to
supper tonight, and I need to get cleaned up before I
go over there."

She nodded. "That's for sure. She'd freak out if she
saw you like this, with blood all over your clothes. I

hope you have some real good concealer, too. You've got a raccoon thing going on."

"Air bag," I explained.

My condo key was on her key ring, mixed in with all her other keys. She separated it, unlocked the door, then stepped back while I went in first and disarmed the security system. She followed Wyatt and me inside. "Mom invited me tonight, too. I figured by the time I got here and back to the office, it would be time to leave anyway, so I left for the day. Do you need me for anything? I'm available."

"No, I think everything's under control."

"Does your insurance company provide a rental until the claim can be settled?"

"Yes, thank goodness. My agent said she'll make arrangements for me to get the rental tomorrow."

Siana was a lawyer; her mind was already moving ahead. "Do you have a mechanic lined up to go over your car, do a postmortem? You'll need a notarized statement—"

"No," Wyatt said. "It wasn't mechanical failure."

"Blair said her brakes failed."

"They did, but they had help. The brake line was severed."

She blinked; then she went pale. She stared at me. "Someone tried to kill you," she blurted. "Again."

I sighed. "I know. Wyatt says it's because I'm a cheerleader." I slanted him a "gotcha" look and took myself upstairs to shower, smiling as I listened to Siana swing to my defense. The smile faded as I climbed the stairs, though. Two attempts on my life were enough. This whole situation was getting on my nerves. MacInnes and Forester had better find that Dwayne Bailey had unaccounted-for chunks of time, and a nice set of fingerprints on my poor car would come in handy, too.

I eased out of my stiff, bloody clothing and let every garment fall to the floor. They were all ruined, anyway. I was amazed that a simple bloody nose could make such a mess. Finally I went into the bathroom and took a good look at myself in the full-length mirror. Bruises were definitely forming across my cheekbones, and across my nose. And on both knees, my shoulders, the inside of my right arm, and my right hip. I ached in every muscle; even my feet ached. Looking down, I saw a big bruise on top of my right foot.

Wyatt came into the bathroom while I was standing there surveying the damage. Without saying anything, he looked me over from head to toe, then gently folded me in his arms and rocked me back and forth for a while. For once, there was nothing sexual in his embrace, but he'd have had to be one sick puppy to be turned on by such an array of bruises. "You need ice packs," he said. "A lot of them."

"What I need," I replied, "is a doughnut. About two dozen of them. I have some cooking to do."

"What?"

"Doughnuts. I need to stop at Krispy Kreme and get two dozen doughnuts."

"Won't a cookie do?"

I eased away from him and turned on the shower. "Everyone was so sweet to me today; I'm going to make a bread pudding to take to them tomorrow. I have a recipe using Krispy Kreme doughnuts for the bread."

He stood frozen, his taste buds already imagining the taste. "Maybe we should get four dozen, so you can make two. That way we'll have one at home."

"Sorry. I can't work out right now, so I really have to watch what I eat. The temptation would be too much if there was a bread pudding sitting there calling to me."

"I'm a cop. I can protect you from it. I'll take it into custody."

"I don't feel up to making two," I said as I stepped into the shower.

He raised his voice to be heard over the running water. "I'll help."

I smiled again at the plea in his voice. He shouldn't have let me know he had such a sweet tooth; now I had him. I thought about torturing him by not letting him taste the pudding until tomorrow at the police station with everyone else, and that kept my mind off the problem of someone trying to kill me. It's just mental dancing, but it works for me.

I heard his cell phone ring while I was rinsing the shampoo from my hair. It was a slow go, since my left arm wasn't really in the game, but I was managing. I listened to him talking, though I couldn't understand what he was saying. Finished, I turned off the water and hooked the towel off the top of the shower door, then began drying myself as best I could.

"Come on out and I'll finish the job," he said, so I stepped out. The first thing I noticed was that he had that grim expression again.

"What's wrong?"

"That was MacInnes," he said, taking the towel from me and gently wiping me down. "Bailey's alibi checks out. Every bit of it. He was either at home with his wife, or at work, with only enough time allowed in between for him to make the drive there and back. According to MacInnes, Bailey's wife has filed for divorce, so she isn't inclined to lie for him. They'll check further, but it looks as if he's clean. Someone else is trying to kill you."

CHAPTER
TWENTY-ONE

We were early getting to Mom and Dad's, even though we stopped for the doughnuts and condensed milk I needed for the bread pudding. Wyatt had everything else at his house, including the size pans I needed. Yes, *pans*. Plural. We bought four-dozen glazed doughnuts. The smell of them made my mouth water, but I was strong and didn't even open the box.

Dad opened the door, paused while he studied my face, then said, "What happened?" in a very quiet tone.

"I totaled my car," I said, going to him for a hug; then I went on into the kitchen to face Mom. Behind me, I heard Dad and Wyatt carrying on a low-voiced conversation and I figured Wyatt was giving Dad the skinny.

In the end, I hadn't tried to conceal the bruises. Well, I did have on a pair of long pants, a light-weave cotton with pink and white stripes, and a white T-shirt tied in a knot at my waist, because if I'd worn shorts that showed the bruises on my legs, someone would have thought Wyatt was beating me and I didn't feel up to defending his honor. But I hadn't put any concealer on the bruises under my eyes, because I figured any makeup would make a mess when Mom did whatever she was bound to do to my face.

She was standing with the freezer door open, staring inside. "I meant to do a roast," she said without looking up when she heard me come in. I'm not certain she knew it was me and not Dad, but it didn't matter. "But I've been fighting with that damn computer for so long I don't have time now. What do you think about grilling—" She looked up and saw me, and her eyes went round. "Blair Mallory," she said in an accusing tone, as if I'd done this to myself.

"Car accident," I said, sitting down on one of the tall barstools at the eating bar. "My poor little car is totaled. Someone cut my brake line and I went through the stop sign into the traffic at that busy intersection just down from my house."

"This has to stop," she said, her voice tight and angry as she closed the freezer door and opened the refrigerator portion instead. "I thought the police caught the man who killed Nicole."

"They did. He didn't do it. He didn't shoot at me, either; after he shot Nicole, he didn't leave his house except to go to work. His wife alibied him, and since she's found out he was cheating on her, she's filed for divorce, so it isn't as if she's protecting him."

Mom closed the refrigerator door without taking anything out, and opened the freezer door again. Mom is scarily efficient, so this dithering told me how upset she was. This time, she pulled out a package of frozen peas and wrapped them in a clean kitchen towel.

"Hold this over the bruises," she said, handing the peas to me. "What other damage do you have?"

"Just bruises. And I'm sore in every muscle. A car T-boned my car on the passenger side, so I took a huge jolt. The air bag hit me in the face and gave me a bloody nose."

"Be glad you don't wear glasses. Sally"—Sally Arledge is one of Mom's closest friends—"drove her car into the side of the house, and when the air bag hit her, it broke her glasses and her nose."

I couldn't remember Sally driving into the side of her house, and I'm sure Mom would have told me. My sisters and I had all called her "Aunt Sally" when we were little, and they palled around together— Mom and the three of us, Sally and her five. That was quite a group when we all went somewhere. Sally had four boys, then a daughter. She'd named the four boys after the Gospels, but didn't find any biblical girl's name that she liked, so they were Matthew, Mark, Luke, John, and Tammy. Tammy always felt left out because she didn't have a biblical name, so we'd called her Rizpah for a while, but she didn't like that either. Personally, I thought *Rizpah Arledge* had a ring to it, but Tammy decided to go back to being Tammy and didn't even have to have counseling.

"When did Sally drive into the house? You didn't tell me about this."

"Put the peas on your face," she said, and I obediently tilted my head back and draped the bag of frozen peas over my face. It was big enough to cover my eyes, cheekbones, and nose, and, damn, it was cold. "As for why I didn't tell you, it just happened on

Saturday, while you were at the beach, and there hasn't been an opportunity since then."

Ah, the beach. I remembered it with longing. It was just a few short days ago, but then my only problem had been Wyatt. No one had been trying to kill me while I was at the beach. Maybe I should go back. Tiffany would like that. So would I, if no one would shoot me or tamper with my car while I was there.

"Did she hit the gas instead of the brake pedal?" I asked.

"No, she did it on purpose. She was mad at Jazz." Sally's husband's name is Jasper, which is likewise a biblical name, only no one calls him that; he's always been Jazz.

"So she rammed her house? That doesn't sound cost-effective."

"She was aiming for Jazz, but he dodged."

I took the bag of peas off my face and stared at Mom in astonishment. "Sally tried to kill Jazz?"

"No, she just wanted to maim him a little."

"Then she should use, like, a riding lawn mower or something, not a *car*."

"I'm pretty sure he could outrun a lawn mower," Mom said thoughtfully. "Though he *has* put on a little weight. No, I'm certain he could, because he was fast enough to get out of the way when she drove the car at him. So a lawn mower wouldn't work."

"What did he do?" I had visions of Sally catching him in the act with some other woman, like maybe her worst enemy, which would make the betrayal doubly bad.

"You know those shows on television where a husband or a wife invites these interior decorators to come into the house and redecorate a room as a surprise for the other one? While Sally was visiting her mother in Mobile last week, he did that."

"Oh. My. God." Mom and I looked at each other in horror. The thought of someone else coming into our houses and undoing what we had done, plus redecorating without having a clue what we like or dislike, was awful. I shuddered. "He got a television show decorator?"

"Not even that. He hired Monica Stevens from Sticks and Stones."

There was nothing to say to that. I was mute in the face of such a calamity. Monica Stevens had a predilection for glass and steel, which I guess was fine if you lived in an laboratory, and she liked black. A lot of black. Unfortunately, Sally's taste runs more toward cozy cottage.

I knew how Jazz had picked Monica, though: she had the biggest ad in the phone book, so poor Jazz would have figured she was very successful and popular if she could afford the biggest ad. That's just how Jazz thinks. He was also hampered by having no clue about a woman's boundaries, despite having been married for thirty-five years. If he'd just thought beforehand to ask Dad if redecorating was a good idea, this whole problem could have been avoided, because Dad has more than a clue, he has it down to an exact science. My daddy's a smart man.

"Which room did Monica do?" I asked faintly.

"Put the peas back on your face." I obeyed, and Mom said, "The bedroom."

I moaned. Sally had worked hard finding just the right pieces for her bedroom, haunting estate sales and auctions to find the perfect antiques. Some of them had been heirloom quality. "What did Jazz do with Sally's furniture?" Technically I guess it was his furniture, too, but Sally was the one who was emotionally invested in it.

"That was the kicker. Monica talked him into putting it in her consignment shop, where of course it sold right away."

"*What?*" I dropped the peas to stare openmouthed at Mom. I couldn't believe what I'd just heard. Poor Sally couldn't even re-create her bedroom. "Forget the car, I'd have rented a *bulldozer* and gone after him! Why didn't she back up and take another go?"

"Well, she was hurt. I told you it broke her nose. And her glasses, so she couldn't see, either. I don't know what's going to happen to them. I don't see how she can ever forgive him— Hello, Wyatt. I didn't see you standing there. Blair, I didn't have time to put on the roast, so we're going to grill hamburgers."

I looked around at where the two men were standing in the doorway, listening. The expression on Wyatt's face was priceless. Dad took it all in stride.

"Fine with me," Dad said affably. "I'll get the charcoal started." He went through the kitchen and out onto the deck, where he kept his monster grill.

Wyatt was a cop. He'd just heard about an attempted murder, though I knew Sally had really intended more to break Jazz's legs than to kill him. He also looked as if he'd just stepped into an alternate universe. "*She* can't forgive *him*?" he asked in a strained tone. "She tried to kill him!"

"Well, yeah," I said.

Mom said, "He *redecorated* her bedroom." Did we have to draw him a picture?

"I'm going outside," he said warily, and followed Dad. Actually, it sort of looked as if he was escaping. I don't know what he expected. Maybe he thought we should be discussing my personal situation, but you know that thing I have about dancing around and not thinking about something? I got it from Mom. It was much better for us to talk about Sally trying to run over Jazz than it was to think about someone trying to kill me.

The topic was like a nine-hundred-pound gorilla, though; we might put it in a corner, but we couldn't forget about it.

Siana arrived, having gone home and changed into shorts and a T-shirt. Jenni breezed in, cheerful in a pale yellow dress that went great with her skin tone, and she had to be brought up to speed on the car accident. That was the topic of conversation at the dinner table, over juicy grilled hamburgers. Actually the dinner table was the picnic table out on the deck, but the principle is the same.

"I'm going to talk to Blair's ex-husband tomorrow," Wyatt said when Mom asked what the plan of action was. "Blair says it isn't him, but statistics say I'd better have a talk with him."

I shrugged. "Knock yourself out. Like I said, I haven't seen or talked to him since the divorce."

"But he called and left a message on her answering machine when it was on the news that she'd been shot," Wyatt told my intensely interested family.

Siana leaned back and said thoughtfully to me, "It's not beyond the realm of possibility that he wants to get back together with you. He may be having trouble with his second wife."

"All the more reason for me to have a word with him," Wyatt said, with a snap in his words.

"I can't see Jason doing anything violent," Mom said. "He'd be too concerned with how it would look. He'd do anything to protect his political career."

"Would he kill to protect it?" Wyatt asked, and everyone fell silent. Jenni toyed with her silverware and didn't look at any of us.

"But I'm not threatening his political career," I pointed out. "Whatever I know about Jason is the same thing I've known about him all along; there's nothing new. So why would he suddenly decide, after five years, that he needs to kill me?"

"Maybe it isn't your situation that's changed; maybe it's his. Maybe he's planning to run for something more important than the state legislature, such as governor, or congressman."

"So he thinks he'll commit murder and get away with it? How likely is that?"

"Depends. Is he a man who's smart, or a man who just thinks he's smart?"

We all looked at each other. The problem was, Jason wasn't a dummy but neither was he anywhere near as sharp as he thought he was. "I'll give you that," I finally said. "But there's still no motive that I can see."

"You can't see any motive, period, for anyone, so that doesn't rule him out."

"I see. Since I can't point you to any specific person, you have to consider everyone."

"But in the meantime, Wyatt, until you catch this person," Mom said, "how are you going to keep Blair safe? She can't go to work; she can't stay in her own home. I'm surprised you even let her come here."

"I thought about canceling," he admitted. "But I had to balance that against other needs. I can guard her coming and going to the car, and I can make certain no one follows us when we leave. Unless this person knows Blair and I are involved, and knows where I live, we're in the clear there. Have any of you told anyone?"

"I didn't even tell Sally," Mom said. "She isn't in any state to listen right now."

"I haven't," Siana said. "We talked about Blair getting shot, but we didn't get into personal stuff."

Jenni shook her head. "Same here."

"Then we're clear," Dad said. "It never occurred to me to talk about her private life."

"Good. Keep it that way. I know my mother hasn't said anything, either. Blair, have you told anyone?"

"Not even Lynn. We've had other stuff to talk about, you know?"

"So we'll go back to the previous arrangement. She'll stay with me, she won't go to work, and after tonight you won't see her until we catch this guy. Talk on the phone all you want, but nothing in person. Got it?"

Everyone nodded. He looked satisfied. "The detectives are canvassing Blair's neighborhood, talking to everyone, even the little kids. Maybe someone was seen around your car, and no one thought anything about it at the time."

I wasn't real hopeful on that front. Because I didn't park at the curb in the front of the building, my car wasn't as readily visible as most of the others. Someone could have approached from the rear unseen, unless a neighbor just happened to be looking out a back window at that exact time, and slid under my car without anyone seeing him from the street.

I hated it, but I'd been banking on Dwayne Bailey being the one who was trying to kill me. He was the only person I knew of with a motive, and even then he hadn't really had one; he just didn't know that I couldn't have identified him. Finding out he had an alibi that was likely legitimate left me mentally floundering, because I couldn't think of any other reason why someone would want me dead. I didn't mess around with other women's men, I didn't cheat anyone, and unless provoked, I tried to be nice to everyone. I didn't even wear white shoes after Labor Day or before Easter. Hey, I saw that movie with Kathleen Turner, and I took it to heart. I don't want the fashion Nazis coming after me.

"If it isn't personal," I said, thinking aloud, "then it's about business, right? Money. What else is there? But I haven't cheated anyone, and I didn't drive anyone out of business when I opened Great Bods. Halloran's Gym had already closed down when I bought the building and renovated it. Does anyone have any ideas here?"

All around the picnic table, heads shook from side to side. "It's a mystery," Siana said.

"What are the usual motives?" Dad asked, and started ticking them off on his fingers. "Jealousy, revenge, greed. What else? I'm discounting politics and religion, because as far as I know Blair isn't political, and she isn't a religious hothead. This isn't a case where someone gets mad and acts without thinking, right, Wyatt?"

Wyatt shook his head. "Both of the attempts were premeditated. If we play percentages, both attempts were made by a man—"

"How do you figure that?" Siana asked, intrigued as always by any intellectual discussion, even one that involved someone trying to kill me.

"The weapon used wasn't a handgun, not from that distance. We know where the shooter positioned himself, because we found the shell casing. It was a twenty-two rifle, which is common as grass in these parts, not a lot of stopping power to it, but with an accurate shot it'll kill. It's also a subsonic round. Blair bent down as the shot was fired, which is why it hit her arm instead of a vital area. Women may use handguns, but they seldom use rifles, which require practice and skill for distance shooting, and that generally isn't something a woman's interested in."

"What about the brakes?" Mom asked.

"There are four women sitting here. Do any of you know where the brake line is?"

Mom, Siana, and Jenni all looked blank. "Beneath the car," I said. "I saw you looking."

"But did you before that?"

"No, of course not."

"There are several lines and cables beneath the car. How would you know which one to cut?"

"I guess I'd have to ask someone. More likely I'd just cut everything."

"Which proves my point. Women aren't likely to know enough about a car to cut a brake line."

"*Or* I would get a book that showed me where the brake line is," I said. "If I really wanted to cut a brake line, I'd figure out some way to do it."

"Okay, let me ask you another question. If you wanted to kill someone, is that a method you would even think of? How would you do it?"

"If I wanted to kill someone," I mused. "First, I'd have to be really, really angry or really, really scared, like if I had to protect myself or someone I loved. Then I'd use whatever weapon was handy, whether it was a tire tool, a rock, or my bare hands."

"That's the way most women are, and there goes the premeditation down the drain. I said *most* women, not all, but statistically we're looking for a man. Agreed?"

Everyone nodded agreement.

"Now, if I were just pissed at someone, that's different," I said.

Wyatt got a look on his face that said he knew he shouldn't ask, but he did anyway. "How so?"

"Well, that would take some planning. Like maybe

I would bribe her hairdresser to do something really awful to her hair. Things like that."

He propped his chin in his palm and stared at me, half smiling. "You're a scary, vicious woman," he said. Dad snorted with laughter and clapped him on the shoulder.

"Yeah," I said. "And don't you forget it."

CHAPTER
TWENTY-TWO

Mom wouldn't let me leave until she worked on my bruises. Siana and Jenni helped, plastering me with cold packs, vitamin K cream, cucumber slices, and tea bags soaked in ice water. Other than the vitamin K cream, everything else seemed to be just a variation on an ice pack, but doing it made them feel better and being coddled and fussed over made me feel better. Dad and Wyatt were smart enough to stay out of the way while this was going on, entertaining themselves with some ball game.

"I was in an accident once," Mom said. "When I was fifteen. I was on a hayride; the hay wagon was pulled by a pickup truck. Paul Harrison was driving; he was sixteen and was one of the few people in our school who had something to drive. The only problem was, Carolyn Deale was beside him in the truck. I don't know what all she was doing, but Paul forgot to pay attention to the road and ran off in a ditch and turned the hay wagon over. I wasn't hurt at all, I didn't think, but the next morning I was so stiff and sore I could barely move."

"I'm already that way," I said ruefully. "And I haven't even had a hayride. I'm missing out."

"Whatever you do, don't take any aspirin, because that'll make the bruises worse. Try ibuprofen," said Siana. "Massage. A whirlpool tub. Things like that."

"And stretching exercises," Jenni added. She was carefully kneading my shoulders as she spoke. She took some massage classes once—she said just for the fun of it—so she was our go-to girl for sore muscles. Normally Jenni was a chatterbox, but she'd been unusually quiet tonight. Not pouty or anything like that, though she can be on occasion, just sort of thoughtful and withdrawn. I was actually surprised that she'd stayed around to do the massage, because usually she had a group of friends she was meeting, or a date, or some party.

I loved being with my family; I stayed so busy with Great Bods that I didn't have a lot of opportunity to do that. Mom told us all about her problems with her computer, which involved a lot of nontechnical language like "doohickey" and "little thingie." Mom operates computers just fine, but she sees no need to learn terms that she considers silly or stupid, such as "motherboard," and for which other normal words will do just as well. In her version, a motherboard is "that main deal." I totally understand that. Technical support (what a laugh) wasn't living up to her expectations, because evidently they'd had her uninstall everything, then reinstall, and that hadn't solved a damn thing. Mom said they'd made her take everything out and put it back in.

But finally we had to leave. Wyatt came to the doorway; he didn't say anything, just looked at me with that look men have when they want to go, the impatient, "Are you ready yet?" expression.

Siana glanced at him and said, "The look's here."

"I know," I said, and gingerly got up.

"The 'look'?" Wyatt glanced over his shoulder, as if expecting something to be standing behind him.

All four of us instantly mimicked the expression and body language. He muttered something, wheeled, and went back to where Dad was. We could hear them talking. I think Dad was telling Wyatt some of the finer points of how to live in a household with four females. Wyatt was a smart man; Jason had thought he already knew all he needed to know.

But Wyatt was right, and we did need to leave. I wanted to get the bread puddings made tonight, because I knew I'd feel even worse in the morning.

Which brought up the subject of what he intended to do with me the next day, because I had my own ideas. "I don't want to go to your mother's," I said when we were in the car. "Not that I don't like her— I think she's adorable—but I figure I'm going to be so sore and miserable tomorrow I'd rather just stay at your house so I can lie in bed all day if I want."

By the dash lights I saw him give me a worried look. "I don't like the idea of you being alone."

"If you didn't think I was safe at your house, you wouldn't be taking me there."

"It isn't that. It's your physical condition."

"I know how to handle sore muscles. I've had them before. How did you usually feel after the first day of full-contact practice?"

"As if I'd been beaten with a club."

"Cheerleader practice was the same. After the first time, I learned to stay in shape all year long, so it was never that bad again, but the first week of practice was still not a lot of fun." Then I remembered something and sighed. "Scratch staying at home and resting. My insurance agent is supposed to arrange a rental car for me, so I'll have to pick it up."

"Give me your agent's name and number, and I'll take care of that."

"How?"

"Deliver the car to me. I'll drive it home, then have your Dad come pick me up and take me back to work to pick up my car. I don't want you in town again until I find this bastard."

A really bad thought struck me. "Is my family in danger? Could this man use them to get to me?"

"Don't borrow trouble. So far this seems targeted specifically toward you. Someone thinks you've done 'em wrong, and he wants vengeance. That's what this feels like, honey: vengeance. Whether it was something in business or a personal matter, he wants revenge."

I honestly couldn't think of a thing, and in a way not knowing *why* someone wanted to kill me was almost as bad as the actual attempts. Okay, so it wasn't as bad; it didn't even come close. I'd still have liked to know. If I'd known why, then I'd have known who.

It couldn't be business. It just couldn't. I'd been

scrupulous, because I was afraid the IRS would get me if I wasn't. The IRS left all the other bogeymen in the dust, as far as I was concerned. I usually even fudged my returns and didn't claim all my deductions, just to give myself some leeway if I was ever audited. I figured if they ever did audit me and had to pay *me,* that would put an end to the auditing stuff as far as my business was concerned.

I'd never fired anyone. A couple of people had quit, moved on to other jobs, but I'd been careful about whom I hired, instead of just picking any warm body that could fill a slot. I hired good people and I treated them well. None of my employees would kill me, because then there would go their 401Ks.

So that left personal. And I drew a huge blank on that.

"I'm ruling out anything that happened in high school," I told Wyatt.

He coughed. "That's probably safe, though sometimes those teenage things can really fester. Were you in a clique?"

Wyatt and I had gone to different high schools, plus he was a few years older, so he didn't know anything about my school years. "I guess," I said. "I was a cheerleader. I hung out with the other cheerleaders, though I did have this one friend who wasn't a cheerleader and didn't even go to the ball games."

"Who was it?"

"Her name was Cleo Cleland. Say that three times real fast. Her parents must have been stoned on pot when they named her. They were from California, so she didn't fit in real good when they moved here. Her mother was one of those natural-beauty-earth-mother types, with some feminist stuff thrown in, so she refused to let Cleo wear makeup or anything like that. So Cleo and I would both go to school early, and I'd take my makeup with me. We'd go into the girl's restroom and I'd fix Cleo up for the day so no one would make fun of her. She had *no clue* about makeup when she moved here. It was awful."

"I can imagine," he murmured.

"Things got tricky when she started dating, because she'd have to figure out a way to put on her makeup without her mother seeing it. By that time she'd learned how, so I didn't have to put it on for her anymore. But she couldn't wait until she was out with her date, because then he'd see her without it, and that would be a disaster."

"I don't know about that. You're cute without makeup."

"I'm not sixteen now, either. At sixteen, I'd rather have died than let anyone see my natural face. You get convinced that it's the makeup that's pretty, not you. Well, I know some girls who felt that way. I never did, because I had Mom. She taught all three of us how to use makeup when we were still in grade school, so it was no big deal to us. See, makeup isn't camouflage; it's a weapon."

"Do I want to know this?" he wondered aloud.

"Probably not. Most men just don't get it. But at sixteen I did go through an insecure stage, because I had to fight so hard to keep my weight down."

He gave me an incredulous look. "You were pudgy?"

I slapped his arm. "Of course not. I was a cheerleader, so I worked off my weight, but I was also a flyer."

"A flyer."

"You know. One of the ones who gets tossed by the other cheerleaders. The top of the pyramid. See, I'm five-four, so I'm tall for a flyer. Most flyers are five-two, something like that, and they keep their weight around a hundred pounds so it'll be easier to throw them. I could be that slim, and be fifteen pounds heavier, because I'm taller. I had to really watch it."

"My God, you must have been a toothpick." He looked me over again. I weigh about one twenty-five now, but I'm strong and muscled, so that means I look as if I weigh ten or fifteen pounds lighter than that.

"But I also had to be strong," I pointed out. "I had to have muscle. You can't have muscle and be a tooth-pick. I had about a five-pound range where I had muscle but wasn't too heavy, so I was constantly balancing my weight."

"Was it really worth it, to jump around and wave pom-poms during a football game?"

See, he knew absolutely nothing about cheerleading. I glared at him. "I went to college on a cheer-leading scholarship, so I'd say, yeah, it was worth it."

"They give scholarships for that?"

"They give scholarships to guys who carry around a piece of pigskin, so why not?"

He had the wisdom to detour off that path. "Back to your high school days. You didn't steal anyone's boyfriend?"

I made a scornful noise. "I had my own boyfriends, thank you."

"Other guys weren't attracted to you?"

"So what if they were? I had a steady, and I didn't pay any attention to anyone else."

"Who was your steady? Jason?"

"No, Jason was my college guy. In high school it was Patrick Haley. He got killed in a motorcycle accident when he was twenty. We didn't keep in touch after we broke up, so I don't know if he was dating anyone special or not."

"Scratch Patrick. Where's Cleo Cleland now?"

"In Raleigh-Durham. She's an industrial chemist. Once a year or so we get together for lunch and a movie. She's married and has a four-year-old."

He could scratch Cleo, too. Not because she was dead, but because Cleo was my pal. Besides, she was a woman, and he'd said the person trying to kill me was most likely a man.

"There has to be someone," he said. "Someone you maybe haven't thought about in years."

He was right. This was personal, so it was someone I knew. And I was totally drawing a blank on anyone who might want to kill me.

Then inspiration hit.

"I know!" I crowed.

He jerked, instantly alert. "Who?"

"It has to be one of *your* girlfriends!"

CHAPTER
TWENTY-THREE

The car swerved. Wyatt brought it back into the lane and glared over at me. "How did you come up with an idea like that?"

"Well, if it isn't me, then it has to be you. I'm a nice person, and I don't have any enemies that I know of. *However,* when was the first attempt? Right after we came back from the beach. How many people know you followed me there? After the way you acted Thursday night when Nicole was killed—"

"The way *I* acted?" he echoed in outraged astonishment.

"You told your guys that we were involved, right? Even though we weren't. I saw the way they looked at me, and *not one* out of about fifty cops came to my rescue when you were manhandling me. So I figure you lied to them and said we were dating."

His teeth were set. "I wasn't manhandling you."

"Stop latching on to insignificant details. And you were, too. But am I right so far? You told them we were seeing each other?"

"Yeah. Because we are."

"That's debatable—"

"We're living together. We're sleeping together. How in hell is it debatable whether or not we're seeing each other?"

"Because we haven't started dating yet and this is just temporary. *Will you stop interrupting me?* My point is, who were you seeing that you dropped like a hot potato to chase after me?"

He ground his teeth for a few seconds. I know because I could hear them. Then he said, "What makes you think I was seeing anyone?"

I rolled my eyes. "Oh, please. You know you're to die for. You probably have women lined up."

"I don't have women— You think I'm to die for, huh?"

Now he sounded pleased. I wanted to beat my head against the dash, only it would hurt and I had enough aches and pains at the moment. "Wyatt!" I yelled. "Who were you dating?"

"No one in particular."

"It doesn't have to be 'in particular'; it just has to be dating. Because some women have unrealistic expectations, you know. One date and they're picking out a wedding gown. So who was the last person you dated, and who maybe thought there was something serious going on, then went totally postal when you followed me to the beach? Had you been on a date last Thursday, the night Nicole was killed?" Notice how I slipped that in, because I'd been wondering.

By this time we had reached his house, and he slowed to turn in to the driveway. "No, that night I'd been teaching a women's self-defense class," he said absently, to my great satisfaction. "I don't think your theory holds water because it's been . . . God, almost two months since I've gone out with anyone. My social life hasn't been as hot as you evidently think."

"This last person you were with. Did you go out with her more than once?"

"A couple of times, yeah." He pulled into the garage.

"Did you sleep with her?"

He gave me an impatient look. "I see where this little interrogation is going now. No, I didn't sleep with her. And, trust me, we didn't click."

"You didn't, but maybe she did."

"No," he repeated. "She didn't. Instead of digging into my past, you should be thinking about your own. You're a flirt, and some man might have thought you were serious—"

"I'm not a flirt! Stop trying to throw this back on me."

He came around and opened the car door for me, leaning in to scoop me up in his arms so my stiff and sore muscles wouldn't have to go to the effort of climbing out of the car, then gently setting me on my feet. "You're a flirt," he said grimly. "You can't help it. It's in your genes."

He had a lot of "f" words to describe me, and I was getting tired of hearing them. Yes, I flirt occasionally, but that doesn't make me a flirt. Nor am I fluffy. I don't think of myself as a lightweight person, and Wyatt was making me sound like the most frivolous—another "f" word—nitwit walking.

"And now you're pouting," he said, rubbing his

thumb over my lower lip, which might have started to stick out just the tiniest bit. Then he bent and kissed me, a slow, warm kiss that for some reason really melted me, maybe because I knew there was no way he was going anywhere with it, and he knew it, too, so that meant he was kissing me just to kiss me, not to get me into bed.

"What was that for?" I asked a tad peevishly, to hide the fact that I'd melted, when he lifted his mouth.

"Because you've had a bad day," he said, and did it again. I sighed and relaxed against him, because, yes, I'd had a very bad day. This time when the kiss was over, he held me close for a moment, his cheek resting on top of my head. "Leave the police work to us," he said. "Unless you all of a sudden remember a deadly enemy who's been threatening to kill you, in which case, I definitely want to hear about it."

I pulled back and scowled at him. "Meaning I'm such a dumb blond I wouldn't remember something like that right away?"

He sighed. "I didn't say that. I wouldn't say it, because you aren't dumb. You're a lot of things, but dumb isn't one of them."

"Oh, yeah? Just what 'things' am I?" I was feeling truculent, because I was hurt and scared and I had to take it out on someone, didn't I? Wyatt was a big boy; he could handle it.

"Frustrating," he said, and I almost kicked him, because he'd come up with another "f" word. "Annoying. Stubborn. Slick, because you use the dumb-blond routine when you think it'll get you what you want, and I figure it usually does. Your thought processes scare the hell out of me. Reckless. Funny. Sexy. Adorable." He touched my cheek, his hand gentle. "Definitely adorable. And this is *not* temporary."

Man, I wasn't the only slick one around, was I? I'd been on the verge of a major snit; then he'd undercut me with the last three items. So he found me adorable, huh? That's a good thing to know, so I decided to ignore that part about this not being temporary. He leaned down and kissed me again, then added, "To die for."

I blinked at him. "That's a girl thing to say. Guys shouldn't say it."

He straightened. "Why not?"

"It's too girlie. You should say something macho, like 'I'd take a bullet for you.' See the difference?"

He was fighting a grin. "Got it. C'mon, let's go inside."

I sighed. I had two bread puddings to make, and I didn't really feel like it, but a promise is a promise. No, the people at the police department didn't know I was making it, but I had mentally promised it to them, so there you go.

Wyatt got the doughnuts and condensed milk from the backseat, then unlocked his trunk and took out a burlap bag with green strings hanging from it. He closed the trunk, frowning at the burlap bag.

"What's that?" I asked.

"I told you I'd get you a bush. Here it is."

I stared at the poor bedraggled plant. The green strings had to be its limp little limbs. "What will I do with a bush?"

"You said the house didn't have a single plant in it,

like that somehow made it unlivable or something. So here's your plant."

"That isn't a houseplant! That's *shrubbery*. You bought shrubbery for me?"

"A plant's a plant. Put it in the house and it's a houseplant."

"You are *so* clueless," I snapped, reaching to take the poor thing from him. "You've had it in your trunk all day in this heat? You've *cooked* it. It may not live. Maybe I can revive it, though, with some TLC. Open the door, will you? You bought some food for it, didn't you?"

He unlocked the door before he answered with a cautious, "Plants eat?"

I gave him an incredulous look. "Of course plants eat. If anything's alive, it eats." Then I looked at the plant I held and shook my head. "This poor thing may never eat again, though."

My injured arm was protesting holding the weight of the plant, even though I was using my right arm to do most of the work and was mostly balancing the thing with my left hand. I could have given it to Wyatt, but I didn't trust him with it. He'd already proven himself capable of major plant brutality.

While he was bringing in my bags, I had the plant in the sink, gently spraying it with cool water in an attempt to revive it. "I need a bucket," I told him. "Something you won't miss, because I'm going to poke holes in the bottom."

He was in the process of fetching a blue plastic mop bucket from the laundry, but he paused at my last words. "Why are you going to ruin a perfectly good bucket?"

"Because *you* have abused this plant to the point that it may not live. It needs water, but the roots don't need to stand in water. So—it needs to drain. Unless you have a nice planter with drain holes in it, which I doubt because you don't have any houseplants, then I'll have to poke holes in a container."

"See, this is why men don't have houseplants. They're too much trouble, and too damn complicated."

"They make a house look nice, feel nice, and they keep the air fresh. I don't think I could ever live in a house without plants."

He sighed. "All right, all right. I'll punch holes in the bucket."

My hero.

He used a long screwdriver to stab through the plastic, and in short order the bedraggled plant was sitting in the bucket in the laundry room sink, the root-ball soaked and draining. I hoped by morning it would have perked up some. Then I turned on his double ovens and started assembling what I would need to make the bread puddings.

He clasped my shoulders and gently forced me down onto a chair. "Sit," he said, which was totally unnecessary, since he'd already made certain I was. "I'll make the bread pudding. Just tell me what to do."

"Why? You never listen." Now, is there any way I could have resisted saying that?

"I'll make an effort," he said drily. "This one time."

Big of him, wasn't it? The least he could have done,

considering the day I'd had, was solemnly promise that from then on he'd pay attention to what I was saying.

So I supervised the making of the bread pudding, which is really simple, and while he was tearing the doughnuts into chunks, he said, "Explain something to me. Those people your mother was talking about: the man tried to do something nice for his wife, and she tried to kill him, so why were y'all on her side?"

"Something nice?" I echoed, staring at him in horror.

"He had their bedroom professionally decorated as a present for her. Even if she didn't like the style, why didn't she thank him for the thought?"

"You think it's nice that, even though they've been married thirty-five years, he paid so little attention to her that he didn't know how long and hard she worked to get their bedroom just right, and how much she loved it just the way it was? Some of the antique pieces she had, and which were sold before she could retrieve them, were heirloom quality and can't be replaced."

"Regardless of how much she loved it, it was just furniture. He's her husband; don't you think he deserved better than her trying to hit him with her car?"

"She's his wife," I returned. "Don't you think she deserved better than to have something she loved destroyed, and replaced with something she absolutely hates? After thirty-five years, don't you think he should at least have been able to tell the decorator that Sally didn't like metal and glass?"

The look on his face said he didn't care for the ultramodern look himself, though he wouldn't have phrased it that way. "So she's mad because he hadn't noticed what style she likes?"

"No, she's *hurt* because she's realized he doesn't pay any real attention to her. She's mad because he sold her things."

"Weren't they his things, too?"

"Did he spend months searching for each piece? Did he refinish each one by hand? I'd say they were hers."

"Okay. That still doesn't justify trying to kill him."

"Well, you see, she wasn't trying to *kill* him. She just wanted him to hurt a fraction as much as she's hurting."

"Then, like you said, she should have used a riding lawn mower instead of a car. Regardless of how hurt she is, if she'd killed him I'd have arrested her for murder."

I thought about it, then said, "Some things are worth being arrested for." Personally, I wouldn't have gone as far as Sally, but no way would I tell Wyatt that. Women have to stick together, and I thought this would be a good object lesson for him: you don't mess with a woman's things. If he could just get past his tendency to categorize things according to what laws were broken, I was sure he'd see reason. "A woman's stuff is important to her, like a man's toys are important to him. Is there anything you really treasure, like something that belonged to your father, or maybe a car—" It struck me. I stared at him, aghast. "You don't have a car!" The only car in the garage was the Crown Vic, which was city-owned and practically yelled, *Cop!*

"Of course I have a car," he said mildly, looking down at the two big bowls in which he had divided the four-dozen doughnuts, pinched into bite-size chunks. "What do I do now?"

"Beat the eggs. I'm not talking about the city car," I said. "What happened to your Tahoe?" When I'd gone out with him two years ago, he'd been driving a big black Tahoe.

"Traded it in." He swiftly beat two eggs, then broke two more into a separate little bowl and beat them, too.

"For what? There's nothing in the garage."

"An Avalanche. I got it three months ago. It's black, too."

"But where is it?"

"My sister, Lisa, borrowed it two weeks ago while hers was in the shop." He frowned. "I expected to have it back before now." He picked up the cordless phone, dialed a number, and tucked the phone between his chin and shoulder. "Hey, Lise. I just remembered you have my truck. Is your car still in the shop? What's the holdup?" He listened for a moment. "Okay, no problem. Like I said, I just remembered." He paused, and I could hear a woman's voice, but I couldn't tell what she was saying. "She did, huh? Could be." Then he laughed. "Yeah, it's true. I'll give you the details when we get them ironed out. Okay. Yeah. See ya."

He punched the *off* button and put the phone back

on the table, then surveyed what he'd done so far. "What comes next?"

"A can of condensed milk for each batch." I stared suspiciously at him. "What's 'true'?"

"Just a problem I'm working on."

I had a hunch I was the problem he was working on, but I needed to be at full speed to win an argument with him, so I let it go. "When will her car be ready?"

"She hopes by Friday. I suspect she likes driving my truck, though. It has all the bells and whistles." He winked at me. "Since you like driving pickups, too, you'll love my truck. You'll be cute as hell in it."

If I wasn't, then I seriously needed to work on my image. Because I was fading fast, I directed the addition of the remaining ingredients: salt, cinnamon, more milk, and a touch of vanilla flavoring. He mixed it all together, then poured each bowlful out into a baking pan. The ovens had already preheated, so he put both pans in to cook and set the timer for thirty minutes. "That's it?" he asked, looking surprised because it was so simple.

"That's it. If you don't mind, I'm going to brush my teeth and go to bed. When the timer dings, take the pans out and cover them with foil and put them in the refrigerator. I'll do the butter sauce icing in the morning." Tiredly I got to my feet. I was almost at the end of my physical rope.

His expression softened and without a word he lifted me in his arms.

I laid my head on his shoulder. "You're doing this a

lot," I said as he carried me upstairs. "Carrying me around, I mean."

"It's a pleasure. I just wish it wasn't under these circumstances." The soft expression faded from his face, leaving his expression grim. "It makes me sick that you're hurt. I want to kill the son of a bitch who did this to you."

"Ah-ha! Now you know how Sally feels," I said triumphantly. Anything to score a point, though I don't generally recommend getting shot and having a car accident to do it. On the other hand, since those things had happened, why not use them? It's silly to throw away a trump card, no matter how it got in your hand.

I brushed my teeth; then he helped me undress and actually tucked me into bed. I was asleep before he left the room.

I slept all night, not even waking when he came to bed. I woke when his alarm went off, and sleepily reached out to stroke his side as he stretched to shut off the clock. "How do you feel this morning?" he asked, rolling onto his back and turning his head toward me.

"Not as bad as I thought I would. Better than last night. Of course, I haven't tried to get out of bed yet. Are my eyes black?" I held my breath, waiting for the answer.

"Not really," he said, studying me. "The bruising isn't any worse than it was last night. All of that voodoo y'all were doing in the kitchen must have worked."

Thank God. I'd do the ice-pack thing again today,

just to be on the safe side. I wasn't very fond of the raccoon look.

He didn't get out of bed right away, and neither did I. He stretched and yawned, then sleepily settled down again. There was an interesting tent thing going on just below his waist, and I wanted to check it out, but that seemed cruel considering my stated position of not wanting to have sex with him. No, that wasn't accurate; it wasn't that I didn't *want* to, but that I knew we shouldn't until we had a lot of things settled between us. I really, really wanted to, though.

Before I succumbed to temptation—again—I forced my attention away and gingerly sat up. Sitting up hurt. A lot. Biting my lip, I slid my legs off the side of the bed, stood up, and took a step. Another. Hunched over and hobbling like a very old person, I made it to the bathroom.

The bad news was, my muscles hurt worse today than they had the night before, but that was to be expected. The good news was, I knew how to deal with it. Tomorrow I would feel much better.

A warm soak in the tub while Wyatt was cooking breakfast helped. So did a couple of ibuprofen, some gentle stretching movements, and that first cup of coffee. The coffee helped my feelings more than it helped my muscles, but feelings are important, too, right?

After breakfast I made the butter sauce to pour over the bread puddings. It was fast and simple, just a stick of butter and a box of powdered sugar, with rum flavoring. The sugar content had to be off the charts, but my mouth watered just thinking about that first bite. Wyatt didn't resist temptation; the butter sauce wasn't cool before he'd dipped a large spoonful onto a saucer and dug in. He half closed his eyes and made an appreciative humming sound. "Man, this is good. I may keep both pans for myself."

"If you do, I'll tell."

He sighed. "All right, all right. But you can make this for me on my birthday every year, okay?"

"But you know how to make it for yourself," I said, wide-eyed, but my heart was doing a little happy dance at the thought of being with him for all of his birthdays, year after year. "When is your birthday, exactly?"

"November third. When's yours?"

"August fifteenth." Oh, dear. Not that I believe in astrology or anything, but a Scorpio and a Leo can be a pretty explosive combination. Both are stubborn and hot-tempered, though I'm out of the norm there because I'm not hot-tempered at all. I plead the Fifth on the stubbornness part, though.

"What's the frown for?" he asked, lightly rubbing between my eyebrows.

"You're a Scorpio."

"So? That's a scorpion, right?" He put his hand on my waist and pulled me close, leaning down to kiss under my right ear. "Wanna see my stinger?"

"Don't you want to know what's bad about being a Scorpio? Not that I believe in astrology."

"If you don't believe in it, why should I care what's bad about Scorpios?"

I hated when he was logical. "So you'll know what's wrong with you."

"I know what's wrong with me." He cupped my

breast and nipped the side of my neck. "It's a five-four blond with an attitude, a smart mouth, and a round, bouncy ass that drives me crazy."

"My ass does not bounce," I said, instantly indignant. I worked hard to keep my butt tight. I also had to work hard to stay indignant, because of what he was doing to my neck.

"You haven't seen it from behind when you're walking."

"Well, duh."

I felt him smile against my neck. Somehow my head had tipped back and I was clinging to his shoulders, and I was forgetting how much it hurt to move. "It moves up and down like two balls bouncing. Haven't you ever turned around and noticed men wiping the drool off their chins?"

"Well, yeah, but I thought that was an evolutionary problem."

He chuckled. "Could be. Damn, I wish you weren't so bruised and sore."

"You'd be late to work." I didn't bother protesting that I wouldn't let him make love to me, because I'd proven to have truly pitiful self-control where he was concerned. I could try, but—

"Yeah, and everyone would know what I'd been doing, because I'd have a big grin on my face."

"Then it's a good thing I'm bruised and sore, because I really frown on being late to work." And if my self-control wouldn't work against him, maybe I could play this hurt-and-bruised thing for all it was worth. Yes, that's a tad manipulative, but this was war—and he was winning.

He nibbled on my neck again, just to show me what I was missing in case I needed reminding. I didn't. "What will you do today while I'm gone?"

"Sleep. Maybe do a little yoga, to stretch and loosen my muscles. Prowl through your house and snoop through everything. Then, if I have time, I may alphabetize your canned goods, rearrange your closet, and program your remote control so it turns the television to the Lifetime channel whenever it's turned on." I didn't know if that was possible, but the threat sounded good.

"Dear God." His tone was full of horror. "Get dressed. You're going to the station with me."

"You can't put it off forever. If you insist I stay here, you have to suffer the consequences."

"Now I see how this works." He lifted his head and looked down at me, narrow-eyed. "All right, do your worst. I'll get my revenge tonight."

"I'm hurt, remember?"

"If you can do all that, you're in better shape than you're letting on. Guess I'll find out tonight, won't I?" He lightly rubbed my butt. "I'll look forward to it." Oh, he was so sure of himself.

I followed him upstairs and watched him shower and shave, then sat on the bed while he dressed. Today's choice was a navy suit, white shirt, and a yellow tie with narrow navy and red stripes. He was a spiffy dresser, which I really like in a man; then when he topped the outfit off with the shoulder holster and the badge clipped to his belt, it was almost too much for my self-control. All of that authority and power turned me on, which is not very feminist of me, but what the hell. You take your turn-ons where you find them, and Wyatt was mine—no matter what he was wearing.

"I'm taking your bread pudding to the boys and girls—which will make them very happy—then I'm going to see your ex," he said as he shrugged into his jacket.

"It's a waste of time."

"Maybe, but I want to see for myself."

"Why aren't MacInnes and Forester talking to him? How do they feel about you horning in on their case?"

"I'm saving them some legwork, and besides, they know it's personal, so they're cutting me some slack."

"Were the others very resentful when you were promoted over them?"

"Of course they were. Hell, they wouldn't have been human if they weren't. I try not to tread on their toes, but at the same time, I'm their boss and they know it."

And he didn't worry if he had to tread on their toes. He didn't say it, but he didn't have to. Wyatt wouldn't take any crap from them.

I walked with him to the garage, and he kissed me good-bye at the door. "Don't throw away anything you find when you're snooping and prowling, got it?"

"Got it. Unless it's letters from an old girlfriend or something; then I might accidentally set them on fire. You know how things like that happen." He should; he was interrogating Jason for suspicion of attempted murder mainly because he'd heard the message Jason had left on my answering machine.

He grinned. "There aren't any letters," he said as he got into the car.

I looked, of course. The day stretched peacefully before me; I didn't have to go anywhere or do anything, didn't have to talk to anyone. With that much time on my hands, I *had* to look. I didn't organize his closet or arrange his canned goods, though, because that required moving and lifting.

Instead I pampered myself that day. I watched television; I napped. I put in a load of laundry, and moved the somewhat recovered bush near a window so it could get some sunshine. That also required lifting and moving, which hurt, but I did it anyway because the bush needed all the help it could get. I also called Wyatt on his cell phone and got his voice mail. I left him a message to pick up some plant food.

He called at lunch. "How're you feeling?"

"Still stiff, still sore, but otherwise okay."

"You were right about Jason."

"Told you."

"He has one hell of an alibi: Chief Gray. Your ex and the chief were in a foursome playing golf at the Little Creek Country Club on Sunday afternoon, so there was no way he could have taken a shot at you. I don't guess you've thought of anyone else who might like to kill you?"

"Not a clue." I'd been thinking about it, too, but hadn't been able to come up with anything. I'd come to the conclusion that someone was trying to kill me because of a reason I knew nothing about, and that's not a good thing at all.

CHAPTER
TWENTY-FOUR

When Wyatt came home late that afternoon, he was followed by a green Taurus. I stepped out into the garage, expecting to see Dad get out of the rental, but instead Jenni climbed out. "Hi," I said in surprise. "I thought Dad was going to drive the rental here."

"I volunteered," Jenni said, pushing her long hair behind her ears. She stood back as Wyatt kissed me hello. His mouth was warm, his touch gentle, as he held me against him.

"How did the day go?" he asked, cupping my cheek.

"Uneventful. Just what I needed." The peace had been wonderful. Not one thing had happened to make me think I might die, which was a nice change of pace. I smiled at Jenni. "Come in and have something cold to drink. I didn't realize how hot it is until I came out."

Wyatt stepped aside for Jenni to enter. She looked around, her gaze frankly curious. "This is a great house," she said. "It looks old and modern at the same time. How many bedrooms are there?"

"Four," he answered, shrugging out of his suit jacket and draping it over the back of a chair. He tugged the knot of his tie loose, and unbuttoned the top button of his shirt. "Nine rooms total, three and a half baths. Do you want the nickel tour?"

"Just downstairs," she said, smiling. "That way if Mom asks me anything about your sleeping arrangements, I can honestly say I don't know."

Mom wasn't a prude—far from it—but she had impressed on her daughters that a smart woman didn't sleep with a man unless they had a committed relationship, and by committed she meant at least an engagement ring on the finger. She was of the opinion that men, simple creatures that they are, value most that for which they work the hardest. I agree in principle, though maybe not completely in application. I mean, look at my current situation. Wyatt didn't have to work hard for me at all; all he had to do was kiss my neck, and I rued the day he'd discovered that weakness of mine. To be fair to myself, though, he was the only man I'd ever met who could so easily undermine my self-control.

Jenni dropped the keys to the rental on the kitchen counter, and followed Wyatt as he gave her the short tour around the ground floor of the house, which consisted of the kitchen, breakfast room, formal dining room (which was empty), living room (ditto), and family room. He had a small office just off the kitchen, as I had discovered that day, but he didn't bother with that; it was very small, maybe six-by-six, more suited for a pantry or a walk-in closet than an office, but he had the essentials in there: desk, filing cabinet, computer, printer, phone. There was nothing interesting in the filing cabinet. I'd played some games on his computer, but hadn't investigated any of his folders. I do have *some* limits.

I didn't follow the two of them, but I heard him pause in the family room and turn on the television—checking to see if I'd messed with his remote, huh? I grinned to myself. I'd thought about removing the batteries, but I figured I'd save that for when we had an argument. No, he probably had a huge supply of batteries, just in case. Instead it would be smarter if I just went shopping . . . and accidentally dropped the remote in my bag before I left. You should think of these things ahead of time, so you won't have to hesitate. She who hesitates gets caught.

I had glasses of iced tea sitting on the table when they came back to the breakfast room. Wyatt picked up one of them and chugged down half of it without pausing for breath, his tanned throat working. As affable as he'd been with Jenni, I could see the lines of frustration in his face. Evidently the police were getting nowhere in finding out who was trying to kill me, or why.

When he finally lowered the glass, he looked at me and smiled. "Your bread pudding was a hit. The pan was empty within thirty minutes, and everyone was on a sugar high."

"Did you make doughnut bread pudding?" Jenni asked, then groaned. "And there isn't any left?"

Wyatt smirked. "It just so happens *two* were made, and one of them is still in the refrigerator. Want some?"

She accepted with all the enthusiasm of a hungry wolf, and Wyatt pulled the pan out of the fridge. I turned to the cabinet and got out two saucers and two spoons. "Aren't you having some?" Jenni asked with a little frown.

"No. I can't work out right now, so I have to watch what I eat." I wasn't having any fun doing it, either; I would much rather work out for an hour or two every day instead of counting calories. I wanted some of that bread pudding, but it wasn't as if I'd never again have any—just not right now.

We all sat at the table while Wyatt and Jenni ate. I asked Wyatt if they had any leads at all, and he sighed.

"The forensics team did find a footprint in the dirt behind your condo, and we ran it through analysis. It's a woman's athletic shoe—"

"Probably mine, then," I said, but he shook his head.

"Not unless you wear size eight and a half, and I know damn well you don't."

He was right. I wore six and a half; none of the women in my family wore that size shoe. Mom was a six, and Siana and Jenni both wore size seven. I tried to think of any of my friends who might wear an eight and a half and who might also have been behind my condo, but no one sprang to mind.

"I thought you said it probably wasn't a woman trying to kill me," I said accusingly.

"I still don't think it is. Sniper fire and tampering with a car's brakes just aren't generally the way a woman would go about it."

"So the shoe print probably doesn't mean anything?"

"Probably not. I wish it did." He rubbed his eyes.

"I can't hide out forever." I didn't say it accusingly, just stating a fact. I had a life, and if I couldn't live it, then this creep had killed me in one sense even if he hadn't managed to kill my body.

"Maybe you won't have to," Jenni said hesitantly, staring at her spoon as if the meaning of life was written on it. "What I mean is—I volunteered to drive your rental out because I've been thinking and I've come up with a plan. I could wear a blond wig and pretend to be you and be the bait in a trap so Wyatt can catch this creep and you'll be safe again," she finished in such a rush that she ran her words together.

My jaw dropped so far it almost hit the floor. "What?" I squeaked. Never in a hundred years would I have expected Jenni to make such a preposterous offer. Jenni was really good at looking out for number one, and no way was that *my* number. "I can be my own bait, and I won't even need a wig!"

"Let me do this for you," she begged, and to my surprise tears welled in her eyes. "Let me make it up to you for what I did. I know you've never forgiven me and I don't blame you; I was a selfish bitch and didn't think how much I'd be hurting you, but I've grown up, I truly have, and I want us to be close the way you and Siana are close."

I was so flabbergasted I couldn't think of anything to say, and that's not an everyday occurrence. I opened my mouth, then closed it again when my brain remained in neutral.

"I was jealous of you," she continued, still talking fast, as if she had to get it all out before her courage failed. "You were always so popular and even *my* friends thought you were the coolest person they knew; they all tried to do their hair like yours, and buy the shade of lipstick you wore. It was sickening."

Now *there* was the Jenni I knew. I felt comforted, knowing the aliens hadn't taken over my little sister's body. Wyatt was sitting quietly, taking in every word, his gaze sharp. I wished he would go into another room, but I figured I had a better chance of growing wings and flying.

"You were the best cheerleader, you were cute, you were athletic, you were the class salutatorian, you went to college on a cheerleading scholarship, you pulled down really good grades and got a degree in business administration, and you married the handsomest guy I'd ever seen," she wailed. "He's going to be governor someday, maybe a senator or even president, and he fell into your hand like a ripe plum! I was so *jealous*, because no matter how pretty I am I'll never be able to do everything you did and I thought Mom and Dad loved you more. Even Siana loves you more! So that's why when Jason made a pass at me, I took him up on it; because if he was looking at me, then it must be because you weren't that great after all, and I *was*."

"What happened?" Wyatt interjected quietly.

"Blair caught Jason and me kissing," she confessed in a wretched tone. "That's all it was, and that was the first time, but everything blew up at once and they got divorced. It's all my fault, and I want to make it up to her."

"You'll have to find another way," he said, his words matter-of-fact. "There's no way in hell I'd set up either you or Blair as bait. If we used that plan at all, one of our female officers would masquerade as Blair. We'd never risk a civilian."

Jenni looked stricken that her grand plan should be so summarily turned down, not just by me but by Wyatt, too; in the end, his was the approval that counted, because he had the authority to either nix the plan or put it into motion. He'd nixed it.

"There must be something I can do," she said, and a tear streaked down her face. She looked pleadingly at me.

"Well, let's see." By this time I'd found my voice. I tapped my bottom lip with a fingernail while I thought. "You could wash my car every Saturday for the next year—after I get a car, that is. Or you could regrout my bathroom, because I really hate doing that."

She blinked at me as if she couldn't quite make her mind wrap itself around what I was saying. Then she giggled. In the middle of the giggle she hiccuped a sob, and that was a very strange sound combination. It startled me into my own giggle—which I've tried hard to stop doing because of the image thing. I'm blond; I really shouldn't giggle.

Anyway, we ended up hugging and laughing, and she apologized five or six times, and I told her she was family and I'd choose her over Jason Carson any day because he was a lowlife bastard who made a pass at his seventeen-year-old sister-in-law and I was better off without him.

Whew. Family dramas wear me out.

Wyatt had to take Jenni home. They asked me to come along, but I elected to stay because I felt that I needed some alone time to get my emotions settled. I had tried to forgive Jenni and to some extent I had, because the lion's share of blame belonged to Jason; he'd been an adult, and married, while teenagers aren't the best in the world at making rational decisions. Still, it had always been there in the back of my mind that my own sister had betrayed me. I had tried to act normally toward her, but I guess she knew there was a difference between Before and After. What surprised me most was that she cared. No, what really surprised me most was that she'd ever been jealous of me; Jenni is gorgeous, and has always been gorgeous, from the day she was born. I'm smart, but not as smart as Siana. I'm pretty, but not in the same class with Jenni. I was sort of middle-of-the-road in our family. Why on earth would she be jealous?

I started to call Siana to talk things over with her, but decided that I'd keep this private between Jenni and me. If she was serious about mending our relationship—*really* mending it—then I wasn't going to sabotage the opportunity by maybe blabbing something she wasn't comfortable with others knowing.

Wyatt was back within the hour. His dark brows were drawn down in a scowl when he came in the door. "Why the hell didn't you tell me you black-mailed your ex into giving you everything you asked for in the divorce? Don't you think that's something that could be considered as motive?"

"Except Jason didn't shoot at me," I pointed out. "And he thinks he got the negative."

He did the green-eyed laser look. "He *thinks*?"

I blinked my eyes at him, and put on my most innocent expression. "I mean, he knows he got the negative."

"Uh-huh. Does he *know* he got all of the copies?"

"Um . . . he thinks he did, and that's what's important, right?"

"So you blackmailed him, then double-crossed him."

"I look at it more as insurance. Anyway, I've never needed to use the picture and he doesn't know it still exists. I haven't had any contact with him since our divorce was final, and that was five years ago. That was why I knew Jason wasn't trying to kill me, because he wouldn't have any reason to."

"Except he does have reason to."

"Well, he would if he knew, but he doesn't."

He pinched the bridge of his nose, as if I'd given him a headache. "Where are the copies?"

"In my safe deposit box. There's no way anyone saw them by accident, and no one else knows I have them, not even my family."

"Okay. I strongly suggest that, when this is over and you can come out of hiding, that you get those copies and destroy them."

"I can do that," I allowed.

"I know you can. The question is: Will you? Promise me."

I scowled at him. "I said I would."

"No, you said you could. There's a difference. Promise me."

"Oh, all right. I promise I'll destroy the pictures."

"Without making any extra copies."

Sheesh, he wasn't the most trusting guy in the world.

It pissed me off that he'd thought of that, too. Either Dad had been giving him advice again, or he had an unnaturally suspicious mind.

"*Without making any extra copies,*" he repeated.

"All right!" I snapped, and made plans to maybe accidentally drop his television remote in the toilet.

"Good." He crossed his arms over his chest. "Now, are there any other little secrets you're keeping from me, anyone else you're blackmailing, any revenge thing going on that you neglected to mention because you didn't think it was relevant?"

"No, Jason's the only person I've ever blackmailed. And he deserved it."

"He deserved worse than that. He needed to have his ass kicked up around his shoulders."

Slightly mollified by those sentiments, I shrugged. "Daddy would have done it, so we didn't tell him why Jason and I got divorced. That was to protect Daddy, not Jason." No way was stomping Jason worth my dad spending even one minute under arrest for assault, which is what would have happened, because Jason is the petulant type and he'd have filed charges.

"Agreed." Wyatt watched me for a moment, then gave a rueful little shake of his head and pulled me into his arms. Comforted, I slid my arms around his waist and laid my head on his chest, and he rested his cheek on top of my head. "Now I understand why you need so much reassurance," he murmured. "That was a big hit you took, finding your husband kissing your sister."

If there's anything I hate, it's people feeling sorry for me. In this case, there was no need. I'd moved on, and left Jason in my dust. But I couldn't say, "Oh, it didn't really bother me," because that would have been a big fat lie and he'd have known it and thought I still hurt so much I couldn't let myself admit it. So I muttered, "I got over it. And I got the Mercedes." Except I didn't have my Mercedes now, because it was just a hunk of crushed and twisted metal.

"You may have gotten over the hurt, but you didn't get over the experience. It made you wary."

Now he was making me sound like some poor wounded bird. I pulled back and scowled up at him. "I'm not wary; I'm smart. There's a difference. I want to be sure there's something solid between us before I sleep with you—"

"Too late," he said, and grinned.

I sighed. "I know," I said, and laid my head back on his chest. "Gentlemen don't gloat."

"What does that tell you?"

It told me he was way too cocky, and I needed to shore up my defenses. There was a big problem, though: I didn't want to shore them up; I wanted to tear them down. Common sense said I might as well abandon my stance on not sleeping with him, since I was doing nothing but wasting my breath. On the other hand, it went against the grain to let him have his way in everything.

"It tells me I should probably go stay in a motel in another town," I said, just to wipe the smile off his face.

It worked.

"What?" he snapped. "What gave you a harebrained idea like that?"

"I should be perfectly safe in another town, right? I could check in under a fake name, and—"

"Forget it," he said. "There's no way in hell I'm letting you run away." Then he realized that I now had wheels, and he had no control over what I did during the day while he was at work. He didn't anyway, because if I wanted to leave, all I had to do was pick up the phone and call any of my family and they would come pick me up. For that matter, his own mother would, too. "Ah, shit," he finished.

He was so eloquent.

CHAPTER
TWENTY-FIVE

I had a nightmare that night, which isn't surprising considering all that had happened. Probably I should already have had several nightmares, but my subconscious is as good at ignoring things as my conscious is. I don't have many nightmares; my dreams are usually about everyday stuff, with weird little details, because that's what dreams are for, right? Like I'd be at Great Bods trying to take care of a mountain of paperwork, but the members would keep interrupting me because half of them wanted to be able to ride the stationary bikes in the nude, and the other half thought this would be a total gross-out, which it would. Stuff like that.

I didn't dream about being shot. There was nothing to dream about that, except the sound and then the burning in my arm, which isn't very much to build on, but the auto accident had a wealth of details for my subconscious to resurrect. I didn't dream about going through another stop sign; instead I was in my red Mercedes, the one I had got when Jason and I divorced and had since traded in for the white one, and I was driving over a high, arching bridge when all of a sudden the car went out of control and started spinning. Car after car kept hitting me, and each hit knocked me closer and closer to the rail, and then I knew the next one would push me over. I saw that last car coming at me, in slow motion; then there was a horrible jolt and my red Mercedes hit the guardrail and tipped over it.

I woke with a start, my heart pounding, and shaking all over. I was shaking, not my heart. Maybe my heart was, too, but I didn't have any way of knowing; all I could feel was pounding. And Wyatt was leaning over me, a big, protective shadow in the darkness of the room.

He stroked my belly, then gripped my waist and eased me into his arms. "Bad dream?"

"My car was knocked off a bridge," I muttered, still half asleep. "Bummer."

"Yeah, I can see where it would be." He had his own technique of comforting, and it involved tucking me under him. I wrapped my legs around his hips and pulled him close.

"Do you feel okay enough for this?" he murmured, but he was a tad late with the question because he was already sliding inside me.

"Yes," I answered anyway.

He was careful, or tried to be. He kept his weight braced on his forearms and his strokes were slow and even—until the very end, when there was nothing slow or even about it. But he didn't hurt me, or if he did, I was too turned on to notice.

The next day was sort of a repeat of the one before, except I did more stretching and yoga and felt lots better. My left arm still hurt if I tried to pick up anything and put strain on the muscle, but I had pretty much full use of it if I kept the motions slow and didn't do any jerking around.

The bush Wyatt had bought for me was going to live, I thought, though it needed a full week of TLC before it would be able to stand the shock of being planted in the yard. Wyatt might not understand the concept of *house*plants, but he had bought it for me and I treasured the poor thing. I was getting cabin fever from my enforced inactivity, so I walked around outside and selected the spot where I wanted the bush planted. Because of the age of the house, the landscaping around it was mature and lush, but it was all shrubbery and no flowers, so it would benefit from some color. It was too late in the season now to plant flowers. Next year, though . . .

The heat and sun felt good on my skin. I was bored with being an invalid and craved the high of a good workout. I wanted to go to work so much I ached, and it made me angry that I couldn't.

The dream from the night before kept nagging at me. Not the part about going over the bridge, but the fact that it was the red Mercedes, which I had traded over two years ago. If you believe in the prophetic nature of dreams, that probably meant something, but I didn't have a clue what it could be. That I regretted not getting another red car, maybe? That I thought white was too boring? I don't, and anyway white was more practical in the south because of the heat.

In terms of coolness—the quality, not the temperature—I would even rank red third, with white second, and black first. There's just something about a black car that makes a statement of power. Red was sporty, white was sexy and elegant, and black was powerful. Maybe my new car would be black, if I ever got a chance to shop for one.

Because I was bored, I rearranged the furniture in the family room, pushing the furniture around with my legs and my right arm, and just for the hell of it moved Wyatt's recliner from its place of honor in front of the television. There was nothing wrong with the way he'd had it arranged and I didn't care if his recliner took the prime spot, but like I said, I was bored.

Since I'd opened Great Bods, I seldom had the time to watch much television, except for maybe the eleven o'clock news at night, so I'd gotten out of the habit. Wyatt didn't know that, though. I might be able to have some fun whining about missing my favorite shows, which of course would be on the channels like Lifetime, Home and Garden, and Oxygen. The bad part about that was, if I won the battle for the remote, I'd have to watch the shows, too. There's always a catch.

I went out to the road and fetched the newspaper from the box, and then sat down in the kitchen and read every item. I needed some books. I needed to go shopping and buy some makeup or shoes. New makeup and shoes always lift my spirits. I needed to find out what Britney was doing these days, because that girl's life was such a mess she made getting shot at look downright sane.

Wyatt didn't even have any flavored coffee. All in all, his house was woefully ill-equipped to keep me satisfied.

By the time he came home that afternoon, I was ready to climb the walls. Out of sheer frustration I had even started another list of his transgressions, and the number one item was his lack of my favorite coffee. If I was going to stay there for the duration, I wanted to be comfortable. I also needed more of my clothes, and my favorite bath gel, and my scented shampoo, and all sorts of things.

He kissed me hello, then said he was going upstairs to change clothes. To get to the stairs, you have to go through the family room. I stayed in the kitchen, and listened to his footsteps come to a dead stop as he registered the change in his living environment.

He raised his voice and called, "What's with the furniture?"

"I was bored," I called back.

He muttered something that I couldn't understand, and I heard him continue upstairs.

I'm not a helpless decoration. I had also gone through the contents of his refrigerator and found some hamburger meat in the freezer section. I'd browned the meat and made spaghetti sauce. Because he never came home at the same time two days in a row, I hadn't put on the spaghetti to boil, so I did that now. He didn't have rolls, but he did have loaf bread, and I buttered the slices and sprinkled them with garlic powder and cheese. Something else he didn't have was the makings for a green salad. This was not what I considered a healthy meal, but considering the contents of his pantry and refrigerator, it was either that or beans from a can.

He came downstairs wearing only a pair of jeans, and my mouth watered when I saw him, with those tight abs and that muscled, hairy chest. To keep from drooling and embarrassing myself, I turned away and slid the baking sheet with the slices of bread on it into the oven. By the time they were nicely browned, the spaghetti would be done.

"This smells good," he said as he set the table.

"Thank you. But unless we go grocery shopping, there's nothing else to cook. What do you usually eat for supper?"

"I usually eat out. Breakfast here, supper out. It's easier that way, because by the end of the day I'm tired and don't want to fool with cooking."

"I can't eat out," I said grumpily.

"Well, you could, if we go to another town. Want to do that tomorrow? That would count as a date, right?"

"No, it won't." I thought we'd covered that ground at the beach. "You eat anyway. A date would be if we did something you don't normally do, like go to a play or a ballroom dancing exhibition."

"How about a ball game?" he countered.

"There's nothing going on now except baseball, and it's stupid. There aren't any cheerleaders. When it's football season, then we'll talk."

He let my insult to baseball pass and instead filled our glasses with ice, then poured tea into them. "Forensics found something today," he said abruptly.

I turned off the heat under the spaghetti. He sounded puzzled, as if he didn't know what to make of whatever it was forensics had found. "What?"

"A couple of hairs, caught in the underside of your car. It's a miracle they're still there, considering the shape your car is in."

"What can a couple of hairs tell you?" I asked. "If you had a suspect you could test for DNA, they would come in handy, but you don't."

"They're dark, so they tell us the person is a brunette. And they're about ten inches long, so that raises the strong possibility that we're looking for a woman after all. Not a certainty, because a lot of men have long hair, but they're testing the hairs for hair spray and styling gel, that sort of stuff. That should help, because not many men around here use stuff like that."

"Jason does," I pointed out.

"Jason is a girlie bastard with more vanity than brains," was his succinctly delivered opinion.

Man, he didn't like Jason. It warmed my heart.

"Do you know any women with dark hair who might want to kill you?" he asked.

"I know a lot of women with dark hair. It's the last part that throws me." I shrugged helplessly. The whole thing was a puzzle. "I haven't even had a parking lot incident in years."

"The reason may not be anything recent," Wyatt said. "When Nicole Goodwin was murdered and you were named as a witness, someone probably saw an opportunity to kill you and blame it on Nicole's killer.

But Dwayne Bailey confessed to the murder, so there's no reason for him to kill you."

"Then why didn't this person stop when he was arrested? Obviously it can't be blamed on him, now."

"Maybe, since she didn't get caught, she figures she can do it and get away with it."

"Have you thought about your dates for this past year or so?" I asked. "Were any of them brunette?"

"Yeah, sure, but I'm telling you, there was nothing serious going on."

"Haul 'em all in and question them anyway," I said in exasperation. This had to be personal, because I hadn't done any of the other things that provide the usual motives for murder.

"How about the guys you've dated? Maybe one of them had an ex who was crazy about him—'crazy' being the important word here—and got a real hate going for you when her guy started dating you."

"That's possible, I suppose." I mulled it over. "I don't remember anyone mentioning a crazy ex-girlfriend, though. No one said anything about being stalked, and this type of person would be a stalker, right?"

"Maybe, maybe not. We have to look at everything now, so I'll need a list of everyone you've dated in the past couple of years."

"Okay. Let's start with you." I smiled sweetly at him. "Let's check out your girlfriends."

You can see we weren't going anywhere with that subject, so we abandoned it while we ate supper and cleaned up the dishes afterward. Then Wyatt shoved his recliner back in front of the television and settled in it with the newspaper, happy as a clam. I stood in front of him and glowered until he finally put the paper down and said, "What?"

"I'm bored. I haven't left this house in two days."

"That's because you're smart. Someone is trying to kill you, so you should stay where you can't be seen."

Did he think *that* was going to deflect me? "I could have gone somewhere today, to other towns, but I thought you would worry if I went out by myself."

He gave a brief nod. "You're right."

"You're here now."

He sighed. "All right. What do you want to do?"

"I don't know. Something."

"That narrows it down. How about a movie? We can make the nine o'clock showing in Henderson. That'll count as a date, right?"

"Right." Henderson was a town about thirty miles away. It was almost seven now, so I went upstairs to get ready. The bruising on my face was already turning yellowish, thanks to Mom, and I used enough concealer to hide most of it. Then I dressed in long pants and a short-sleeved blouse, and tied the ends of the blouse at my waist. I brushed my hair, put on earrings, and I was set.

Wyatt, of course, was still reading the newspaper. And he was still half-naked.

"I'm ready," I announced.

He glanced at his wristwatch. "We have plenty of time." He went back to reading.

I found my list and added *inattentive*. You'd think he'd have wanted to make a better impression on our first date in two years. See, I knew sleeping with him so soon had been a big mistake. Already he was taking me for granted.

"I think I'll move into one of the other bedrooms," I mused aloud.

"Jesus. Okay. We'll leave." He dropped the paper to the floor and took the stairs two at a time.

I picked up the paper and sat down in his recliner. I'd already read it, of course, but I had no idea what movies were currently out. The listings were for our town, but I figured Henderson would have the same ones.

I was in the mood to laugh, and there was a new romantic comedy out that looked both cute and sexy. Wyatt came down the stairs, buttoning a white shirt. He stopped and unzipped, then tucked in his shirttail and zipped back up. "What do you want to see?" he asked.

"*Prenup*. It looks funny."

He groaned. "I'm not going to see a chick flick."

"Well, what do you want to see?"

"That one about the mob after the survivalist guy looks good."

"*End of the Road?*"

"Yeah, that's it."

"We're set, then." Wyatt's choice was a typical shoot-em-up, with the hero fighting for his life in the mountains, and of course there was the requisite half-naked beautiful woman whom he rescues, though why he'd bother when she's always so cosmically stupid was beyond me. But if Wyatt liked it, that was his choice.

We went in the Taurus, and I breathed a sigh of relief at the change of scenery. The sun was very low, the afternoon shadows long, and the heat still intense enough that the car's air-conditioning was working full blast. I angled the cold air toward my face because I didn't want to sweat off the concealer over my bruises.

We arrived at the theater almost half an hour before showtime, so Wyatt cruised the streets for a little while. Henderson was about fifteen thousand people, just big enough to have the one four-screen theater. It was a nice theater, though, renovated a couple of years back to stadium seating. Being a typical man, Wyatt hated waiting for a movie to start, so we made it back to the theater with just five minutes to spare.

"My treat," I said, taking out my money and stepping up to the ticket window. "One for *Prenup* and one for *End of the Road.*" I slid a twenty in the window.

"*What?*" I heard Wyatt say in outraged tones behind me, but I ignored him. The ticket clerk tore both tickets and pushed the two stubs through the window, along with my change.

I turned and gave him his ticket. "This way we can both see what we want," I said reasonably, and led the way inside. Luckily, both movies started within minutes of each other.

He looked furious, but he went off to watch his choice and I sat in the dark by myself and had a very nice time, watching silly antics and not worrying about whether or not he was bored. The sex scenes were nice and hot, too, just the way I like them. They made me think about jumping Wyatt's bones on the way home; I hadn't made out in a car since I was a teenager, and the Taurus had a respectable backseat. Not a great one, but respectable. Nice suspension, too.

When the movie was over, I walked out smiling, having enjoyed the hour and fifty minutes. I had to wait a little while for Wyatt's movie to finish, but I passed the time by looking at all the posters.

The movie hadn't improved his mood any; he was still scowling like a thundercloud when he came out about ten minutes later. Without a word he seized my arm and marched me to the car.

"What in hell was that about?" he barked when we were in the car and no one else could hear him. "I thought we were going to see the same movie."

"No, you didn't want to see the movie I was interested in, and I didn't want to see the one you liked. We're both adults; we can go into movie theaters by ourselves."

"The whole idea was to spend time together, to go out on a *date*," he said between clenched teeth. "If you didn't want to see the movie with me, we could have stayed at home."

"But I wanted to see *Prenup*."

"You could have seen it later; it'll be on television in a few months."

"The same goes for *End of the Road*. You didn't have to sit in there if you didn't want to; you could have watched the other one with me."

"And been bored out of my mind by a chick flick?"

His attitude was getting to me. I crossed my arms and glared at him. "If you won't watch a chick flick with me, give me one good reason why I should watch a dick flick with you. Unless I want to see it, too, that is."

"And everything has to be your way, huh?"

"Now wait just a damn minute. I was perfectly happy watching the movie on my own; I didn't insist you go with me. If anyone is insisting on things being her way, it's you. 'His way,' I mean."

He ground his teeth together. "I knew it would be like this. I knew it. You're so damned high maintenance—"

"I am *not*!" I was abruptly so furious with him I could have smacked him, except I'm a nonviolent person. Most of the time.

"Honey, if you look up 'high maintenance' in the dictionary, your picture is there. You want to know why I walked away two years ago? Because I knew it would be like this, and I figured I could save myself a lot of trouble by getting out early."

He was so angry he was practically spitting out the words. My mouth fell open. "You threw us away because I'm *high maintenance*?" I shrieked the words. I'd thought his reason would be something deep, something important, like maybe he'd been going on an undercover job and he'd made a clean break with me in case he got killed, or something. But he'd dumped me because he thought I was high maintenance?

I grabbed the shoulder strap of my seat belt and twisted it as hard as I could, to keep myself from doing the same thing to his neck, or trying to. Since he outweighed me by about eighty pounds, I didn't know how that would turn out. Well, I did know, and that's why I strangled my seat belt instead of him.

"If I am high maintenance, you don't have to worry about it!" I shouted at him. "Because I don't depend on anyone; I take care of myself and do my own maintenance! I'll get out of your hair and you can go back to your nice peaceful life—"

"Fuck that," he said savagely, and kissed me. I was so angry I tried to bite him. He jerked back, laughed, and kissed me again. He threaded his fingers through my hair and tugged my head back, exposing my neck.

"Don't you dare!" I tried to wriggle away from him, releasing my grip on the seat belt to push against his shoulders.

He dared, of course.

"I don't want a nice peaceful life," he said against my throat a few minutes later. "You're a lot of trouble, but I love you and that's that."

Then he settled me back in my seat, started the car, and drove out of the parking lot before we drew someone's attention and the cops were called to us. I was still pouting and near tears, and I don't know how far he drove before he pulled off the road and parked the car behind some big trees where it couldn't be seen from the road.

Oh, a Taurus has very nice suspension.

CHAPTER
TWENTY-SIX

You'd think that because he said he loved me I'd be happy as a lark, but he'd made it sound as if I were a dose of nasty-tasting medicine that he had to take or die. Never mind that he'd made love to me in the backseat of the car as if he couldn't get enough of me; my feelings were hurt. Not only that, after I had a chance to think about it, I was very uneasy about the state of that backseat. I mean, the car's a rental; there was no telling *what* had been back there, and now my bare butt had been added to the list.

I didn't speak to him all the way home, and as soon as we were inside, I raced up the stairs to take a shower, just in case I'd picked up some rental-car cooties. Well, I hurried up the stairs; I still wasn't in racing shape. I also locked the bathroom door so he couldn't join me in the shower, because I knew how that would end and I hate being a pushover.

I should have planned ahead and taken some clean clothes into the bathroom with me, but I didn't, so I had to put on what I had just taken off. No way was

I walking out with only a towel wrapped around me. I knew Wyatt Bloodsworth, and his motto was: Take Advantage.

He was waiting for me when I came out of the bathroom, of course, leaning against the wall as patiently as if he didn't have anything else in the world to do. He didn't shy from an argument; I'd noticed that about him.

"This isn't going to work," I said, forestalling him. "We can't even go to the movies without getting in a major argument, which you then try to solve with sex."

His brows lifted. "There's a better way?"

"That's just like a man. Women don't like to have sex when they're angry."

The brows went even higher. "You could have fooled me," he drawled, which wasn't the smartest thing he could have said.

My lower lip quivered. "You shouldn't throw that up to me. It isn't my fault you have my number, but when you know I can't resist you, it's really snotty of you to take advantage the way you do."

A slow smile curved his lips and he straightened from the wall. "Do you have any idea what a major turn-on it is when you admit you can't resist me?" Quick as a snake he coiled one arm around my waist and locked me to him. "Do you know what I think about during the day?"

"Sex," I said, staring straight ahead at his chest.

"Well, yeah. Some of the time. A lot of the time. But also how you make me laugh, and how good it is to wake up beside you in the morning and come home to you at night. I love you, and swapping you for the most even-tempered, uncomplicated, low-maintenance woman in the world wouldn't make me happy because the spark wouldn't be there."

"Uh-huh," I said sarcastically. "That's why you dumped me and stayed away for two whole years."

"I got cold feet." He shrugged. "I admit it. After just two dates I could tell there would never be a peaceful minute around you, so I decided to cut my losses before I got in too deep. At the speed we were going, I figured we'd be in bed within a week, and married before I knew what was going on."

"So what's different this time around? *I'm* not."

"Thank God. I love you just the way you are. I guess I faced the fact that no matter how much trouble you are, to me you're worth it. That's why I'll chase after you when you go to the beach, why I didn't walk out of the movie theater even though I was so mad I don't remember a single thing about the movie, and why I'll move heaven and earth to keep you safe."

I wasn't ready to stop being mad, but I could feel my temper slipping away. I tried to hold on to it, and scowled at his shirt so he wouldn't know his sweet-talking was working.

"Every day I learn a little more about you," he murmured, pulling me closer so he could nuzzle my temple. I hunched my shoulders to keep him from getting at my neck, and he laughed softly. "And every day I fall a little more in love. You've also eased some tension in the department, because the guys who resented me before are now sympathizing with me."

I scowled harder, but this time it was real. He needed sympathy because he loved me? "I'm not that bad."

"You're hell on wheels, honey, and they figure I'm going to spend the rest of my life scrambling to put out your forest fires. They're right, too." He kissed my forehead. "But I'll never be bored, and I'll have your dad to teach me the finer points of surviving in the middle of a tornado. C'mon," he cajoled, moving his lips to my ear. "I bit the bullet first. You might as well say it: you love me, too. I know you do."

I fidgeted and fussed, but his arms were warm and the smell of his skin was making me dizzy with want. Finally I heaved a sigh. "All right," I said sulkily. "I love you. But don't think for a minute that means I'm going to turn into a Stepford wife."

"Like there was ever a snowball's chance in hell of that happening," he said wryly. "But you can bet the farm that you're going to be my wife. I've been serious about that from the beginning . . . the second beginning, that is. Thinking you might have been killed was a real eye-opener for me."

"Which time?" I asked, blinking at him. "There've been three."

He squeezed me. "The first time. I've had enough scares in the past week to last me a lifetime."

"Oh, yeah? You should try it from my side of the situation." I gave up and leaned my head on his chest. My heart was doing that flutter thing he could make it do, but in stereo. Confused, I concentrated, and abruptly realized that I was hearing his heartbeat while I was feeling mine—and his was racing, too.

Delight bloomed in me, filled me like water in a balloon until I felt all swollen with it, which may not be a really great description but kind of fits, because I felt as if my insides were too big for my skin. I tilted my head back and gave him a huge beaming smile. "You love me!" I said triumphantly.

He looked faintly wary. "I know. I said so, didn't I?"

"Yeah, but you really do!"

"You thought I was lying?"

"No, but hearing and feeling are two different things."

"And you're feeling . . ." He let the words trail off, inviting me to fill in the blank.

"Your heartbeat." I patted his chest. "It's jumping around just like mine."

His expression changed, became tender. "It does that whenever I'm anywhere near you. At first I thought I was developing arrhythmia, but then I realized it acts up only when you're around. I was about to go in for tests."

He was exaggerating, but I didn't care. He loved me. I had longed for and hoped for and dreamed of this practically from the moment I'd met him, and he had devastated me by dumping me the way he had. Oh, I'd have been devastated no matter how he'd done it, but he'd really done a number on me by not telling me *why*. I'd made things as difficult as possible for him this past week because he deserved it for treating me the way he had, and I didn't regret one moment of it. I just wished I could have made things even tougher by not rolling over for him every time he touched me, but what the hell; sometimes you just have to go with the flow.

"Do you want to get married as soon as we can, or do you want to plan some sort of shindig?" he asked.

There wasn't any doubt which one he'd prefer. I cocked my head and thought about it for a minute. I'd had the big church wedding and loved every minute of it, but church weddings are a lot of trouble and cost a lot of money—and they take time to plan. I was glad I'd gone through it once, even though the marriage itself hadn't held up, but I didn't feel any need to go through all of that pomp and ceremony again. On the other hand, I wanted more than just a quickie marriage.

"Shindig," I said, and he managed to stifle his groan. I patted his arm. "But not a big one. We have to think of our families and have some sort of to-do, but we don't have to do a big deal with ice sculptures and a champagne fountain. Something small, no more than thirty people—if that many—maybe in your mother's garden. Would she like that, or would she be terrified her flowers would get trampled?"

"She'd love it. She loves showing off that house."

"Good. Wait, what if you can't find out who's shooting at me and tampering with my car? What if I have to stay in hiding until *Christmas*? There won't be any flowers then, and besides, it'll be too cold to have a garden wedding. We can't even pick out a date!" I wailed. "We can't plan anything until this is settled."

"If we have to, we'll take the entire family to Gatlinburg and get married in one of those little wedding chapels."

"You want me to get ready in a motel?" I asked, my tone letting him know I wasn't crazy about that idea.

"Don't see why not. You aren't planning on wearing one of those long, big-skirted things, are you?"

I wasn't, but still . . . I wanted my stuff around me when I was getting ready. What if I needed something and had forgotten to pack it? Things like that can ruin a woman's memories of her wedding.

"I have to call Mom," I said, pulling away from him and going to the phone.

"Blair . . . it's after midnight."

"I know. But she'll be hurt if I don't tell her right away."

"How will she know? Call her in the morning and tell her we decided over breakfast."

"She'll see through that in a heartbeat. You don't decide to get married over breakfast; you decide to get married after a hot date with making out and stuff."

"Yeah, I really liked that 'stuff' part," he said reminiscently. "It's been eighteen, nineteen years since I'd done it in the backseat of a car. I'd forgotten how fucking uncomfortable it is, and vice versa."

I started dialing.

"Do you want your mom to know about the 'stuff' part?"

I gave him a "you're kidding me" look. "Like there's any way she doesn't already know."

Mom answered on the first ring, sounded harassed. "Blair? Is something wrong?"

Caller ID is a wonderful thing. It saved so much time, bypassing the need for identification. "No, I just wanted to tell you that Wyatt and I have decided to get married."

"What's the big surprise about that? He told us when we first met him in the hospital, when you were shot, that y'all were getting married."

My head whipped around and I glared at him. "He did, huh? Funny thing, he didn't mention it to me until tonight."

Wyatt shrugged and looked totally unrepentant. I could tell I was going to have my hands full with him over the years. He was way too sure of himself.

"Well, I wondered why you hadn't said anything," Mom said. "I was beginning to feel hurt."

"He'll pay for that," I said grimly.

"Oh, shit," Wyatt said, knowing good and well I was talking about him, but without knowing exactly what his transgression was. He could probably get in the ballpark, since he knew what we were talking about, but he hadn't yet realized what a no-no it was to hurt Mom's feelings.

"There are two schools of thought concerning these situations," Mom said, meaning she had considered two angles of approach. "One is that you come down hard on him, so he'll learn how to handle things and won't make that mistake again. The second is that you cut him some slack because he's new to this."

" 'Slack'? What's that?"

"That's my girl," she said approvingly.

"Why are you still awake? You answered the phone

so fast you must have been sleeping with it." I was a
tad curious, because Mom always slept with the phone
when she was anxious about any of us. It was a habit
she developed when I started dating at the age of fifteen.

"I haven't slept with the phone since Jenni gradu-
ated high school. No, I'm still working on these damn
quarterly taxes, and this stupid computer keeps freezing on me, then losing touch with its parts. Now it's
typing gibberish. I'd love to send in the taxes typed in
code, since the IRS instructions and rules are so clear
even they don't know what they're doing. How do
you think that would fly?"

"It wouldn't. The IRS has no sense of humor."

"I know," she said glumly. "I could have done this
by hand much faster if I'd known this stupid machine
was going to go bananas, but all of my files are in the
computer. From now on I'm going to keep a paper
copy."

"Don't you have a backup disk?"

"Well, of course. Ask me if it'll work."

"I think you've got a major problem."

"I know I do, and I'm just about fed up with the
whole mess. But it's become a point of honor now not
to let this demented monster win."

Meaning she would keep at it way past the point
where any normal person would have thrown in the
towel and taken the thing to a computer hospital.

Then I thought of something, and looked at Wyatt.
"Is it okay if I tell Mom about the hair y'all found?"

He briefly thought about it, then nodded.

"What hair?" Mom asked.

"Forensics found some dark hair, about ten inches long, stuck under my car. Can you think of anyone with dark hair about that length who might want to kill me?"

"Hmmm." That was Mom's thinking sound. "Is it black hair, or just dark?"

I relayed the question to Wyatt. He got that expression that said he wanted to ask what the difference was, but then he thought about it and realized the difference. "I'd say black," he said.

"Black," I relayed.

"Natural or dyed?"

Mom was on a roll here. I said to him, "Natural or dyed?"

"We don't know yet. The evidence will have to be analyzed."

"The jury's still out on that," I said to Mom. "Have you thought of someone?"

"Well, there's Malinda Connors."

"That was thirteen years ago, when I beat her out for Homecoming Queen. Surely she's over it by now."

"I don't know about that; she always struck me as a vindictive girl."

"But too impatient. She couldn't have waited this long."

"That's true. Hmmm. It has to be someone who's jealous of you about something. Ask Wyatt who he was dating before y'all started going together."

"I've already thought of that. He says there aren't any candidates."

"Unless he lived like a monk, there are candidates."

"I know, but he won't even give me their names for me to check out on my own."

He came to sit beside me on the bed, looking worried. "What are y'all talking about?"

"You and your women," I said, turning my shoulder to him and scooting farther away so he couldn't eavesdrop.

"I don't *have* any women," he said in exasperation.

"Did you hear that?" I asked Mom.

"I heard it; I just don't believe it. Ask him how long he was celibate before he met you."

Notice my mother assumed he was no longer celibate. The fact that she was so unconcerned about my current love life told me that she thoroughly approved of him, which is a big thing. Having Mom's approval goes a long way toward keeping our family life smooth and happy.

I looked over my shoulder at him. "Mom wants to know how long it had been since you'd had any, prior to our engagement."

He looked deeply alarmed. "She does not. She didn't say that."

"Yes, she did. Here. She'll tell you herself."

I extended the phone to him, and warily he took it. "Hello," he said; then he listened. I watched two spots of color start to burn on his cheekbones. He put his hand over his eyes as if he wanted to hide from the question. "Uh . . . six weeks?" he said sheepishly. "Maybe. Could be a little longer. Here's Blair."

He couldn't hand the phone back to me fast enough. I took it and asked, "What do you think?"

"Six weeks is a long time to wait if you're crazy and

fixated on someone," Mom said. "He's probably in
the clear. What about you? Have you had any former
semi-boyfriends who have since hooked up with some
nutcase who may have developed intense jealousy over
his former relationships?"

Semi-boyfriend means a couple of dates, maybe
several, but nothing serious developed and we both
sort of drifted out of each other's orbit. Since Wyatt,
I'd had a few of those, and at the moment I wasn't
certain I could even remember their names.

"I haven't kept in touch, but I guess I can find out,"
I said. If I could remember their names, that is.

"That's the only other possibility I can think of,"
Mom said. "Tell Wyatt he'd better get this settled in a
hurry, because your grandmother's birthday is coming up and we can't celebrate if you're still hiding
out."

After I hung up the phone, I relayed that message to
him and he nodded his head as if he got it, but I'm
pretty sure he was still in the dark about Grammy. He
had no idea of the wrath that would come down on
our heads if she felt the least slighted. She said that at
her age she didn't have many more birthdays left, so
if we loved her, we'd better make the most of them.
Grammy is Mom's mother, if you haven't already
guessed. She'll be seventy-four on her birthday, so she
isn't even all that old, but she plays on her age to get
what she wants.

Huh. Genetics is a funny thing, isn't it?

I gave him the beady eye. "So. What's her name?"

He knew exactly whom I was talking about. "I knew
it," he said, shaking his head. "I knew you'd latch onto

that like a leech. It was nothing. I ran into an old acquaintance at a conference and—it was nothing."

"Except you slept with her," I said accusingly.

"She has red hair," he said. "And she's a detective in—no, hell no, I'm not saying where she works. I know better than that. You'd be on the phone with her tomorrow, either accusing her of attempted murder or comparing notes on me."

"If she's a cop, she knows how to shoot."

"Blair, trust me in this. Please. If I thought there was the slightest possibility she would do something like that, do you think I'd hesitate for a second before hauling her in for questioning?"

I sighed. He had a real knack for phrasing things in a way that left me little wiggle room, and he'd picked it up fast.

"But it's someone who's jealous of me," I said. "Mom's right. I'm right. It's something personal."

"I agree." He stood up and began stripping off his clothes. "But it's after midnight, I'm tired, you're tired, and we can talk about this after we get the analysis on the hair. Then we'll know if we're dealing with a real brunette or someone who may have dyed her hair as a disguise before acting."

He was right about the tired part, so I decided he was right about that, too. I pulled off my clothes and crawled naked between the cool sheets. He turned the thermostat down to Stage Two Hypothermia, turned out the lights, and got under the covers with me, which is when I found out he'd been lying about the tired part.

CHAPTER
TWENTY-SEVEN

I dreamed about my red Mercedes again that night. There wasn't a bridge in this dream, just a woman standing in front of the car pointing a pistol at me. She didn't have black hair, though. Her hair was a light brown, the shade that is almost blond but doesn't quite get there. The weird thing was, I was parked at the curb in front of the apartment where Jason and I had lived when we first got married. We hadn't lived there long, maybe a year, before buying a house. When we divorced, I was happy to let Jason have the house and the attendant payments, in exchange for the capital to start Great Bods.

Even though the woman was pointing a pistol at me, in my dream I wasn't very frightened. I was more exasperated with her for being so stupid than I was scared. Finally I just got out of the car and walked away, which shows you how silly dreams can be, because I would never have abandoned my Mercedes.

I woke up feeling puzzled, which is a strange way

to feel when you just wake up. I was still in bed—
obviously—so nothing had happened yet to puzzle me.

The room was so cold I was afraid my butt would
get frostbite if I got out of bed. I don't know why Wyatt
liked to turn the air-conditioning so cold at night, unless he was part Eskimo. I lifted my head so I could
see the clock: five oh five. The alarm wouldn't go off
for another twenty-five minutes, but if I was awake, I
saw no reason why he shouldn't be awake, too. I
poked him in the side.

"Uh. Ouch," he said groggily, and rolled over. His
big hand rubbed my stomach. "Are you okay? Another bad dream?"

"No, I had a dream, but it wasn't a nightmare. I'm
awake and the room feels like a meat locker. I'm afraid
to get up."

He made a half-grunting, half-yawning noise, then
got a look at the clock. "It isn't time to get up yet," he
said, and burrowed back into the pillow.

I poked him again. "Yes, it is. I need to think about
something."

"Can't you think while I sleep?"

"I could, if you didn't insist on putting a layer of
frost on everything at night, and if I had a cup of coffee. I think you should turn the thermostat up to, say,
forty, so I can start thawing out, and while you're up,
you could get one of your flannel shirts or something
for me to wear."

He groaned again, and flopped over on his back.
"Okay, okay." Muttering something under his breath,
he got out of bed and walked out into the hall where

the upstairs thermostat was located. Within seconds, the blower stopped. The air was still cold, but at least it wasn't moving around. Then he came back into the bedroom and reached deep into his closet, coming out with something long and dark. He tossed it across the bed, then crawled back under the covers. "See you in twenty minutes," he mumbled, and just that easily went back to sleep.

I grabbed the long dark thing and pulled it around me. It was a robe, nice and thick. When I got out of bed and stood up, the heavy folds of fabric fell to my ankles. I belted it around me as I tiptoed out of the bedroom—I didn't want to disturb him—and turned on the light over the stairs so I wouldn't break my neck on the way down.

The coffeemaker was set to come on automatically at five twenty-five, but I didn't intend to wait that long. I flipped the switch, the little red light came on, and the thing began the hissing and popping sounds that signal help is on the way.

I got a cup from the cabinet and stood there waiting. The floor was cold beneath my bare feet, making my toes curl. When we had kids, I thought, Wyatt would have to get out of the habit of turning the air-conditioning so low at night.

The bottom dropped out of my stomach, just the way it happens when you go over that first steep hill in a roller coaster, and a sense of unreality seized me. I felt as if I were occupying two planes of existence at the same time: the real world, and the dream world. My dream was Wyatt, had been from the moment I met him, but I had accepted that I'd lost my chance. Now, all of a sudden, the dream world was also the real world, and I was having a hard time taking it all in.

In a little over a week's time, everything had reversed. He said he loved me. He said we were getting married. I believed him on both counts, because he'd told my parents the same thing, and his mother, and the whole police force. Not only that, if his feelings for me were anything like my feelings for him, I could understand getting cold feet at first, because how do you deal with something like that?

Women can handle those things more easily than men, because we're tougher. After all, most of us grow up expecting to get pregnant and have kids, and when you think about what that really means to the female body, it's a wonder any woman ever lets a man within a country mile of her.

Men feel put upon because they have to shave their faces every day. Now, I ask you: In comparison to what women go through, is that wussy, or what?

Wyatt had wasted two *years* because he thought I was high maintenance. I'm not high maintenance. *Grammy* is high maintenance. Of course, she's had a lot more practice. I hope I'm just like her when I'm that age. What I am now is a reasonable, logical, adult woman who runs her own business and believes in a fifty-fifty relationship. It just so happens there'll be times when I'll have both fifties, such as when I'm shot or when I'm pregnant. But those are special occasions, right?

Enough coffee had dripped into the carafe to fill my cup. Thank heavens for the automatic cutoff on coffeemakers today. I pulled out the carafe, and only one little drop escaped to sizzle on the hot pad. After pouring the coffee, I slid the carafe back into place and leaned against the cabinets while I began to mentally worry at what had been puzzling me in my dream.

My feet were freezing, so after a moment I went into the family room and got the notebook in which I'd been listing Wyatt's transgressions, then curled up in his recliner with the robe tucked around my feet.

What Mom had said last night—well, a few hours ago—had triggered some chain of thought. The problem was, the links weren't connected yet; so technically, I guess, there wasn't a chain, because they have to be linked to make a chain, but the individual little chunks were lying there waiting for someone to put them together.

The thing was, she had said pretty much what I'd already been thinking, but phrased it just a little differently. And she had gone way back, all the way to my senior year in high school when Malinda Connors threw a screaming hissy fit because I was voted Homecoming Queen even though I was already Head Cheerleader and she thought it wasn't fair for me to be both. Not that Malinda would have gotten Homecoming Queen anyway, because she was, like, the poster girl for Skanks Unlimited, but she had a real high opinion of herself and thought I was the only obstacle in her path.

She hadn't tried to kill me, however. Malinda had

married some moron and moved to Minneapolis. There's a song in there somewhere.

But Mom had started me thinking that the roots of this could go back quite a while. I'd been trying to think of something recent, such as Wyatt's last girlfriend, or my last boyfriend, which didn't make sense at all because *Wyatt* had been the last one who mattered and he hadn't even technically been a boyfriend, because he got cold feet so fast.

I started writing items down in the notebook. They were still the individual links, but sooner or later I'd hit on the one thing that turned them into a chain.

I heard the shower running upstairs and knew Wyatt was up. I turned on the television to check the local weather—hot, fancy that—then stared at the notebook some more while I pondered what I was going to do that day. I'd had enough of sitting in the house. The first day had been great; yesterday had been not so great. If I had to stay here all day again, I might get into all sorts of trouble, out of sheer boredom.

Besides, I felt fine. The stitches in my left arm had been in for seven days and the muscle was healing nicely. I could even dress myself. The soreness from the car accident was mostly gone, taken care of by yoga, ice packs, and general experience with sore muscles.

After about fifteen minutes Wyatt came down the stairs and saw me sitting in front of the television. "Making another list?" he asked warily as he approached.

"Yeah, but it isn't yours."

"You make lists of other people's transgressions?"

He sounded a little insulted, as if he thought he was the only one who deserved a list.

"No, I'm making a list of the evidence."

He leaned over and kissed me good morning, then read the list. "Why is your red Mercedes on the list?"

"Because I've dreamed about it twice. That has to mean something."

"Maybe that the white one is a total wreck and you wish you had the red one back?" He kissed me again. "What would you like for breakfast this morning? Pancakes again? French toast? Eggs and sausage?"

"I'm tired of guy food," I said, getting to my feet and following him into the kitchen. "Why don't you have any girl food? I need some girl food."

He froze with the coffee carafe in his hand. "Women don't eat the same things that men eat?" he asked cautiously.

Really, he was so exasperating. "Are you sure you were married? Don't you know anything?"

He finished pouring his coffee and set the pot back on the hot pad. "I didn't pay that much attention back then. *You've* been eating what I eat."

"Just to be polite, because you were going to so much trouble to feed me."

He thought about that for a minute, then said, "Let me drink my coffee and I'll get back to you on this. In the meantime, I'm going to cook breakfast, and you'll eat it because that's all I have and I refuse to let you starve yourself."

Man, he gets testy over the least little thing.

"Fruit," I said helpfully. "Peaches. Grapefruit. Whole

wheat bread for toast. And yogurt. Sometimes a cereal. That's girl food."

"I have cereal," he said.

"A *healthy* cereal." His taste in cereal ran to Froot Loops and Cap'n Crunch.

"Why worry about eating anything healthy? If you can eat yogurt and live, you can eat anything. That stuff's disgusting. It's almost as bad as cottage cheese."

I agreed with him about the cottage cheese, so I didn't leap to its defense. Instead I said, "You don't have to eat it; you just need to have girl food here for me to eat. If I'm going to stay, that is."

"You're staying, all right." He fished in the pocket of his jeans and pulled out something, which he tossed to me. "Here."

It was a small velvet box. I turned it over in my hand but didn't open it. If this was what I thought it was—I tossed the box right back at him. He fielded it one-handed and frowned at me. "Don't you want it?"

"Want what?"

"The engagement ring."

"Oh, is that what's in the box? You *threw* my engagement ring at me?" Boy, this was such a big transgression I would have to write it in block letters on its own page, and show it to our children when they grew up as an example of how *not* to do something.

He cocked his head while he gave this a brief consideration, then looked at me standing there barefoot, dwarfed by his robe, waiting narrow-eyed to see what he would do. He gave a quick little grin and came to me, catching my right hand in his and lifting it to his mouth. Then he went down gracefully on one knee and kissed my hand again. "I love you," he said gravely. "Will you marry me?"

"Yes, I will," I replied just as gravely. "I love you, too." Then I threw myself at him, which of course knocked him off balance, and we sprawled on the kitchen floor, except he was on bottom, so that was okay. We kissed for a while; then I sort of came unwrapped from the robe and what you might have expected to happen, happened.

Afterward he retrieved the velvet box from near the door, where it had skittered when he dropped it, and flipped the top open. Taking out a simple, breathtaking solitaire diamond, he took my left hand and gently slid the ring onto my ring finger.

I looked at the diamond and tears welled in my eyes. "Hey, don't cry," he cajoled, tilting my chin up to kiss me. "Why are you crying?"

"Because I love you and it's beautiful," I said, and gulped back my tears. Sometimes he did things just right, and when he did, it was almost more than I could bear. "When did you get it? I can't think when you would have had the time."

He snorted. "Last Friday. I've been carrying it around for a week."

Last *Friday*? The day after Nicole was murdered? Before he followed me to the beach? My mouth fell open.

He put a finger under my chin and pushed up, closing my mouth. "I was certain then. I was certain as soon as I saw you on Thursday night, sitting in your office with your hair up in a ponytail and wearing that little pink halter top that had all the men's tongues dragging the ground. I was so relieved to find out you weren't the one who'd been murdered that my knees nearly buckled, and I knew right then that all I'd been doing for two years was avoiding the inevitable. I made up my mind right then to get you corralled as soon as possible, and I bought the ring the next day."

I tried to take this in. While I'd been busy protecting myself until he decided he loved me the way I knew he would if he just let himself, he'd already made up his mind and had been trying to convince *me*. Reality altered once more. At this rate, by the end of the day I wouldn't have a real good grasp on what was real and what wasn't.

Men and women may belong to the same species, but this was proof positive to me that we are Not Alike. That doesn't really matter, though, because he was trying. He bought a bush for me, didn't he? And a gorgeous ring.

"What are you doing today?" he asked over breakfast, which consisted of scrambled eggs, toast, and sausage. I ate about a third of what he did.

"I don't know." I twined my feet around the legs of the chair. "I'm bored. I'll do something."

He winced. "That's what I was afraid of. Get ready and go to work with me. At least then I'll know you're safe."

"No offense, but sitting in your office is even more boring than sitting here."

"You're tough," he said unsympathetically. "You can take it."

He wouldn't take "no" for an answer; his track record on that so far was pretty damn consistent. So I decided my arm hurt after all our rolling around on the floor and he had to help me put on some makeup to cover my bruised cheekbones; then my hair just wouldn't do what I wanted it to do and I told him he'd have to braid it. After two attempts, he growled something obscene and said, "All right, that's it. You've punished me enough. We need to leave or I'll be late."

"You might as well learn how to braid hair," I said, giving him the Big Eyes. "I just know our little girl will wear her hair in braids sometimes, and she'll want her daddy to do it for her."

He almost melted under the onslaught of Big Eyes and mention of a little girl; then he caught himself. He was made of some stern stuff, to withstand the double whammy. "We're having all boys," he said as he hauled me to my feet. "No girls. I'll need all the reinforcements I can get without you bringing in a ringer."

I grabbed my notebook before he hustled me out to the garage and practically stuffed me into the Crown Vic. If I had to sit in a police station, I might as well work on my clues.

When we got to City Hall and he ushered me into the police station, the first person I saw was Officer Vyskosigh. He was wearing street clothes, so I guessed he had just finished his shift. He stopped and gave me a little salute. "I enjoyed the dessert you sent, Ms. Mallory," he said. "If I hadn't been late getting off my shift, I wouldn't have gotten any. Sometimes things work out for the better."

"I'm glad you enjoyed it," I said, smiling at him. "If you don't mind my asking, where do you work out? I can tell you do."

He looked faintly startled, then preened a little. "The YMCA."

"When this is over and I can go back to work, I'd like to show you around Great Bods. We offer some programs that the Y doesn't, and my facilities are first-rate."

"I looked around last week," he said, nodding his head. "I was impressed with what I saw."

Wyatt was gently herding me forward with his body, and as we turned the corner to the elevator, I looked past him and called, "Bye, now," to Officer Vyskosigh.

"Would you stop flirting?" Wyatt growled.

"I wasn't flirting. I was drumming up business." The elevator doors opened and we stepped inside.

He pressed the button for his floor. "That was flirting. So cut it out."

Chief Gray was talking with a group of detectives that included MacInnes and Forester, and he looked up when Wyatt steered me toward his office. The Chief was wearing a dark taupe suit and a French blue dress shirt. I gave him a big smile and a thumbs-up, and he self-consciously stroked his tie.

"Maybe this wasn't such a good idea," Wyatt muttered as he parked me in his chair. "But it's too late now to change my mind, so just sit there and make lists, okay? There are some guys here who have high cholesterol, so try not to smile at them and give them heart attacks. Don't flirt with anyone who's over forty, or overweight, or married, or under forty, or single. Got it?"

"I'm not a flirt," I said defensively, and pulled out my notebook. I couldn't believe he was being so dog-in-the-mangerish. That might be list-worthy.

"The evidence says otherwise. Since you told him he'd look good in blue, Chief Gray has worn a blue shirt every day. Maybe you should clue him in on some other colors."

"Oh, how sweet," I said, beaming. "He must have gone shopping that very day."

Wyatt studied the ceiling for a moment, then said, "Do you want some coffee? Or a Diet Coke?"

"No, I'm fine right now. Thank you. Where will you be, since I have your desk?"

"Around," he said unhelpfully, and left.

I didn't have time to get bored. Several people popped into the office to thank me for the bread pudding, and ask for the recipe. The women asked, that is; I don't think it occurred to the men. Between interruptions, I doodled in my notebook and wrote down other things that might or might not be relevant, but didn't hit on that magic detail that would tie everything together.

Around lunchtime, Wyatt returned with a white sack containing two barbecue sandwiches, and with two soft drinks hooked in his fingers. He moved me out of his chair—I don't know what it is about him and his chairs, that he can't share—and looked over my list of clues and my doodles while we ate lunch.

He didn't seem impressed by my progress. He did like where I'd written his name, then drawn a heart around it and an arrow through the heart. He scowled, though, when he found his new list of transgressions.

After we had eaten he said, "The lab guys say that the black hairs are original, not dyed. And that they're Asian, which is a big break. How many Asians do you know?"

Now I was really puzzled. There aren't many Asians in this part of the country, and though I'd had some Asian friends in college, we hadn't kept in touch. "None since college, that I remember."

"Remember, Native Americans are of Asian heritage."

That put a whole new light on things, because this close to the Eastern Cherokee Reservation, there were a lot of Cherokees around. I knew a lot of people with Cherokee heritage, but I couldn't think of one who might want to kill me.

"I'll have to think about this," I said. "I'll make a list."

After he left, I did make a list of all the Native Americans I knew, but even as I was writing the names, I knew this was a waste of time. None of them had any reason to kill me.

I went back to my clues. I wrote down: *Asian hair.* Wasn't that what all good-quality human-hair wigs were made of? Asian hair was heavy and straight and glossy; anything could be done to it, in terms of color and curl. I wrote down *wig*, then circled the word.

If the person trying to kill me had been smart enough to wear a wig, then we shouldn't be paying any attention to the color of the hair. This threw the field of suspects wide open again. A wild idea struck me and I wrote down a name, with a question mark beside it. This was taking jealousy to the extreme, but I wanted to think about this person some more.

Around two o'clock, Wyatt stuck his head in the door. "Stay here," he said brusquely. "We have a call about a murder/suicide. Turn your cell phone on and I'll call you when I can."

If my cell phone is with me, it's always on. The big question was, when would he be back? I'd seen how long it takes to work crime scenes; he might not be back to fetch me until midnight. There is no good that comes of not having your own wheels.

The constant noise in the big room outside Wyatt's office had lessened considerably; when I went to the door, I saw that almost everyone had left. They were all probably going to the scene of the murder/suicide. If I'd been given the choice, I would have gone, too.

To my right, the elevator dinged, signaling someone's arrival. I looked around just as the person stepped out, and I froze in shock as Jason, of all people, came into view. Well, not shock; that's too strong a reaction. More like surprise. And I wasn't frozen, either, if you want to get literal about things.

I thought about ducking back into Wyatt's office, but Jason had already seen me. A big smile lit his face and he came toward me with long steps. "Blair. Did you get my message?"

"Hello," I said with a lot less than enthusiasm, and didn't bother answering his question. "What are you doing here?"

"Looking for Chief Gray. Same question back atcha."

"There were some details to clear up," I said vaguely. This was the first time I'd spoken to him in five years, and I felt uneasy about speaking at all. He was so firmly out of my life I could barely remember anything about our time together.

He was still handsome, but his looks didn't speak to me at all. The state legislature wasn't in session, but now that he was a state representative, he did things like play golf with the chief of police, and even when he was casually dressed, as now, he went for a higher fashion statement than he had before. Though he was wearing jeans and docksiders—no socks, of course—he also had on an oatmeal-colored linen jacket. Some linen blends now don't wrinkle so horrifically; he hadn't been smart enough to find one. His jacket looked as if he'd slept in it for a week even though he'd probably put it on fresh just that morning.

"I haven't seen the chief since this morning," I said, stepping back so I could terminate the conversation by closing the office door. "Good luck."

Instead of going on his way, he stepped forward into the office doorway. "Is there something like a break room where he'd go for coffee, or anything?"

"He's the chief," I said drily. "He probably has his own coffeemaker. And someone to pour it for him."

"Why don't you walk with me while I look for him? We could catch up on old times."

"No, thanks. I have paperwork to do." I gestured toward Wyatt's desk, where the paperwork was all his except for my notebook, but of course I'd gone through all his paperwork again, so in a way it was mine.

"Aw, come on," Jason cajoled. He reached into his pocket and pulled out a snub-nosed pistol. "Walk with me. We have a lot to talk about."

CHAPTER
TWENTY-EIGHT

Obviously I would never have gone with him if he hadn't had that pistol jammed in my side, but he did, so I did. I was sort of in shock, trying to wrap my mind around what was happening. Thinking about something else until my subconscious felt ready to face this obviously wasn't going to work this time. By the time I realized he wouldn't have shot me in front of witnesses—and there had been a couple of other people still in the department—it was too late; I was already in his car with him.

He made me drive, while he kept the pistol trained on me. I thought about driving him into a telephone pole or something, but I flinched at the idea of being in yet another car accident. My poor body was just now recovering from the last one. I didn't want to get hit in the face by another air bag, either. Yeah, I know, a bruise is temporary but a bullet can be forever, so maybe I didn't make the best choice. Just in case I had to drive into a telephone pole, though, as a last resort, I glanced down at the steering wheel to make certain there was an air bag there. The car was a late model Chevrolet, so of course it had one, but after the week I'd had, I wanted to double-check.

The funny thing is, I was alarmed but not terrified. See, the main thing to know about Jason is that he'll do anything to protect his image. His whole life is built around his political career, polls, and his ambition. How he thought he could get away with murder when at least two people had seen me leaving with him, I don't know.

I followed his directions while I waited for him to realize this, but somehow he seemed to be in his own alternate reality. I didn't know where he was taking me; in fact, we seemed to be driving aimlessly around town while he tried to think of somewhere to go. He kept pulling at his lower lip, which, I remembered, was a habit he had when he was worrying about something.

"You wore a black wig, right?" I casually asked. "When you cut my brake line?"

He shot me a nervous glance. "How did you know?"

"Some hairs got caught on the undercarriage. The forensics team found them."

He looked faintly puzzled, then nodded. "Oh, yeah, I remember sort of catching the wig on something. I didn't think about any hair coming out because I couldn't feel anything pulling."

"They're checking now for a list of people who bought black wigs," I lied. He gave me another nervous glance. Actually, it wasn't much of a lie. When Wyatt found my notebook with the word *wig* circled, he would definitely check it out.

"People saw me leaving with you," I pointed out. "If you kill me, how are you going to explain that?"

"I'll think of something," he muttered.

"What? How can you dispose of my body? Besides, they'll hook you up to a lie detector so fast your head will spin. Even if they can't find enough evidence to bring you to trial, the publicity will ruin your career." See, I know Jason; he has nightmares about anything that might threaten his career. And even though he'd cut my brake lines, I simply couldn't see him killing me in person.

"You might as well just let me go," I continued. "I don't know why you're trying to kill me—*wait a minute*! You might have cut my brake lines, but you definitely didn't shoot at me last Sunday. What's going on here?" I jerked around to stare at him and the car swerved. He cursed and I hurriedly straightened the wheel.

"I don't know what you mean," he said, staring straight ahead and forgetting to keep me covered with the pistol. See? Jason is just not cut out for a life of crime.

"Someone else shot at me." My brain was racing, and all the separate little links were knotting together, forming a chain. "*Your wife!* Your wife tried to kill me, didn't she?"

"She's crazy jealous," he blurted. "I can't stop her; I can't reason with her. This will ruin me if she gets caught, and she will, because she doesn't know what she's doing."

That made two of them.

"So you thought you'd sort of kill me yourself so she wouldn't have to? Beat her to the punch?"

"Something like that." Frazzled, he raked a hand through his blond hair. "If you're dead, she'll stop obsessing about you."

"Why on earth would she obsess about me? I am so totally out of your life; this is the first time I've spoken to you since our divorce."

He mumbled something, and I threw a glare his way. "What? Speak up." He mumbles when he feels guilty about something.

"It might be my fault," he mumbled, slightly louder.

"Oh? How's that?" I tried to sound encouraging, when what I really wanted to do was beat his head against the pavement or something.

"When we argue, I might say something about you," he confessed, and now he was staring out the passenger window. Really. I thought about simply reaching over and taking the pistol away from him, except he had his finger on the trigger, which is so totally stupid if you aren't an expert, and Jason wasn't. If he had been, he would have been watching me like a hawk instead of staring out the window.

"Jason, you dummy," I groaned. "Why would you do something stupid like that?"

"She's always trying to make me jealous," he said defensively. "I love Debra, I really do, but she isn't like you. She's clingy and insecure, and I got tired of the way she tried to make me jealous and I started firing back. I knew it made her mad, but I didn't know she'd flipped out about it. Last Sunday night, when I got home from playing golf and found out she'd actually shot at you, we had this huge argument and she swore she'd kill you if it was the last thing she did. I think she's been staking out your house or something, trying to find out if there's something going on between us. Nothing I said made any difference to her. She's crazy jealous, and if she kills you, I probably won't even be reelected as state representative. I can kiss the governorship good-bye."

I mulled all this over for a minute.

"Jason, I hate to tell you this, but you married a nitwit. That's fair, though," I added judiciously.

He looked at me. "How's that?"

"So did she."

That made him sulk for a few minutes, but finally he groaned and said, "I don't know what to do. I don't want to kill you, but if I don't, Debra is going to keep trying and she'll ruin my career."

"I have an idea. How about you have her committed to a mental institution," I suggested sarcastically. I meant it, too. She was a danger to others—namely, me—so she met the criteria. Or criterion. Whatever.

"I can't do that! I love her."

"Look. It seems to me you have a choice: if she kills me, it may ruin your career; but if you kill me, the results will be way more serious because you've made a prior attempt and this shows premeditation, which will get you in serious hot water. Not only that, I'm engaged to a cop, and he'll kill you." I took my left hand off the steering wheel and held it over for him to see the ring.

"Wow, that's a rock," he said admiringly. "I didn't think cops had that kind of money. Who is he?"

"Wyatt Bloodsworth. He questioned you the other day, remember?"

"So that's why he was so nasty. I get it now. He was the football player, wasn't he? I guess he has plenty of money."

"He gets by," I said. "But if anything happens to me, he'll not only kill you—and the other cops would look the other way, because they like me—he'll burn your village and sow your fields with salt." I thought I'd throw in a little biblical warning just to impress him with the seriousness of the consequences.

"I don't have any fields," he said. "Or a village."

Sometimes Jason could be stupendously literal. "I know that," I said patiently. "It was a metaphor. What I meant was, he'll totally destroy you."

He nodded his head. "Yeah, I can see that. You're looking hot these days." He tilted his head back against the seat and groaned. "What can I do? I can't think of anything that will work. I called in that murder/suicide to get the cops out of the building, but not all of them left. You were right; there were witnesses. If I kill you, I'd have to kill them, too, and I don't think that would work because by now the cops have probably found out that call was a false alarm and they're back at the station."

As if on cue, my cell phone rang. Jason jumped a foot. I started to fish around in my bag for the phone, but Jason said, "Don't answer it!" and I pulled my hand out.

"That will be Wyatt," I said. "He'll go ape shit when he finds out I left with you." That wasn't biblical, but it was accurate.

Sweat beaded on Jason's brow. "You can tell him we were just talking, right?"

"Jason. Get a clue. You've been trying to kill me. We have to get this settled or I'm telling Wyatt you made a pass at me, and he'll take you apart all the way down to your molecules."

"I know," he groaned. "Let's go to my house so we can talk, come up with a plan."

"Is Debra there?"

"No, she's watching your folks' house, figuring you'll turn up there sooner or later."

She was stalking my parents? I'd scalp the bitch for that. Hot fury zipped through me, but I controlled it, because I needed to keep my head. I had talked Jason around, but I knew Jason and I wasn't the least bit afraid of him. Evidently his wife was crazy as a loon though, and I didn't know what we could do about her.

I drove to Jason's house, which of course is the one we'd bought together, and which I'd given him in the divorce. It hadn't changed much in five years; the landscaping was more mature, but that was about it. The house was red brick, two-story, with white shutters and trim. The style was modern, with interesting architectural details, but there was nothing about it to make it stand out from the rest of the neighborhood. I think developers have at the most five house plans and styles that they use, so subdivisions have a cookie-cutter look to them. The garage doors were down, so Debra wasn't at home.

When I pulled into the driveway, I said thoughtfully, "You know, it might have been smart to move rather than expect Debra to live here."

"Why's that?"

Like I said: clueless. "Because this is where we lived when we were married," I said patiently. "She probably feels like this is my house instead of hers. She needs her own house." Weird, but for the first time I felt a gleam of sympathy for her.

"There's nothing wrong with this house," he protested. "It's a good house, nice and modern."

"Jason. Buy the woman her own house!" I yelled. Sometimes that's the only way to get his attention.

"All right, all right. You don't have to yell," he said sulkily.

If I'd had a wall right there, I'd have beat my head against it.

We went inside, and I rolled my eyes when I saw he still had the same furniture. The man was dense beyond saving. *He* was the one Debra should kill.

Now, I knew the cavalry was on the way; the first place Wyatt and the guys would check would be Jason's house, right? They knew Jason wasn't the one who had shot me, but Wyatt would also see my notes and put two and two together the way I had. The person who was jealous of me was my ex-husband's new wife, only she wasn't so new, since they'd been married four years. How much more obvious could it be? Jason hadn't shot at me, but he'd left that worried message the next morning—after five years of no contact at all. Wyatt might not catch on immediately that Jason was the one who had cut my brake lines, but that didn't matter. What mattered was that I could probably expect the first patrol car to come rolling up within five minutes.

"So," Jason said, looking at me as if I had all the answers, "what can we do about Debra?"

"*What do you mean, what can you do about me?*"

The shriek made me jump about a foot straight up, not only because I hadn't been expecting it, but because it obviously meant Debra was home, after all. On the list of things that were not good, that was at the top.

Jason jumped, too, and dropped the pistol, which didn't go off—thank you, Jesus—because my heart probably would have stopped. It came close to stopping anyway when I turned around and faced the former Debra Schmale, now Mrs. Jason Carson, who appeared to be dead serious about her status. She was holding a rifle, and she had the stock up to her shoulder and her cheek against the stock as if she knew what she was doing.

I swallowed and put my tongue in gear, though my brain was still stuck in park. "He meant how could we convince you that you don't have any reason to be jealous of me. This is the first time I've talked to Jason since our divorce, so he was just trying to get back at you for trying to make him jealous, by throwing me in your face to make you jealous, and really you should shoot him instead of me because I think that was a really shitty thing for him to do, don't you?"

Under the circumstances I think that was a masterpiece of a speech, if I do say so myself, but she didn't even blink. She kept that rifle aimed right at my chest. "I hate your guts," she said in a low, vicious tone. "That's all I hear—'Blair, Blair, Blair.' Blair this and Blair that until I want to throw up."

"Which, I'd like to point out, isn't my fault. I had no idea he was doing that. I'm telling you, shoot him instead of me."

For the first time Jason seemed to realize what I was saying. "Hey!" he said indignantly.

"Don't 'hey' me," I snapped. "You're the one who caused this. You should get down on your knees and apologize to both of us. You've driven this poor woman almost crazy, and you've caused me to almost get killed. This is all your fault."

"I'm not a *poor woman*," Debra snapped. "I'm pretty and I'm smart, and he should appreciate me, but instead he's still so in love with you he can't think straight."

"No, I'm not," Jason said instantly, taking a step toward her. "I love *you*. I haven't loved Blair in years, since way before we got divorced."

"That's true," I said. "Has he ever told you he was cheating on me? Doesn't sound to me as if he loved me, does it to you?"

"He loves you," she repeated. Obviously she wasn't about to listen to reason. "He insisted we live in this house—"

"Told you," I said in an aside to Jason.

"*Stop talking to him.* I don't want you to ever speak to him again. I don't want you to ever *breathe* again." Furiously she stepped closer, so close the rifle barrel was almost jabbing me in the nose. I drew back a little, because the bruises from the air bag were fading and I didn't want a fresh set. "You got everything," she breathed on a sob. "Oh, I know he kept the house, but he can't bear to change it, so you might as well still have it. You got the Mercedes. You drive around town with the top down like you're hot shit, and I have to drive a *Taurus* because he says it's good for his image that we drive American cars."

"A Taurus has really good suspension," I said, trying to deflect her. See? Somehow my subconscious knew the car was important.

"I don't give a shit about the suspension!"

Huh. She really should try it out before being so dismissive.

I thought I heard something outside, but I didn't dare turn my head to look. Besides the obvious points of entry into the house—the front door and the back door and the windows—there was a set of French doors leading onto the patio from the breakfast room. From where I was standing, I could catch a glimpse of the French doors and I thought I saw movement there, but I couldn't look directly at them or she would know something was up.

Jason, standing to my right, didn't have the same angle and couldn't see anything except the stairs. Debra could see out the living room window, but her view was restricted because of the angle of the house and the sheer curtains that were drawn over the windows to let in light but provide a measure of privacy. I was the only one who knew rescue was at hand.

But what if they busted in the way cops do and scared Debra, and she pulled the trigger? I was dead, that was "what if."

"How did you learn how to use a rifle?" I asked,

not because I cared but just to keep her talking, keep her focused on something besides shooting me right now.

"I used to go hunting with my father. I also shoot skeet, so I'm very accurate." She gave a fleeting glance at the bandage on my upper arm. "If you hadn't bent down when you did, you'd have seen how accurate I am. No, wait—you wouldn't. Because you'd be dead."

"I wish you'd get off this dead stuff," I said. "It's boring. Not only that, you won't get away with it."

"Sure I will. Jason won't tell, because he doesn't like negative publicity."

"He won't have to tell. Two cops saw him kidnap me."

"*Kidnap?*" Her eyes rounded.

"He's been trying to kill me, too," I said. "So you won't get caught. See, he does love you, because I wouldn't do that for anyone."

She glanced at him. "Is that true?" she asked hesitantly.

"I cut her brake line," he admitted.

She stood very still for a moment, then tears began to well in her eyes. "You do love me," she finally said. "You really love me."

"Of course I do. I'm crazy about you," he assured her.

Crazy was a very apt word under the circumstances, don't you think?

I blew out a relieved breath. "Good, that's settled," I said. "Y'all have a nice life. I think I'll just be going—"

I took a half step back, and several things kind of

happened all at once. When I moved, Debra reacted automatically and swung the rifle at me. Behind her came a crashing sound as the French doors were kicked in, and as if in slow motion, I saw her jump, startled. When she swung the rifle at me, my body sort of reacted all on its own, without any command from me. Muscle memory, you know? She swung, I jerked back, and years of training took over. I kept on going, my body bending back, legs tensing for the spring that would take me over, my arms going out for balance. The room turned upside down; then my legs and back muscles took over and provided the thrust and twist.

As a backflip, it was a disaster. Both my legs came up and Debra was way too close: my left foot caught her under the chin and the other knocked the rifle flying. Unfortunately, her finger was on the trigger and the motion pulled it; the sharp crack was deafening. Because she was in the way, my legs couldn't complete their proper rotation and I fell flat on my back, hard. My kick under her chin sent her stumbling backward, completely off balance, her arms windmilling. She lost the battle to regain her balance and hit on her butt, skidding across the polished hardwood floor.

"Ouch!" I shrieked, grabbing my left big toe. I was wearing sandals, which is not the best choice of footwear for kicking someone in the chin.

"Blair!" The house was suddenly full of cops, pouring in from every opening. Uniformed cops, plainclothes cops—and Wyatt. He was the one who had literally burst through the French doors when he thought she was about to shoot me, and he scooped me up off the floor, holding me so tight to his chest I could barely breathe. "Are you all right? Did she hit you? I don't see any blood—"

"I'm fine," I managed to say. "Except you're squeezing me to death." The iron band of his arms loosened just a bit, and I added, "I hurt my toe."

He drew back and stared at me, as if he couldn't believe I was all in one piece and had come out of this without even a scratch. After the example of this past week, he must have been expecting me to be bleeding from a dozen bullet wounds.

"A hurt toe?" he said. "Good God. This calls for a cookie."

See? I told you he was a fast learner.

EPILOGUE

You know who got shot? Jason. Can you think of anyone more deserving? Debra's wild shot creased his head, since the rifle barrel had been flying upward when she pulled the trigger, and he'd hit the floor as if he'd been poleaxed. Everyone says that, but I don't really know what a poleax is. If I had to guess, I'd say it's something to do with cutting timber, but if that was the Final Jeopardy! answer, I wouldn't bet all of my money on that question.

She didn't kill him, but he was bleeding like a stuck pig, because heads do that when something tears up the scalp. Both of them started blabbering away, sort of blaming each other but at the same time trying to take the blame on themselves, and none of it made any sense, so I explained everything to MacInnes and Forester, and Wyatt, and even Chief Gray, who for some reason had come along. I think almost the entire police department was there. The SWAT team was, in their cool black fatigues, and when the medics came, my pal Keisha was one of them. We greeted each other like long-lost girlfriends.

Getting things sorted out took a while, so I went into the kitchen and put on a pot of coffee for everyone. I hobbled a little bit because my toe hurt, but I didn't think it was broken.

About six o'clock, Wyatt took me home.

"Do me a favor," he said during the drive. "For the rest of our lives together, don't put me through another week that's anything like this past one, okay?"

"None of this was my fault," I said indignantly. "And I'm the one who's had the worst of it, you know. I've been shot and bruised and battered, and if you hadn't kept my mind off how much I hurt, I probably would have cried a lot."

He reached over and caught my hand, held it tight. "God, I love you. The guys are going to be talking about that karate kick you gave her for the rest of their lives. Even the SWAT guys were impressed, and they try to be real hard-asses. Where did you take lessons?"

"I provide all sorts of lessons at Great Bods," I said demurely. What, you thought I was going to tell him I sort of automatically did a backflip and didn't intend to do what I did? Not in this lifetime.

This proves beyond a doubt, however, that you never know when you'll need to do a backflip.

We called all the family and told them the crisis was over, which involved lots of explaining, but Wyatt and I didn't want any company. My latest close shave had been a hair too close, because there's something more immediate about a rifle in your face than a car accident, even though the accident had been horrific enough and that was what I dreamed about. I didn't dream about the rifle at all, maybe because Jason was the one who got shot, so that made it a good outcome, right? But we spent that evening cuddling and kissing and making plans for the future, sort of giddy with relief. Plans weren't all we made, of course. I'm talking about Wyatt, the horniest guy in the county. If he was happy, he wanted sex. If he was mad, he wanted sex. He celebrated everything with sex.

I foresaw a very happy and contented life with him.

The next day he took me car shopping. His sister, Lisa, delivered his Chevy Avalanche to him, thanked him for the loan of it, and asked me a million questions. Thank goodness I liked her immediately, but she was a lot like his mother, so there was no reason why I wouldn't have. I also liked his truck, and that's what we drove to the Mercedes dealership.

Of course I wanted another Mercedes. You don't think I'd let Jason and his nitwit wife stop me from buying my favorite car, do you? Picture me in a black convertible. Black is a statement of power, remember. The insurance company hadn't come through with the check yet and since it was Sunday, my bank wasn't open, but the salesman promised to hold my car until Monday evening. I was a happy camper when we arrived at Mom and Dad's house.

Dad answered the door, and held his finger up to his lips. "Shhh," he cautioned. "We've had another computer disaster and Tina has gone quiet."

"Uh-oh," I said, pulling Wyatt inside. "What happened?"

"She finally got her computer straightened out, she thinks, and this morning her monitor went blank. I just got back from the computer store with a new monitor, and she's in her office hooking it up."

Jenni came into the family room, and gave me a big hug. "I can't believe that stupid Jason," she said.

"I can. When you came by Mom's office, could you hear anything?"

"Not a word," Jenni said, looking worried. When Mom's mad, she mutters to herself. When she's beyond mad, she gets very, very quiet.

We heard Mom coming down the hall, and we all sat silently as she marched past without saying a word, or even glancing in our direction. She was carrying a large roll of plastic, which she took out into the garage. She came back in empty-handed, and again marched past us without saying anything.

"What's up with the plastic?" Wyatt asked, and we all shrugged in the classic "Who knows?" gesture.

There was a heavy thump, then a strange sliding noise. Mom came back down the hall, her expression grim and set. She had a thick cord clutched in her hands, and she was dragging the offending monitor behind her. We watched in silence as she dragged it to the garage door, down the two steps with more heavy thumps, and into the middle of the plastic she had spread on the garage floor.

She went to where Dad had his tools, attached to a big pegboard on one wall of the garage. She selected a hammer, weighed it in her hand, then returned it to its spot. She moved to what looked like a small sledgehammer or a mallet of some sort. I don't know tools, so I can't say for certain what it was. She took it down from the wall, considered it, and evidently decided it would meet her requirements. Then she returned to where the monitor was sitting on the plastic, and beat it to smithereens. She hammered it until it was nothing more than a pile of pieces. Glass flew; plastic splintered. She beat it almost out of existence. Then she very calmly returned the sledgehammer to its place, dusted her hands, and walked back into the house with a smile on her face.

Wyatt had the weirdest expression in his eyes, as if he didn't know whether to laugh or run for the hills. Dad clapped him on the shoulder. "You're a smart man," he said encouragingly. "Just keep a regular check on your list of transgressions so you'll know if there are any major problems you need to handle, and you'll be okay."

"You promise?" Wyatt asked drily.

Dad laughed. "Hell, no. I have all I can handle; if you get in trouble, you're on your own."

Wyatt turned and winked at me. No, he wasn't on his own; we were in this together.